HANDS DOWN

BY TOM FIGEL

Reputecture, LLC

HANDS DOWN

ISBN 978-0-578-89021-0

Ebook ISBN 9780578285573

Library of Congress Control Number: 2021907800

First Printing, 2022

Published by Reputecture, LLC
455 East Ocean Boulevard, #202
Long Beach, CA 90802-4936
www.reputecture.com

Printed by IngramSpark

Design of cover: Robert W. Jahn, Creative Works, Daytona Beach, FL

Photo credits:

Chapter 5:
    Amish buggy - Hutch Photography, Shutterstock
    Grazing cows - Mel Theobald

Chapter 9:
    Main Street - Leigh Trail, Shutterstock

Chapter 19:
    Centennial Bridge - Ryan Brohm, Shutterstock

Chapter 22:
    Path in cornfield - Paul Clarke, Shutterstock

Chapter 24:
    Farm field horizon - Mel Theobald

Back cover:
    Iowa map - Alexander Lukatskiy, Shutterstock

For

Nancy Carlin,
the poet who is poetry

A Caution

Hands Down is a self-published novel, a book in the category of vanity press. Vanity press is a true term for a kind of work that does undergo some manner of review but is still in existence because of the author's presumption that the manuscript merits publication. While some manuscript readers encouraged publication and made good suggestions, there were others whose answers were tepid or worse. A writer who self-publishes many novels of his own advised the discarding of the manuscript before beginning an entirely different work. My wife said, "Tom, your book is better than I expected."

Hoping that knowing my own taste provides some guidance, I provide this list of admired writers: Fyodor Dostoevsky; William Styron; Tom Wolfe; Albert Camus; Mark Twain; Alexsandr Solzhenitsyn; J.D. Salinger; Chaucer; Norman Mailer; Arthur Miller; Nathan Hill; H.L. Mencken; Ken Kesey; Carl Hiaasen; Tennessee Williams; Milan Kundera; Ignazio Silone; William Faulkner; Martin Luther King, Jr.; Abraham Lincoln; Bret Stephens; Eugene O'Neill; Flannery O'Connor; Tom Robbins; Jonathan Dee; Hillary Jordan; Luke Mogelson; Robert Penn Warren; Irwin Shaw; Matthew Stewart; Dorothy Wickenden; Joan Didion; John Stuart Mill; Dan Wakefield; Michael Lewis; Henry Fielding; Charles Portis; Thomas McGuane; Mordecai Richler; Frederick F. Reichheld; poets T.S. Eliot; W.B. Yeats; Howard Nemerov; James K. Flanagan; Gwendolyn Brooks; and Wallace Stevens.

CHAPTER 1

C130 rollin' down the strip.
Airborne daddy gonna take a little trip.

Ronnie Tonti had no plans beyond what he had been doing since tucking his ETS documents in a pocket of his fatigue pants and walking on his hands past an envious line of personnel clerks at Fort Bragg.

The day of his discharge, he flipped back upright, showed the laughing clerks a grin as large as an endless R&R, and then returned to the barracks for retrieval of his packed duffel bag.

"Had best get your sorry ass out of here, Tonti," the company clerk told him. "This is off limits for civilians."

"Rogah that," said Tonti, still grinning.

"What's your DOB? You twenty-four? Get yourself re-upped and . . . " The clerk calculated a moment. "Uncle Sugar start paying you that sweet pension time you're 42."

"Negative. See you laytah, lifah. Aihbawn!"

"Lifer! Sixty-seven days."

Tonti laughed. "Gettin' shawt."

"Damn straight. 'Bout two months and a wakeup."

Tonti shook hands with the clerk, saluted the 82nd Airborne banner strung across the back wall of the little company office, and slung the duffel bag to his shoulder. Everyone knew the clerk was more likely to re-up with a bonus and a hope of combat pay, but Tonti only grinned, said, "Sweet Army" and left.

Tonti's thumb, duffel bag, big smile, and the military look of his short, red-brown hair easily secured rides from other veterans: a trucker taking U.S. mail to Atlanta, a happy, new contract-in-the-pocket manufacturer's rep speeding home to his wife and newborn son in Montgomery, and then a former Navy medic heading to New Orleans.

At first, Tonti followed the plans that were no plans, only laissez faire sampling of the civilian life that had ended soon after Ernestine divorced him and, for spite, contacted the Selective Service. Arrived in Slidell on a humid afternoon trying hard to throw rain from a blackening western sky, Tonti took up residence with his brother Francois, a grumpy, square-faced man living in his same small, silver trailer near the town. Franky shrugged and welcomed Ronnie with a can of Busch from the fridge. In their old, oil and water, Esau and Jacob way, the brothers resumed old habits. With enough money in his pocket from one little job after another, Tonti soon was having a fine time each evening at whatever bar or party he landed.

But now, for four days since Franky correctly suspected that Tonti had gone to bed with Lucille, Franky, dark and testy at the best of times, was tearing through the whole of New Orleans like the enraged bear he was.

Anyone who knew that crazy coon ass Cajun could foresee the trouble when Franky did manage to catch his younger brother at entertaining play among college kids or conventioneers buying beer for him in the jazzy heat of a Quarter bar. Careful of Franky and of the knife he carried on him somewhere, mutual friends gave the fearsome man true but incomplete information in hopes that the passage of some days would see everyone returned to custom:

square-faced, dour Franky arriving with his perfumed petite amie
Lucille, a woman not so pretty as ten or 15 years before but, all in
all, not bad to look at with her bawdy way of showing breasts and a
meaty figure that still had vestiges of those times, and everyone
around them amused by whatever Ronnie was telling or doing.

And how had Franky become aware of the simple, exploratory
tryst, anyway? Who but the vine-ringed cedars and a few pecan trees
at the edge of the small clearing, some jumpy waxwings, had caught
Lucille entering the trailer in search of Ronnie, only hours after
seeing Franky off to meet Henri for a couple of nights of gigging
frogs out in Honey Island Swamp?

She had gone back to bed, not due at work till late afternoon
but, unable to sleep, she soon rose, restless and excited. Then, as she
worked her face with Oil of Olay, brushed her lashes, and studied
the blue shading around her eyes, she let the impulse propel her.

She drove to the trailer. Wearing an unbuttoned cotton dress she
only pretended to gather around the nakedness of her round, busty
form, she entered, and came right up to Ronnie's bed. For just a
moment, she watched him, boyish and slightly round-faced with
the thinnest of red-brown, two-day growth along his jaw. He lay on
his back in white, GI boxers in a pool of mid-summer Louisiana
damp. Just as Tonti's eyes opened, she took his head and pressed his
startled face into her crotch.

If the man had any better angels, they couldn't make themselves
heard with Lucille's hands clasping his ears. From then on, it was
wham bam thank you ma'am, nothing Franky needed to know.

But vampy Lucille couldn't keep the secret. At the Piggly Wiggly
that afternoon, when her smiles and a large hickey drew notice, she
saw no harm in telling some co-workers, a coterie of women as
likely to hold a secret as New Orleans was to overlook Mardi Gras.

Lucille's husband took in the tidbit with no more visible reaction than an alligator slowly sinking back into the metronomic

regularity of a 7:05 a.m. departure the next morning, enough time allowed for hearing the LSU farm report and a Paul Harvey installment along the way to the little shoe store where he worked in Hammond.

Not so Franky. He had not heard but, arriving at the trailer and finally catching the sense of the hints in Lucille's chatter, he clopped her a blow that reddened the whole side of her head and made blood flow from the gums holding her irregular, discolored teeth.

Ignoring her crying and heated shouts, Franky went immediately in search of his brother.

Ronnie had seen Franky's cold-eyed fury before and expected the same pattern this time: be found and any kind of violence could result. Sure to have his big jackknife on him and maybe a pistol, a Franky deranged with anger would supplement his own power with whatever was at hand. While that kind of violence was always latent in Franky, he had never been able to sustain the level of rage gripping him now.

And so, the whispers and outright finger-in-the-chest warnings from Ronnie's friends hardly put a dent in his customary optimism. Laissez les bons temps rouler! The sun was shining, the red beans were soaking, the shops and bars had shade, and all the streets – Bourbon, Chartres, Decatur, all of them - were flowing with roisterous groups of Texans, Georgians, good-humored people from all over the country and the world.

Ronnie avoided a few places but not all. Franky would settle back into his gruff, miserable self and the two brothers would resume their loose family companionship. Wasn't that the irritable brother's pattern? In the meantime, spicy Irene or someone else would have room for Ronnie at her place.

And what was the harm, anyway? Sure, Lucille had plopped suddenly on Ronnie's lap and run her tongue deep into his ear that time but they were all happy, tipsy drunk and daring. Franky had his own hand running up that Covington woman's thigh.

Without full awareness of it, Ronnie benefited from the gregarious, entertaining spirit that sent him to the center of many celebrations, especially those of the New Orleans visitors ready to abandon for a time whatever they had left at college, at home, at work, at the Army, Air Force, Navy base.

As an ex-paratrooper himself, an ex-GI with stories from his Basic Training at Fort Polk near Alexandria, his tour in Germany and his short-timer service with the 82nd Airborne at Fort Bragg, Ronnie was an easy comrade for the young servicemen coursing through New Orleans. His cheerfulness also made him a nexus for the college students, conventioneers, and middle-aged revelers attracted to the free-wheeling fun and potential of New Orleans.

Welcome everywhere with his stories, his laugh and his hand-walking, Ronnie Tonti was everywhere or had just been there, or was nearby, Franky learned as he carried his angry search from one place to another. Franky had never bothered to know where his younger brother was scrubbing pots or hosing walks or sweeping floors owned by some amused, forgiving patron serving up New Orleans in plates of oysters, étouffée, blackened fish and alcohol. With haphazard persistence, Franky searched all the spots he suspected.

Ronnie left a whiff of himself in the aftermath of one of his best tricks: to the hoots and encouragement of whatever group had adopted him for an evening, he earned an evening's drinks, food and maybe a bedmate by climbing onto one of New Orleans' long, polished, crowded bars and traversing the length of it, sometimes back and forth, on his hands.

On the fourth night, Ronnie joined up easily with a small pack that included two young GIs putting a New Orleans cap on some final nights of leave before they reported to airborne training. They were with a Georgia frat brother and his sister, a light-hearted Tulane co-ed who had her hair cut in straight, black bangs almost to her big, dark eyes. She wore a one-piece, white shorts outfit. Despite her girlish manner and her youthful clothing, Tonti and Melinda's proud brother saw clearly a pretty girl gelling into a head-turning woman.

Tonti came upon the slightly giddy foursome where they had been detained by a couple of adolescent Negro boys.

"I knows where you gots those shoes," said the taller of the two boys. Puberty had given him a long face and a defined adam's apple. Against the darkness of his skin, the pink of his mouth was pronounced.

"How do y'all know that?" a heavy-boned, ruddy GI answered. He had a booming manner, a big laugh. Like the other young men, he was dressed in civvies: bermuda shorts, t-shirts, and, in his case, shiny penny loafers.

"Yeah, that's a bunch of hog shit," said another, his voice marking him as an out-of-state visitor.

"Y'all don't even know where he's from," said the frat member. He and the big GI had the same accent.

By then, the four, already merry, were laughing.

"Ain't no matter," replied the Negro. "I knows where you gots those shoes. Don't matter you's a Yankee. I knows where you gots those shoes."

"Huh! Ain't no damn Yankee." The solid GI laughed at the silliness of the Negro's confusion.

"Yankee, shit. Yankee?" added the Georgia frat member.

"I bets you he does," said the second Negro boy. His skin was brown, light enough to show freckles along his forehead and beneath his eyes.

"How much you want to bet?" asked the big GI. His name was Owen.

"Yeah. How much? You're crazy," said the second GI.

"I bets you ten dollar."

The solid GI looked quickly at his companions, then raised the wager. "Make it twenty. Put your money where yeh mouth is."

The four young people laughed as the smaller Negro boy pulled twenty dollars from his back pocket and held it in front of everyone.

Owen did the same after he quickly accepted five dollar bills from two of the others. "Okay," he said. "Twenty dolla."

The tall Negro boy stooped and studied the GI's penny loafers carefully before he pronounced, "You gots your shoes on Decatur Street rights here in N'Awlins."

Silence, then bursts of laughter from the four victims.

"He got you, Owen. Damn."

Owen held out the bills, let the smaller of the two Negro boys take the money.

"Rights here on Decatur Street," the first Negro boy repeated.

Then the Negroes grinned and moved along Decatur Street as the four friends stood, laughing at themselves and regrouping.

Into their aimlessness stepped Ronnie Tonti.

"On Decaytaw Street," he said.

Startled, then sheepish, they turned to enjoy the sight of the man sharing their own laugh. They saw his grinning face and caught the sympathy in the little shaking of his head. He was not as tall as two of the boys, slightly more than five nine, but he had shoulders broader than any of them. The breadth emphasized the slimness of the rest of him. Most of all, the man, probably in his middle twenties and probably familiar with New Orleans, had a companionable air of juvenile adventure. Attractive, too, was the way his grin broadened as he returned their stares.

Tonti soon knew that Owen and Bill, the GI's, were about to begin jump school at Fort Benning in Columbus, Georgia. Owen and Daniel were childhood friends. Melinda, Daniel's sister, was letting her brother and his friends stay with her in her apartment while two roommates were gone for the summer.

Tonti was leaving the Quarter for a meeting with Irene at a neighborhood place close by on Dauphine Street but, easily deterred by his interesting new friends, he decided to go with them for awhile before he walked up Esplanade in whatever early evening cool could be found under the spread of live oak branches and palm fronds.

"Damn, it's hot out here," said Owen. The heat was enough reason for ducking into the shade of a bar looking out on Jackson Square.

"Mr. Ron, who's that?" asked Daniel. Like the others, he was drinking an iced tea.

Tonti saw Daniel's gaze on the statue of the man seated on a rearing horse. With a laugh, he said, "That's Andrew Jackson. Andrew Jackson himself."

Melinda's face took on a serious look.

"What's on your mind, darlin'?" Ronnie asked.

"Tonti is your name, Mr. Ron?" she asked.

"What my daddy tells me."

"Are y'all one of those Tontis? The explorer Robert LaSalle Henri de Tonti Tonti?"

"Wouldn't doubt it," Ronnie answered. "All I know, there been Tontis raising hell and bons temps roulayin' in N'Awlins since befaw. . . N'Awlins. . . befaw Gen'ral Jackson."

"I took New Orleans history last semester. Henri de Tonti was . . . remarkable. He cut his own hand off when someone shot him. This was before he ever came to the New World, before he joined Robert Sieur de LaSalle up in Montreal. Ever after that, Tonti, he wore a hand made out of iron. And he was just bold as brass. One time, he didn't like the pile of skins the Indians were trying to trade and he just kicked the whole pile over, right in front of about a thousand of them."

"We try to have bettah mannahs now," Ronnie said. "My brotha Franky, though. Darlin', he'd flat take on a thousand Indians. Do it in a instant. You don't want to get on the wrong side of that boy, I'm tellin' you."

"Sounds like a Sigma Chi to me," said Daniel. "The brothers in that frat are just plain uncivilized."

"Your brother doesn't seem like a fella any a us are takin' home to momma," said Owen.

"Rogah that," said Tonti.

They finished their drinks, Daniel paid, and the four resumed an aimless walk that took them off sunny Decatur Street into the mildly shaded Chartres and Royal Streets before they came back to Jackson Square. From the shaded front of the old Spanish trading center, the Cabildo, they leaned against the cool stone of the building, and watched the coming and going of tourists and worshipers at the neighboring entrance of St. Louis Cathedral.

"Y'all getting hungry?" Owen asked.

"Chow sounds good to me," said Bill.

"This is N'Awlins," Melinda said. "We don't have 'chow' in N'Awlins."

Whether New Orleans had chow or not, it did have Franky Tonti, who had turned into the Quarter and suddenly discovered his brother.

Carrying a load that was not entirely confined to the rattling mess of bolts and car parts in the bed of his truck, Franky cranked the vehicle onto the sidewalk, screeched to a stop, and almost falling, came lumbering around the truck in pursuit of Tonti.

"What the hell?" Bill, like the rest, looked in surprise and anger at the thick-chested Cajun. Franky's stubbled face, long-sleeved blue workshirt and green pants had splotches of oil fallen from whatever vehicles had been hoisted above him in his shop that week.

Tonti didn't delay. He scrambled around the side of the Cabildo and then into a back entrance of St. Louis Cathedral. Once inside the church, he remained near an exit at the front and kept alert to the sound or the appearance of Franky entering. He could hear sounds of tourists at the rear. A woman with a lacy white scarf covering her hair prayed with lowered head in a front pew at his left. Minutes later, a group led by an entertaining priest in a long black cassock began receiving instructions for a wedding rehearsal that was about to start. Caught up with themselves, the members of the group talked, laughed and concentrated on their roles.

After twenty minutes, Tonti exited and moved quickly away from Jackson Square to the St. Anthony's Garden at the Cathedral's rear. There he waited another few minutes against a shady line of summer green forsythia. A thin, wrinkled man busy with a freshly lit cigarette passed through and then the garden was quiet again except for the muffled sounds of normal Jackson Square activity.

Resuming his path toward North Dauphine, where he would look for Irene, Tonti was not very far along when he heard Owen and the others calling him.

"Bet I know where you gots those shoes, Mr. Ron," said Daniel as they came together at the front of a small, open-to-the-street bar.

"The police didn't like your brother's parking place," Bill said.

Tonti could imagine.

"He skedaddled pretty fast," Owen said.

For the first time, Tonti was pessimistic about Franky banking the fire of his anger. When it came to Lucille, Franky could hold rage the way a gator held a nutria. With the lengthening shadows of early evening came the shocks of seeing, and then not seeing Franky in dark spots beneath oak branches bearing thick, sunlight-warping tatters of moss, in the doorways of shops, in the hazy distance among people moving through the New Orleans Streets.

Angry enough, smart enough to hunt him for so many days in so many places, Franky could remember Ronnie's friend Irene. When they were together one night at a place Franky liked in Covington, Franky and Irene had talked about the food at Nina's, the place where Irene was supposed to be in wait for Ronnie. Everyone in New Orleans was looking for him!

Worried of a sudden, Tonti stayed with Owen, Melinda and the others. In deference to Tonti's unease and his local knowledge, the five rode a shaking streetcar to the end of Charles Street. Near the high river levee, they bought po'boy sandwiches and sat on a small, uneven patio fragrant with night-blooming jasmine. In the shadowy corners, an occasional cockroach skittered across an open space. Some chameleons made stop and start passage along the stucco of a neighboring shop.

Bill, who was from Iowa, amused the rest with the way he kept a wary eye on the insects and lizards.

"We're near the river here," Melinda said when they had finished. "Let's go there."

The others didn't care, so they let her lead them up the levee and down the other side. There were barges and a few high-riding cargo ships on the far side of the river, all seemingly stopped.

Melinda made her way through a thin strand of river's edge saplings until she could dip her hand into the Mississippi.

"Y'all watch for snakes," Owen said.

"What you want to put your hand in the river for?" Daniel asked. "Time the Mississippi gets traveled all down here, it's half cat spit and Yankee butt wash."

"Yeah, it's even dirty in Iowa. I've seen it out east of us in the Quad Cities," Bill said.

A dreamy look on her face, Melinda ignored him.

"I love N'Awlins," she said. "I'm going to live here forever."

Her quiet, firm statement struck Tonti with its prediction of exciting years of knowing and enjoying the city to its heart. The girl, not yet a woman, could choose, had chosen her home.

Suddenly, he realized that he was leaving, at least till Franky came to his senses. While Franky was on his tear, there was no Irene, no fun in the Quarter, no truly safe place to earn a few dollars or get up and dance.

But Tonti would come back. The way Melinda's breasts fell against the front of her outfit made Tonti sure he would only be gone long enough for the girl to finish becoming a woman. Smart already, she would have her whole très jolie self glowing from all the knowledge she was taking in at Tulane. When the evening ended, after they had listened to a small group led by a bony, long-fingered man with a squeeze box perform tunes in Louisiana French, the five of them rode the street car almost as far as the Quarter and walked a few blocks to Melinda's apartment. In the darkness, they heard the clicking of cockroaches scattering from their path. Two shirtless Negro boys sped past on a small bike. Jazz, blues, country, all kinds of music flowed from small shotgun homes and from two-story places supporting wide, upper galleries. The sounds mixed along the street overhung with long, horizontal branches of live oaks.

As a small fan made noisy, ninety-degree sweeps of the living room and an aggressive moth flew against the screen of a large window, Tonti talked some more with Owen and Bill, who were making beds of their Army-issue sleeping bags. Then, with his feet extending over the arm of a short couch, he fell asleep.

In the morning, he woke with his normal ebullience pressed under the hands down realization that, with Franky so enraged, there was no family for Tonti in Slidell, in New Orleans, in Louisiana. The offer from Daniel made sense. Tonti accepted the chance to ride north into Georgia with the three men. After that, he would go where the rides went, and away from Franky.

Owen, Bill and Daniel waited in front while Tonti stopped at Irene's little apartment for his duffel bag. Irene was already at work, her apartment left carelessly unlocked ever since the second time she forgot her keys. Tonti thought of her, a light summer dress fluttering a bit over her legs in the breeze of an office fan as she took dictation from a young lawyer trying to prolong the simple correspondence while he watched the fan reveal, and hide, the sight of Irene's knees.

Regretting the end of the New Orleans time, Daniel exited the city by way of Decatur Street so that, with Tonti partly hidden in the back seat of the new, white Mustang, they could see the people seated at Cafe Du Monde with their servings of beignets and coffee. Under a sky holding a far line of white cumulus clouds, Jackson Square was fresh with sunlight that would soon drive everyone to shadows.

"Good-by, N'Awlins, hello, black hats," Owen said, as they passed out of the Quarter. He was speaking of the jump school instructors waiting for Bill and him.

"You folk're fresh from AIT," Tonti said. "Look a ya. Bran' new eleven bravos, kick ass 'n take names infantry troops. Y'awl make it. And when y'awl get up in one of those scary C-130s, y'awl won't care you're jumpin' out of a perfectly good airplane because y'awl won't be in one."

As they crossed the twenty-five mile expanse of flat, silvery, sun-glinting Lake Pontchartrain on the causeway, Tonti took mental stock: about eighteen dollars in his pocket plus a paycheck of slightly more than eleven.

Louisiana, Mississippi, Georgia, Florida, he could imagine. Picturing the United States, he saw Iowa in the unknown other country, the up north one that sent tourists and GIs. He'd need more than Franky and eighteen dollars before he saw that part.

Tonti wondered if Lucille would miss him. He wondered if Irene would. He wondered if Melinda would.

He knew one thing: he'd a damn sight jump out of a plane before he cut his own hand off.

CHAPTER 2

You had a good home but you left
Your left... your le-eft

For Kevin Francis O'Geara, it was another day at the office, one marked, as always, by the whistling screech of full volume battle summons bagpipe music as he made his way down the aisle. After waving his shillelagh along the way and stopping for some flexing of his tremendous shoulders and biceps in front of three lady friends, he tossed the shillelagh to one of the beefy Irishmen in the front row. Dipping under the top rope and stepping into the ring as Muscles Muldoon, he pulled back against the top rope for a few quick knee bends and then stood for a glowering look that took in the patchy illumination of the lights as well as the satisfying size of the crowd in the seats.

Reflexively, Dennis Spuhn stood with Jim Clayton, Tony Szabo and Joe Yoder when the Central High School gym in Davenport, IA began sounding with boos and cheers for the burly wrestler. Shouting as loudly as they were able, the St. Sebastian's classmates continued to ignore Spuhn's distracted air.

Clayton, Szabo and Yoder mistook Spuhn's distance as concentration on the Marine Corps induction he faced the next morning.

Instead, Spuhn was foggy from the collection agent's call that afternoon. Spuhn interrupted the woman, promised to pay the charge - four months of overdue winter gas expense – yes, pay it before the first of June, yes, and went to meet his friends at Stubby's Pool Hall. Before leaving, he endorsed his Outing Club salary payment, the one enlarged with the tip from the Marycrest seniors' spring dance, and put the check with some cash in the cigar box where his mother kept household bills.

For Spuhn, the certainty of boot camp, the specificity of a three year military service promised relief from the viewing of his family's financial condition coming unwrapped, game by game, in his father's vulnerability to the slick men at the Coopershill Country Club.

Meanwhile, amid the noise of a gym filling with men whose shifts had just ended at the Alcoa and International Harvester plants, clusters of students, already in summer vacation spirit, were acting up near some St. Ambrose or Marycrest or Augustana coeds. Vacantly, Spuhn watched as he brooded about the phone call from the debt collector. His mother would have an exaggerated cheerfulness as she prayed to St. Theresa, the Little Flower, and pushed the three children - Spuhn, ten year old Mike and seven year old Veronica, through their routines of scouting, sports and everything else.

Coming to the River Rumble Spectacle this evening had been Spuhn's idea, a diversion of his friends' curiosity.

"Tank Vetrov is wrestling Muldoon tonight," Spuhn said as Yoder set a new game in the rack. The announcement had been running for days in the sports section of the *Davenport Morning Democrat*.

"Tank will flatten him," Szabo said. "Remember the way he slaughtered Rain Cloud that time? So much for the Red Man's revenge. No scalping that time."

"He kicked his ass. Hands down, he kicked his ass," said Clayton, his eyes fixed on the chalking of his cue.

"Fuckin' A," Yoder said, using much of his conversational vocabulary. He scattered the balls, took a puff from his cigarette and placed it back on the edge of the table before scanning the lay of the solids and stripes.

The evening fell into place. The highlight would be another Spuhn plan, the 11 o'clock meeting with Clayton's older brother Bob, who would have with him three quarts of Bud and a pint of sloe gin. Before then, the four friends closing in on the June, 1964 conclusion of high school years would watch Tank Vetrov take on Muscles Muldoon, cruise some loops on the one-ways paralleling the riverfront, make an appearance at Mike's Drive-In for cherry Cokes, a Green River for Yoder, and a large onion rings for sharing.

Clayton, Szabo and Yoder were glad for the regularity that let them stop dwelling on the jump Spuhn would make the next morning, when he stepped across the narrow chasm separating high school and adulthood. Spuhn's decision was so knife-sharp that it forced everyone else to know his own aimless crawl through graduation, summer jobs, college until mature American life took form.

But that was Spuhn. For good or ill, he would make a decision, and no backing down about it.

The day he turned 18, the previous April 27th, Spuhn walked into the U.S. Marine Corps recruiter's office, presented himself to the straight-backed corporal and added himself to the regional tally. Spuhn would leave, be done with the draft, send money home and whatever happened while he was away would happen. After that, Spuhn would find a way to have enough money for protection from the worries that had become part of the family's previous years.

Within a week, paperwork in order, Spuhn sat with, but apart from the others in class at St. Sebastian.

Now Spuhn reflexively touched his left shoulder, the spot of the healed smallpox shot, and looked about the gym.

He did not expect to recognize anyone who could be one of the prosperous men his father knew from the client's country club but, just the same, Spuhn scanned the rows. In a crowd ready to be raucous, many faces were familiar. Two teachers from St. Sebastian's had come: Mr. Hayes, the freshman math teacher, and Dr. Veysey, who taught biology and coached the j.v. wrestlers. Other men and some of the women were parents known from crowds at Pony League games or passed in the stands on nights of the St. Sebastian football season. Some were kids Spuhn recognized as students at Central or West, kids from baseball or swimming, known to him only by a first or last name, or a nickname.

One college student waved a Goldwater banner, while some couples seated in the adjacent section wore buttons in support of Goldwater's primary opponent Rockefeller.

Two small, merry women wearing black were familiar from the St. Sebastian cafeteria. With their long brown hair wound up into buns pinned beneath lace-fringed black bonnets, they clutched their handbags with a firmness that would have done credit to any wrestler on the night's card.

The rows near the ring held couples out for a night, some of the men in coats and ties. There were also some pretty women sitting near Muldoon's big Irish friends and watching for chances to catch the wrestler's attention. Regularly, they checked their lipstick and makeup with looks at small compacts taken from their purses.

Not far away, on the KTQC-TV platform, announcer Ned Conway was nodding in sycophantic bliss as the Romanian Ripper, victor of the bout just ended, predicted the following week's dismantling of Tex Adams.

At sight of the small, agitated announcer, Clayton spoke Conway's favorite phrase, "He'll feel that in the morning!" The others laughed.

Anna Adamski drew the Spuhn pack's notice right away. Eat crackers in bed? Neither Spuhn and his friends, nor the other men keeping track of her, would complain. She was a looker, with rich, brown hair, lively blue eyes, full lips, and a movie star's figure. As popular during her years at Iowa as she had been during her time at St. Sebastian's, her beauty and twinkling manner made her the sweetheart of one fraternity after another. When she punctuated her conversation with touches of her date's arm and brushed her knee against his leg, rows of watching men could feel something that made blood rush. Even Muscles Muldoon, suffering the press of his corner man's fingers and the flow of the corner man's instructions, had his grim, liquid eyes on her.

"Look who's here," Clayton said, elbowing Spuhn and nodding up toward the left, where a former St. Sebastian's classmate and two younger boys were getting settled.

Spuhn's mood soured as he saw Greg Benson removing his St. Sebastian sweatshirt and folding it for a seat cushion.

"That shit for brains," Spuhn said.

"He was so lucky," Clayton said. The previous fall, with a reverse at the very end, Benson had outpointed Spuhn and won the 138 pound slot for their senior season. Spuhn, naturally weighing a little more than 150, had crash-dieted down in order to avoid Pat Higgins, unassailable at the 145 pound slot. Even the night before wrestling Benson, as Spuhn bussed trays of untouched chicken and whole servings of roast beef at his Outing Club restaurant job, he stuck to the two day, pre-weigh in fast he had imposed on himself.

"Benson was farting so much, I don't see how you kept from passing out," Yoder said. "Jackass."

"Yeah," said Spuhn. "I was dragging. My job went pretty late."

"Yeah, you were pretty dead," said Clayton. A beat later, he said, "Man, Benson was lucky, though. You were so close to the pin that one time."

Then the noise began in the tight basketball gym with its corners left shadowy and the main lights squared on the ring set atop the letters of Central High School

"Tank, Tank, Tank," shouted Spuhn's group, immersing their own calls in the chanting that also had "Mul-doon!" coming from pockets of that wrestler's supporters.

"Tank, Tank, Tank!" On their feet, they said the name like a prayer and a threat.

"Benson wants Muldoon," Yoder told Spuhn.

Taller than Muldoon by an inch or two and just as massively broad without the tapering of Muldoon's form, Tank Vetrov entered the gym to the sound of a frenetic Russian dance. His gray-blue eyes were set in a solid face under thick black eyebrows. His hair, equally dark and thick, was cut short in no particular fashion. Across his shoulders was a shaggy cloak of brown fur, only large enough to suggest the Siberian cold, and not enough to hide the savage Cossack, hairy-chested bulk of his frame. Willing to be what he had been called from childhood – Tank - Nikolay Antonovich Vetrov had been inflexible about the league's plan for a cold war, Communist history: Russian he was, yes, but the Russia of long winters and absorbing dimension.

Ignoring the shouts of the crowd as well as the theatrical taunts of the waiting, red-faced Muldoon, the Russian Tank moved at measured, blank-faced pace to the ring. Then, dramatically sounding his weight as he set each foot steady on the canvas, he halted the other wrestler's abuse with a threatening look and rested against the turnstile of his corner with his forest timber arms at rest on the top rope. His own corner man, a large, flushed man with a solid Irish jaw and an anchor tattoo on the back of one hand, spoke little as he worked Tank's shoulders.

"Three minutes," Szabo predicted, running his small black comb through his dark hair, same as he had done several times since the four arrived. "Tank uses his Tartar Twist, man, and Muldoon will be begging."

Spuhn, Clayton, Szabo and Yoder were berserk. "Muldoon is in trouble tonight," Spuhn said, an opinion that earned "Fuckin' A."

This time it was Yoder. "Fuckin' A, he'll feel that in the morning!"

Spuhn's Uncle Jerry, not long out of the Marines then, not long back from Korea, had been a freshman at Iowa eight years before, in 1956 when Tank Vetrov was the top name of a wrestling squad that seemed unstoppable. Match after match, Vetrov, O'Brien, Walters, Henry, all of them on that spectacular team, they flattened the Big 10 along with records for points and pins. Tank, the heavyweight, simply dominated. He was strong, of course, but he was also as agile as the scrappiest lightweight, able to control the previously untouched Michigan star as soon as the contest got under way. The cheers from the crowd showed that others in the room remembered those stardust days, right up to Tank's brave effort against Sam Elwin, who finished up his Oklahoma career as national champ before going on to the Olympics.

Spuhn let his mind go to the next day as the ring announcer, a bespectacled man with the boom of a preacher, began the main River Rumble Spectacle with a reciting of upcoming River Region Professional Wrestling matches. Behind him, an athletic, crewcut official in a tight white T-shirt began the ritual of patting down Muscles Muldoon, then Tank Vetrov for knives, hammers, chains and other instruments.

The whole Quad Cities population knew the forces that had shaped the two powerful men in the ring: Tank Vetrov, the grandson of a Cossack chief, smuggled to the Free World in the arms of his sister, the two of them hidden by their young parents, the father and mother soon imprisoned and sent to perish in Stalin's Siberia; and Muscles Muldoon, raised in the bleakest and roughest neighborhood of Philadelphia by a single mother who earned some of the household's scant livelihood by besting man after man in tavern arm-wrestling tourneys.

Spuhn dwelt on the looming days: Marine boot camp's famous yellow footprints leading on. . . hair cut to the scalp, strong, angry men shouting orders and insults from inches away, unknown exercises and challenges that would leave everyone in limp panic, more shots, unpredictable, strange military companions, and then orders to be, learn, do, go for the remaining time of the enlistment. Meanwhile, lanky, gruff Yoder would either flunk out of Iowa or be serious about his business courses; upbeat, brilliant Szabo, with his sense of the world and command of several languages, would keep fixing his intense dark eyes on the texts of his engineering courses; handsome, wavy-haired Clayton with his chin dimple and long lashes would wheedle and charm his way through whatever course and fraternity he fancied; and Mary. . . Mary Siemons, about to move on to Iowa and new realms of social life, had already set Spuhn's picture in her memory's closet. She had always been brazen about the way she noticed who was noticing.

"Well, here we go," Clayton said.

In the ring, an insistent Muldoon was interrupting the progress of the event with his ritual of maternal gratitude. Leaning over the top rope above his two standing brothers, he received in reverence the silver-framed photograph the oldest one, Patrick Brennan Muldoon, unwrapped from a green velvet cloth. The second brother, Eamon Francis Muldoon, had the candle and matchbook. His face stiff with pent agony, Muldoon placed the image against the turnbuckle in his corner, set the lit candle before it, and then knelt with closed eyes for a prayer. At his own pace, ignoring the fussy, time-conscious announcer, Muldoon rose, turned first toward the KTQC-TV camera platform, and shouted up into the lights above him, "Mother, me dear mother, tonight in your honor, I promise that this son of the proud Muldoons will be victorious over the Russian Tank and-any-army-he-tries-to-bring-along!"

Noisy shouting ensued, each faction reacting.

The Russian Tank let a small smile escape his lips while he rested his arms on the top ropes in his own corner of the ring. He gave his black trunks a final, quick snugging, then came forward and bent into a crouch as the referee organized the two combatants for the start of the match.

Spuhn, Clayton, Szabo and Yoder stood. Szabo gave his hair a quick pre-match grooming.

The bout began. Both wrestlers crouched forward, testing one another with short feints of their arms and circling until they suddenly locked in an ox-pull contest of pushing and pressing. Spuhn's group and the rest of the crowd were now shouting instructions at the two straining men.

A headtwist takedown and a pressing arm bar gave Muldoon early dominance. With the tendons in his neck growing to cable size and his face screwed into a look of steely purpose, he avoided the sweep of Tank's free arm while he pressed and pressed on the captive one. A minute, maybe two minutes later, suddenly losing patience, he flung one leg across the other man's torso, wrenched Tank's arm into a painful new twist, and settled into a hold that had his own legs scissored over the tiring legs of the straining Tank.

Soon, with a miracle of closed-eyes determination, Tank reversed the force of the leg hold and flung himself free of Muldoon.

With the shouts of the audience rising and falling, the match see-sawed through intense, canvas-thumping falls and holds, neither wrestler able to gain complete control.

Here and there, they broke apart for aggressive circling of one another.

Of a sudden, Muldoon sprang forward into a somersault that ended with his legs flung over the shoulders and around the neck of his rival. As the caught wrestler struggled to stay upright with the 215 pound Muldoon squeezing, Tank snatched at Muldoon's arms but was not able to catch hold. With Muldoon tightening the grip of his legs and the crowd in the gym turning frantic, Tank stumbled about the ring.

Mistakenly coming into range of the ringside brothers, Tank suffered a quick clubbing of Patrick's shillelagh before the referee managed to make his warning heard.

Tank shook his head, cleared it, and gathered himself under Muldoon's weight. Increasing his speed as he progressed, he moved forward.

Muldoon became aware but too late for a full avoidance of the force Tank directed at one of the turnbuckles. Again, Tank slammed into the corner. Again, as Muldoon's grip weakened and his arms dropped. Again, as the referee pressed so dangerously close that he could not escape the force that flung him into the turn-buckle, immediately before the weight of the two wrestlers ex-ploded over him.

Szabo laughed. "He'll feel that in the morning!"

Tank suddenly had the ankle of Muldoon, an advantage that presently had Muldoon's face to the canvas as Tank sat astride him with his weight on the bent left leg pressed beneath the center of Muldoon's body. Biceps bulging, alternating gasps of pain and gulps of air, Muldoon strained to raise his chest and turn. Nearby, his corner man was gesturing and calling with visible alarm.

"Tank, go. Pin that fish," Szabo shouted. "Pin that fish."

"He'll feel that in the morning!" said Yoder. "Fuckin' A!"

Tank bore down, driving his weight against Muldoon before leaning back and locking his hands under Muldoon's chin. Tank pulled back until Muldoon was bent with his face raised toward the high, far corner of the gym.

The referee crouched beside them on the canvas, pressed his face close for a look and telegraphed with his rigid intensity the looming end of the wrestler's struggle.

Muldoon's frantic eyes took in the sight of his brother Patrick at the end of the ring.

"For herself, "Patrick shouted, presenting the framed image of their mother Peggy Mary Banion Muldoon. "For herself."

A moment later, catching Tank unaware, Muldoon not only managed to extricate himself but began avenging himself with a solid chokehold. For a moment, it was Tank looking wild-eyed and desperate but then, with his free arm, he grabbed enough of Muldoon's shoulder that Muldoon, reacting to the shock of Tank's grip, released his own hold and rolled away.

Glad to catch their breaths, the two men stalked about the ring. Wary of one another, they took quick opportunities for looks out at the crowd in search of remedy. The corner men and the Muldoon brothers waved and shouted, one voice overwhelming the other as the crowd intensified its own wave of noise.

Ned Conway, gripping his microphone tightly, was waving his free arm and talking like someone describing a double-feature of Armageddon.

Muldoon suddenly backed hard against the ropes and raced across the ring, where he sank backward into those ropes before hurling himself against Tank, now bewildered at center ring. At the last moment, Muldoon leapt feet first so that his legs wrapped fully around Tank's midriff. The force of the assault took the battle to the canvas, where Muldoon was able to grab Tank's wrists and pull his arms back as the scissoring grip of the legs kept Tank from breathing.

Ned Conway, unable to hear his own voice in the shouting of the crowd, was in full Apocalypse, Last Days form as Tank slowly lapsed into unconsciousness brought on by the squeeze of Muldoon's legs as well as the pain Muldoon was inflicting through his hold on Tank's twisted arms.

Exultant, glistening, Muldoon stood and flexed as he circled the ring.

The crowd was in full cry.

Patrick Muldoon unwrapped the photograph of his mother and held it toward his preening brother.

At center ring, Tank blinked, raised his head slightly and fell back with his eyes shut in pain. Alerted by frantic Patrick and Eamon, Muldoon took notice of the awakening Tank. Muldoon kicked his opponent viciously in the chest, then heel-stomped him twice in the windpipe for good measure. After that, arms up and flexed again, Muldoon strode in triumph toward Patrick, still waiting with the photo of their mother.

"Mother, it's time. It's time for the kiss of surrender," roared Muldoon, holding the photo high.

"Kiss and respect the photo of me Mother Muldoon," he said, bending and holding the image toward Tank's face. "Kiss me Irish angel," he said, kneeling and raising Tank's head.

With that, all hell broke loose. Roused and furious, Tank rolled back and kipped to his feet with such force that Muldoon, turned craven, hastened on hands and knees to where his brothers were brandishing the shillelagh and shouting. Tank bolted forward. He snatched the shillelagh from Patrick and flung the rod to the canvas as Muldoon, still trying to become small, slid away on his knees. Then Tank, impregnable at the ring's center, rolled his shoulders and fixed a terrible, unblinking gaze, his Siberian Death Stare, on Muldoon.

"Here it comes," Clayton said. "He's started the stare."

. Muldoon cowered, near to sniveling. With metronomic intensity, Tank moved slowly forward, grabbed Muldoon under the arms, flung him into the air, and held him aloft while turning in a slow, triumphant circle.

Patrick and Eamon pounded the canvas and clasped their meaty hands in a futile entreaty.

With a decisive thud, Muldoon crashed to the canvas and lay there, twisted, unmoving. Tank grabbed the man's ankles, straightened him on his back. With quick movements, in workmanlike fashion, Tank snatched first Patrick, then Eamon, by their arms, raised them one at a time overhead and flung them to the canvas.

Then, with the crowd roaring above the foaming torrent of Ned Conway's reporting, Nikolay Antonovich Vetrov, the Russian Tank, piled the three Muldoons in a heap and dropped across them with all the force of the Russian winter.

CHAPTER 3

People say we're crazy 'cause the crazy things we do!
I'm a Hard Core leather neck, now who the hell are you?

Boldly, Jim Clayton poked Tank Vetrov's arm as the wrestler moved, eyes straight ahead, along the aisleway toward a waiting Ned Conway and a KTQC-TV cameraman. Then, hooting, Spuhn, Clayton, Szabo and Yoder moved into the stream of people leaving the match.

Spuhn saw a little ahead of them Greg Benson and the two freshmen with him.

"Watch out," Spuhn said to the others. "Don't want to smash into the Farter."

Benson wheeled and, barnyard excited, stopped directly in Spuhn's path.

Benson's young round face was set. The center of his chin bunched white around a couple of delicate reddish hairs curled up from a cluster of tiny acne boils.

"You asshole," Benson said. "Shut your mouth."

"Spare me," Spuhn said. "Too bad the Tank wiped out that grappler of yours." Ready himself, rowdy with anger from the afternoon's call and the excitement of the wrestling, Spuhn saw Benson's shoulders harden and his short, thick arms tighten.

Spuhn feinted a movement that made Benson flinch. Spuhn feinted again, as if to snatch the Goldwater for President button from Benson's shirt collar.

The pin was another deliberate widening of the fissure that separated Benson from most of the other St. Sebastian classmates. Except for Benson, they were content with a political awareness composed of the assassination of President John F. Kennedy the previous fall, the fixity of the country's global stare-down with the Soviet Union, and a rising consideration of racial relations, something brought on by television reports of young Negroes and earnest white college students ignoring shouting groups of Southerners. In the sky some nights, people could see the glimmer of satellites designed by engineers of the USSR and US.

"Wiped out?" said Tony Szabo. With a nonchalant ease, he was rubbing the lenses of his glasses with a white handkerchief. "Wiped up, you mean."

Yoder started with his own fusillade, one that earned a scolding stare from the black-garbed St. Sebastian cafeteria women.

A couple inches taller than Benson, with an angular, wiry reach that outstripped the other boy's, Spuhn settled his weight forward and stood ready for whatever was about to boil over. Ordinarily contained, this night he was ready to mix things up right there and then, a proper goodbye to a jackass who had been a nuisance for four years. Benson, he knew from practices, was strong. He had a neck built up from religious regimens of neck bridges and arms expanded from lifting of a Sears weight set, but Spuhn had quickness and an advantage that came from anticipation of what any opponent was about to do. Besides, Spuhn was enjoying the way his unconcern made Benson so imprudently angry.

"I have to be home by nine-thirty," one of Benson's friends said, yanking Benson's sleeve. Clayton, Szabo and Yoder had arranged themselves against the two freshman boys.

When Greg Benson arrived at St. Sebastian as a freshman boy among freshmen boys – pimpled, babyfat plump, speaking in the tones of puberty – his average height, round face and reddish crew-cut were nothing exceptional. Even his voice, unsure and given to a nervous rise at the end of a statement, was within the norms of the class.

Spuhn, though, simply tossing something into the general banter, was the first to make some fun of a pattern Benson couldn't help.

"Will this be on the test?" Spuhn had asked Benson within the first week. Spuhn's agreeable face was not mean when he mimicked the Benson question but, once out in the open and overheard, the question became a matter of fact, universal definition of Benson the rest of his high school career.

Without meaning more than a quip, Spuhn had established a personal zero sum game that would have the other boy forever fretting miserably about the importance draining from his own account into Dennis Spuhn's reservoir of popularity.

"Will this be on the test?" raised Benson's temper every time he heard it.

Then, during senior year, Benson's oft-voiced embrace of the John Birch Society made him easy pickings.

John Birch Society, John smirch society, as far as Spuhn and most of his classmates were concerned. They had no particular feeling about the group and had no particular interest in knowing anything about its concerns for a Supreme Court surrendered to false doctrines or a foreign policy riddled with wasteful aid to Communist allies. Benson's excited advocacy of any idea or opinion or cause was enough to damn it.

Even Benson's success in the competition for the 138 pound slot on the wrestling team had come off as a surprising letdown by Spuhn. Despite pinning Bettendorf's 138 pound contender in the first meet, Benson grew to know that, no matter if he tore the arms off the eventual state champion from Muscatine, the achievement would only count as something junior to what the popular, always competent Spuhn would have done.

Simply joining the Marines had affronted the dip. Benson could see that while Spuhn's enlistment enraged a Mary Siemons suddenly left without a date for all the graduation events, other senior girls had new hope evident in the way they lingered nearby or came up to Spuhn as Benson's green-eyed, long-lashed nemesis was horsing around with his regular pals Clayton, Szabo and Yoder.

When Spuhn enlisted, news of it whipped around St. Sebastian's before the start of classes.Mr. Hayes, not so long out of the service himself, swerved on the way to one of his mid-morning math classes and tousled the wavy, brown hair Spuhn kept combed straight back. Immediately, Spuhn pulled a small black comb from his back pocket.

"You can say goodbye to this stuff," the teacher had said, messing up Spuhn's part again and tugging at a lock at the front of Spuhn's head. "And don't bother packing that comb. You won't need it. Give it to Yoder. He can stand some grooming."

Mr. Hayes had a little smile from the private thought that the determined Spuhn's eyes were just about the color of money. What if money had been gold or red instead of green?

Other students besides Spuhn were transforming from child to adult. At least three senior girls, maybe four, were getting married within weeks of graduation. Half a dozen boys had either enlisted, or were expecting to enlist then, in one of the military branches. Jerry Strebinski and Doug Carson were leaving the morning after graduation for Los Angeles, where Strebinski's uncle was foreman on a construction project with some laborer slots open. They'd be catching a train and be gone from the Quad Cities by six a.m.

But Spuhn always drew the most pleasing notice, notice that, in their personal zero sum game, Benson took as a withdrawal from his own account. Neither Spuhn nor anyone around him worried about how, but just knew he was going to do better than get along. From years of birthday and holiday gifts, from methodical saving of sixty percent or more of his salary from afternoon and weekend jobs, from poker winnings, he had built a savings account approaching two thousand dollars. If he wished, he had the means to pay, from his own pocket, for college, or to buy a new car.

Clayton, of all Spuhn's friends, was the closest to suspecting the use Spuhn was making of some of his savings.

All of a sudden, the fight shaping up between Spuhn and Benson had the attention of a security man.

"You boys settle down. Behave yourselves," said the fatherly policeman who was covering some small family expenses with a night of security duty. He forced himself between Spuhn and Benson. "Nobody needs this kind of crap from you two. Don't you kids have school tomorrow? Get on home. Settle down."

"He's going in the Marines tomorrow," Clayton told the officer.

The policeman took a moment for a kindly lookover, then put his hands on Spuhn's shoulders and gave him a light shake. Moving his face close, the man said, "Save all that piss and vinegar for the service, young man. Good luck to you. Keep your head down."

The moonlighting policeman glanced along the corridor, saw that Benson and his two friends were gone. With a light push, the man guided Spuhn toward a second exit way.

"Benson nearly got his ass kicked there," Yoder declared once they were walking toward Yoder's cream and brown, dual exhaust '53 Chevy. The car looked dark, attractively evil and wild from all the black magic Yoder was sanding smooth along the doors and fenders.

"Didn't none," said Szabo.

Yoder had left an electric sander along with some ratchet
wrenches that slid around in the trunk with a tire jack as he gunned
the car loudly away from Central High School and toward their 11
p.m. riverfront connection with Clayton's brother. Spuhn had the
honor of riding shotgun, no need to claim it. He brushed aside the
Time Magazine from the seat and, idly noticing its cover photo of
New York Governor Nelson Rockefeller, kicked the magazine out
of the way on the floor. No question, this was Spuhn's night.

But Benson was now sharing some of it, and was also adding to
the irritation of the woman's call for payment.

That worthless, addle-brained Benson had, in his customary
way, landed right in the night's activity.

From his younger brother Michael, a friend of Mary Siemons'
brother Kevin, Spuhn already knew of Benson's phone call to her,
an unsuccessful date proposal wrapped up in a mishmash of
sympathy over Spuhn's enlistment.

"That prick," Clayton said, a statement sufficient to loose an
acid review of Benson aggravations.

Killing time and also watching for cars driven by any of the girls
they knew, Yoder moved into the light, Thursday night flow of cars
and a few motorcycles circling the one-ways that paralleled the
riverfront. Szabo was watching for the white Chevy station wagon
his girlfriend Sheila D'Agostino was able to use some nights. Clayton's girlfriend Karen, a Grinnell College sophomore he met at a
J.C. Penny's counter, wouldn't be home for another two weeks. To
his annoyance, Spuhn was keeping an eye out for the cream-and-
turquoise Pontiac that Mary Siemons' friend Fran Hasenberg drove
when the two girls made their one-way rounds.

"Are you coming back to work for Klein? Klein Construction?"
Clayton asked.

Spuhn's friends knew of the startling conversation in the Outing
Club dining room one night that month.

Mr. Klein, his wife, and another couple, all dressed in the suits and shined shoes of the mainstay Outing Club patronage, were talking and smoking as they waited for the arrival of dessert. Mr. Klein suddenly interrupted the table conversation and Spuhn's invisible efficiency when he addressed Spuhn with "I hear you're going in the Marines."

Used to being heard when he spoke, the man's authoritative voice caused conversation to dip slightly at the nearby tables.

"Yes, sir," Spuhn answered, surprised that Mr. Klein knew his plans, or of him.

Now, startled by Mr. Klein's attention, Spuhn self-consciously gazed at the prominent Outing Club member.

About five foot eight in height and solidly broad, Mr. Klein was a physical man who carried himself like a six-footer, a gritty business founder ready to launch forward from the secure foundation of his Klein Construction company. His graying flattop, starting to thin, was in good order over a face that was slightly round and this early in the season, already a bit colored. His eyebrows were a rampage of black above the silver frames of his glasses. Beneath his right eye, pushing dangerously into the socket, was a horizontal, raised line of red scar. Mr. Klein shaped the ash of a cigar held in a large hand with an American flag tattoo across the back of it.

"A jarhead," Mr. Klein said. He had a small smile as he looked intently at Spuhn, held in polite mid-service beside the table. "They're a tough outfit."

"Yes, sir," Spuhn agreed.

"I'd like you to see me when you get out," Mr. Klein said.

"Yes, sir," Spuhn replied.

"I mean it," Mr. Klein said.

"Yes, sir," Spuhn said again. Known to Mr. Klein, Mr. Fred Klein, such an important man! Spuhn was anxious to turn away and resume the clearing before his smile became a disrespectful, giddy grin.

"Tell the lady to bring us some more coffee, will you, son?" the other man with Mr Klein asked. The man wore a Goldwater for President pin.

Spuhn rushed to tell the waitress, saw soon after that the Kleins and their friends had gone back to their visiting. The four rose and left while Spuhn was delivering trays of bussed dishes on one of his runs to the kitchen. So that had been that, the conversation alone, and no catching of Mr. Klein's gaze for a respectful verification of what had been invited.

Restless in the front seat as Yoder smoked and occasionally changed to a new station, Spuhn regretted not going after Benson wherever he had parked at the wrestling match.

"What time is it now?" Szabo asked.

Spuhn looked. From where they were near the river levee, he could see the clock on the pale, white tower of the tall First National Bank building. "We have about an hour and fifteen minutes," he said.

Yoder agreed. "Yeah, the guy on the radio said it's nine-thirty a minute ago."

Spuhn was quiet, an idea forming as Yoder drove them along the riverfront. At the levee rail here and there to the right side of the car, groups of men fished for catfish, gar, crappie and companion-ship. Between Davenport and the shapes of buildings and illumina-tions on the Rock Island side, the Mississippi passed in strips of currents and backwash, the press of its flow pushing, pushing, moving toward the dark lands between the Quad Cities and the Gulf of Mexico. Near the Rock Island side, a powerful white tug guided a line of barges making their way toward the north.

"Let's go by Benson's," Spuhn said.

"I don't care," said Yoder. "We're pretty close."

No one else objecting, Yoder continued along the river. Five minutes later, as they left Davenport for Bettendorf, Yoder downshifted and abruptly headed off to the left, up one of the streets that curved along the front of the high river bluff where lawns rose to the porches of grand homes. Three stories in height, variously lit up in each room or solidly dark around a single living room lamp, the homes sat on lots of large, irregular size along streets gracefully following the contours of the bluff. Crowned with elms and oaks, Benson's neighborhood eventually gave way to level tracts of small worker homes and then the regularity of fields, barns, white houses and silos laid out under a deep Iowa sky. The view down the hill, from the rooms and the porches of the large, solid bluff homes as well as from the windows of Yoder's Chevy, showed the Mississippi flowing black and wide between Iowa and Illinois.

Spuhn, Clayton, Szabo and Yoder were quiet as Yoder rounded a curve onto Benson's street and slowly passed the tall, gray stucco house belonging to the Bensons. From the road, the boys looked up the slope of the long yard, with its clusters of iris beds, abundant forsythia and a trellis supporting budding rose bushes. The porch of the house was dark except for a dim lamp above the wide front door and the illumination from a lamp in the front room. A stand of lilac bushes, their season of bloom beginning, grew between the house and the asphalt driveway reaching toward the rear, where the former horse stable was a two-car garage. There, in front of the garage, in light partially blocked by the bushes, Benson's maroon 1960 Chevy was parked beside the white Cadillac his father drove.

"Stop," Spuhn told Yoder, who promptly wheeled into a pocket of roadway hidden from the Benson house by some trees and, just above them, the shape of a small hill. "Wait here a minute, you guys. I'm going to put something on Benson's windshield." Spuhn grabbed the *Time Magazine* from the floor.

Yoder laughed. "Hell, yes," he said.

As Spuhn neared the Bensons' house through the shadowy protection of a line of hedge, a beagle owned by a neighbor began to bark. When the dog remained agitated, Spuhn retreated.

Back at the car, Spuhn said "That dog knows we're here."

"No shit, Sherlock," Szabo responded. His voice was anxious.

Spuhn was still thinking. "There are some big railroad ties next to the garage," he said.

The dog continued barking.

"How can they stand that dog?" Spuhn said in a moment.

"Little beagle dog?" Clayton asked. "Margie Kehoe lives there. That dog's Lucy. Let me try."

Clayton swung out of the car and moved quietly up the lawn, just ahead of Spuhn.

When the dog barked, Clayton and Spuhn paused, watching the Bensons' house for a reaction. No one was paying attention.

Clayton whistled a few times, slapped one hand against his thigh and called in a low voice, "Lucy! C'mere. Girl! C'mere." In a moment, the dog, now growling, approached to sniff the back of Clayton's hand. Soon, Clayton was petting the happy, wriggling animal. "Lucy, good dog," Clayton repeated, rubbing the dog's neck.

Watching Benson's house, they saw nothing changed.

Quickly, Spuhn returned to the car for Szabo, Yoder, and the jack from Yoder's trunk.

Szabo and Clayton kept lookout as Spuhn and Yoder jacked up the back of Benson's Chevy, then the front, over railroad ties they dragged from beside the garage. In less than ten minutes, Benson's car rested immobile, violated. Before they finished, Spuhn propped the *Time Magazine* on the steering wheel.

In Yoder's car again and descending the bluff, the four became silly and loud.

"Benson will shit a brick," Szabo said. "He will shit a brick."

"Fuckin' A," said Yoder.

With the radio tuned to big Quad Radio KQUD's Top 10 Countdown, they circled the one-ways twice, not finding any familiar cars, before they went to meet Clayton's brother at the riverfront.

The rest of the night drained away in laughs, memories, smoke rings, speculations about graduating classmates, and attempts to say meaningful things about the experience Spuhn would begin the next morning. He was to be at the southeast corner of the Post Office lobby at 6:30 a.m.

"Two years'll go fast," Clayton said.

"You comin' back here when you're done?" Szabo asked. The sloe gin had made him warm and quick to giggle.

"Oh, yes," Spuhn said. "Hands down." He thought of Mr. Klein.

Arrived at his family's bungalow less than four hours before induction, Spuhn walked to the side door past his sister Veronica's bicycle lying on the little strip of side yard. Once inside, he stood for a moment in the hush and looked into the living room, where his father had fallen asleep over an open *Saturday Evening Post*. In the light of the table lamp, Frederick Spuhn's wavy brown hair had a tiny gleam of Vaseline.

Spuhn was used to being told how he resembled his father, ordinarily a steady man who was careful about everything, from the obligation of his family to the care of the brown dress shoes he wore to church and business. In sleep, he did not show the deference that emanated from a sad, inner reckoning of an ambition beached at a modest rail freight company. He breathed easily, his solid chin bearing a soft stubble.

"Don't wake him," Spuhn's mother said. "You need to get to bed. Where have you been? We were getting ready to call the police." Dark-haired and brisk, she gathered her light blue robe around herself and kissed him quickly on his cheek before they both headed to sleep. "We were worried about you."

"You didn't need to be," Spuhn said.

His brother Michael, ten years old, did not wake as Spuhn stripped from his clothes and rose to the top bunk.

No, no one needed to be worried about him, Spuhn thought. Before dark sleep a moment later, he felt the liquor whirl him about in the room.

CHAPTER 4

Mama, Mama can't you see?
What the Marine Corps' done to me...

Hoo-rah!

The Greyhound buses Dennis Spuhn had taken, first from Los Angeles to Des Moines, and then to Davenport, had brought him home foggy but still alert enough to sense the promise in the note taped to the refrigerator: "Jim Clayton is home. Called twice. Important. Call him."

What Spuhn found at home quickly dampened the homecoming, no matter what plans Clayton could have.

The house had signs that Frederick Spuhn's flighty gin and poker playing was affecting everyone. Spuhn detected wariness. The living room held a Sylvania color TV now, the mahogany-colored console the outcome of a notably successful night. But why did Veronica leave a pair of her pajamas on one of the beds in the room Spuhn and his brother shared? "Veronica comes in and sleeps there some nights," Mike said. "She can hear Mom and Dad argue sometimes."

As soon as Spuhn had his seabag in the bedroom, he made the phone call. Within the hour, Clayton was in front of the house, where he honked long, twice, at the curb.

Spuhn was relieved to leave the house and get into the dark brown '55 Chevy the Clayton brothers and their mother shared.

"Son of a bitch, that is a haircut," Clayton said.

"Screw you, shitbag," said Spuhn. "Had best watch your mouth when you're talking to a United States Marine."

Both laughed. Then they went on to news that Clayton couldn't discuss with Spuhn over a telephone, not while Spuhn stood at the kitchen counter near someone working on school or household chores.

Hoo-rah!

Clayton's sexy friend Karen, the Grinnell student, had her best friend Janet coming from Peoria for a stay before Grinnell's new school year got underway. Janet, who took on the form of a panting pinup nymphomaniac in Clayton's telling, had broken up with a guy in the Navy.

"She puts out?" Spuhn asked.

"She is hot to trot, hot to trot," said Clayton, with happy emphasis. He punched at a radio button and changed stations as a commercial began. "Karen didn't say so in those exact words but they are roommates."

Roommates. Q.E.D. Janet must be cut from the same, free-wheeling cloth as Karen. And Clayton was still going with Karen, at least the whole summer. Q.E.D. Hoorah!.

The four of them would meet on Saturday night. The next afternoon, Spuhn would catch a bus back to Camp Pendleton and the beginning of his combat training.

Before then, the rest of Saturday, Clayton was going to. . .

"You're shitting me," said Spuhn. "You? In a rodeo?"

"Three events," said Clayton. "Bareback bronc, saddle bronc, and bullride."

"Are you crazy?" asked Spuhn. "You're out of your mind."

"This is going to be neat. A guy where I work does it. If that clod can ride the things, I know I can. He is a dip."

Spuhn gave Clayton a long stare. Clayton, a big smile on his face, looked straight ahead as he drove into downtown Davenport on the way to the river.

"Szabo and Yoder are coming, too," said Clayton.

"They're doing this, too?" Spuhn asked.

Clayton laughed. "No, to watch. Yoder's getting me stuff I need from their farm. You have to bring your own bronco riding gear, spurs, and like that. I have a pair of boots. A hat, too. "

Enough of that. Spuhn's thoughts returned to Saturday night and Janet.

"Janet's the same age as Karen?"

"Yeah. Juniors. So?"

"So I don't look like someone that age." Spuhn, his hair barely more than scalp, shaved his light beard a few times each week, even in Marine Corps training, and that out of hope as much as from need. Clayton, on the other hand, had a beard that grew dark by nightfall. He'd been that way for a year.

"She won't care," Clayton said. "Karen thinks I go to Iowa. Don't worry. Karen thinks I play on the football team, third string halfback."

Spuhn grinned. He returned to the rodeo plan.

"Where'd you get this big rodeo idea?" Spuhn asked.

"I don't know. End of summer, something to do. . . Got to try this sometime."

"Yeah, like never."

"You're the one joined the Marines."

"That's different."

"Maybe. You try the Marines, I give the rodeo a whirl."

The next morning, Spuhn slept past eight o'clock, right through the sounds of the radio as his mother went about breakfast making, right through her conversation with his father, who had lingered in wait for Spuhn before going out the door toward work. Veronica had just gotten up, this time in her own room. Mike was still asleep when Spuhn came into the kitchen. The "civvies" Spuhn wore, a white t-shirt and a pair of jeans, felt good.

"Mary Siemons asked about you, Denny," Veronica told him. "She works at Lake Gordon. She's a lifeguard."

When he received the letter from Mary the second week of boot camp, Spuhn wrote back to her in the same casually interested tone of her own letter. She was going with a boy from Davenport Central right now, a sophomore at Iowa who already had asked her to a fraternity dance. He was a Phi Kappa.

Spuhn wished she and two other girls who wrote to him had sent pictures. In contrast, a raw-boned galoot of a kid, a pimpled boy from New Mexico, had almost daily letters from a pretty girl who enclosed tormenting photos of herself. Spuhn's own mail dropped to letters from home and one funny note from his uncle Jerry, a reminiscence about his own drill instructor.

"What'd you say?"

Veronica shrugged her shoulders and grinned. "I said you were in the Army."

"Marines."

"Marines. What's the difference, anyway?"

"There's a difference. Those sorry Army guys go to war. Marines win them."

"Same thing." Veronica became caught up in reading the back of the Cheerios cereal package.

"Hell it is."

No drill sergeant looming, free to scan his world in arcs instead of crisp 90 degree swings from "Attention!" to "Left face!" or "Right face!", Spuhn luxuriated for a time in drinking coffee and riffling through the newspaper his father had left.

In her direct way, his mother asked about training, about the food, about people he was meeting, about Davenport friends and. . . about plans. She was short, cheerful but uninformative when Spuhn asked about his father's work and how things were going in Davenport.

Nearly 43, Spuhn's mother was slender, and among the mothers of the sports teams and school events, pretty. A pair of reading glasses with dark brown frames hung from a silver chain around her neck. This morning, one already turning humid, she wore a favorite rose house dress as she tied the strings of her checked apron in readiness for baking Spuhn's favorites, a crumb top coffee cake and several loaves of bread.

At some point, Spuhn's mother would read the newspaper's business section and major news articles. An avid bridge player who had passed the love to Dennis and was now working on his brother Mike, she would be sure to read the Goren column, then discuss it with Spuhn's father, an instinctive player who should have stayed with the bridge group instead of succumbing to the men at the country club. Spuhn couldn't understand why a man so competent at bridge would be so vulnerable in other games.

When she asked, Spuhn responded that he and Clayton would be doing something Saturday.

After dropping his late-rising brother Mike at a friend's that morning, Spuhn had the use of his mother's old Ford Fairlane station wagon, a swaying, squeaking thing his father had obtained, almost as a gift, from a client.

With Mike in need of no ride till six p.m., Spuhn had transportation for his own errands: the deposit of some pay and card winnings in his bank account. . . a look around. . . and the buying of some rubbers he would be using Saturday night.

California had been hot, but Davenport in early September, just on the vacation side of Labor Day, was hot and Midwest humid.

Good for the corn, he had heard in common conversation his whole life. Still, as he drove, he had the windows down as far as they would go. The passenger window in front remained stuck at the midpoint.

Depositing money in his Davenport National bank account always pleased him, even though the posting of transactions this early afternoon showed a reduction in his balance. The woman at the teller's window snuck looks at his Marine haircut.

"Where are you in the service?" she asked him. She wore her dark hair long, tightly pinned along the temples.

"Camp Pendleton, ma'am," Spuhn answered. "I'm on leave."

"God bless you, young man," she said.

Spuhn customarily enjoyed his effect on the adults who always reacted to his respectful manner and confident, groomed appearance, but this time he was eager to get on with his day's plan. He was soon back in the station wagon. Somewhat taking the measure of the September Quad Cities, he looked for a place to buy the condoms he would need Saturday.

After a summer of Marine Corps boot camp, the movement of pedestrians along the downtown blocks and of cars and trucks along the streets seemed capricious. One man, struck by a thought in mid-crossing while Spuhn sat at a light, turned and hastened back to the same corner where he had been. The Marine Corps had heightened Spuhn's liking for plans, direction, days that ended with something done.

During the bus ride from California, he had re-read *Think and Grow Rich*, a seventeenth birthday gift from his father. At one point, before turning back to the book from a long, bored study of the desert's golden emptiness, he met the curious glance of the man seated across the aisle. "The Bible?" the man asked, eager to have conversation. About the age of Joe Yoder's grandfather, the man had a tired air, with a broad, veined nose and cheeks drawn in over several missing teeth. He had put a weathered cream Stetson on the rack above his head.

"No," Spuhn answered. "*Think and Grow Rich.*"

"Oh, it's black. The cover of it. I thought it looked like the Bible."

For a while then, they talked. The man was going to Albuquerque, where he had a daughter and two grandsons. Once a truck driver himself, he had been all over the country.

"I imagine you're meeting all sorts of folk yourself in your line of work," the man said to Spuhn.

Spuhn agreed that, yes, he was.

"You can saw New York and New England, most of the East Coast, right off the map," the man said. "You're wondering why I say that."

Again Spuhn agreed. Yes, he was.

"Those folks think they're important because of all the big heroes, the explorers and the generals and so on and so forth, who used to live in this house or next to this little pond. But out in the rest of the country, where the regular folk live, people are important because of what they're going to do. They don't care much about what used to be."

The bus traveler's regional bias came back to Spuhn as he drove in a sweep along Davenport's northern edge and then beneath the bluff of grand Bettendorf homes toward the Rte. 6 bridge. The day, though humid, was bright, full of smells coming from the western farms, the riverside baking plant, and the wet of the river.

Among billboards for car dealerships and banks were some arguing for Johnson or for Goldwater, the presidential candidates. He saw "Klein Construction" on signs where men in hardhats moved earth or set framing in place for new buildings: a medical office building near the hospital, the sidewalks of a residential development begun on a slightly elevated spot Spuhn had never noticed before, an entire line of retail spaces leading to one large area where a new IGA food store would open soon.

Spuhn kept his eye out for Mr. Klein, but didn't see him among the people at each site.

At a Standard station after crossing the river, Spuhn found a restroom with a machine vending Love Magic and French Ticklers. He bought one of each, then changed a dollar, and bought another Love Magic. Musing over Janet, imagining her as Clayton described her, Spuhn returned to the Davenport side of the river, and then home, where he hid the condoms in the toe of a shoe.

Spuhn's father, either unaware of or unsure how to acknowledge the family breakage becoming visible, contrived to have Spuhn with him the next morning for a stop at the office. "Everyone wants to see you," he said. His voice was cheerful. As always, he had the brown waves of his fading hair combed back and smelling of a dab of Vaseline.

After the quick visit, including introduction to a new sales manager who seemed made up of steak, liquor and horse laugh, Spuhn learned that the rail freight services work had become clouded by the graceless opportunism of the same man, Kelly, who had re-ordered the sales territories. Spuhn's father was now going to Muscatine south of Davenport and developing new clients. The news of his father's separation from the Coopershill cardplayers cheered Spuhn. But then he heard his father say, "The clients aren't so happy about the new plan," he said. "In fact, a couple of them have begun doing their buying through their Muscatine offices."

Through Yoder, Szabo, Clayton and a call from Mary Siemons' information-gathering factotum, Linda Brozek, Spuhn was aware of his high school group's quickening college pulse. Now readying for college life, their thoughts were full of fraternities, sororities, new pledges (Clayton and all), beer parties with Coors brought from Colorado (Yoder), events, and then the beginning of the football season on September 26th (jealous Szabo, the St. Ambrose student). The Hawkeyes would play Idaho.

As he always did, Spuhn felt able to enter such a swirl if he wished but now, from his Marine Corps vantage point, he felt no disappointment that he had gone a different way. The way of the Marine Corps made futile thinking about his family difficult. At Camp Pendleton that summer, he had been with people who knew Korean battle, had visited Japan and Europe, had impacted small and large spheres with simple, unrelenting determination. He had watched a command spread through a whole parade ground of attentive Marines as certainly as rain came across a field. He had seen officers and non-coms – without degrees, with nothing more than good sense and character – gain the following of others.

The Marine Corps also prized action over talk, a bias in concert with Spuhn's family worries and his anticipation of the Saturday plans.

Clayton had the Chevy for that night. He would pick Spuhn up along the way to Karen's house. From there, they would go to the drive-in movie.

First, though, Clayton would live out the rodeo dream set in motion by his summer job co-worker. Saturday morning, typical of Clayton, he showed up grinning and so cowboy-attired that his garb spoke more Halloween than cattle drive. He wore a white silk shirt, a big, beige Stetson, and a pair of brown cowboy boots abundantly stitched with looping red designs.

Nothing said by Spuhn, Szabo and Yoder affected Clayton's happy confidence as they drove among cornfields and pastures brightening in early Iowa sunshine.

In his wildest dreams, Spuhn had never expected to spend part of his first U.S. Marine Corps leave seated on a wobbly bleacher seat in the country nearly an hour away from Davenport. But, there he was, along with Szabo and Yoder, ready to watch would-be cowboy Jim Clayton compete in the first of three events.

"Well, folks, let's welcome this fancy Quad City cowboy," the rodeo announcer said, introducing and mocking the grandly outfitted Clayton at once.

Up until then, until he was atop the fence and watching for the moment to drop onto the back of the gray bronco, Clayton had been all whoop and mischief. Now, unsmiling and serious, Clayton succeeded in settling himself with the reins in his left hand while the infuriated animal lunged hard against the holding push of two rodeo cowboys.

The small crowd on the bleacher rows and watching along the fences of the tiny rodeo arena waited.

"Clayton. Man!" Szabo said in a drawn-out whisper.

"Clayton is going through with it," Spuhn thought, repeating "Clayton is going through with it."

Except Clayton wasn't.

The gate suddenly opened, the horse leapt forward, dropped on stiffened legs and separated from Clayton, who rose high before helplessly flailing as he fell away. With a breath-knocking whump, Clayton landed nearly flat on his back. For a moment, as the rodeo assistants raced toward him and as dust settled over and around him, Clayton lay still.

Then, assisted by one of the sturdy cowboys, Clayton stood, dazed, trying to get a good breath as he acknowledged the crowd's applause with stiff nods. Favoring his right leg, he made it from the arena with his arms thrown over the shoulders of the two cowboys.

"Let's give this young fellow credit, folks," the announcer said. "He has a lot of guts, a lot of guts. Anyone who gets onto the back of Snowstorm like that is a brave young man." Clayton, Spuhn, Szabo and Yoder left soon after Clayton regained his breath and tried walking.

In the fall, he had struck the side of his right knee.

Even without the wincing expression as he put weight on the leg, Clayton was transformed. His dark blue bandanna and the entire back of his shirt were layered with dust that also grayed his face and the back of his pants.

Clayton took over the front passenger seat and let Yoder drive.

"You tried, man," Spuhn said.

"Fuckin' A," said Yoder.

"No harm in trying, huh?" Clayton said.

"Once is enough, though," Szabo said.

"No shit," Clayton agreed. He grinned as he cautiously swung his head for a glance at the others.

Then Clayton laughed. "I guess I'll have to give Karen the bad news tonight. Can't be the third string halfback while my leg is hurting like this. I'll have to go on the disabled list for a while."

Spuhn and the others whooped.

"Clayton, you are crazy," Szabo said.

After resting and soaking his leg for the afternoon, Clayton showed up as scheduled at Spuhn's house that evening.

"You drive," he told Spuhn. "I told Karen we would go to Top Place before the movie. It doesn't begin till eight."

"Fine with me," said Spuhn, his thoughts on Janet. He was wearing a short-sleeved madras shirt and tan wash and wear slacks. After shaving, he had been generous with Old Spice, maybe too much so, he thought as he followed Clayton's directions to Karen's house near St. Sebastian High School.

Janet lived up to Clayton's promises.

She entered the car and settled against Spuhn like a garment, a small, perfumed, talkative garment with a giggling laugh. Janet's face was round, framed by short-cut brown hair deliberately curved at the ends of her bangs and around her ears and slender neck. She wore white Bermuda shorts and a sleeveless lime green blouse that revealed the white edges of her bra.

She told Spuhn right away that she admired him for joining the Marines. She thought that was neat. An old friend of hers was in the Navy. She giggled.

When she handed him a book of matches and asked him to light her cigarette, she wrapped her fingers around his and held his cupped hands for a moment.

In the back seat, Karen, graceful and long-legged, dark-haired, pressed equally tightly against Clayton while she delicately touched his swollen knee.

"Live and learn," Clayton said.

While they drove the little way to the Top Place restaurant, they talked date talk: boot camp, Clayton's rodeo ride, Hawkeyes football, Janet's excitement at visiting Karen and Davenport, a frightening Grinnell class soon underway, the prettiness and immensity of the river. Janet's touch, light at first, then probing, on Spuhn's knee and thigh, overrode any topic. He tightened his own reach around her shoulders and stroked the slender shape of her arm.

Distracted, Spuhn pulled into the Top Place lot and parked – right next to Greg Benson, who had driven up at the same moment in a light blue Cadillac bearing front and rear Goldwater bumper stickers. With him was Marsha Tredwell, a popular, blond member of their St. Sebastian's class. Tanned and her face carefully made up, Marsha gave a smile of recognition that contrasted with the dagger look on Benson's face.

"Dennis!" Marsha called. Benson's anger deepened.

Spuhn and Clayton smelled blood.

Separating immediately from all of them, Benson took Marsha to a small table against the window on the far side of the big restaurant. There, as he and his date talked and ate, he shot glances toward the others.

While Janet and Karen visited the ladies' room, Spuhn explained his plan to Clayton, who guffawed and said, "Hell, yes."

Then Spuhn crossed the restaurant to engage Benson and Marsha in a catching up of summer news. Long-lashed, green-eyed and Boot Camp fit, he affected a sincerity that the thin St. Sebastian bond would never support. Caught, Benson grunted answers, angrier and angrier as pretty, personable Marsha warmed to the conversation. She had great curiosity about the Marine Corps. Was it hard? What was it like?

"A whole lot of running, lot of harassing. They keep you busy," Spuhn said.

Then he bent and pretended to find something on the floor beside the table.

"Oh, here, Greg. This fell out of your pocket," Spuhn said, placing a French Tickler package at the center of the table.

CHAPTER 5

I said MP, MP, don't arrest me
Arrest that leg behind the tree
He stole the whiskey, I stole the wine
All I ever do is double-time

Mickey Jaspers, careful to have bulky Randy Cahill and Strangler Walker with him, rose when Tank Vetrov came from his last appointment into the small reception area of the Louisa Psychiatric Care Center in Wapello, Iowa. The big wrestler was quiet, distant and, to Jasper's relief, calm except for the twitching of his left leg. Flanking him as he entered and then dropped onto the thin purple cushions of a wooden bench were two staff members: a tall orderly carrying Tank's gray Samsonite suitcase and a stout, cheerful nurse who carried a clipboard and a manila envelope. She had flecks of sparkle in the dark green frames that held lenses curving up at the round edges of her face.

Except for Tank, the room in the brightening light of a fresh day was full of purposeful activity.

Three months, the first one spent in some section of the small, red brick building and the other two as an out-patient attending counseling sessions, had elapsed since the incident, the night Tank rose in a Muscatine tavern, babbled threats, and pushed a heavy table the length of the room.

"You look good, Tank," Jaspers said. Randy Cahill and Strangler agreed.

Strangler took Tank's big gray case from the orderly.

"You need to stop back at your place?" Jasper asked.

"No," said Tank. He had packed up that morning at the rooming house, before the ten-minute walk up Franklin Street.

Once they were in Jasper's pale green Cadillac, Strangler, a powerful young wrestler still awed by everything about his new life on the circuit, including his conversation now with Tank Vetrov, asked from the back seat "What was it like there?"

What was it like?

Yes, what was it like?

Tank didn't remember much of the first couple of days, except for the burning absence of liquor and the way the orange bomb, what everyone called the concoction of tranquilizers, set him hovering in detachment from his own twitching, mumbling form. What was it like? The question brought to mind what was already there: the leather straps that held him in the big gray chair fixed near the light brown wall as he sat, unable to grasp his own thoughts or speak coherently through his own dry lips as the full-volume sound of Wesley's clock radio played a series of the same 50 songs and, a short distance away, Willie's radio boomed its own roster of 50 tunes.. What was it like? A stubbled, creased veteran of many 30-day respites said it was 30 days in a place designed to make sure the world never ran out of crazy people.

It was like the heating of a gas held in a tight container. Now, with his new regimen of medication making his leg twitch and his liquor need a little blunted in a space too confined, he was ready to burst.

But burst where? Jaspers had driven down from Davenport the first week, to tell him something that broke on the sedated Tank with as little force as a dandelion puff brushing into a fence railing: Jaspers had dropped Tank from the circuit. Jaspers thought the world of Tank, would always remember the time at the Iowa Invitational when Tank came back hard and took down, then pinned that undefeated Drake wrestler. But something's wrong now. All that strength and no control. People getting hurt. Andrews' shoulder maybe never the same. And the drinking! The drinking! God almighty, Jasper was no one to be pointing fingers but just plain shit-faced or hung over from being shit-faced, that didn't cut it.

So no wrestling then. No wrestling with its tedious script of good versus evil, its testing and eventual breaking of strong, agile men, its small fame and, in his case, the undercurrent of Russian Commie emotion. In his dozen years, Tank had seen powerful men succumb to inevitable decline. In his own case, he knew, he had let the drinking turn from college celebration, from a feature of a completed workday, into a life increasingly solitary and furtive and bleak.

"A treatable, mild bipolar disorder" was Dr. Stanley Gilmore's assessment. He was on the teaching staff of the Iowa Psychopathic Hospital at Iowa City. No one doubted him at the Louisa Psychiatric Care Center.

Yes, the prescriptions did return control of Tank's thoughts, a reasonable trade for the arrival of a leg that was twitching right now as the car moved quickly along Iowa route 92 through corn-rich fields and warm grassy smells toward the cluster of trees and a courthouse steeple marking Washington, Iowa. There Tank would catch a Greyhound for his return to western Iowa and the small farm where his mother still lived.

More than a year had passed since Tank had been there. He had not needed Dr. Gilmore or the program for the shame that bore down on him the times he remembered his mother's whispers as she stroked his hand. She had found him with his head down, crying, full of his mysterious sadness, his cheek against the white enamel table of her kitchen. She stroked him and touched his hair with a persistence that finally broke his gloom enough that he could wash his face, hug her as she kissed his cheek, and leave in his big, cream-colored Oldsmobile for the next match on his circuit. The drinking had worried her for a long time. He knew the hopelessness she saw that early morning terrified her.

Before transferring in Des Moines, he would have time for a meeting at a Lutheran church Tank's sponsor had found for him. The same man – a taciturn, Marlboro-smoking shop foreman Tank knew as Dick – had found Tank a lifeline of emergency numbers and then an AA group right in nearby Harlan, only a short trip from unaffiliated, tiny Navalny. Marked by no stoplights and only one speed sign in each direction from a corner where a tiny domed church and a windowless shed had turned gray and misshapen, Navalny had its name from a fable. The first Russian immigrants fleeing Russia of the early 1900s had named the spot Navalny after a hero who freed his followers by dropping pebbles that finally blocked the swing of a despot's castle gates. Eventually, after Navalny and his neighbors escaped, the ruler and his henchmen perished when their fortress became a flaming prison.

Over the years, the Navalny farms had combined into large tracts. A population shrinkage begun soon after World War II continued through the 50s and now the 60s as young men and women left for university study and for jobs with big enterprises providing manufactured goods and processed food.

Tank's sister Galina, now in her late twenties, was one of them. Settled in Omaha with her husband Jim Casper, a second shift millwright at a metal fabrication firm, Galina had embraced all the changes that came her way, including her three busy children. For his part, Jim, raised on a farm east of Sioux City, Iowa and everlastingly surprised that life took him from the same future, relished the visits he and his family made for the sake of looking in on his mother-in-law, Mrs. Vetrov. No matter that, even before Tank's father, quiet Anton Zakhar Vetrov, fell so hard from the barn and began his uncomplaining hobble into dying, the Vetrov farm had given way to little more than a house, a pen and a vegetable garden surrounded by leased fields, Jim Casper always came to it with joy. He studied the state of the boarded livestock, the condition of the mouldering little sheds and the old barn, the quality of the corn and beans in surrounding fields.

Tank was too big for comfortable rest in one of the Greyhound's gray and blue seats, so he planted himself in the center of the seat at the bus' rear. Alone, still except for his twitching leg, he leafed twice through a discarded copy of the *Rock Island Argus* newspaper before turning his vacant gaze on the flat scenery of a sunny late September day in Iowa. President Lyndon B. Johnson was campaigning in California while his opponent, Senator Barry Goldwater, was waving to supporters in Ohio.

The rows of tall green corn plants fanned past in continuous, curving radians. Occasionally, the bus slowed and shifted around a big tractor moving along the road to another field. In the Amish country, the highway had a parallel road of stones and hard clay for the buggies of black-garbed, bearded Amish farmers who watched as their dark horses worked toward whatever destination was known from the pull and release of the reins. Billboards touted car dealers and candidates for sheriff. A few announced Jesus as Lord or warned of Hell for the unrepentant sinner.

In the warm rear of the bus, a couple of flies moved about on the panel framing one of the windows.

Tank was hungry when the bus completed its hissing turns into a stall at the Des Moines station but he put off eating. Instead, he asked directions of a wiry Negro baggage handler and made his way to the St. John's Lutheran Church on Sixth Street. He entered behind a woman who had light brown hair tucked under a small dark hat with a pheasant feather for adornment. His size and his darkness frightened her. The nervous woman quickened her pace as he followed her down a stairway into a big corridor where a dozen people, mostly men, were waiting in and just outside a room marked for AA.

The meeting was soon underway, a relief to Tank, who knew how prone he was to turn a missed session into a descent. He could tell some of the others recognized him as he sat among them on the folding chairs fanned around a big lunchroom table.

Grim as he ever was in the ring, he concentrated on his sobriety, now spanning more than 92 days, including the two nights he had thrown himself around a cell in the back of the Muscatine police station.

"I am Nikolay. I'm a recovering alcoholic," he said in his turn. Recovering. Recovering.

Dave's whispered reading, Darlene's patient guidance of an honest action discussion were familiar to him, and encouraging. Others could repair themselves, be happy. He could, too. The simple meeting settled him.

With the others, he spoke the Serenity Prayer - ". . . grace to accept with serenity the things that cannot be changed, courage to change the things which should be changed, and the wisdom to distinguish the one from the other." Then, he returned to the bus station, where he ate a hot dog and sat in tumbling thought on a scratched wooden bench until twenty after two, when a tidy, crew-cut man with a coffee thermos cranked open the door of the silver bus that would stop in Harlan along the route to Omaha.

With his size and his introspection making him a poor choice for a seatmate, Tank again had the wide back seat of the bus to himself. For a while, he stared at the city passing away into a broad scene of prairie. There were white farmhouses, red barns, white barns, silos, lines of Chinese elms flanking entrance roads, barbed wire, Burma Shave messages on arresting series of reddish-brown signs, and over the soft hills of central, then western Iowa, cornfields relieved now and then by grazing herds of fattening steers. "See Rock City" called from some barn sides, "Chew Red Man Tobacco" from others. Absently, Tank took in the narrow, quick crossing of the Raccoon River before stretching out on the seat for a sleep that made time pass without resting him. He woke with his cheek resting in saliva.

When he looked out the window, he saw that the bus was passing through Guthrie Center. The sight of two boys in football pads made him remember the freshman year, only his second match, when he surprised the strong, 165 pound spark of the Guthrie Center Tigers' team with the wrestler's first pin in two seasons. Furious, the defeated boy had leapt up and jammed his shoulder into Tank's as they shook hands. That had been the end of state hopes for the boy, a thickset kid with yellow hair and large, dark freckles down the back of his neck and the backs of his arms.

Wrestling. Such a lift in high school and then at Iowa, It had become just wrestling, the job organized by Jaspers into training leading to the clashes or the fights for survival or the free-for-alls or whatever Jaspers named the exhausting series of them.

Against his wishes, Angie came into Tank's mind. She had the graceful fingers of one hand twisting a strand of her dark hair as she stood her ground in his thoughts. Even here, she had her eyes looking past him as she openly took in the attention of the men who always had eyes on her. Annoyed with himself, Tank pictured her as he first saw her, a striking chiropractor-in-the making, a healer who moved him with ease as she probed the soreness of his back and then adjusted his spine. The second time he went to the clinic of the Palmer School of Chiropractic, Angie brought her face close to his ear, whispered things and touched him with such mischief he waited more than an hour for her in his car. She stayed that night, another and another, before they married at the Davenport City Hall and began their decline into mean-spirited, mutual contempt. His wife for less than nine confused months, Angie remained lost and unchecked on his AA list, her mother in Indianapolis now dead and her sister returning no calls from Nikolay Vetrov.

Tank's mouth felt sour and dry as the bus entered Harlan, circled the square in front of the gray county courthouse building and stopped before the Woolworth's.

Arrived and apprehensive about the conversation lying ahead, Tank delayed. He took a seat at the lunch counter of the small, familiar store with its creaking, wooden floor and tin ceiling. A high school girl with a natural friendliness came to take his order. Bearing his dour, indecisive study of the plastic-covered menu pages, she filled a water glass that rattled with cubes, set it before him, and waited. "That pork sandwich platter is really good," she said. "It comes with fries."

Good enough. Still bewildered, Tank sat, filled with the hollowness that massed from the past months as well as from the lost familiarity of the small store. He was just beginning to shed "wrestler," replacing that definition with whatever he was: hurt, solitary, recovering, anxious about the pill jars carried in a pocket of his bag.

When the food came, he finished the sandwich before taking a swig of Coke and polishing off the french fries. He tipped the girl 35 cents, and returned to the courthouse square, where the sunshine had the slant of late afternoon. Tank sat heavily on a bench facing the gray court building. There Nina Bjornson saw him and called to him through the passenger window of a dusty white Ford pickup. "Nikolay!" Her voice was strong and cheerful, sincere, as authoritative as it had been when she was an eighth grade bus monitor keeping Nikolay and the other young students in line. "Nikolay!"

Immediately, Nina offered Tank a ride to his mother's place, "right on the way" to her sister Kathy's place. When he hesitated, Nina pressed him. "C'mon," she said, stretching across the seat and pushing the door open. "Get in. It's right on the way. C'mon. I want to hear all about everything you're doing."

A sledgehammer and garden tools rattled with two large buckets and Tank's suitcase in the bed of the truck as she drove toward Navalny. Once pretty, even a dream girl for Nikolay and the other boys she mothered as a responsible adolescent, Nina now had her hair turning gray and a modest expansion of stomach showing against her overalls. She still had her sure way, an evident comfort with the double chin and the roundness of her maturing body.

Nina's warmth raised Tank's spirits, too, as she acquainted him in a torrent with the happenings of the families and places they both knew. Her husband Chet now worked for the State Agricultural Department and one of her sister's sons was selling for Monsanto. Nina and Chet's son Dan, who got polio as a youngster, had a new leg brace and was now in his second year at Drake. Dan wanted to be a therapist. The Stendovs had the Budweiser distributorship that used to belong to Alex Stendov's father-in-law. The little Schmidt girl was married and had five children: one boy and the rest girls, all as darling as their mom. Summer was wet at first. Nina was used to talking without having full attention. "Oh, look at that. Isn't that pretty?" she said, slowing as they approached a stretch of homes where a large maple was turning grandly red.

Tank was startled. He looked at the tree and saw its beauty without understanding what Nina noticed.

Resuming her speed, Nina continued her patter of names and stories.

Outside of Harlan, they turned onto a single-lane concrete strip and, watching for any oncoming vehicle, drove to the end of the Mattingly's old farm. The roadbed there became a gravel surface that tossed Nina, Tank and the things on the truck bed from side to side as a rooster tail of dust rose behind them. Two shaggy farm dogs came roaring to the roadside from a dismal little farm with a leaning barn and a small house covered in failing gray shingles.

Tank looked for the apple orchard where he and the Taylor brothers used to play with the trees' misshapen, pocked fruit, good for throwing at barn sides, tree trunks and birds. But the corn was high and green along the road. If the little orchard existed, it was hidden from view. Along the road, a line of sumac had taken hold, the leaves turned wine red from the dipping September temperatures.

The color caught Tank's eye the way the maple had delighted Nina. This time, the friendly woman did not comment, only continued her news about one event or another.

A son with polio as a child and then a lifelong twist in his leg, Tank thought, wondering about Nina's pleasure at everything from seeing a childhood friend to seeing a tree in fall color.

Where was the woman finding the joy she made so evident?

They crossed the culvert bearing the lazy flow of Little Creek and arrived at the drive leading to Tank's old home. Some rose showed in the glass of small front windows framed by Russian-style, blue ornamentation. The sky reflected there was turning from sunny afternoon to a great horizon of pink and orange.

Out of politeness, Nina only drove Tank to the edge of the small, weedy yard. Scattering a half a dozen hens, she turned around short of the two big oaks that gave the house, barn and pen a portal. The leaves of the trees were become dry, soon to show brown.

"Your mother will be so glad to see you, Nikolay. We used to see her but that's been a good long while now. I hope her health is good. You be sure to say hi. Don't be a stranger."

Chickens scattered again and regathered at mid-yard as Tank picked up his suitcase. The evening air felt cool. To his right, a mottled cat with its belly low to the ground quickened across a short open space into the shaded barn. Some wrens flitted about the branches of bushes along the barbed wire fence of the field now leased to a father and son named Schoepke. At the gate of the small pen, a worn white horse swished its tail and rippled its flanks.

The shiny gloss of the fresh window trim made Tank wonder: who had done that? He crossed the yard, intent on kissing his mother's cheeks, apologizing in blunt admission of the sadness he had inflicted.

The door opened. In the golden light of the descending sun, he saw his mother, lovely still at nearly seventy years, with large, very dark eyes under firm eyebrows remaining black as her soft hair, wound in pinned circles, grayed. Along with the musk of the closed-in front room, he smelled the familiar odor of the garden on her. Her delicate hands held fast on the strong arm of her smiling companion Otto Traugott, who carefully supported the light weight of the tall, thin woman.

"Nikolay," she cried. "God's love. My son."

She spoke in Russian, her meaning clear even though Nikolay remembered the words imperfectly. "Николай! Люблю Бога! Николай! Мой сын!"

Russian! The mother who had forged with such determination into full replacement of her native tongue with the new American language was looking lovingly, happily at Tank. Her hands shook, her cheeks pinkened, and, expecting an answer, she greeted him in Russian.

CHAPTER 6

They say that in the Marine Corps,
The chow is mighty fine.
Chicken jumped off my tray once,
And started marking time!

The plan Jesus Hernandez cooked up made sense, even though Spuhn could tell the big Cuban with the friendly, dark eyes was concocting half of it as he watched Spuhn's own face.

When they were done with Fort Lee and their training as Food Technician Specialists in twelve days and a wakeup, end of January, 1965, they would get to Miami in the Volkswagen bug Hernandez was buying from a guy going to Okinawa. Driving straight through from where they were south of Richmond to Miami would take about a day, including all the stops for gas, chow and the head. They'd go to the beach, they'd relax, see the sights, chase some tail and have a good little vacation before they reported to the West Coast for transport to Okinawa. Lieutenant Solomon was already counting on Spuhn helping him drive back from Miami to Chicago. From there, Spuhn could get to Davenport for time with his family before leaving for Japan.

Hernandez was hard to counter once some plan occurred to him. Just having the idea became for the big, always smiling Marine the certainty of all the good consequences, as if simply turning the key in the ignition of whatever shaky car he was picking up for fifty dollars and the balance from the next month's paycheck would roll the two of them into all the easy living times Hernandez foresaw. In fact, Hernandez already owed his bunkmate twenty of the fifty dollars paid to the Okinawa-bound Marine.

With his exuberance, Hernandez was able to wear the practical Spuhn down quickly. Spuhn was glad his friend had not used what he knew of the trouble in Davenport as a reason for being elsewhere. A few days of home visit would be enough for Spuhn.

Part of the appeal, the challenge for Hernandez, two years older than Spuhn, was the chance to guide. Spuhn, so deliberate, so thoughtful, so very mature about the life ahead of him, needed to put the pedal to the metal, skip and go naked. Spuhn needed to get laid.

He also needed to get a Marine Corps tattoo, something accomplished at a wrinkled Navy veteran's small parlor toward the end of the Food Technician school training.

Hernandez, along with the rest of the boots, had come to trust Spuhn's easy recognition of the cords and persuasions that grouped disparate Marines – New York punks, some California pretty boys, Idaho country boys, a Miami hombre with Cuba in his voice, a puertorriqueño whose understanding of English was less than his grasp of the Marine Corps – into cohesive teams of trench diggers or volleyball powers. Toward the end, even the DIs, conscious of it or not, made use of Spuhn's practical leadership.

By the end of the third week of Boot, Hernandez and Spuhn had a bond that continued through combat drills and then into the training at Fort Lee. Some amused clerk in the Marine Corps chain had playfully steered U.S. Marine Private Dennis Spuhn into a military occupational specialty that would assure him a true spoon, or cook, name for the remainder of his U.S. Marine Corps life. At that, Hernandez signed on for the same training, and at the expense of another year added to his enlistment.What did Hernandez care? He'd see what the Marine Corps and life dished up. Okinawa? Even Vietnam? As Spuhn knew, Hernandez wanted to invade Cuba. There was little that Hernandez took seriously, but Cuba fired his eyes. Hernandez wanted to go back and get his mother, to set her up among amigas and some familia in Miami.

Hernandez had the Volkswagen in his possession as soon as the training ended.

The car showed wear in the dings of its hood and in the frozen fuel gauge but it responded to Hernandez's full out, pedal-to-the floor driving.

Hernandez wore aviator sunglasses and, under his fatigue coat, a shirt bedecked with flamingos. The runs and pushups and press of the Marine Corps training had trimmed him but had not leaned him down like the hardened Spuhn, who had gained three pounds. Hernandez's face kept a small trace of the roundness from his pre-Marines time. With him in the car, he had a sack of some of his own baking – cookies and bread dressed up with spices from his store of island flavors - and some oranges from the duty he had pulled in the mess hall the previous day.

Hewing to the 200 mile driving stints Spuhn established, they fell into the rhythm of the trip, stopping to stretch, use the head, and buy gas when Spuhn determined. Spuhn checked the oil stick reading each time they bought gas.

With Hernandez still sleeping, slack-jawed in the other seat, Spuhn pored over new thoughts – of Davenport, of the enlisted club time with a gunnery sergeant who had been a lied-about-his age Navy corpsman in the World War II Pacific. Sure of U.S. might and Vietnamese insignificance, the veteran of so much war force made his view clear. Some chinks had stirred up a bigger fight than they could handle. If Spuhn and the rest of them got to Vietnam at all, it wouldn't be for long. The Fighting Third? Leave the engine running. The Fighting Third would kick those little, yellow asses in a hurry.

Nearing Columbia, South Carolina, Spuhn began falling in among trucks, eighteen-wheelers, tankers, and flatbeds bearing loads of steel rods or immense engine parts.

The rear doors loomed high, most of the truck doors empty of anything but stickers, occasional lines of numbers, and silver bands marking cargo secured.

As he followed and, when he passed, Spun began to see.

The caravans of trucks hauled doors that could be advertising billboards, signs that would convince highways of following or passing drivers that this would be the place to eat, that the place to sleep, and this the car or the sofa or the cereal to choose. Spuhn imagined national banks, insurance companies, bakers, the U.S. Marine Corps speaking through the backs of presently under-utilized semi-trailer doors.

Spuhn began to calculate. Was he averaging three minutes behind a truck before he became able to pass? And then three minutes for absorbing the ad on the next truck. And the next. And if he overtook six trucks every eighteen minutes, eighteen or twenty trucks an hour, would that matter to Coke-a-Cola, to 7-Up, to the First National Bank, to McDonalds? Who owned all the trailers, and where were they found at the times – either empty or loaded – they were awaiting hook up to a truck tractor?

By the time Spuhn swung into a Shell station doing a side business in boiled peanuts and pecans, he had ideas and numbers washing through his thoughts. Beside him, Hernandez woke, looked around, muttered "in a moment", and exited the car in search of the head. When he returned, he was awake, happy again with the increased warmth of the air, which smelled of diesel from the passing trucks and of country. The puffs of breeze coming over the station were rich with odors of silage and of the cargos of cattle and hog transporters.

"Where are we?" Hernandez asked as he began to drive.

"About here," said Spuhn, folding the map for Hernandez's glance. "We must be fifty, sixty miles from a place called Statesboro. We're in Georgia."

In Georgia they were but not in the range of a radio signal Hernandez liked. After skittering through shrieks of static, a moment of Christian Power Hour, and weak signals from two stations that seemed to be in Savannah, Hernandez turned the radio off and beat a quick rhythm on the steering wheel.

"Did I miss anything?" he asked.

Spuhn told Hernandez about the truck signs idea he had been mulling.

"You and my father will like each other," Hernandez said.

They turned to other talk. They ought to eat barbecue. Hernandez didn't care what the weather was, he was going to the beach. Hernandez knew this girl.

"You always know this girl," Spuhn said.

"No, man, I do. And she'll have someone tasty for you, too."

Once more, Hernandez beat on the steering wheel.

By the time they reached Statesboro and the next leg of Route 1, Spuhn had fallen asleep. He woke again when Hernandez found a radio station playing pop hits. He had the volume high and was accompanying The Beatles' "I'll follow the sun" with beating on the steering wheel and his own "I'll-follow-the-sun."

They were driving then in moonlight under a sky that had filled with stars. The highway was easy to find amid the flat, black fields, its path marked by the taillights of cars and trucks ahead, the headlights of others approaching. Off to the sides and ahead, Spuhn and Hernandez could see the lights of farmhouses and farmyards as well as the bunched, shadowy illuminations of small towns.

With the dark had come cool weather, chilly weather.

"We're in Florida," Hernandez said. "Near Jacksonville."

"Why's it so cold?" Spuhn asked.

"How it is up here in Georgia," Hernandez said.

They were hungry when they stopped shortly after for gas at a St. Augustine Stuckey's. The waitress, a woman with large hands who called them "Hon", quickly poured coffees and readied her order pad as they made up their minds. The sound of two new arrivals caused her to look up and nod to a nearby booth. "You men be fine right there. With you right quick," she said.

Spuhn had come to like grits, so he was pleased to find them served along with the eggs, ham and toast he had ordered. He was starting on them when the conversation of the two men with the waitress began nearby.

"So this is Florida," a man of about fifty was saying in a resonant, center-of-the-stage voice. Carefully groomed, with an aristocratic bearing and a peppery Van Dyke beard, he wore clothes that were unusually fine: pleated, beige pants, a dark blue, V-necked sweater over a starched yellow shirt. The other man, perhaps in his late twenties and smaller than his companion, was fit, with his muscular chest and arms showing under a tight, long-sleeved cashmere shirt of an orange color found in sunsets. "Right arry out tonight, ain't it?" the waitress agreed.

"Airy! Is that what it is?" the man responded.

Quickly, he glanced down one side of the menu, then down the other. "What do the natives survive on here?"

"People like our pork sandwich," the woman answered. To Spuhn, she seemed surprisingly patient.

"What are you having, Edward?"

"Goodness," Edward said. "The soup and sandwich? Yes, the tomato with the grilled swiss cheese, please."

"I suppose I can endure the same," said the first man. "I assume you accept traveler's checks."When the waitress left them, the man in the blue sweater addressed Spuhn and Hernandez. "And what is the destination for you weary pilgrims?" the man asked. "And I hope that you will not use the detestable 'y'awl' in your answer."

Hernandez understood and answered. "No, we're Yankees. Going to Miami."

"Palm Beach," the man replied. "Edward's been pleading for this tropical vacation ever since his client invited him."

"George, you know that's not true," Edward said. Spuhn noticed Edward put his hand on the other man's knee. "That's not true at all. Ponzio and Graham simply adore you."

"Graham is an insipid, vapid little bitch. Insufferable."

Edward smiled, his part completed in a familiar conversation performance.

Soon, the two pairs' table-to-booth conversation had gone far enough that George and Edward knew Spuhn and Hernandez as Marines on leave, while Spuhn and Hernandez vaguely knew George and Edward as a homosexual, New York City couple on their way to a working vacation at the home of a Palm Beach client. Edward was an interior designer fascinated by the foliage of the Florida winter season. He had been to Palm Beach before this trip.

"What are your next orders?" George asked.

"Okinawa," Spuhn answered. "Third Marine Division."

"The Fighting Third."

"The scuttlebutt is Vietnam," Hernandez said.

"Vietnam," said Edward. "I am so confused about all these places in the news these days. Where in heavens is Vietnam?"

George reached into his sweater for a small leather-enclosed notepad and an expensive-looking fountain pen. In a moment, he had drawn a simple map showing Vietnam at the end of a peninsula south of China, across a sea from India on the west.

Edward lost interest almost as soon as the map had been drawn but Spuhn, noticing the heading of the note, "From the desk of George N. Forrest II, Principal, Madison Alberts Investments," became very interested.

"Keep it," George said to Spuhn, once the map had served its purpose. "In case your G-2 is not up to snuff. Or in case you are lost in New York someday."

"Yes, sir. Thank you, sir," Spuhn said. He folded the map and put it in his wallet.

When they were done with their meals, George took the check from Spuhn and Hernandez's table, paid that bill along with the other. "This is for you, dear," he said, leaving the pleased waitress with a five dollar bill from the change she brought him.

In answer to Spuhn and Hernandez, the man said, "Please. It's trivial. Let a grateful citizen repay two of the country's fine young warriors."

The chill outside made their good-byes and thank yous quick. George and Edward had parked their car, a right-off-the-dealer's lot white Lincoln, beside the VW. In the Lincoln, a small, gray French Poodle jumped about and whimpered in excitement as Edward began opening the door of the driver's side. "Arzshant, shhhh. Arzshant," he said, trying to calm the happy pet.

"Godspeed," George said to Spuhn and Hernandez. Then, with a pointed look that revealed part of his own history, he said, "Carry on, Marines", waited a beat, and, with a satisfied air, settled in the passenger seat of the big car.

Back on the road, now at the wheel while Hernandez adjusted the radio, Spuhn said, "A few good men."

"Mariposas," Hernandez said. "My neighbors. There're lots of queers in Coral Gables. . ."

Miami. Big deal. More babes for you and me."

For a moment, Spuhn mused about the way the world fit together, so interesting and hopeful with people who could be
surprisingly able, able as almost anything: customers, providers,
partners, neighbors, entertainment, patrons. . . Marine veterans.

The night went by in loneliness as the moon traveled toward the
western horizon and the VW, though burning an increasing
amount of oil, continued performing. They were small in a landscape, under a sky of immense scope. Spuhn drove, then slept as
Hernandez took his shift. The eastern sky had become grandly
pink, then rose, then bright with sun by the time, just before the
heaviness of the morning commute, they came to Miami.

Hernandez had weary pits of dark under his eyes but he was
excited, infectiously so, as he drove along Miami's downtown and
instructed Spuhn to notice one sight after another. A causeway led
off toward islands of large, white, tile-roofed homes. Palm trees,
pink and rose camellia hedges, bougainvillea two stories high in
purple or white or yellow against house walls, and tall, cement-
trunked Royal Palm trees caught morning light, the same light
splashing onto the glass and coral and aquamarine and yellow of
Miami's architecture.

So taken with the wonder of the Miami sights along their way,
Spuhn was not as startled as he could have been when Hernandez
pulled into the wide, circle driveway of an extraordinary house in
Coral Gables.

"La casita," Hernandez said, as Spuhn looked at the house, with
its sheltered exterior walkway, its sprawl of bougainvillea pouring
over the stucco wall of a courtyard containing numbers of tall
palms, its handsome wooden front door bearing a door knocker
and hinges suited to a Spanish castle. The sides of the house and the
walkway held arrangements of tiles with delicate designs and lively
colors.

Hernandez's family was rich.

The house was empty. Spuhn and Hernandez would not hear "Jesus!" and the excitement of arrival until they had slept and arisen to find Hernandez's father, Antonio Hernandez, reading in a large, stuffed chair under an arch of deep green fronds moving in the slight breeze through the big screen separating the room – the Florida room, Spuhn would learn – from the shaded courtyard. Pots of red begonias were in a sunny row just inside the house.

Hernandez's father was the sign of his son's future. Not so tall as Jesus, Mr. Hernandez was approximately the shape of Jesus, with thinning dark hair combed back, not entirely covering a bald spot at the back of his head. He had thick, dark eyebrows, bright, dark eyes and a large black mustache. Like his son, a smile, large and confident, was natural to him.

His face showing pleasure, he folded his reading glasses, set his magazines aside and came to greet them. With dignity, he shook Spuhn's hand firmly and welcomed him. "What will you have? Something cold?" he asked. "How was your trip?"

Pleased with all the answers, Mr. Hernandez directed Spuhn to a phone, encouraged him to call his parents. "Fathers and mothers worry," he said. "Call. Tell them you are fine. Please give them our regards."

Veronica answered. Her cheerfulness made Spuhn glad he would see her the next week. She would tell everyone Dennis called and was all right.

They ate at home that evening, joined by Hernandez's bouncy, dark-haired half-sister Maria Ernestina, a fourteen year-old clearly entranced by Jesus and eager to have his attention once she had shed her plain school uniform and dressed in a polka-dotted, long-sleeved blouse and a pair of close-fitting jeans.

The Hernandezes spoke English, except when addressing Florentina, the deferential, efficient friend-servant-family member who had prepared the meal. The English was not because of Spuhn, Hernandez explained later, but because the family spoke English. Jesus' father spoke French and a little German, too, but he spoke English very well because of the years he attended a boarding school in Indiana. His father and other Cuban students had attended Culver Military Academy. His father was very fond of that school and the friends he made there.

With the help of some of those friends, the Hernandez family had been able to leave Cuba, and had been able to do so without losing what the family owned. They had arranged for Mr. Hernandez, a professor of chemistry, to spend a year teaching in Miami, not long before Castro and his forces took over the country. Even when she still had the chance, Jesus' mother had not come. She wasn't a Communist, at least not then, but she was glad about the necessary arrival of justice and wanted to stay through the revolution. Then, she would be with her family again in their Matanzas house or in Miami.

In the polite, all-things-available comfort of the Hernandez's home, anyone would have found welcome. No surprise to Jesus, Spuhn was drawn to Mr. Hernandez and the steady confidence displayed in the well-regulated pattern of the man's habits. When he was not in conversation or away from the home, Mr. Hernandez took his glasses and turned his attention to reading of the business and technical magazines stacked beside his chair. Among the furnishings of the house were two bookshelves holding plenty of books on chemistry subjects, in Spanish, English and other languages, as well as novels, poetry, Shakespeare, histories, travel books, government and philosophy volumes. Jesus pointed out a book about Esperanto.

"Way my father is," Hernandez said.

Mr. Hernandez, who would have been courteous to any guest in his home, was pleased with Spuhn, too. When Jesus told of Spuhn's ideas for advertisements on the rear doors of trucks, Mr. Hernandez took interest. The young man's ambitious nature and astute curiosity were youthful and unformed but they existed. Valuable qualities, they made a fortunate brace for the spontaneity of the likable, drifting Jesus. Who knew what lay ahead for the two of them in the military, in Vietnam, in life? Mr. Hernandez was glad that the two had met and formed their friendship.

When Mr. Hernandez took his son and Spuhn to visit the paint manufacturing company he had founded under the name Beautiful Florida Paint Company, Jesus suffered the time while Spuhn thrilled to it. Jesus separated from his father and Spuhn for loud reunions with his friends among the workers, Spanish-speaking men and some women at work mixing, moving and labeling paint. Meanwhile, Spuhn's interest in the materials, the process, the promotion, lab and patents of Mr. Hernandez's products struck directly to the man's pride. The interest Spuhn took in all the activity in and around the company's quonset hut plant solidified Mr. Hernandez's certainty that his son had found someone whose feet were on the best path.

"You're going to be fixed, man," Spuhn said to Hernandez later, once Mr. Hernandez had left them at the entrance of La Flor, where he would be having dinner with a friend. Spuhn would learn about the friend, Mr. Hernandez's mistress Maria Anastasia, mother of Maria Ernestina.

"I suppose," Hernandez said. The tone of resignation made Spuhn look at him, away from the sights of Miami and Miami Beach, spread out for them as they crossed the causeway for a look at the beaches.

Hernandez's mood was back at his normal top register by the time they had passed along the main Miami Beach street, Collins Avenue, its beach flank occupied by curved, high, grand destination hotels and its facing side showing moored houseboats and graceful sailboats. "Let's try here," Hernandez said, pulling into the entrance of one large hotel, the Eden Roc, as if he owned it. In a moment, a uniformed attendant had taken Mr. Hernandez's butterscotch-colored Cadillac, given Jesus a ticket and a Spanish-inflected "thank you", and they were in the hotel lobby, on their way to the beach area with their suits.

Mr. Hernandez's name and a signature gave them access to a locker room and then the beach area, where they piled their clothes on the sand near groups of sunbathing young women in their late teens or early twenties. The beach was beautiful, broad and true to the postcards that had been Spuhn's only experience of any such swimming place. The afternoon waves came in surges that panicked small, long-legged birds pecking at whatever the water had deposited.

Overriding the ocean was the sight of the three languorous women in bikinis. Their laughter and chatter eclipsed for Spuhn the soft sounds of the ocean hitting and drawing back from the sand, the cries of seagulls overhead. As if feeling the physical touch of Spuhn's stare, a red-haired woman rested on her elbows and looked at him, just as he was noticing with equal intensity her and the plunge of her bikini top. The other two women, equally interested in Spuhn and Hernandez, twisted into positions for furtive glances. They were legs, knees, hair, breasts, skin: soft and young, mesmerizing.

On the way back from a quick ocean plunge, Spuhn's first, despite his months of proximity to the Pacific, the two Marines approached close beside the three pretty women.

"You missed a spot," Spuhn said to the bold, red-haired woman.

She took her bottle of tanning oil and held it out. "Would you get it for me?" she asked. The directness made her friends giggle as they exchanged a look.

In a moment, Spuhn was kneeling beside her and massaging the area of her back between her shoulder blades. She was softly round and, Spuhn observed, she was wearing what he took to be an engagement ring, one with a sizable diamond.

"Oooh, you're dripping. That's cold," the woman said, pulling away and rising on her knees. When she combed her curls into place with her fingers, Spuhn saw again how her breasts and hips and form moved, all barely contained in her black-and-white, polka-dotted bikini.

They settled on the beach and progressed into conversational dance. The red-haired woman Lauren was with her cousins, sisters Naomi and Sarah, the three of them in Miami Beach from suburban New York and Connecticut for the bar mitzvah of another cousin. The Marines? They wanted to know about the Marines.

Very soon, the three women let it be known that they were restless, done with being cooped at the hotel with other little cousins and a few uncles and aunts who had not gone shopping. They wanted to do something, to go somewhere, to see Miami.

Pretty on the sand, the women were striking when they came from the lobby and met Spuhn and Hernandez at the car. In a rush, but seeming to take their sweet time, the trio had fixed their hair and put on jewelry and fine, close-fitting skirts and blouses. Lauren, who sat with Spuhn and Naomi in the back seat, wore perfect perfume in a perfect application. When she moved her legs, Spuhn heard the soft sound of rubbing nylons. As Hernandez drove toward the causeway and Miami, then into the Calle Ocho Little Havana neighborhood with its array of neon, stores, restaurants, and people, Lauren sat easily against Spuhn, unlike Naomi, who kept a careful space on Spuhn's left.

Calle Ocho pleased Lauren. Noticing this sight, that restaurant, that dignified, very elderly man in a pressed white suit, this workman drinking from a small cup at an open counter, she asked Hernandez a stream of questions, with each answer prompting a delighted cooing, an enthusiastic "neat" or "never seen that." She was infectious, intent on seeing everything through the car's every window. Hernandez pulled into the lot of La Esperanza and, using his father's name again, bought a dinner that introduced Spuhn to a gamut of seafood and then to flan and Cuban coffee. Lauren praised it all, but, like her cousins, turned down any shellfish in favor of red snapper and grouper.

When they left La Esperanza, Hernandez resumed a tour along palm-lined Flagler Street in Miami's downtown and along upscale Brickell Avenue. At the request of Naomi and Sarah, who were tired, Hernandez drove back to their hotel. Leaving Spuhn and Lauren in the car, Hernandez went into the lobby for use of a phone.

"They think they're in the way tonight," Lauren said to Spuhn He felt her leg against his, smelled her perfume, felt her hair soft on his cheek when she leaned his way.

"You should see Coral Gables," Hernandez said as he entered the car. "And Elvira wants to meet you. My friend Elvira is getting off work in about ten minutes."

Elivira, a dark-haired, exciting woman with her mouth open in a great smile, came right to Hernandez and then wrapped her arms around him through the car window. In a moment, she was pressed against him in the front seat, with her face turned toward Spuhn and Lauren in the back seat. She extended her hand, gave each of them a deep, smiling inspection as they shook. "I'm Elvira," she said.

Spuhn and Lauren later agreed that Elvira reminded them of an easy-going aunt: very pretty and also a forced grown up with her round cheeks bright with makeup, her full lips reddened with lipstick, and her whole presence ringed in perfume. Her breasts were blouse-bustingly ample. Typical of the women Spuhn had seen with Hernandez, Elvira had jewelry that included a gaudy wedding ring.

She talked steadily and happily, asked questions and interrupted herself to remark upon sights as they moved toward Coral Gables and the Hernandez house.

"You lost weight. So many muscles now," she said, raking her bright red nails across Hernandez's chest. She bit his ear, pulled into the arm that he tightened around her.

Spuhn did learn from Elvira's curiosity that Lauren was in her third year at Barnard, an economics major, engaged - "sort of" - to a senior at Columbia. "Our families are very good friends," Lauren said. "The Steins and the Singers, we do everything together."

At the house, Hernandez turned the blank-faced Florentina from waiting on them, told Spuhn and Lauren where to find things, and soon disappeared with Elvira, who had been pressing her hip against his and rising to speak things in his ear.

Spuhn and Lauren, each with a bottle of beer, went into the courtyard, to a cushioned bench partly obscured from the sight of the house by ropes of aerial roots hanging from the branches of an immense banyan tree.

"Sort of?" Spuhn asked.

"Sort of," she said. She said no more, soon rested her head on his shoulder and let him play his fingers along her arm as he held her in the moonlight and shadow smelling of the garden's night-blooming jasmine.

Was he worried about going to Asia? Would there be a war in Vietnam? Would he go to college after the Marines?

They talked. Spuhn didn't know. He wanted to be in business. He wanted nice things, a house like this one. In his mind, he called up the plan he had made with *Think and Grow Rich* advice: a millionaire by his thirtieth birthday from his own company.

Spuhn finished his beer. She put hers on a table decorated with mosaic.

They kissed, pressed, kissed long with their tongues tangling, kissed and pressed and stroked again.

When Spuhn moved to cup his hand over her breast, she blocked his hand, kept her tongue moving in his mouth.

The next night, while Lauren attended the bar mitzvah and prepared for the early morning flight to New York, Elvira fixed Spuhn up with a delicate, Jamaican friend whose laugh was easy and whose teasing hands in the back seat of the Cadillac went from his thigh to his crotch as soon as Hernandez and Elvira left for a walk on the beach. As Spuhn and Caryne pushed against each other, Spuhn imagined at moments Lauren, her breasts, her knees raised, her mouth.

Three weeks later, aboard the troop ship taking Hernandez, him and the rest of the Marines toward duty with the Third Marine Division at Okinawa, Spuhn reread Lauren's mail and pictured her, listened to her light, straightforward laugh amid the slosh of the separating ocean.

CHAPTER 7

One, two, three, four, one, two, three, four
We like it here
We love it here
We've finally found a home
A home
A home
A home away from home (Hey!)

The elderly congregants, all two dozen or so of them, kept curious watch on Nikolay Vetrov as the big man sat in shadowy pastel illumination at the end of the third pew on the left. Tank's brooding presence in the weak November light making it through a stained glass window of commandments on stone did not surprise any of the church members. Largest city in its region as well as a county seat, Harlan still was a small town. Harlan felt slight disturbances instantly – glimpse of a strange car in a driveway, the summer arrival of college students selling magazine subscriptions – the way a leaf dropping on a pond can turn a school of minnows.

To his embarrassment as he sought quiet invisibility, in Navalny and in the vicinity of Harlan, Tank remained a celebrity as well as a curiosity. Mention of his return in the newspaper's "Over the Fence" column was unnecessary. People greeted him when they found him in town, enthused over him, remembered his matches, reminded him of his photo and his trophies on display at the high school. They were neighborly to him. They sympathized about his mother, remembered sweet Klara Vladimirovna's beauty as well as the gentleness and strength of Tank's father. Wordlessly, they compared their expectations about the young wrestling titan with the powerful, quieted man now living among them again.

Everyone, including the pastor John Sherman, knew it would be only a matter of time before the big, private man sampled the wares of this church, same as Nikolay had ventured into the area's other places of worship. They also knew his pitted Oldsmobile as they knew all the cars of the town, knew approximately or even precisely what he paid John Hayes for the raggedy red thing. The car's presence on part of the lumpy, gravel pad outside the building this overcast morning would become an item of lunchtime conversation.

Today, as the congregants rose and sat, prayed and sang, Nikolay rose and sat with them, each time returning to fix his gaze on the back of the pew before him. His haircut was fresh and close, even and black, except for a healed gash from a childhood fall. With his big hands clasped, his large frame bent forward, and his cropped hair, Nikolay Vetrov had an appearance that made John Sherman see in Nikolay a repentant sinner, a libertine or high official transfixed by awareness of his savior Jesus Christ.

The minister could not help studying the man he remembered as a hell-raiser during those years in the early 1950s. Nikolay wasn't the worst of the lot but everyone was aware of the way he and a few of the other wrestlers tore around with some of the girls. Proper, decent and reserved, always a little confused about America altogether, Nikolay's parents had their hands full with that one, the pastor remembered. Thank God Galina had been of another stripe.

Tank this day was reflective, still.

"Job," the pastor thought, remembering the Scriptural passage as he observed the big man's sadness. "Ah, could my anguish but be measured and my calamity laid with it in the scales, they would now outweigh the sands of the sea!"

When the worship ended, only Randall Grant ventured close to Tank. Then he stopped. Seeing the large man so absorbed in thought, the retired farmer turned away.

After the members of the congregation had visited in the crisp of a low-hanging day before going off in their pickup trucks and sedans toward the Country Platter for their Sunday fare, John Sherman re-entered his small church. As aged as his congregation, his tall frame hunched over the light walker he used, the pastor came to Nikolay Vetrov's pew. Careful not to rock the pew or make a sound, he sat at the other end. With hands shaking from the Parkinson's that was sapping him, he removed his glasses and rubbed them with his handkerchief as he patiently, quietly prayed on Jesus Christ for guidance.

Very soon, Tank looked up, and met the pastor's kindly gray stare.

They knew one another from the Ten O'Clock Club, the morning gathering of store owners and other business people – men except for two women - who gathered at the Woolworth's for a coffee break that blended Chamber of Commerce with discussion of news, crop conditions, socializing and mutual appreciation. Greg Beutel, an outgoing insurance agent who had been a classmate of Tank's sister Galina, talked Tank into joining him after one of the AA sessions the two attended at the Lutheran church. Tank began to appear several mornings each week, as soon as the AA session ended. He soon had his own cup among the Ten O'Clock array displayed on the lunch counter wall.

"I'm thinking about all the places the seed went," Tank said. Pastor Sherman had spoken that morning about the way the seed had grown or gone to waste on good ground or bad, amid weeds, with or without water.

The minister waited.

"The world has lots of places the seed can't get a start." As he spoke, Tank broke from the pastor's gaze and looked down at his clasped hands.

The pastor waited.

Tank traveled in his mind through a number of the places. His thoughts at the farm, in this church were going everywhere: his years at the University of Iowa, his time with Angie before she left him, parties he crashed with some of the other wrestlers. Most of all, he thought about the hours he had been spending seated near his mother as she read and dozed, read and dozed, bewildered, with a bible or other religious book in her hands. At times, she spoke to him in English, and knew him.

"Almighty God tucked in lots of spots where the seed will do just fine, too," Pastor Sherman said. "Sometimes, the seed just sits there for awhile and doesn't start growing. It rests in our hearts. Under the snow. In the cold soil. It just seems like the seed has landed in the worst possible spot. No one has any hope for it. But our God is a patient God, a good and loving God. All of a sudden, the seed pops, and it keeps popping. Turns out the seed just needed a little, friendly breath of heavenly air, something to get the seed set up just right in the dirt."

"Yes." Tank's expression was thoughtful. The minister's words put in Tank's mind the image of a sure, serious man in white robes, his lips pursed as he directed the nearby world with blasts of his breath.

"You and I can't know where Almighty God is sending us, why my Josephine and I got the call to come here instead of Mason City or Ottumwa or anywhere else back then in 1934, why the blessed spirit moved you to come home and look after your mother last fall.

I have faith, I know that a man who is looking for God is good soil. The seed is growing in you, Nikolay. I know it. The Psalm tells it just right: 'The Lord is near to all who call upon him, to all who call upon him in truth.' You just wait, Nikolay. Here in Iowa, our loving, powerful God gives us plenty of water. We just have to let our growing season start."

Tank returned to the church twice more, in two weeks and then in mid-December. He and Pastor Sherman had no lengthy talk either time, nothing more than a welcoming smile and the second time, the feel of Pastor Sherman's shaking hand upon his shoulder. Even in that short time, Tank could see the minister's health deteriorating. Before the new year 1966 arrived, a daughter living in West Des Moines came for him, helped him gather things from the little house she would return to close up, and took him to live with her family. The church closed, its members dispersed to a few other faiths or simply prayed at home and, consciously or not, made their own progress along the aging process taken by their pastor.

Fully aware over these months of his own drifting, Tank kept himself to precarious management of his own condition. What began as going home to see his mother had turned into going home and staying with, caring for his mother. What began, too, as being with his mother had turned into a curiosity about God – to be precise, the rising whisper of divine purpose in the forces affecting him. Soon after his return, when his mother's nap interrupted the reading of a Gospel story about some Pharisees' sly questioning of Jesus Christ, he took another bible from a table in the front room and finished the reading in the barn. Thereafter, he kept the bible in a barn cabinet and came to think of the area – a crate for a seat, an overhead light on a hanging cord, and the cabinet with the bible - as the place for knowing God.

When he took stock of himself, Tank noticed that the twitching in his resting leg had diminished. The look on his face, noticed as he shaved, had evolved into just a look, no longer the hollow-eyed appearance of a big man with dark hair and thoughts all askew. Always before, he had lived a life that simply rolled out ahead of him in all respects: match after match, Angie and other women, places he would go, things he would do, could do.

But now, he felt content to wait, to concentrate on understanding big questions that could be condensed as "What next? And for what?"

Some days, he realized, he woke up happy, ready to address and understand the big thoughts rolling in his mind.

He had taken his mother for granted, expected her to be there, in the house, on the farm, unchanged. Instead, he had found her changing. . . and precious to him.

Sometimes speaking in Russian, sometimes just looking at him, Klara Vladimirovna took pleasure in his presence. She rested her fingers on the back of his big hand, holding him at her side as she read in a soft voice from a black-covered book of prayers. Some parts were recognizable to Tank, from repetition over the weeks and from hearing the words in his childhood. Determined to be English-speaking Americans, his parents were religious people who often let their prayers sail toward heaven in the Russian words that bound them to their ancestry at the same time the words lifted them toward the Almighty.

In his mother's presence many afternoons, with her fingers light and trembling on his hand, Tank felt calmed. While the western wind made deep winter sounds against the house and shaped the snow in curving trenches around fences and tree trunks, Tank could take optimism from the strength of his mother's spirit. She believed! Nearing the end of a life so difficult, so uncertain, she could talk to a God who was protector and companion.

Out of idleness, as he released his strength in lifting of the simple weights and a large stone where he had worked out in the barn as a boy, he gave thought to the prayers his mother repeated, thought about the world she saw with its seasons, its generations, its struggles and satisfactions affected by a God she felt close.

And where was he going, beyond settling into control of his impulses, his behavior? The days went by, with the regularity of them freeing Tank to begin small contact with people and things beyond the tiny farm.

At least once each month, Galina and her family drove from Omaha so that Galina could see her mother and Tank while Galina's husband Jim Casper and their busy young children, Anton, Mike and Pam, swarmed over the small farm property. Jim went to the tasks while the young children, dark-haired and stair-step close in age, headed into the barn for pursuit of the wary cats. To please the children, Tank had gathered a litter of four kittens in some peach baskets.

"Remember Dad and his baths?" Galina asked as she and Tank walked one cold, sunny January day along the path beside Little Creek. They had come to the small structure, dry and neglected, the banya their father had built for himself when he and Klara Vladimirovna came into possession of the little property. The air was still, quiet and fresh with the scent of deep winter on the surrounding fields. The snow around them and over the deep pool of Little Creek had the tracks of rabbits and a deer.

A strand of Galina's hair, Cossack dark, fluttered at the edge of her babushka, lively with purple and yellow flowers around her ruddy face. Pretty and energetic with long, athletic limbs, she had grown up into a fresh, healthy young mother.

"The Coopers thought he was a Commie," said Tank.

"Not really," Galina said. "They just thought Russians were Commies, Commies were Russians. They liked Dad, though."

"Everyone did," said Tank. He thought of his father, of his gentle smile, the strength of his thick body. Never fully comfortable with English, he always gave way to a big smile as he sifted through a companion's words for the meaning in them. His hands were big with thick fingers. Even so, his touch on an animal's neck or withers was always calming and very often healing. People knew Anton Zahkar Vetrov for the way he managed the bodies and moods of their animals, from dairy cows and riding horses to hogs and sheep.

The next morning, Tank went to the barn for the wooden tool box and carried it to the neglected banya. His father had built the banya carefully; once Tank had the entrance knocked and pushed back into plumb, the removal of silt and some dank, heavy boards made the three rooms of the little building reappear. Beyond the entrance chamber were a central washing room and a steam room. With strength and concentration, after a week of replacing and tightening the fit of planks, of restacking the rocks his father had gathered together for the throwing of steam, Tank began seeing the little retreat come back to rights.

The project cleared his mind for examination of ideas and memories he had never valued during his childhood, certainly not when his strength and quickness brought him notoriety as a wrestler. Unlike Galina, he never took interest or prized any bits from his parents' occasional revelations about their lives before Iowa. They were Russian, from Russia, among some other immigrants and many other people who did the ordinary things of U.S. families: worked, prodded children through school, waved hello, favored Harlan teams, and occasionally acquired a television, a car and other American comforts.

His mother had always been steady in her religion, even effusive, rapturous when there had been a priest celebrating the Divine Liturgy in Navalny's simple Orthodox church. Tank remembered her crossing herself, touching her fingers to the ground, crossing herself again and again as the priest and deacon moved about in golden vestments.

Now, grown feeble, she remained just as steadfast. The path that had brought her into old age remained firm ahead of her. She prayed, she read, she stayed true.

While his mother napped many late afternoons, Tank worked at the banya. If he found Otto Traugott settled for a visit, Tank eked out an additional hour or two before returning to the house. Tank's mother and Otto were well-acquainted from the years of Iowa life. Widowed for almost ten years, Otto and his wife had raised their children in a small trailer at the back of a farm owned by Otto's main employer. The widower was an old, familiar friend, a comfort to Klara Vladimirovna. An immigrant like she was, he knew the Baltic from the northern shore of his native Germany.

Often, Otto brought bread and vegetables, then remained to eat with Klara and Tank before driving back to the Navalny home where he was one of the boarders. After seeing the work begun on the banya, Otto, who was skilled in carpentry and plumbing, began a deferential oversight of the restoration. On his own, he repaired the bench of the entrance chamber and built a solid replacement for the rotted bench in the washing room.

"A little project is good," Otto said when Tank thanked him.

Otto kept track of Klara Vladimirovna's doctor visits, too, and each time contrived to have need of going over there, fifty miles west to Council Bluffs, right near Edmundson Hospital for a call on one of his cousins. A little confused but trusting and excited, Tank's mother took her seat easily in Otto's navy Buick.

With the ability to spend extended time at the brute portions of the work, and with Otto managing the repair of the stove and piping in the steam room, Tank was able to give a good report when Ten O'Clock friends asked about the state of the repair.

"Pretty soon," he said. "Won't be long."

"Bet you can't wait to jump through the ice so you can run inside and roast yourself," said one store manager. "Hell of a way to take a bath."

"Gonna need a rider on his insurance," said Greg Beutel.

The crack amused the others.

"Wonder where he can get one of those?" one man asked. They all liked Greg, who was making inroads on the insurance needs of the bunch. The young man had given his wife and little boy a rough go of it for a time, but now seemed to have his affairs back on track. He certainly worked hard.

From there, conversation went to business – decent the previous Saturday when the weather was accommodating – to the good soil moisture from the winter snow, the draft notices received by three new Harlan boys, and the wrestling team.

Everyone brightened.

The high school team was doing well. In addition, two of the Ten O'Clock members who had sons on the team frequently arrived with news from the boys' practices. Still, those men and all the others deferred to Tank as they discussed the wrestlers and their prospects.

Tank remembered those days very well: exercising or simply sweating in layers of clothing before he reached the heavyweight level and no longer had to make weight for a match.

The discussions lifted him along with the others. With enthusiasm, he joined in the conversation as the group considered the risk of letting a powerful wrestler such as Jim Morris crash down as much as twenty pounds in order to take on the quick, little sophomore from the Red Oak squad.

"Fort Dodge is here Saturday," said one of the team fathers. "You should take a look, Tank. These boys have some stuff."

Friday afternoon, recognizing that he had gotten as far along in the banya work as he could go without Otto's skill, Tank decided that he would show up for the wrestling match.

His appearance in the gym drew looks from men who remembered watching Tank – or, in the case of one heavyset old teammate, competing against Tank. Tank returned the smiling man's wave, then sat in the bleachers next to Greg Beutel, who had brought his seven year old son John.

Being inside felt good. Outside, the day was dry and bitter with a white sun the only relief in high gray clouds. The parents and young people arriving in the gym entered with their faces reddened and their coats drawn tight.

After warming up, the wrestlers gathered around their coach, the mainstay biology teacher Phil Cole, for the familiar advice to take the fight to the opponent: "You've done the work, hard work. Today, you have fun. More fun than your opponent. Way more! Get 'em! For your family! For you! For Harlan!"

In the stands, Tank and the rest could not hear the coach clearly but they felt the excitement, too, when the Harlan wrestlers cheered, broke from the circle, and fell in line for the singing of the Star Spangled Banner, led this afternoon by a hard-faced Marine recruiter in perfect dress blues.

"Glad you're here, Tank," said Tom Daniels. The school principal, a small, wiry man of about 50 years of age, had come to rest for a moment on the seat to Tank's left. Tank saw him still catching his breath, warming up and wiping cold-drip from his pink nose with a handkerchief.

As Tank was saying hello in return, the principal continued. "Very glad. Listen. We have something to talk about with you. You coming to the Ten O'Clock Monday?"

Respected and liked for his resolute, pure loyalty to everything at the school, the principal also amused the school community with his birdlike moves from matter to matter. His excitement made the skin showing at the crown of his head pinken. His Adam's apple, pronounced as a buckeye on his slender neck, moved with his words and with his thoughts. Students and parents alike, most knew the principal as Knobby.

Once he had accomplished his purpose with Tank, the principal went on to sit for a moment with one person or another, just long enough to get something done with a parent, a board member, a big team supporter.

Greg Beutel's son had been asking his father, "Dad, can we go now?" Soon after the match began with the narrow victory of a quick Fort Dodge 95-pound wrestler over a frustrated Harlan hothead, Greg Beutel stood and shrugged, then explained to Tank, "John and I are going to McDonald's. He's not so interested in this sport yet. But I know I'll see you Monday."

Tank smiled. "This is Iowa," he said. "You wait, John. This is what you'll be thinking about all the time."

"Plus girls," Greg Beutel said.

After that, Tank gave the competition all his attention. The Harlan team had strength, seldom less than the members of the Fort Dodge team. The Harlan boys' moves, though, were sometimes wooden, less reflexive than they should be at the midpoint of a season. Did the coach, Phil Cole, see that? Tank guessed not. The man called steady encouragement during the matches but, in Tank's estimation, very little instruction.

Tank began taking over the role. Loudly, adding his shouts to the noise of the others on the bleacher seats, he began directing the boys out on the mat. "Get behind him. Behind him!" he shouted at Harlan's 125-pound wrestler, a compact, flushed boy who was levering his weight dangerously against a slippery Fort Dodge opponent.

"Pull it in. Now! Pull it in! Flip him!" he shouted, directing another tired boy to drive against the shoulder of a boy set to ride a one-point edge for another 30 seconds. In alarm soon after, Tank shouted at another wrestler who was leaving his arm carelessly vulnerable to seizure.

During the remaining matches, Tank stood, unconscious of the obstacle he made himself for the parents and a line of high school students who moved right and left behind him for sight of the wrestling.

At the end of the match, a close one taken by Harlan when the heavyweight wrestler was able to escape and reverse a muscular Fort Dodge sophomore, Daniels made eye contact with Tank. He waved from the company of some happy, relieved team parents.

"Talk to you Monday, Tank."

Tank waved back. "Good."

At home, he found Otto's car parked before the house, which was empty. The wind had dropped, the clouds had lowered, and flakes of snow had begun to fall. His mother's absence did not worry Tank. She was with Otto, the two of them probably walking carefully along the paths made in the hard snow of the property as Otto exulted in the weight of Klara Vladimirovna on his arm and she exulted in the smells and bird activity of a winter day's late afternoon.

After checking the barn, fragrant with the shut-in smells of hay, soil and the presence of the cats hanging warily back near the far wall, Tank moved down the path for a look at his nearly-restored banya. Snow rested almost a foot deep on the frozen Little Creek, defined among the empty-limbed trees as a snowy road.

He found Otto beaming, showing the renovated banya to a pleased Klara Vladimirovna.

"It's ready, Nikolay," Otto said, a proud expression on his face as he took in the accomplishment. The stove and piping he had dis-

assembled and cleaned now stood assembled, repaired with a length
of new pipe as well as the refitting of the door. Otto pressed his
weight down on the stove and demonstrated the solidity of his
work. Everything was ready. The stove had a stack of hard wood
next to it. The damaged section of the roof had been replaced. The
benches were firm and in place at two heights along the wall of the
steam compartment.

The next morning, once the stove had come to baking heat and
Tank had gathered enough switches from the frozen ground at the
base of the nearby birches, he would chop an opening in the ice
over the deep spot in the creek. After steaming, he would drop into
the water and return to the banya. Repeating the procedure two or
three times, he would let his mind run with memories of his father
and, he felt sure, with the pondering of the big questions that
opened up with each reading of his mother's black-covered book of
Bible passages and prayers.

Beside him, Tank's mother, happy and a little lost, had a smile
she could not contain. With joy, she gestured about the interior.
She seemed to be looking for someone.

"The starets," she said. "Grigori Yefimovich, the starets."

CHAPTER 8

Come on. Let's go.
We can go. Through the snow.
We can run. To the sun.

Ike Johnson, tight-lipped intimidating with his gun showing in an obvious bulge under his jacket, signaled toward the upstairs with a nod. He kept a steady stare on the two nervous Iowa coeds.

"Up there?" asked the tall one.

Ike nodded again, each dangerous, fierce look of his unblinking eyes moving the coeds like a charged prod. His bulk, his impatience, and his black skin had the women terrified. They better not bother him again about something so simple as going up the stairway right there in front of them, ready for their skinny little white butts.

The coeds hastened away from him, up the stairs. He nodded when they came to the door.

There, Jewel, her face a somber match of his, met them and led the women into a bedroom. Three children paused and watched from a tired sofa where they were eating cereal and giving bored attention to schoolwork. Ike swept his glance across them and then returned to his station at the building's front door.

Jewel closed the bedroom door.

In less time than Marjorie Haas and Jenny Adamski expected, Jewel had worked the coat hanger into Marjorie and made the baby go away in a pool that collected in the sheet Jewel had draped across the bed. Then they were out of the bedroom, past the children, down the stairs and back on the street. As much as bewildered, introspective Marjorie was able, they fled - away from notice of any police staked out around the drab three-story apartment building, away from the neighborhood where white women only went for trouble, away from the horrible ending of Marjorie's condition.

When they were driving in the little Corvair belonging to one of the awkward boys from her World History class, Marjorie gave into crying. "Shit," she repeated, wiping at her eyes and turning away from Jenny each time for staring out her window at the dirty snow frozen in shoveled piles and rivulets across Iowa City. The sky hung gray over them.

"I'm fine," Marjorie said, each time Jenny asked. "I'm fine."

The dorm was still Saturday morning quiet when they returned to their room. Marjorie sank on her bed, drew her blankets around her and faced the wall. A moment later, she pushed aside the elaborate quilt made by her grandmother and said she was going to take a shower. Small except for the disproportion of breasts that always excited men, Marjorie was weak and unsteady under the weight of sadness. Her beautiful face, usually bearing full, smiling lips, ordinarily made up carefully, was tear-streaked and wan, vacant. Instead of being gathered in a pony tail, her dark hair was untended, surrendered to disarray.

While her roommate showered, Jenny gave cursory attention to the term paper she was writing for her course on Western Civilization. One thousand words, one thousand words on museum men who had lived, orated, postured, attacked, protected, inspired and disappeared thousands of lives away from her. The Romans, the

Carthaginians, they were as distant from Jenny this gray morning as she was from the January weekend that would begin unfolding in a couple of hours across the Iowa campus. The basketball team was hosting Minnesota. The wrestling team was hosting the NWCA Duals tournament. Even the library would be a gathering place for more flirting and seeking than pre-finals researching and studying.

After her June, 1966 completion of four quiet St. Sebastian years recorded in one track meet photo, Jenny had come to Iowa with an unworded hope that the environment would transform her somehow into an easy-going version of Anna, whose celebrity was still present, still showing in the way people hearing "Adamski" paused a beat or two as they studied Anna's little sister. Jenny could tell that, more often than not, the comparison was unfavorable. The seniors and grad students who had known Anna, even some of the professors who heard Anna's name, were disappointed that this Adamski was someone else, not a replica of the curved, light-hearted, ready-for-anything beauty who had spent her four Iowa years at the center of so much student life and fantasy.

Dutifully, Jenny answered the questions, the same questions. And what is Anna doing now? Is she married?

She lives in the Twin Cities, works for an ad agency. Which one? McGregor Stanton. A good one? Yes, I suppose it is. Anna likes it. She's an account executive. Yes, made for it.

Occasionally, the questions went to additional depth and Jenny answered that, no, she was the baby, there were no other Adamski sisters. Their brother Bob graduated from Iowa ten years ago. He went to New York, works for a big bank. He's married.

And what am I, anyway? Anna's secretary? Go talk to her yourself.

Did Jenny ever talk with her sister? Well, yes, but not the way you hope. How do you think we found out about Jewel?

Before Marjorie came back to the room from the shower, Jenny put aside her notebook and returned to a sketch begun in a class the previous Wednesday. With a charcoal pencil, she labored to bring dimension to the bowl and cooking items that had been arranged before the students as subjects for practice of hatching technique.

Little cheerleader that she was, Marjorie scoffed at Jenny's view, refused to accept interpretations that had the boys, the grad students, the professors overlooking the appeal of an Adamski whose own shape had something of Anna's bosom plus legs of remarkable length and form. Short, buxom Marjorie, always comfortable with men, always circled by students and professors finding pretexts for drawing her gaze, maybe a touch of her fingers, her cheerful laugh upon them, envied Jenny the legs that gave her such height, such a dramatic womanly shape. "They are talking about Anna, honey, but they are thinking about you," Marjorie said. "Those horny frat boys are thinking about you."

Through Marjorie's introduction, through Marjorie's persistence, Jenny had become one of the life models hired for art classes. There, her nakedness sometimes partly wrapped in loose windings of a gauzy shawl and other times full, she never approached Marjorie's unashamed stances. Time could drag, the air around Jenny too warm, too cold as a serious young professor circled among quiet men and women intent on lines, highlighting, color of the woman objects before them.

The work provided spending money and, unlike the cafeteria jobs or the minor clerk positions, the responsibilities were limited to being there, just being there. A person could read, study, daydream.

For Marjorie, the sessions could be paid study periods or paid revery moments. Rarely was Jenny able to immerse herself in a textbook or class notes, not while young men and women her age were so close by, so focused on the bones showing along her back, so focused on the chiaroscuro of her breast, arm and leg curves, the way her yellow hair fell to touch her shoulders.

As Marjorie slept, wrapped in her grandmother's quilt, her sad face toward the wall, Jenny sketched, working shadows and shapes from the grids of lines made with her pencil. Time passed. Knocks at the locked door twice went unanswered. The light of a gray day rose and subsided as the winter sun moved away from their east-facing room. Footsteps and exaggerated exclamations, conversations sounded as students passed in the hallway.

By two o'clock, Marjorie was awake. She was coming around. A red line from a sheet fold ran across one pale cheek and her eyes were puffy from sleep. But her expression was turning back to normal, her full mouth near to a smile as she drew her hair into place and slid a rubber band over a fresh pony tail.

"Well, that's over," she said.

During the weekend, mostly staying in the room, Marjorie continued to recover. Her color returned, she made funny, complaining comments about the readings she was completing for her English Composition I assignment, and, on Sunday afternoon, she convinced Jenny to attend the French language department's showing of new films from a Parisian school of visual art.

Marjorie's conversation became light, steady, and without Jerry. In the brightly lit auditorium, four boys chose seats behind them and talked at a performance volume meant to draw Jenny and Marjorie into their banter about the tedium of a Sunday night on a winter campus. "It's Siberia," said the most voluble, a remark that led to snickering about "comrades" and "revolution" and then to discussion of a film the voluble one had seen in New York at Christmas. Had the others seen it? Peculiar but compelling. He addressed Marjorie and Jenny with the same question.

Pretending they had not been listening, Marjorie asked "Which film?"

"*Repulsion.* Roman Polanski directed it."

"No," Marjorie answered, turning to look at Jenny. "It hasn't come here yet, I don't think."

"Where is here?"

Marjorie was from near Oskaloosa in Mahaska County. Her grandfather had mined coal until he was able to begin farming.

At other times, Jenny would have watched Marjorie joined in gregarious interaction, with excitement showing in her expressions as the effect of Marjorie's charm and voluptuousness drew young men toward her. She was innocently generous. Tonight, though, she let the invitation drop, simply turned away and ignored what soon would have led to questions about majors, and eventually an exchange of names with addresses.

The strange, imaginative student shorts with their drum beating or sound of surf or honking horns, their hard-faced city characters and little cars carrying young women with long cigarettes went by, accompanied by subtitles, everything shown in little more than an hour and a half.

Marjorie, asking about the time, withdrew again from the young men, who looked toward Marjorie and Jenny in hope that a conversation would now begin.

But Marjorie wanted to go. Jenny was not surprised when Marjorie admitted that she was meeting Jerry at eight o'clock.

"Why?" Jenny asked.

Marjorie's look was sad again. "I don't know. I said I would tell him how it went. He asked me to."

Jenny didn't say anything.

"Do you think I'm crazy?"

"It's a free country."

With Marjorie gone, Jenny gave in to the pull she had been feeling for several days. Ashamed of her helplessness and also looking forward to the respite, she moved along in a wet wind that was pushing her and flecks of snow along a diagonal path. At the student center, she went in a ladies room and combed her hair. She had let it grow thick and long enough that the curls, once she removed her plaid scarf, rested almost at her shoulders. She applied lipstick and then some blue eyeliner that brought attention to the delicacy of her slender nose and cheekbones, a face that was turning from adolescence into striking young adult.

She was glad she had put on the ribbed beige sweater and the short, racing green woolen skirt, even though her tights did little to protect her from the wet, windy cold. It was an outfit Val liked.He had said he could not see her this weekend because of his job interview for the summer internship in Chicago. When he got back on Sunday afternoon, he knew he had to begin studying for the torts exam the next day, thirty percent of the whole grade.

Jenny decided to try, anyway. Even if he were already started on an all-nighter, at least she would have a moment with him, a moment for quick making out, for knowing the next time they would lie together in the space he had claimed for his own room beneath the stairway of the apartment he shared with a senior and two other graduate students.

Wanting to trust him, she did trust him, thrilled each time by the dreamy things he revealed about his plans for their life together in the someday, the time he would be hired, working, able to begin married life as an attorney with a career that would permit time for representing the impoverished and for helping her own art benefit from the introductions he would make. He would make the law dance, exert its power for the benefit of those now deprived, and for the benefit of deserving clients, while she would have the freedom to pursue and achieve her own powers as a painter.

Jenny took immediate hope from the sight of Val's building, a Victorian holding four apartments on a plain street of student housing. The first floor apartment of Val and his roommates was ablaze with so much light that the snow of the front yard was in full view beyond a scraggly, snow-crusted evergreen hedge at the height of the windows.

On the front porch, facing the line of mailboxes beside the heavy wooden door to the building foyer, Jenny heard loud music coming from upstairs and from the first floor apartment: The Supremes from upstairs and The Beach Boys from below. The volume of sound masked her entrance to the foyer, high-ceilinged and small, lit by a low wattage bulb turned on and off with a pull of a dangling chain. Jenny knocked, waited, knocked hard enough at the cracked enamel surface of the door that one of Val's roommates, a small, red-haired law student with a flat Irish nose, heard her.

After a hesitation, remaining in the doorway with the door only partly opened, he first asked if Jenny was looking for DiCosta, then said to wait while he looked for him.

The music was so loud that Jenny couldn't hear clearly but she thought there was a shout, laughter and sounds of some scurrying before Val came to usher her inside.

"I've got the exam," he said. He was barefoot, dressed in a pair of jeans and a red sweatshirt reading Washington Redskins.

As they stood in the living room of the apartment, among its mismatched assortment of stuffed chairs, an arched lamp, a vinyl-topped coffee table holding pads, law books, a can of Cherry Blend next to a brown pipe, and an open *Playboy*, Jenny was aware of Val's roommates watching them like leering forest creatures from other doorways and from the other side of the room. The student who had opened the door pressed tobacco into the bowl of a pipe and prepared to light it.

"I know. I won't bother you. Just a moment," Jenny said.

Jenny saw grins spreading on the faces of the other roommates as Val led her to his own space, a large triangular closet, his room formed by the slant of the building's stairway. She had been in the space before, knew of its floor, all but a strip of it taken up by a mattress bunched at the rear wall, the little room's low, slanted ceiling bearing an overhead light connected to an exterior outlet by a white string of cord. There was no room to stand, only room to be near, to feel the close presence of Val.

Jenny wanted to tell Val about Marjorie but he disliked her and her dislike for him, so Jenny fell away from that subject as Val stripped her of her coat and began to kiss her neck. He was unshaven, maybe more than a day, and she was being scratched by the stubbled growth. She tried to turn into him but he was already heated, making low grunting noises as he pressed her into position with her face on a pillow smelling of sweat. Just as she had foreseen, he became unstoppable, his fingers strong on her hips and into the softness of her stomach and breasts as he grunted and breathed. Then he rolled onto his side, let her reach under his sweatshirt and stroke the dark hair growing on his chest and stomach.

She smelled tobacco on him, felt the weight of the hairy forearm he draped loosely across her shoulders. His beard grew unevenly across a bubble of second chin.

"Was Chicago fun?" she asked.

"It was okay," he said. He was looking blankly at a freckle on her shoulder, not at her. He wanted her to go.

Before he began guiding her, she lay back and wriggled her stockings and skirt back into place. When she had the room of the door open and was standing, she reached back in for the coat he handed her.

"Good luck with the test," she said.

"Yeah," he said.

"Okay." Then she left.

On the way back to the dorm, her face nestled into her buttoned coat collar against the oncoming wind and bits of snow, Jenny felt miserable. With his dark features and black-framed glasses, Val was excitingly grown up, sexual, seemingly taller than his five nine frame really was, perfectly oriented in a life that already was leading to exotic places and people. Gesturing and touching with easy movements of his firm, short arms, he conversed endlessly at high levels: the workings of legislation, the strategies of conglomerates, the Lautrec exhibit that would open at the New York Met. Like a painter himself, he smothered the grayness of Jenny's own, pedestrian world with the colors that showed her New York, his hometown of D.C., celebrities and ideas. He matched stories with stories, observations with opinions at the few parties they had attended together, one of them at the freshly renovated home of a law professor and his wife; they had spent more than six months on the removal of four layers of old paint from intricate door frames and cabinetry, removed carpets and sanded original flooring back to oaken hues, then painted all the walls and ceilings art gallery white. Being with Val was living in a movie, a movie full of touches, grand plans, encounters with out-of-the-ordinary people.

But who else appeared in such a movie? Jenny suddenly looked at everything through Marjorie's betrayed eyes and saw that all the cameras in Val's life pointed at him. In the twisting and pushing of the sex, there had become visible at the pillow's edge an open *Glamour* magazine, something Val was unlikely to read. The grinning and open stares of Val's roommates had been more than leering; they had been looking, she knew, at a fool. Nor was this night the first time: they had looked from the first glance, from her first privileged entry to the little nest of a room beneath the stairway, at a fool.

Looking through Marjorie's eyes, she saw Val as nothing more than Jerry: bright, handsome enough to attract notice, horny, and then, in the end, fickle.

Yet. Yet. He spoke in lies, spoke with the intensity of his stare and the nearness of his mouth, the masculinity of his Brut or Old Spice aroma on a shining new shave, the steering touch of his thick fingers. But he spoke lies that were dreams, dreams that Jenny's tenacious, sincere love could will into truth. She could will it, wanted to will it.

As she thought about Val, she couldn't trim the image to him alone. At the sides, roommates smirked. Other girls smiled, touched him suggestively and freely. The sounds as she left now sorted into one of the roommates saying, "That didn't take long." And seen from the porch of the apartment building, across the street, the car Val had driven to Chicago lay entrenched in a blanket of Friday's snow.

When Jenny got back to the dorm, she found Marjorie's mood matched to hers.

Damn it! They had begun making out. Marjorie never wanted to see Jerry again and then it just happened. He was so sad and then they were making out.

Marjorie wasn't going to see him again, though. He had burned his bridge, the way he acted about the baby, the weaselly fuss he made about paying for the abortion, the way he . . . didn't. . . marry her after all his talk.

Marjorie held to her resolve as the routine of the week progressed. On Monday, one of the boys who had been at the showing of the film shorts intercepted her after her math class and clumsily bent his path enough that they walked together toward their next classes. His name was Dan, he was majoring in chemistry, and he asked if she would go to a game with him.

On Wednesday, Marjorie decided to drop out, just for a semester, just until she could figure things out, get her mind back on school.

The next day, as the earnest, silent art student sat a few feet away, sketching Jenny at rest on her elbows with her eyes closed and her head tipped back, she gave her thoughts to the worries that had been troubling her for days.

What was the matter with her? She hoped she had not gotten pregnant.

CHAPTER 9

Late last night, it was drizzling rain,
Lying in bed I was feeling no pain.
I heard a ringing in my head,
It was the telephone, so I jumped from my bed.
I tripped, stumbled, and said hello,
My first sergeant said it was time to go.

Tom Daniels had his administrator's cunning on display as the Ten O'Clock Club reacted to the arrival of Tank and Greg Beutel the Monday following Harlan's victory over the Fort Dodge wrestlers. Tank and Greg Beutel were hardly at the door of the Woolworth's and stamping February snow off their shoes before conversation dropped. Briefly, the interruption became an expectant silence as everyone looked their way. Then amid a warm hail of greetings, Tank and Greg took the seats reserved for them.

"Colder than a witch's titty 'is morning," said Duane Swift, the heavyset retailer whose bad hip gave him such a wobbly walk that he used his car for everything, even the short trip down the block from his appliance shop to the Woolworth's. The sharp fins of his white Cadillac poked from one of the angled spots at the door.

"Then some," agreed another of the group, tamping a new cigarette on the counter and feeling with his other hand for the lighter in a front shirt pocket. "Tonight, 'll be eleven."

"Eleven!" came the reply.

In Tom Daniels' assumed role as chairman of the day's assembly, he took over then. "The boys pulled it out other day, didn't they?" he asked.

Conversation passed through general mention of some matches before coming to rest at Tom Daniels again.

He placed his small hands palm down on the counter before him and assumed a worried look as he made eye contact up and down the lunch counter.

"We're losing our coach. Season ends, Phil Cole's calling it quits." Tom Daniels put his fingers to his cheeks, rubbed his face for a moment and then, with a decisive tone, cut through an undercurrent of worried reactions. "But the timing might be just perfect, just perfect."

What Tom Daniels said next was what the members had been hoping. Even before the superintendent called him, Greg Beutel had been insistent about going to the Ten O'Clock with Tank once the AA session ended that morning.

"How's that?" asked Marty Seider, on cue.

By then, Tom Daniels and all the others were looking at Tank.

"Over the weekend, I talked with the board, with some of the parents. Your name came up a lot, Tank."

Tank had sensed something of the sort as soon as Tom Daniels sought him out at the Saturday match.

"Long and short of it is, Tank, we think you should take over from Phil. And Phil does, too. He made sure I understood that when we bumped into each other at worship."

The others chimed in with "Good idea" and "You're the one" as Tank understood what Daniels and others had in mind was more than helping out. They wanted Tank to be more than a former team member come back to help with some practices and meets. They wanted Tank to be the coach.

Sensing Tank's shoulders on the mat, a pin imminent, the Ten O'Clock members pressed.

"My Richie, he's stubborn, can't take advice from anyone," said Ellen McTigue. "But Tank, you yelled at him to get his arm in, and you see how quick Richie did that? He had that arm in right now. In a blink."

"Yeah, Tank, hands down, these boys listen to you," the father of one of the wrestlers agreed.

When the gathering broke up, Tom Daniels took Tank aside. Phil Cole thought Tank should start right away, as assistant coach for the rest of the season, and then head coach.

"You come to the school Wednesday morning? Nine o'clock?" Tom Daniels asked. "We'll get a contract together for you to coach, teach Iowa history, maybe debate."

A teacher? Of what? And with what capability? The principal's plan set Tank's mind to confused sorting of the surprising idea. Still, Tank promised to meet at the high school on Wednesday morning.

Before they separated and Tank walked back to the Lutheran church for his car, a delighted Greg Beutel added his own endorsement. "Tank, you can't be sittin' around on your ass like you are. Time to get up and get it. I'm serious. You'll be good at coachin', and you need to be doin' something besides just thinking."

As Tank sat beside his mother that day, while listening to Klara Vladimirovna's soft voice at prayer and helping her turn the pages of her book, the thought came to Tank that life for him, life for anyone had divine pressure on it. The god he could vaguely picture, but was beginning to hear, had Klara Vladimirovna at ease, ready to go and do whatever instruction came to her from the words she read each day.

The thought continued when Nina Bjornson parked her white Ford pickup at the end of the driveway and, accompanied by Lady, her collie, picked her way over the rest of it on foot. "Nikolay, Nikolay," she greeted him happily when he came to the door. In an instant, she had placed a bag with two bread loaves in his hands.

"Can Lady come in, too?" Nina ran a hand lightly through Lady's coat, over a lump at the top of the dog's right front shoulder.

Despite the gentleness of Nina's touch, the dog flinched from it.

"The vet thinks Lady and I are going to hear bad news today. We're on our way there," Nina said.

Klara Vladimirovna looked at Nina with pleasure but without recognition as Nina removed her coat and settled with Tank and Lady for a visit at the table in the kitchen. "How are you, Mrs. Vetrov?" Nina asked. She wore a heavy white sweater and overalls that had become wet at the bottom of each leg from the snow. "Nikolay taking good care of you? I've been in the mood to bake bread and my family is not keeping up. I figured you can use it, unless Nikolay's stopped eating so much."

Smiling as she did so, she studied his solid appearance, the calm that had replaced the nervous look Tank brought home to Navalny in September.

While they talked, Tank pet Lady, who was pressing her nose against him each time he stopped. Tank began a careful massage of the tender place on the dog's shoulder.

After a quick spurt of news about some boys getting drafted and a farmer getting treated for pneumonia, Nina showed she was up to date on the Ten O'Clock Club discussion, too.

"They want you for the coaching job, I hear," she said. "You should say 'yes'. I'm praying on it."

Soon after that, she gathered up her coat and prepared to leave. When her coat was buttoned to her round chin, she gave Tank's hand a squeeze. "Don't be a stranger, Nikolay. You're too young to turn into a hermit."

Lady hung back, though, reluctant to leave Tank.

"Let's go, girl," Nina said.

Lady jumped up against Tank, who bore the weight easily.

"She hasn't moved like that in a long time," Nina said, reaching to put her hand on the dog and direct Lady out the door. Then Nina noticed the change in the animated collie. "Her sore's different," Nina said, feeling for the lump. "It's all smooth here."

Lady no longer flinched at the touch of her shoulder.

"You've got your father's gift," Nina said to Tank. "You're a healer. You are."

Then she left, in a hurry to make it back down the track of the driveway and continue the errands of her day.

Tank watched from the house as Nina, her heaviness magnified by the thickness of her work coat and a big gray hat that framed her round face in warm earflaps, navigated the cold walk to her truck. From the truck, she turned and waved, then stood to the side as Lady leapt up into the cab. The vet would confirm that day what Nina already discerned: the frisky, untroubled Lady had no growth atop her right front shoulder.

"Isn't that pretty?" Nina had said the September before, when they passed the bright maple. "How beautiful" as she and her husband Chet took care of each other and their son Dan, the Drake sophomore with the polio-weakened leg. "How beautiful" as she brought two loaves to Tank and his mother, as she moved about, ever-smiling and happily warm when anyone saw her.

And she was praying on it, she said. Tank knew Greg Beutel was, too. So many of them, his mother included, were "praying on it", for guidance to a big, ex-wrestler who had begun coming to grips with alcohol and the consequences of a random existence.

The realization of all the praying struck him as he checked on, then fed, the half dozen hens waiting in their coop for the conclusion of the Iowa winter. Galina had seen something when she gathered eggs, had told Tank to keep watch for pecking. Sure enough, the Plymouth Rock hens, barred with strips of white and black, and one of the Rhode Island Reds sat close together, while the remaining Rhode Island sat pressed into a corner along the floor. Tank would begin watching, in case the young hen needed a separate cage.

Even as Tank lifted the old weights and the heavy boulder in the barn late that afternoon, he felt small. Who was he, that these people were praying on him? Just the morning before, as he left with the others who had listened to Reverend James preach to his Baptist congregation about "Being Afire for the Lord", a young mother he didn't recognize touched his arm and said "We're praying on you, Mr. Vetrov."

Amid such thoughts, he became conscious of the prayer now entered into his workout, the words of it broken and paced to the lifting and his breathing in the barn. "God, give. . . " *grip tight. . .* "us grace. . . " *lift, hold . . .* "to accept. . . " *breathe, breathe . . .* "with serenity. . . " *change. . .* " The prayer punctuated his lifting, bending, stretching and his thinking until he completed his workout, placed the set of weights back in their place and sat on an overturned crate with the old bible he kept among an assortment of tools in an old wooden cabinet.

Beneath a bulb hanging from a support of the barn's upper floor, Tank flipped randomly through Psalms and then the account of Moses wandering. Tank gave the pages small attention as he simultaneously mulled the questions prompted by his mother's practices, the discussions of the AA meetings, and the memories of his life.

His mother's favorite readings and his own picking through the New Testament were bringing him to a new and comforting opinion of God. This God, this Jesus Christ healing, listening, forgiving, forgiving again was generous. This God set things up so people who had made a mess of things could go at it again, could go back in the ring.

"In an acceptable time I heard you, and on the day of salvation, I helped you," Tank read, then reread to the sound of the barn door catching the force of a low, steady wind. Within the barn, the cats that had been watching from the back shadows ventured to the edge of the light and settled next to a folded tarp. There, in patient expectation, they groomed themselves.

They scattered again to the shadows when Tank rose and left the barn for the banya where, before entering and stripping for a sweat, he chopped a hole in the ice over the pool where Little Creek curved.

By the time he had sweat himself ruddy, dropped in and out of the creek, and returned to the banya, he was content in the decision Tom Daniels already took for granted: Tank would begin coaching – and teaching! - at the high school. His mother, Nina, Pastor Sherman, so many others, they all discerned divine intention, even kindness, in the link of events making up their lives. The same, he thought, must be the case for him. The imminent depletion of the money remaining from his wrestling, that alone was an unmistakable sign that he needed to find a job. For this, was he present in Navalny?

The principal must know about AA, about the time at Louisa Psychiatric Care Center, about a raft of things that must not matter as much as having Tank coach the wrestling team.

"I place my trust in my Lord and Savior, Jesus Christ," Tank prayed as he hurried along the path to the house through the snow. "I place my trust. . . "

His happiness grew the next morning when, very soon after he came back from the morning AA meeting, Galina turned into the driveway and churned her heavy aqua Mercury two-thirds of the way to the house. She was alone this time, in a rush to deliver a warm, cream-colored winter coat and other winter clothing she had found for her mother at a mid-winter cleanout sale. Galina wanted to get back to Omaha before the children came from school.

Full of purpose and urgency, Galina bustled around the kitchen and the rest of the house. "You're letting it get like this?" she complained to Tank as she reorganized supplies in a kitchen cabinet, as she took stock of the things on the refrigerator shelves. With authority, she swept him into her work of straightening.

Klara Vladimirovna, lucid and pleased, protested from her kitchen seat that Galina should sit, relax, visit. In front of her mother, Galina had set a cup of tea.

By then Galina was around the corner, in her mother's bedroom. "Mom! What is all this?" Galina scolded. "Tank, you have to pay attention."

Galina returned to the kitchen with a stack of random photographs, letters, prayer tracts and clippings she then placed in front of Tank. "Straighten this up for Mom, will you, Tank? This is a mess."

Galina took a container of scouring powder and some rags into the bathroom. "How can you two live like this?" Tank's sister called as she put the little room to rights.

"Leave that. Galina. Come sit," Klara Vladimirovna called. "Your father and I, we do that ourselves."

Soon, Galina came into the kitchen, took her own cup of tea and sat down at the table, where Tank had made a small effort to organize the stack of his mother's papers. "Do you need these?" he asked his mother. "Who are these people?" He showed Klara Vladimirovna a photo of a row of young women and some young men at table with a dark, deep-eyed man.

"The starets," Klara Vladimirovna said, extending her hand to touch the face of the man in the photo. A twisting black beard lengthened the man's already long countenance, which had a staring air of sure authority.

"That means a holy one," Galina said. "That's from St. Petersburg."

Galina tapped the image of one of the serious young women. "This is you, isn't it, Mom?" Galina asked. "Mom, this is you? Look."

Tank studied the appearance of the woman in the photo and recognized his mother, her young face rounder then than it became in maturity, her hair richly thick and gathered in braids that wound over the top of her head.

"Dad is in that photo, too," Galina said. "See him?"

Yes, Tank recognized then Anton Zakhar Vetrov, who stood broad-shouldered and deferential at the far right edge of the group.

"You've never seen this before?" Galina asked her brother. "Mom keeps that in the front of her prayer book."

"I don't remember," Tank answered.

"You were too full of yourself," Galina said. "The star wrestler. You didn't pay attention to anything."

Tank could tell his confusion amused Galina, who was shaking her head in pretend annoyance. Her blue eyes, though, gave her away. She rolled them, and then raised her voice to her mother.

"Mom, isn't that right? Nikolay paid no attention at all."

Klara Vladimirovna smiled, not understanding, but happy to have the company of her Nikolay and Galina.

"They were visiting the monk then, Rasputin. Grigori Rasputin. Right, Mom?"

Tank had no trouble remembering the main facts, the time of living in St. Petersburg, of working for the Tsar at the family's St. Petersburg palaces, his father having great respect, a reputation even reaching up to the Tsar, for the way quiet, strong Anton Zakhar Vetrov had with horses and other stock. In a vague way, Tank knew of troubles: waves of Russian soldiers battling Germany, the government of the country uneasy with dishonesty, assassinations and looming revolution.

"The starets," Klara Vladimirovna said, beginning to cross herself until Galina put her own hand comfortingly on her mother's.

"You know about Rasputin, don't you?" Galina asked Tank. "The healing? The way he was with Tsar Nicholas and the Tsar's wife?"

"Sort of," Tank said.

"The Tsar and his wife had a little boy who was a hemophiliac. If he got a cut, he just bled. No stopping. He could die. But Rasputin could fix all that. He pretty much had his way with the Tsar because of that. You can imagine. Someone keeps your son alive and that means something. Well, Rasputin had his ideas about how things should be. The Tsar listened. Right, Mom? Rasputin could get away with saying things no one else could. Right, Mom?"

Galina stood up and turned on the gas beneath the samovar. Taking her seat again, she held her mother's wrist and continued.

"Well, things were going from bad to worse in Russia with no food, people cold, soldiers dying by the truckload, everything just all mixed up. Then some enemies of Rasputin killed him. Pretty soon, the lid blew off everything with the government all mixed up, revolution coming, the Tsar and his family holed up in one of their palaces, and nobody in charge.

"Mom and Dad escaped with some other friends. They all went to Lithuania somehow first. Mom and Dad got married."

Tank knew that part of the history, of the daughter Emma who died right at birth, in Lithuania, before Anton Zakhar Vetrov and Klara Vladimirovna arrived with a few other Russian couples in Navalny. The others – the Markovics and the Orlovs, the other families who came after that - were no longer in Navalny. Death from old age, some movement for the sake of work in Mason City and in Omaha, the wandering of grown children had drawn the other families from their Navalny settlement.

After Galina left for the drive back to Omaha, after his mother had fallen asleep, Tank went to the barn, where he read about accepting the kingdom of God as a little child. On impulse, after completing his workout with the weights and the boulder, as the cats crept back from the shadowed rear of the space, Tank stretched face down on the barn floor.

He was tired, too tired to work through the complexities of the ideas running into one another as he suppressed the wish to drink, as he remembered Angie, and the times before Angie, when, as Galina said, he was full of himself, a powerful Russian hedonist running amok. With his face feeling the cold of the floor, with the smell of farm decay – soil, grain, animal odors, manure – strong in his nostrils, he surrendered himself to the happiness of trusting that he knew, that he would know, even if the knowing came as mysteriously as breath.

Tank's detached air remained with him during the meeting with Tom Daniels at the high school Wednesday morning. The principal noticed something but ascribed the change to Tank's appreciation for what Phil Cole and the board had created. Tank signed the contract presented, agreed to begin assisting Coach Cole the following week, and to teach the state's required Iowa civics course the next school year. Within twenty minutes, the meeting ended with a handshake and the principal's transfer of Tank to the woman who had been tasked with compilation of his employment documents.

When he left the school, he found the air warming into a thaw that was softening the snow and causing rivulets along the highway. In places, the Oldsmobile splashed through puddles that had collected in the low spots of the gravel road leading to Navalny.

As Tank looked across the landscape of the flat farms and lines of windbreak trees, the sight of gray houses and silvery silos, he felt a sense of belonging. He knew Navalny. He knew Harlan. He knew high school wrestling.

At home, a young man with an unhappy expression was waiting for Tank in the barn. Barely twenty, putting an end to a Marlboro in long, hard draws, the man spoke in a low voice, not much louder than the sound of the dripping snow flowing from the warming roof of the barn. His face and his whole body were softly round, babyish.

Tank had not recognized the man, but he recognized the family.

"My aunt Nina told me to come see you. I'm Jimmy Bjornson," he said. "My arm is all screwed up from the Army."

Here, the man extended the arm as far as he could.

"My aunt says you're a healer."

"I'm not. I'm not that," said Tank. The contradiction caused a flash of pain across the visitor's face.

"She says you are."

Tank had his friend's nephew seat himself on the crate beneath the dangling bulb in the knowing God space. Jimmy Bjornson, near to tears, sat with heavy resignation. He kept his unhappy gaze on the barn floor a few feet away from him. Lighting another cigarette, he resumed smoking in hard draws.

By then, Tank had his bible in hand. Seated on an old chair pulled from a barn corner, Tank began reading, interspersing the random landings on psalms and passages with unvoiced prayers. In a few minutes, with his own breath turning forced, he found himself reading ". . a certain woman, who for twelve years had had a hemorrhage. . . came up behind him and touched the tassel of his cloak", the cloak of the generous, sympathetic Lord Jesus Christ, Savior.

Tank read the passage again. Again.

Unaware of anything but a certainty flowing into him, a stirring of imminent, erupting force, he gave way to a staring trance.

The melting snow of an ordinary February thaw dripped from the barn roof. The cats crouched in their ordinary watchfulness.

Of a sudden, Tank stood, causing the chair to fall, the cats to draw back.

Taking Nina's nephew by the back of his shirt and the seat of his pants, Tank raised him aloft, held him shrieking and flailing with the young man's alarmed face toward the overhead beams.

"Jesus Christ, Jesus Christ, Jesus Christ," Tank called. "Something you can do about this?"

"You're crazy! God! Stop!" Jimmy Bjornson shouted, moaned, shouted, begged. "Stop, you asshole."

Tank felt strong, sure, loved. "Jesus Christ," he called, pushing the light weight of the frightened man toward the heavens.

CHAPTER 10

Gimme that eagle, globe and anchor
gimme that eagle, globe and anchor
gimme that eagle globe and anchor
cause it's good enough for me

Spuhn had decided, would remain decided. He stood at iron attention.

Outside, the January rain sounded. A jeep squished past the spare headquarters office where Lieutenant Kip Travers was reading Lance Corporal Dennis Spuhn's application for extension of his Vietnam assignment and term of enlistment.

"At ease, Marine," the lieutenant said, still studying the paperwork. Lean and solid, only a couple of years older than Spuhn, the lieutenant was sweating along his jaw and at the beginnings of a widow's peak in his thin reddish hair.

"You are aware that, if I approve this, once you've had your thirty days, Uncle Sugar is going to have your ass for an extra four months? You're going to extend your service till . . . September 27, 1967?"

"Aye aye, sir," Spuhn responded to each question. He kept his green-eyed stare on the lieutenant's forehead.

"Just can't get enough of this tropical adventure, is that it, Corporal? So much better here than. . . what's your home of record? . . . than Davenport, Iowa, that it?"

"Guess not, sir," Spuhn answered.

Strange decisions were not surprising to the officer. This was another Marine extending in country, maybe for the combat pay benefit, maybe for whatever at home was worse than Vietnam.

Jody, thought the lieutenant. Jody. A Marine so anxious to get home and pull Jody away from some hot pussy that he's willing to extend his time in country. And in this country. He knew the troop, a good Marine with his gig line straight, his boots cleaned, the set of his chin and his whole athletic form bespeaking Corps. Spuhn was steady, squared away, able to get along, a kid with something in mind when he had survived the Marine Corps, the Nam. He also had a reputation for edible chow. He could make the standard ingredients into something different from the slop offered up in other mess halls.

"You're short in country now, Corporal," the lieutenant said.

"Yes, sir," Spuhn said. "May third. One hundred nine days and a wakeup, sir."

"But you want the thirty day leave. You want the benny."

"Aye, sir."

"Where's Uncle Sugar going to take you on this leave, Corporal?"

"New York City, sir."

New York City, so that's where the girl was, the girl listening to the sweet bullshit of some chickenshit draft-dodging Jody. There were Marines would rather fight than fuck. Lance Corporal Dennis Spuhn was another kind: if he had to fight to fuck, he'd fight. The Marine Corps would take it however it came. Lieutenant Travers signed all three copies. He stood up and extended his hand.

"Good luck here. Good luck in New York," the lieutenant said as they shook hands. "Give these papers to the CQ. "

At the sandbagged headquarters mess hall, Spuhn had a number in his mind – 109 days plus now another 147, altogether 258 days – as he went about the work of the food operation. "Lifer," one after another of the platoon members taunted him.

"How it starts," the mess sergeant told him. "Six months here, a year. Pretty soon, you're in for six, ten. Lifer." Still, the sergeant's tone was kindly and approving. Spuhn knew something of the alternative life the man had passed up himself: a girl who didn't wait at home near a little somewhere in Missouri, an unskilled labor assembly line something for the rest of his life with high school classmates who were tired of one another even then. The Marine Corps had become home. Semper fi.

Nothing came from Lauren. Nothing. Nothing in answer to Spuhn's delicate blue letter telling of his extension, telling of his upcoming travel to see her in New York City.

He did receive mail from his mother, a letter that came just before he departed Da Nang for Travis Air Force Base and then New York. She knew to reduce a letter's weight with small script. Her two pages held much on the four sides, including her wish that he be careful, assurance of everyone's prayers, and the plan to use the money Dad won at cards for a new linoleum floor in the kitchen. As Spuhn suspected, his father remained in the game with the men at the country club. Spuhn hoped the extra six months of combat pay he arranged would cover the inevitable need.

Clayton wrote one of his quick letters about parties, a class giving him trouble, and much about girls, mostly their shapes and tits, and willingness to put out. In bits, Clayton told of the others: Tony Szabo spent lots of weekends at Iowa, was having no trouble with his Ambrose courses. Joe Yoder nearly failing a bunch of things. Benson brown-nosing his way everywhere, now one of the junior officers at his frat, Delta Chi; Benson's father was a muckety muck with the national organization. As he read, Spuhn could hardly feel sorry for a guy who was being put to sleep by a visiting professor with a German accent; Clayton, after all, was sitting in a classroom with numbers of sexpot coeds on a campus, in a country where he could do whatever he wanted whenever. On top of that, Clayton's rodeo injury had given him a medical deferment for an almost undetectable injury: he didn't even have the draft board worrying him.

Spuhn finally reached Lauren by phone from Travis.

"Don't come," she said.

"I'm comin'. I have a ticket."

Lauren was silent.

"Lauren?"

"I'm here."

"I get there tomorrow morning. Pretty early."

"Where are you staying?"

"I don't know. Somewhere."

"You can stay with us," Lauren said. Her voice was flat, soft.

"That's good."

"But, Dennis. . . I'm engaged. You know that. I wrote you."

"Yes." Spuhn had read the letter the month before he put in his paperwork for extension of his Marine Corps enlistment and Vietnam station.

"Lauren? You there?" he asked.

"Yes." Then, sounding forced, she gave him directions to the Oyster Bar on the lower level of Grand Central Station. "When you get to Grand Central, ask anyone."

"I will."

"I have a class at two o'clock. It's one I can't cut."

In the best of his restless imaginings during the nighttime flight east, Spuhn greeted Lauren with such a hug, such an arousing kiss, and just the right arguments that the two of them, resuming the close pleasure of the time in the Hernandez garden, would then walk around New York with their arms about one another until they found a place to be alone in love. Spuhn worked over his arguments, what he could say in order to disrupt a marriage shaped in family expectation. Face to face, would Lauren understand the letters he wrote from Okinawa and Da Nang?

His eyes hurt and he had a small headache as he rode a shuttle-bus from LaGuardia Airport into Manhattan the next morning. From visits to Chicago and one wrestling event in the Twin Cities, he knew skyscrapers and the immensity of the urban places shown in *Life* or *Look* magazine photos of things like a parade for astronaut John Glenn or for a victorious Yankee team. But New York in reality was grander than them all. Even if he had wanted, he could not have napped. Around the bus, and ahead of it, cars, vans, taxis and other buses made practiced, often honking, progress toward Manhattan. Once in Manhattan, with the bus lurching forward in short, hard accelerations within inches of other vehicles, Spuhn watched unending, intimidating vectors of pedestrians making their ways from subway openings toward one or another of the buildings. Even honking taxis had negligible effect on the vectors as they flowed along the narrow sidewalks of the city.

Slinging his seabag strap over his shoulder, feeling the sharp February chill of a gray New York day, Spuhn made his way through a vector coursing out of Grand Central Station and, just as Lauren said, went down the big staircase to the Oyster Bar restaurant. A group of sturdy workers in yellow hardhats made room for him on a bench.

"Get the Marine a coffee," a man, probably a foreman, said to one young worker who had moved to sit on a large toolbox. The foreman took a bill from his coat pocket.

Just as the construction crew rose and gathered around another project manager wearing a hardhat and a tie, the foreman paused to tell Spuhn, "Semper fi. Take care of yourself, Marine."

Then Spuhn, in a motionless stupor, with his eyes smarting and his head hurting from jetlag, spent the next hour searching the lines of hurrying pedestrians for sight of Lauren.

He saw pretty women, beautiful ones, smartly dressed ones, but none that dwarfed Lauren and her long, soft, russet hair, the wonderful, light sweetness of her perfume, the shape of her form.

Then he saw her at the far end of the big space, just as she noticed him.

He rose, grabbed his seabag and hurried to meet her with an embrace and a kiss worthy of a *Life* photographer.

She shrank from him though, only glancing at him obliquely and near to tears as she spoke in a controlled pattern of polite acquaintance. Her face was pale.

They sat down. She held herself stiff as he kept his arms around her and tried to capture her direct gaze.

"Why did you come?" she said. "Dennis, why? We only met that one time, that one time."

"I'm like that, I guess," Spuhn said. "I get my mind made up that way, that's all she wrote."

Lauren took his hands in her own.

"I think you are remarkable," she said. "You're nice looking. Handsome. Exciting. I was glad we met that time. I do think about you. I have feelings for you. Yes. But you're so serious. Your letters. . . they made me think."

"I liked your letters, too," Spuhn said. "I pretty much tore your letters out of the mail clerk's hand."

"No, I mean your letters made me sit down and think." Lauren looked hard at him, then looked down at her hands as they held his.

"You made me serious. Like you are. You're serious. What was I doing? That's what I had to ask myself. And I did. I've thought about this a lot. How could I be good for you? We're different. I know David. I've known him and his family since forever. He's known me and my family like that, too. Our families are always together. I know what life with David will be."

Lauren paused. Her eyes were tearing. She collected herself, waved her hand to keep Spuhn from talking.

"And I want that life. You see? It was wrong of me to play around with you in Miami. I just can't do that to you. I can't."

Without speaking, as she cried, Spuhn held her.

Confused and sad, his misery only intensified when Lauren occasionally consoled him with the resting of her head on his shoulder and, once, a soft kiss that came into their clumsy day like an escaping animal. Spuhn followed her without noticing where they went, and what she showed him. The weight of his travel, the strangeness of being away from the Marines and from Vietnam pressed heavily on him. They ate sandwiches she bought for them at an automat and then rode the subway north to Barnard. At times, he dozed.

Before going to her class, Lauren led Spuhn to a gray townhouse that had been converted to apartments for Columbia students. As she expected, one of the friends who occupied a second floor unit was home. Of course, the boy agreed. Spuhn could camp out there, catch some winks until Lauren came back from her class. Then she left.

Friendly and curious, the boy, a senior named Pittsburgh, wanted to talk with Spuhn about Marine life and about Vietnam but when Spuhn's yawns became long and continuous, Pittsburgh gave up the effort.

"Here," he said, showing Spuhn a room with two single beds and wall art that included a semester of Playboy foldouts. "My roommate's on campus till tonight and I can do my studying in the living room."

As he fell asleep, Spuhn heard Bob Dylan singing, same as Da Nang.

A few hours later, in the room now dimming with gray evening light, Spuhn awoke in Vietnam confusion. For a moment, he tensed and shrank from whatever was happening around him at the base. Then the sound of Lauren talking with someone in the living room brought him to New York.

Coming into the living room, he found Lauren and a young, pipe-smoking man in a red sweatshirt looking at him.

"Finally!" Lauren said. "You were tired."

"I am tired," Spuhn said. "Man."

"This is Wally," Lauren said. "Wally and Pittsburgh share that bedroom."

"Dennis Spuhn," Spuhn said, shaking the student's hand. "Thanks for the place to sleep."

"Anytime."

Wally had a friendly way about him. To Spuhn, he seemed very intellectual with his straight, brown hair, his dark-rimmed glasses, and his ease among shelves and shelves of books. The boy's straight, brown hair was many times the length of Spuhn's fresh Marine white walls and brush, probably because of neglect. Wally and Pittsburgh, these were smart people, smart in a different, more substantial way than the couple of Marines Spuhn knew who maintained their own libraries of single authors: Isaac Asimov for one, Ayn Rand and Ian Fleming for another.

Lauren rose and spun her cream-colored scarf close around her neck and chin. "Thanks, Wally," she said. Then, to Spuhn, "You ready, Dennis?"

"That's a rog," said Spuhn. "Let me grab my gear."

The cold New York air was strange to him after the months in Da Nang but he enjoyed the way it roused him and brought him awake.

"Let's hang around in the city for awhile before we catch the train," Lauren said. "You're in charge," Spuhn said. He was glad that Lauren seemed righted again, full of her spark, instead of sad and weepy.

As they walked and then when they rode the subway to Chinatown for dinner in a small, noisy place that made Spuhn think of Vietnam, she wouldn't let him press into conversation about them.

"I did write you," she said. "I was about to mail it and then I didn't. I wrote you again. I didn't mail that one, either. I wasn't nice to you at all."

"I know how you can make it up," Spuhn said.

"In your dreams," she said. "I'm getting married, Dennis. To David."

"When?" Spuhn asked.

"In a year, when I graduate. David will be in law school then."

"He won't get drafted?"

"He's joining the reserves. He goes in at the beginning of June. At Fort Dix, so we can see each other sometimes."

Lauren didn't explain directly but she said enough that Spuhn knew David and his family had the means of living – in fact, living well. Lauren spoke of city habits: theater, concerts, and of chances to use her parent's place in Miami Beach.

Lauren had said they were different. Spuhn knew that but had not thought about the difference as a barrier, just a difference.

Even so, the opulence of the Steins' Tudor home when they arrived in Westchester was beyond what Spuhn had imagined. Rivaling the Outing Club in its grandeur, the house had grounds as extensive as some that crowned the river bluff in Bettendorf. The white of a gazebo reflected light from the line of lamps along a circular driveway and from the front entrance.

Inside, Spuhn saw a hallway and living room giving way to other grand spaces, each hung with striking color-splashed oils. The living room also had a weighty block of granite carved into a complex, interlocked twist of geometric forms.

Lauren led Spuhn into the house, to a guest room with a private bath beside the large, brilliantly white kitchen.

"Get some sleep," she told him. "My first class is not till eleven, so we don't have to rush."

When he tried to kiss her, she stiffened and gave him the side of her face.

"Get some sleep," she said.

The next morning saw polite interrogation by Lauren's mother, a thin, pretty woman with streaked hair, perfect jewels and a full schedule of volunteer committees. Lauren's mother knew that Spuhn and Lauren had met in Miami at the time of the bar mitzvah but what now, and what might this portend for the wedding of Lauren and David Singer? A Marine, a Catholic boy from Iowa. What was Lauren doing?

And what could the Steins do to ensure that the young Marine knew the magnificence of New York?

Almost as confused as Lauren's mother, Spuhn answered in polite, rank-respectful Marine fashion about the friendship he and Lauren had begun. Exuding about New York was easy. The vastness, strength and motion of the city excited him. Spuhn was a willing recipient for every suggestion of things to visit and see while Lauren attended her classes.

He went first to the Empire State Building, where he pressed against the curved bars of the open observation area and poached on the lecture of a guide pointing out landmarks to a Pennsylvania school group. After her final class that afternoon, Lauren led him into Central Park, where she laughed at his curiosity about the variety of park visitors and activities. There were elderly friends having loud conversations in native languages. Russian? Polish? Serbian? Middle-aged women with dark hair and shawls pushed heavy baby buggies. Some runners came by on long strides. Pretty young women walked Irish setters and poodles. A man of about fifty talked loudly to himself at the end of a bench. Two Jewish men with broad-brimmed black hats and braided locks of dark hair practiced the playing of their trombone and a French horn. A group of boys shouted and bounced a basketball from one to another as they overtook Lauren and Spuhn.

That evening, with Lauren intercepting and deflecting what she could, Lauren's father asked gentle questions of his own. He was a handsome man with gray at his temples and well-used laugh lines around his mouth. Like Lauren's mother, he had become avid about tennis, which he had played that afternoon with a friend and client of the investment firm.

"Is Vietnam as terrible as we read?" Mr. Stein asked, accepting the plate served to him by Mrs. Golarski, the cook whose years in the household had made her Lauren's familiar relative, a stout Polish woman who loved Lauren and the Steins the way she loved her son and daughter.

"It's no picnic, sir," Spuhn replied. "We have good people there, good Marines. They're doing the job. Hands down, they're doin' it."

"They're admirable, all of them," Mr. Stein said. "I'm glad to hear you confirm that. But what about the South Vietnamese leaders? They seem to come and go. As soon as one faction gets too corrupt or too cozy with some group or other, boom, there's a coup and all the leaders go at one another's throats until some strongman gets hold of the reins. For a while. Then the whole thing begins again."

"You're talking about the ones took over from Diem? The junta?" Spuhn asked.

"All of them," said Mr. Stein.

"What I see, Mr. Stein, seems the grunts just keep their heads down and do their best to protect the people from the NVA and the Cong. We don't pay much attention to the shenanigans. That's not our job."

"It's so far away," said Mrs. Stein. "And we've got Cuba right here. I know you are not a Jew, Dennis, but everyone has to be concerned about all the terrible things in Israel."

"There's a lot of trouble all over the place, that's for sure," Spuhn said.

Lauren, ill at ease throughout, intervened. "Let's talk about other things," she said. "Please. Dennis isn't making any of this happen. Just the opposite."

Mr. Stein, pleased with his daughter's boldness, smiled.

"You're right, sweetheart," he said. "Let's get to the real issues. Who's your favorite baseball team, Dennis?"

"We're for the Yankees around here," Mrs. Stein said. "So watch what you say."

"I have to say the Cubs," Spuhn answered. "Ernie Banks gets things going. But that Nellie Fox is exciting, too. He could play some second base. He was my hero when I was in Little League." Lauren was quiet. Spuhn could tell from the color in her cheeks that the pretty woman with the green-blue eyes and long red-brown hair was fuming.

When they rose from the table, Lauren kept going. Wasting no time, she shepherded Spuhn out of the house and into a tan Mustang.

"My mother embarrasses me at times," Lauren said.

"Don't worry," Spuhn said. "She's fine."

Lauren reached the end of the driveway and turned so quickly onto the street that the tires squealed.

"She likes you, though. She thinks you'd be a good match for Naomi."

Spuhn remembered Lauren's cousin with the curly dark hair and happy giggle, one of the trio Spuhn and Hernandez had met the same time Spuhn met Lauren. Naomi was pretty and likable but she was Naomi, not Lauren.

Lauren combed some tresses with absent-minded strokes as she drove here and there in neighborhoods filled with perfect homes on big lots marked with stands of towering hardwoods and dense firs. They had set out for a White Plains area with some bars that could have music but, without saying so, Lauren abandoned that plan in favor of pulling into a park overlooking what she told him was Lake Rye.

After a silence, she worked herself up to tell Spuhn what had been stirring in her.

That afternoon, as he surrendered to the futility of Lauren's distance, he had already decided to leave.

"You need to go, Dennis. I don't mean to insult you. You're something, you are. But I can't do this. David has plans for us tomorrow, then the weekend, and then everything else."

She let him kiss her then, then let him hold her as she gained control of the quiet sobs that shook her.

The next day, before he caught a Greyhound bus at Port Authority and returned to Davenport for the remainder of his leave, Spuhn sought out the Park Avenue address of Madison Alberts Investments. The day was sunny, cold and windless around him. Spuhn looked up at the five-story building with its graceful iron balconies and window boxes.

Then he left, satisfied that he knew where to find the investor and former Marine George N. Forrest II. He knew the same hard way another fact: Spuhn would have a house someday like the Steins'. Hands down, he would.

CHAPTER 11

Your baby was lonely, as lonely could be
'Til Jody provided the company
Ain't it great to have a pal
Who works so hard just to keep up morale

As they waited on the tarmac for the arrival of the Continental Boeing 707 that would take them in hopscotch fashion across the Pacific to Vietnam, Spuhn first fell in with a couple dozen Marines, mostly teen-aged privates assigned straight from infantry training or straight from communications, logistics or some other military occupational specialty training. Boisterous and in varying ways, drunk, they exchanged exaggerated memories of the sex and beer and fighting that had marked their leaves. A few of the Marines and several dozen of the Army and Navy personnel were married, so those waiting included men hugging or kissing women as children pulled at their parents' sleeves.

When one military son, a bold four year old, fixed a stare on him, Spuhn winked, then began a game of peek-a-boo that took his own mind off the waiting and the apprehension. With a giggle, the boy put his small hands over his own eyes and, leaning against his kissing parents, peeked at Spuhn. The game went on, a game that took Spuhn's thoughts away from the vain evening when he had shouted at his father to get his shit together and stay away from the big shot friends who were just having fun with him. "Why is someone as good as you losing? And why do you let the manager steal your accounts?"

"You don't know anything about it," Spuhn's father said. "You just don't."

Spuhn left, ignoring the way his mother tried to stand in the path toward the back door, ignoring her insistence that he speak to his father with respect. Veronica was not home. Spuhn could feel Mike making himself forgotten in his bedroom. Spuhn left without saying that he did know, hands down he sure as shit knew what the cook at the Outing Club told him when she said those men playing cards with Spuhn's father, they cheat when they play, and they laugh. They pretend to have drinks. Everyone hears. The cook's husband is the men's locker room attendant. He hears.

Six months, then 27 days, altogether 210 days and a wakeup. They stretched ahead of Spuhn as a delay, a sentence from which he'd emerge ready to clamber upward into his success: a million dollars by age 30, his own company, house like the Steins', wife who was . . . Lauren.

Marine parlance made death capricious: "Your number's up, it's up." Spuhn's number wasn't coming up. No toe tag and body bag for him. He would live, would be unscathed, he knew. He wouldn't shirk anything but neither would he venture into danger the way Hernandez had. Only 19 days from the conclusion of his tour, Hernandez had talked himself onto a patrol in a quiet area of a quiet region, just enough experience for bragging rights when he came back to the world and picked up with the busty women who would want war stories with their horny Marine. Spuhn could imagine Hernandez wanting the taste, wanting the chance to know for himself what the war was for Marines with an infantry MOS.

Of course, the affable, entertaining Hernandez, probably the same age or a year older than his platoon leader, had been able to wangle the favor. A spoon? The platoon leader, the whole squad, would have been amused by the incongruity of a crazy spoon joining them as they patrolled the quiet, pacified area just outside Phu Bai.

But then, only two clicks from the conclusion of the patrol, a sniper's bullet tore through the achilles tendon at the top of Hernandez's left boot, and he went from short to medevacked to hospital ship to rehab and medical discharge. Hernandez was in Coral Gables, where he was limping to and from rehab when he wasn't running after pussy. Hernandez was just sitting in the house, in the garden, in time.

On the tarmac, Spuhn was glad for the crewcut, merry boy. Dressed up in a white, buttoned shirt and brown, creased pants, he hid against his parents, then started the game again by masking his small, happy face with his hands.

The game went on. Spuhn thought of Lauren, of the way his mother held so tightly the bills he put in her hand when he said good-by. He thought of the coarse, pretty, Iowa student Clayton introduced. So unabashed about sex she was uncaring, she surprised Spuhn with the way she kept a lit cigarette at the corner of her mouth while she talked or, bare but for panties, oblivious to anything else, watched black and white quiz shows on the old RCA television in her dorm room.

The plane taxied toward them, its appearance intensifying the farewells of the married couples and provoking noise from numbers of the waiting GIs.

A solidly built Marine captain named Gutierrez positioned himself at the base of the stairs, began asking some of those boarding "Do you play bridge?"

When Spuhn answered that he did, the captain exclaimed "Out-standing!" and escorted Spuhn onto the plane. Once aboard, the officer and Spuhn joined an Army lieutenant named Tomczak and another Marine captain named Sawyer in a forward area with two facing pairs of seats.

"Gentleman, we have a fourth for bridge," Captain Gutierrez announced to the others. "Corporal Spuhn is helping us out."

"Uncle Sugar!" said Lieutenant Tomczak, extending his hand to shake Spuhn's. "Uncle Sugar comes through." He had a round, friendly face that was showing dark, twelve hour growth. Spuhn saw infantry insignia on the small man's collar. His dark-framed glasses gave him the look of a financier or a tax lawyer.

"Three leathernecks in the game," said Marine Captain Sawyer. "You're up shit creek here, Tomczak." The Captain was the freckled Anglo counterpart of Captain Gutierrez, both of them a couple of inches shorter than Spuhn, much more broad than he was through their chests and shoulders.

Gutierrez had very white teeth, often flashed in big grins. There was no sense of Vietnam or apprehension about him.

"I saw you keeping that Navy officer's boy in line," Captain Gutierrez said. Spuhn could tell the officer approved.

"Mommy and Daddy had business," Captain Sawyer said.

Spuhn, the only enlisted man, listened while they waited for the plane to take off and reach cruising altitude. The men were two or three years older than he. The three knew one another from train-ing and then from duty assignments: Gutierrez and Sawyer were Annapolis classmates. Tomczak must have come from the ROTC program at Ohio State. Either that, or he had graduated from Ohio State and then gone through Officers Training. He was a para-trooper: the wings were in display on his shirt. More clear than that, Tomczak liked calling the other officers "legs".

Friendly and genuine, three confident, athletic men heading up the ladders of their military careers, the officers took Spuhn in, trading information about themselves for Spuhn's answers about his home of record – Davenport – and the joke of his MOS, the decision someone had made about turning a Marine named Spuhn into someone with the Military Occupational Specialty Food Specialist. The Marines had made Spuhn a "spoon."

Gutierrez, with self-effacing grace, told of his delight about the muggy, hot Annapolis climate he found when he entered the Academy. "Growing up, I was the coldest Mexican in Minnesota," he said. "You couldn't make it hot enough for me."

"The Nam's got some weather, doesn't it?" asked Sawyer. "Plenty hot enough for me."

Spuhn knew they would be arriving at the end of the good season. From April on, Vietnam would begin getting very hot, and very rainy.

"It does get warm, no lie about that," Tomczak said.

"To say the least," Sawyer agreed.

"You know what, though," Gutierrez said. "There are some unbelievable places. The beaches, the old French buildings. Cam Ranh Bay."

"Oh, yeah, that A Shau Valley is a must-see," said Tomczak. "The excitement there just goes on and on."

Gutierrez laughed, flashed his white smile. Then he continued.

"You watch. There are going to be hotels, people taking vacations."

Tomczak and Sawyer hooted at that. Spuhn only half hid his own amusement.

"We should get set up for your next R and R. The Delta," said Tomczak.

"How about Chu Lai? You like plants? Hot weather? Bugs?" Sawyer said.

"Any spots you recommend, Corporal Spuhn?" Tomczak asked him.

"Chu Lai's not one of them, sir," Spuhn answered. He had been coming up on six months in country when his platoon and the rest of the 3rd Brigade became part of the Operation Starlite action that tore up the hillsides and fields and hundreds of Viet Cong. From his field kitchen operation, Spuhn had heard the thundering artillery, seen the Marines going and coming under a sky full of Huey helicopters hastening to attack or extract. He had seen Marines with their teeth grit or their bodies motionless as medics cut clothes away from flesh turned blood-gushing hamburger. He had dug trenches, served terrifying stretches of guard duty, felt insects crawling inside his drenched shirt. Hotels in Vietnam? A cold day in hell.

"This war's not going to last forever," Gutierrez said.

"From your lips to God's ears," Sawyer said. He was thinking of his wife, married at the time of his Annapolis graduation, the voluptuously curved, long-haired brunette child who had stroked his face on the tarmac. As they waited, they made no secret of their sadness. Spuhn had seen them.

"Meanwhile, troops, let's play cards," Gutierrez said.

"How about Big 10 versus the Academy?" Tomczak said. "Corporal Spuhn, okay with you?"

"Everyone trust me to keep score?" Sawyer asked.

"We don't trust you but you can keep score," Tomczak said.

The flight hit turbulence halfway to Honolulu. Even so, during the five minutes, the ten minutes of it, Spuhn and the three officers played without interruption. Sawyer made a barrier of his extended arm and kept the cards from jouncing off the playing tray onto their laps.

The others were intelligent players, Spuhn found, Gutierrez very much so, but none of the officers was the equal of Spuhn's father.

Spuhn's partner Tomczak revealed himself as a predictable competitor for the playing of a hand: he didn't want to be an observing
dummy to Spuhn's play. But when bidding closed and Tomczak
began the play, he offset the snatching of the bid with an impressive
ability to sense where the dangers lay in the cards held by Gutierrez
and Sawyer.

Spuhn adjusted his own bidding so that Tomczak could veer
toward contracts – four hearts, three no trump – that were safer
than the ones Tomczak would make with his own style.

But not always. Gutierrez's look had recognition in it when
Spuhn succeeded with a four-spade bid, with Sawyer and Gutierrez
holding an ace and a king of the trump suit.

"Airrrr borrrne!" Tomczak said as Spuhn drew the two cards on
a single lead.

Sweetening the win was the bonus from Sawyer's challenging
double. Sawyer posted the score and then rolled his shoulders.
"Let's go, partner," he said to Gutierrez. "Got to press on."

A half hour from Honolulu, Gutierrez and Sawyer won the
third game and, so, the rubber. Spuhn and Tomczak had kept
things close, had forced Gutierrez into bidding and then making a
contract more difficult than the dealt cards indicated.

"Veni, vidi, vici," Sawyer said, smiling this time as he gathered in
the cards.

"Who are you now? Julius Caesar?" Tomczak said.

"Omnia Vietnam in tres partes divisa est," Sawyer replied.

"I can imagine," Gutierrez said.

"Yeah, us, our enemies and the enemies of the enemies of the
enemies," Tomczak said. "It changes every day."

The officers were proper and careful in what they discussed but
their conversation still let Spuhn imagine things occupying them
and other staff of MACV, the joint service Military Assistance
Command in Saigon. This was a trip they had made before – in

fact, made in accord with their military assignments. The three officers were on their way back to the Saigon nerve center from attendance at Pentagon meetings. The Vietnam they experienced had an ambassador, commanding officers, possibly Secretary McNamara in it as well as the all-points touching of the war being conducted by growing numbers of U.S. troops. Spuhn wondered what their security clearances could be.

Before they were aloft again and the game had resumed, Spuhn learned that Captain Tomczak's regular bridge partner, an Army captain, was on compassionate reassignment to Fort Belvoir, VA, close enough to Baltimore that the officer could spend time with his failing mother.

Lieutenant Tomczak had joked that there wouldn't be a crab left in Chesapeake Bay when Johnson got done. Johnson was Special Forces, an Airborne Ranger who had gone from Howard University into Officer Candidate School at Fort Benning, GA.

Captains Gutierrez and Sawyer offered to switch partners but Lieutenant Tomczak and Spuhn were set on evening the standing.

With powerful cards, a strong hearts suit well-played by Tomczak, they took the first game in an orderly succession of tricks.

Tomczak threw down the last three cards, all trump. "Chieu Hoi, motherfuckers," he said.

"One lucky hand," Sawyer answered, gathering the cards and passing them to Spuhn for the deal. "You'll be the ones surrendering."

"Roger that," Gutierrez said. "Time to kick ass and take names."

With exaggerated delight, he picked up each card Spuhn dealt him and assembled his hand.

Gutierrez and Sawyer had strong enough cards for a game-winning three no-trump bid but were two tricks short after the play of the hand. Spuhn had been the factor. After gaining the lead, he was able to ruff a small diamond before driving the lead back into the visible dummy hand Sawyer had set down in front of him. Very soon, Gutierrez had to lead into Spuhn's spades, which were long and commanding. The final cards, all red, fell to Spuhn's four of spades.

"Airrr borrrne!" said Tomczak.

As Sawyer shuffled and dealt, as Tomczak and Sawyer bantered, Gutierrez looked thoughtfully at Spuhn.

Hours later, when they had landed at Ton Son Nhut air base and the plane came to a stop, before they exited, Gutierrez leaned into Spuhn and asked him the name of his commanding officer.

"Lieutenant Travers?" Gutierrez answered. "Good."

A beat later, he leaned into Spuhn again and indicated what had entered his mind.

"Marine, I can't do anything about your name. But we ought to do something about that MOS of yours."

The promise came back to Spuhn's mind two weeks later. On a blue-sky day that had the sounds of a volleyball game wound into the sounds of aircraft and moving patrol units, the CQ runner, another corporal, came to tell him, "Lieutenant Travers wants you, Spuhn."

Spuhn hastened to the Lieutenant's office, reported and kept as deadpan as he could when the Lieutenant explained the orders he was holding in his hand.

"You're going to MACV, Corporal, effective five days. And these orders give you a secondary MOS, too. Intelligence specialist."

"Aye, sir. Thank you, sir," Spuhn said.

Lieutenant Travers looked at Spuhn's orders a moment longer, stripped off copies for Spuhn, and stood up.

"Good luck to you, Marine. Looks like you are to watch this war from up high, up there with the brass."

CHAPTER 12

Mission top secret, destination unknown,
I don't even know if I'm comin' home.
Jump up, hook up, shuffle to the door,
Jump on out and count to four

Ronnie Tonti, whose habitual first stage of intoxication showed in a giddy "all is right with the world" grin and a reddening of his plump cheeks, didn't feel that way as the police car left the bridge behind and drove into Arkansas. Tonti had been docile as the policeman cuffed him in Memphis an hour earlier. Now his mouth felt dry, an ache had begun in his head, and, on top of everything, he needed to pee like a racehorse.

What was going on?

The policeman, amused and sure, had been waiting for Tonti at the end of the bar when Tonti finished one of his handwalking adventures, complete with an entertaining stop over the cleavage of a couple of pretty women stopping in after work from the offices of Summit Transport. Happily, he took a sip from the glass held to his mouth by one of the women, and then a kiss on the lips from her companion. With his friends from Rogers Roadbuilders leading the whoops and nonsense, Tonti navigated through the bar's landscape of ashtrays and beer glasses, some thick forearms and one resting, gray head, all the way to the place where Memphis patrolman Jimmy Dan Ellis had placed himself.

Back in Slidell and other places, including a time in Leesville near Fort Polk, Tonti had been in handcuffs before. The police had their ways. These things happened when a person got to enjoying himself. Offering no resistance, Tonti went like a hero on the path Jimmy Dan Ellis cleared through the men and some women crowding the early evening at Neil's Corner.

Needing no directions, the police officer drove Tonti to the little gray bungalow where Tonti had moved in with a woman named Terry, a slender, long-legged waitress who had been the girlfriend of another Rogers Roadbuilders crew member before she and Tonti found one another.

"Get your things. You're leaving town," the officer said. "This one yours?" he asked as he pulled Tonti's duffel bag from the disorganized mess of an open closet. "Pack."

Soon after, the duffel bag was full of things mostly Tonti's and the patrol car was headed out of Memphis, across the Mississippi River bridge toward a sun disappearing in broad bands of orange and lavender on the Arkansas side.

The policeman didn't talk and didn't respond to any of the voices bursting now and then in the crackling on the car's radio.

His head hurting, needing a bathroom or a tree, rocking a bit with the car's sway along a truck-rutted highway, Tonti stayed quiet.

A couple of miles past the bridge, now pointed north, the patrol car slowed and turned onto the gravel lot of a glowing truck stop. Amid the sounds of passing traffic and the country throbbing of frogs, the low noises of parked diesel engines were in the cool air.

The policeman opened the door and removed Tonti's handcuffs.

"This here road goes in two directions," the policeman said. "Make sure you go in the direction away from Memphis."

Tonti was quiet, eager to relieve himself.

"You got that?"

"Yes, sir."

"You had your fun with the wrong little girl," the policeman said.

Girl?

"Messin' with jailbait, specially the daughter of a city clerk, that's just plain dumb," the policeman said. He pulled Tonti's duffel bag from the back seat, dropped it on the gravel.

"Yes, sir," Tonti said. He knew the girl now. Whooeee! That had been one wild piece of ass. Terry hadn't been happy about that.

"And Blahthville ain't far enough. You get on up least far as Missoorah."

"Yes, sir."

Tonti was in such straits that he rushed to the edge of the parking lot, where he emptied himself near an overhang of forsythia growing among some thorn bushes.

For the next quarter hour, he sat in the darkness and considered his circumstances, familiar ones, as he watched the passing of traffic in both directions. Terry would throw away the rest of his things, anything he forgot. He had left a soft violet shirt he liked but there would be another he could find. As always, there hadn't been money to leave. The Rogers Roadbuilders job was coming to an end, everything hurried along by the sunny, abnormally dry April weather. The summer projects of the crew Tonti was with wouldn't start for another three weeks. After the final pour on the bridge approach the next week, the members would disperse, some to other crews, some to Kentucky and complete indolence for a time. Memphis had been good, same as Macon, Little Rock, some other places Tonti had been since leaving New Orleans. He'd left places before and come out okay with new friends, pussy and ways to get by.

New Orleans? Tonti knew that the years now passed, going on three of them, had not altered his brother Franky's vengeful mood. Three? Three hundred and that crazy coon ass would bust through concrete walls to get at Ronnie or anyone else Franky had on his get-even list. But New Orleans had neighborhoods and hiding places as well as friends and spaces that would keep the two brothers apart. This was as good a time as any. Tonti could go have a look, see what New Orleans was doing, what remained torn up from Hurricane Betsy's walloping in 1965.

Tonti stood up, slung the strap of his duffel bag over his shoulder and, feeling good again, walked across the gravel and into the diner of the truck stop.

He entered to find two middle-aged truckers grinning and ready for fun as they recognized him.

"You're the fellow does all that walking on his hands," said one of them, a thick-chested man wearing a partly buttoned jean jacket over his heavy body.

Tonti remembered noticing somewhere the man and his large, reddish handlebar mustache. The other man, indistinctly average with his scruffy fringe of graying hair and his long, thin face and frame, Tonti didn't remember at all. But he sensed with no trouble their amusement at his arrival.

The first man put a broad hand on the seat of the counter stool next to him. "Here's a place, chief," he said. "Willy and me, we saw you few times at Neil's. Both of us, we pull loads for Summit. Summit. Down the block a little from there. I'm Kevin."

"We all call him Bulldog," said Willy.

"Yeah, I bite," said the first man, with a big smile that made his dark, happy eyes small. He laughed and gave his mustache a fond combing.

"Or Bull something else," Willy said.

Bulldog just shook his head, gave the other side of his mustache a touch.

"Ronnie. Ronnie Tonti." Tonti dropped his duffel bag and took the seat.

"What you doin' here, Ronnie?" Willy asked, taking a pack of Lucky Strikes from his shirt pocket and offering the cigarettes toward Tonti first, then Bulldog. "Smoke?"

Willy's motions were slow and exhausted. The shadows under his moist eyes showed long lack of sleep.

"No thanks," Tonti said. "All those other vices, don't have room for that one."

"Lucky for you," said Bulldog, picking one of the cigarettes from Willy's pack and placing it beside his plate. "Hard to do 'out these cancer sticks once you start on them."

Leaving out the details of his informal arrest and police-escorted departure from Memphis, Tonti explained that he was moving on from Memphis. Where he'd been working, that Rogers job was getting to the end.

Willy was flicking ashes on a finished meal while Bulldog had just begun eating his. Tonti ordered a cheeseburger and a Dr. Pepper from Doris, a sturdy, perspiring waitress in a green uniform smelling of her.

"Doris, how's your boy Johnny?" Bulldog asked.

"He comes home on a leave three weeks from last Tuesday," Doris said. "Soon's he's done with his AIT there at Polk."

"Advanced infantry training," Tonti said. He didn't say it, but he knew along with the other two men and anyone overhearing them from down the counter: with the Vietnam folk and the United States so tangled up these days, someone with eleven bravo in his personnel file would be pretty quick visiting a jungle.

"That's right," Doris answered, topping off Bulldog and Willy's coffee cups from a silver pot. "There's a sergeant there Johnny says they all hate worse than any Viet Cong. He's gonna be happy when he says good-by to that mean ol' son a bitch. Now I got to keep Johnny's little brother home. Roy, he wants to join up, too. I'm tellin' him finish high school and then let's see."

"You're right," said Willy. "Come soon enough."

"Yeah, plenty a time, plenty a time," Bulldog said.

He pushed his plate away and lit the cigarette Willy had given him.

"Willy here's 'bout home on his way back to Memphis but I'm on a St. Louis run tonight," Bulldog said to Tonti. "That helps you, chief, ride along."

Not New Orleans, but a long ride, and to a place Tonti had never been. Might as well have a look.

"Whooee, that'd be flat kind," Tonti said. "'preciate it."

Willy smiled. "You got some hours of whoppers head of you tonight," Willy said to Tonti.

"Got some of that bullshit in me, too," Tonti said.

"I'll keep him awake," said Bulldog. "Not like that hallelujah save-me Jesus, heal-me preachin' he'd hear ridin' with you."

"Oh, I can't be listenin' to that devil talk." Willy laughed, stood up and said good-by. "Back to the barn," he said. "You men be safe. The blessin's of the Lord on you."

"You better call your old lady you get to Memphis," Bulldog said. "Tell her hide that young stud in a closet 'fore you're home."

Willy didn't respond, just grinned broadly, waved good-by and headed toward the door. "Doris, thank you, darlin'," he said.

"Thank you, hon," she replied.

Bulldog finished his cigarette, crushed it in a blot of ketchup on his plate, and picked up the meal check. "I gotta use the little boy's room 'fore we go." Then he put some bills with the check, called to Doris, and gathered himself with a tug of his belt, one with a silver bulldog buckle on it. By the time he was back, Tonti had finished his food and was ready.

"Let you get the coffee in Cape Girardeau," Bulldog said. "Ready to go, chief?"

Outside, the early April night was cool and spread with level, dark fields under a sky full of stars. The air, fresh and a bit wet, felt good to Tonti. His headache had passed along with any regret about his push north.

Once Bulldog had the gleaming purple Peterbilt tractor he called Molly moving in powerful, shaking lunges north, the big man shot a teasing glance at Tonti. "Nice a that policeman give you a lift out of Memphis, chief," he shouted over the engine noise.

"Yeah, real nice fella," Tonti shouted back.

They laughed.

CHAPTER 13

Standing tall and looking good
Ought to march in Hollywood

From habit, Dennis Spuhn came quickly into Mr. Fred Klein's tiny office and stopped three feet from the edge of the nicked-up wooden desk, right in a narrow space between a heavy, padded chair and the cowling from a small machine.

With a laugh, Mr. Klein stood, reached across the spread of the desk's array, and shook Spuhn's hand in a powerful, rough grip.

"Sit down," he said. "I got your letter." He didn't look for the blue tissue of it amid the other papers, though, just kept an amused gaze on Spuhn, dressed today in a navy blue sportcoat, a just-unwrapped, folds-still-showing white shirt and a blue and yellow-striped regimental tie.

Spuhn was glad to feel the recognition and the delight Mr. Klein was taking in the appointment. As energetic and solid as Spuhn remembered him from three years before, Mr. Klein had some gray in his heavy band of eyebrows and a bit of scalp showing in the close cut of his gray flattop. He wore the same silver-framed glasses, touched the red horizontal strip of scar beneath his right eye with a hand showing across its back the same small, American flag Spuhn had seen at the Outing Club.

"You look like hell, death warmed over," Mr. Klein said.

"Tired, sir," Spuhn said. "Flight took a long time."

In addition, his alertness to night sounds overrode travel exhaustion. When his mother passed the door of the bedroom at five-thirty, a shock of alarm brought Spuhn upright, intent on finding his weapon.

Now Spuhn felt some burning in his eyes but, otherwise, he was fully awake, excited about this call on Mr. Klein, less than 24 hours after arriving home in Davenport. In Saigon at MACV, on the flight from Vietnam to California, as he out-processed amid other Marines coming to grips with re-entry, Spuhn had been thinking about Mr. Klein and the instruction three years ago: "Come see me."

Well, here he was, standing tall, all his shit together, anxious to have the chance at any work tidbit Mr. Klein would provide.

Mr. Klein's gaze could have been one of the x-ray machines the shoe store on Third Street had a dozen years before for showing the fit of new shoes around the toes of a foot. Spuhn felt Mr. Klein taking in everything, comparing Spuhn three years before to the nervous, serious twenty-one year old seated with his hands on his knees and his clean, thin face fixed at respectful attention.

Unconscious of the motion, Spuhn quickly touched his scalp, assessed the lengthening of his brown hair. The combing was not doing anything to make Spuhn's hair lie again in the brown waves he had before the Marine Corps set his style. Spuhn was in a hurry for that change, too.

"Where you staying now you're out?"

"Home, sir. At my family's."

Mr. Klein asked questions, took each answer like someone who already knew. Spuhn's health, the little bit of weight and size he had put on. Thinking about it later, Spuhn decided Mr. Klein knew something of the card playing.

"Signing up for school?"

""Tell you the truth, sir, I'm mostly wanting to get going with things, see what studies I'm going to need as things happen."

"Hmmn."

Spuhn hadn't seen Clayton, Yoder, Szabo yet but he had formed an opinion of college from Clayton's letters: lots of people killing time, not getting it done, never trying to look around the corner of their futures, just term papers, labs, parties, lots of getting drunk and now, some getting high.

Mr. Klein pushed some papers aside, matter-of-factly cleared a space on the desk in front of him. He picked up a pencil, and began tapping the eraser end against the desk in punctuation of his words.

"This is what I'm thinking. October's half gone. Most years, we're pretty dead about now but this year, knock on wood, we've got some projects. Kenny's got a spot opening up on his crew."

Spuhn's deliberate, serious expression began to give way.

"It won't be fun. You'll freeze your ass off some a these days we get into the winter."

Spuhn had broken into a grin.

"We'll pay you for that. That's union. On Fridays, I want you to work here in the office, start learning some things you'll need to know. We'll find a little bit of money for that. Won't be much."

"Thank you, sir, thank you."

"And you need to go to school. Night, weekend. Know something about numbers, how to talk with bankers, government. You got the GI bill?"

"Yes, sir."

"You find yourself couple a business courses. Accounting."

"Yes, sir." Spuhn realized: Mr. Klein was hiring him and forming him, directing him on a path aimed at the same summit Mr. Klein himself occupied. Mr. Klein! His own Andrew Carnegie making a path.

Mr. Klein pressed a button on his phone, one that brought an announcement knock on the door and the entering of a thin woman with a pair of pink-framed glasses hanging from a cord over the front of the gray sweater she wore.

The woman came up behind Spuhn and waited in silence for her boss's instruction.

"Mary, you got time this morning? Meet Dennis Spuhn."

Mary looked at Sphun, gave him a smile as she nodded in welcome.

"He's gonna start working Kenny's crew. Get Dennis set up with his paperwork and catch Kenny for me when he comes by."

Spuhn spent the next couple of hours in a happy, uncontained, smiling delirium as he completed the forms Mary gave him for a new employee file – address and work history, Social Security, health insurance, union membership application - and then went for a physical at the nearby office of a physician Spuhn had seen playing cards with Mr. Klein at the Outing Club.

When Spuhn returned to Klein Construction's office, Mary made him wait on an oak chair in a little reception area decorated with a United Fund service award and six framed photos of buildings and a roadway marked as company projects. Mary introduced Spuhn to Kenny when the wiry, weather-burned man came from Mr. Klein's office.

Kenny took the measure of Spuhn with a direct look as they shook hands. Friendly but brisk, Kenny gave Spuhn the location of the work site where Spuhn would show up the coming Monday at 5:30 a.m.

The earflaps of Kenny's green hunter's hat held a record of the concrete, caulk and whatever else had been used at many Klein sites. He removed the hat and passed a rough hand across the smoothness of his scalp.

"Just out of the service?" Kenny asked.

"Yes, sir," Spuhn answered.

"'Sir' was my father," Kenny said. "Call me Kenny."

Spuhn agreed.

"That's good you're through with the service. Damn draft board's been taking everyone."

"Well, they've had their whack at me," Spuhn said.

Yes, he had served. He was done. Now, he was getting his life started. Everyone out of the way! He was starting with Klein Construction Monday and already getting direction from Mr. Fred Klein himself.

By the time he arrived Monday morning and joined Kenny and his four man crew at the site of what would be the new Davenport location for the Roberts menswear chain, Spuhn had enrolled in two evening classes at newly opened Scott Community College. As Mr. Klein had advised, Spuhn would take Accounting 1 and Marketing.

The announcement of the success with Mr. Klein pleased Spuhn's mother and father, even though they asked him separately about college.

"You don't think you should get your college done first?" Spuhn's father asked as they sat together in front of a Walter Cronkite news report. "You've got the GI Bill. You don't want to let that get away from you. It's nothing to sneeze at."

Spuhn looked at his father, then shifted to a painting his mother had in progress, a paint-by-number arrangement of two ducks rising from a misty pond.

Now grown to six one, Spuhn had a couple of inches on the man who was watching the television at the same time he was reading the *Davenport Times-Democrat*, folded to the Goren on Bridge column.

Nothing had changed the resemblance: Spuhn would continue to hear remarks, compliments that he looked like his father – same fine nose, brown hair the way his father's was, same waves in it, even a voice with his father's depth.

"I feel like I need to get started," Spuhn said. He reminded his father about the accounting course, the marketing course.

"Just keep an open mind," Spuhn's father said. "Fred Klein, he's certainly one can teach you a lot."

The weekend went by slowly, as Spuhn read ahead in the textbooks and organized the work clothes he'd wear Monday morning.

This was how people spent their time? What they did back here, back here so unlike the tense, hot, noisy, pay attention, keep your shit together Vietnam?

Saturday afternoon, Jim Clayton's older brother Bob, unshaven, wearing a white t-shirt, only got off the couch when Spuhn rang the bell a second time and rapped on the window of the closed-in sleeping porch. This is how people spent their time? Clayton's brother had been watching a return of *The Fugitive* as he waited for a basketball game and then departure to his second shift, extra weekend time at International Harvester.

Then Clayton took Spuhn to do. . . nothing.

They spent a drizzly afternoon playing pool and then looking for Szabo, who had moved from home into a big apartment made from the third floor of an aging Victorian in an aging neighborhood overlooking the river from west of downtown.

The place had an air of impending crisis in the dozen or so picket notice flyers dropped on a chair and the floor, or taped to the outside of the bathroom door. One of Szabo's three roommates, already notified of induction, had taped that letter on the wall of the entrance hallway. The living room, where a sagging brown sofa faced another relic of splotched rose color, had walls with posters protesting discrimination and the military draft. Amid them, at a corner where a scarred table held a large phonograph with wires leading to speakers at the other ends of the two couches, there were tour posters of Bob Dylan and of Peter, Paul and Mary. An empty, open guitar case had been left beside a window with a thick white candle on the sill.

Spuhn received tight, reserved looks from the sturdy roommate and his companion, who were talking and listening to a Dave Van Ronk album when Spuhn and Clayton arrived. Ken, a friend of Szabo's from St. Ambrose, was attempting to grow a mustache, so far just a thin scattering of uneven yellow hairs. The woman was small and dark-haired. She wore large hoop earrings and, with her glasses off, was looking at the arrivals with squinted eyes.

Szabo said good-bye to them and went with Spuhn and Clayton to do. . . nothing.

Clayton told Spuhn later that Szabo was thinking of going to Canada.

While they were together that evening, before they rounded up another Iowa friend of Clayton's named Slick and went to Spuhn's for poker, Szabo probed in guarded questions at Spuhn's Vietnam experience.

They hadn't gotten very far before Spuhn began answering, "You should go see for yourself." Vietnam, Vietnam, Vietnam. Over and done for Spuhn, the war had turned into dark matter everywhere in the country, a depressing, misunderstood thing mixed with any subject, everything from getting out of bed to getting married.

For his part, Spuhn was curious about Yoder, about Mary Siemons and some other St. Sebastian's girls, even about Benson.

The draft had everyone uneasy. Yoder, who had dropped out of Iowa after pretty much doing nothing the second semester, was still living with some friends in Iowa City and waiting for his notice. Benson, safely tucked into the reserves through some string-pulling by his father, remained set on law school; Benson would go through Basic Training the next summer. Clayton saw Benson all the time.

"Will this be on the test?" Spuhn spoke in Benson's old, worried cadence.

They laughed.

"He says that all the time," Clayton answered.

"That's true. He does," Slick confirmed.

Mary Siemons was around. She had gotten serious with a guy from Mason City who was a Marine. He had been in the ROTC program.

The weekend dripped away, with Spuhn thinking at times of Gutierrez and the others still at MACV. The lack of urgency Spuhn was finding at home heightened his own urge to begin, to progress.

The whole lot of them, naive Szabo at the front, had their heads up their ass and their minds in Arkansas. Three years along now since Spuhn left and what? They had taken enough courses to reach junior year, had gone to Ft. Lauderdale - some of them - for a spring break, had readied for moving on to law school with the same weak purpose. That was it? Well, maybe not the lawyers: Clayton, smart and with his good looks, his smooth way, was Clayton and Benson was the same, clumsy beneficiary of everything his father could do for him.

Spuhn was ready for Monday, ready to immerse himself.

That day, he still woke up in Vietnam, only partially swallowing a low cry as he felt for a weapon. Outside the door, his mother said, "It's time. You said to tell you when it was."

That morning instinct would stop, Spuhn promised himself as his eagerness for the beginning of his Klein Construction work flooded him. He promised himself again. Quietly, he dressed in the workclothes already laid out during the weekend.

Very soon after, Spuhn took the lunch and the hug his mother gave him, and, using his mother's Ford stationwagon, arrived twenty minutes early at the block where a rickety line of small worker cottages had been removed.

162 - BY TOM FIGEL

A panel truck with its side reading Klein Construction, Building the Future, was parked beside stacks of pre-fab panels and bundles of shiny metal studs.

Spuhn didn't have long to wait for Kenny and the other members of the crew.

While a few of the men waited another five minutes or so in the warm cars and a pickup truck they had driven to the site, Kenny and his passenger replenished their silver cups from a large green thermos and began walking a line marked with stakes and string. When they returned, Kenny introduced Spuhn to the other four crew members.

By midday, Spuhn, now known as "Professor" because of the community college courses, was part of them, part of building the retail center future on a block that lay clear, with only some roots and rotted pieces of timber poking from the clay and black dirt that had been scraped by a bulldozer parked in the center.

CHAPTER 14

Mile one, just for fun.
Mile two, good for you.
Mile three, good for me.
Mile four, let's run some more.
Mile five, I feel alive.

"Hey, Prof," Greg said, indicating with a head nod the arrival of Mr. Klein's unmistakeable, gold-colored Chevrolet in front of the 12-unit apartment building where Kenny's crew was working. Even though the empty building had no heat and many windows had been removed, the project was inside work, a good place to be during the mean January part of winter. The workers had wrapped up the retail project just as the winds of a looming December storm started ripping the last leaves from the city's oaks and maples.

Mr. Klein had a friendly way with the men of his crews, and liked being out on the job, away from the paperwork and phone calls of the office. If need arose, he was ready to install drywall or show his old skill with electrical work.

Now, as his steps sounded on the stairs of the empty building, Mr. Klein heard Rolly having fun with Lee about a public scolding Lee's old lady had given the quiet, muscular worker a couple of nights before. Weakly, laughing himself, Lee tried to argue his own facts as the two hung doors in the apartment where Spuhn was helping Greg install window frames.

"If your dick was as big as your mouth, you'd be quite a boy," Mr. Klein hollered at Rolly by way of greeting.

Rolly, continuing to hold the door in place as Lee set the position, was quick with a reply. "Well, and if your mouth was big as your dick, you wouldn't be able to talk."

Mr. Klein laughed the loudest of them all.

Efficiently, he scanned the room and then walked into the other areas of the apartment for an assessment of the progress.

"Kenny," Mr. Klein said. "Spare the kid for a bit?"

While Mr. Klein and Kenny walked on an inspection of the first two completed apartments and then the next two that would be rehabbed, Spuhn went to the basement, washed at the sink where the water lines had been left connected, and did his best to brush rehab debris from his jeans. He changed socks and put on a pair of loafers. Tucking the tail of a blue, button down dress shirt into his pants, he hurried to wait for Mr. Klein at his Chevrolet, a V-8 Caprice he kept perfectly washed and waxed.

Greg, Rolly, Lee and the others working for Klein Construction liked Spuhn. Spuhn knew they laughed at his haste, the way he hustled for the shovel or another tool at a site, the way he drew on his galoshes, snapped them, and hastened to stand in the wet concrete as Rolly directed the flow of it into the forms from a succession of cement trucks. The kid, Prof, could keep up. Liking him, they admired without resentment the understanding he was gaining so quickly of the entire business.

In a way that paralleled Mr. Klein's attention, Greg, Rolly and Lee, along with Kenny and others, kept track of the college courses and the company privileges that were drawing Spuhn up from their own level. Only Greg had completed high school. The crew teased

Spuhn, called him Prof as they observed his down-at-the-
groundlevel ignorance of tasks, and, as firm as parents, made sure
that he kept up with the class work they put before him.

Mr. Klein took a half-smoked cigar from the ashtray and relit it
before he pulled away from the Klein project.

"Got to make a stop," he said. Spuhn was accustomed to ending
up just about anywhere on such drives with the construction
company owner. He also knew that each stop, each person visited,
held some meaning in the curriculum Mr. Klein was following for
development of Spuhn's experience.

This time, after a drifting look at two blistered Victorians near
the border with Bettendorf and then a studied circling of the
surrounding blocks, Mr. Klein asked Spuhn "What do you think?"

Spuhn knew from other tours what he was meant to analyze:
the location and state of shopping, schools, evidence of neighboring owners' attention to their properties.

Mr. Klein seemed to like Spuhn's answer, seemed pleased that
Spuhn had seen evidence of the city's improvement to lighting of
the nearby commercial street, that Spuhn had taken in the sound-
ness of the block's other homes under their skins of flaking paint.
The two Victorians as well as the neighbors had solid, high wooden
doors and porches with bluffside views, maybe even grand sight of
the river from a Davenport neighborhood giving hints of up-
grading. From the street, the roofs of the houses seemed snug, the
layer of snow even, no circles of melt from escaping heat.

Spuhn added a proof of Mr. Klein's instruction, received as he
worked in the office on days when heavy near-winter rain interrupted projects in the field. "Depends on the cost, and when it has
to be paid, how it has to be paid."

"Precisely." It was a signature word for Mr. Klein, one he liked
to use, sometimes with the extra emphasis of a hand on the table or

the stubbing of a cigar in an ashtray. "Precisely," he repeated. At the office, they found Mr. Klein's principal banker talking amiably with Mary.

"Jack," Mr. Klein said to the slender, gray-haired man who had been waiting for him. "Meet Dennis Spuhn. Dennis, Jack Michaelson."

They shook hands and went into a conference room where some of the chairs held unopened tan parts boxes. The banker moved one box to the floor and waited for Mr. Klein and Spuhn before sitting down. His gray suit and the match of his navy tie showed care.

The banker looked at Spuhn.

"You Fred Spuhn's boy?"

"Yes, sir."

"The Fred Spuhn plays cards with Wally Meadows, the fellow owns the Chevy dealership over in East Moline? Over at Coopershill Country Club?"

The banker kept his gaze on Spuhn another beat while the fact settled amid all the other relationships in Spuhn's mind. Wally Meadows Chevrolet: the name appeared on the rear license frame of Mr. Klein's car and on most of the Klein Construction vehicles.

Spuhn knew the ads: Who will make you a deal? Wally will!

Who will screw you at cards? Wally will! Or someone else would. Or all of them would.

For just a moment, the banker seemed about to say something. In a blink, the look went away, replaced by the ready, neutral expression of a visitor awaiting his host's turn of conversation.

After some catching up on family, Mr. Klein and the banker got down to business, a purchase of a 40-acre site far west on Locust Street, outside Davenport's city limits. Mr. Klein was ready for documents, a contract, but the banker, playing with the flexible silver band of his watch and looking unhurried, maintained that the bank was ready, as soon as the bank completed appraisal of the collateral.

"Those properties are sound. They're full up leased," Mr. Klein said.

"You know that. I believe you," said the banker. "It's just I have to have everything tied in a bow the way the committee wants it."

When the banker left, Mr. Klein took Spuhn back to the conference room.

His contentious mien had passed. He drummed his fingers on the table and showed Spuhn a small file.

"We each have to have our little show," Mr. Klein said. "Michaelson knows. Some other banks want this but Michaelson's good to deal with. We'll be turning dirt come spring. Have to."

After asking Spuhn about school, Mr. Klein arranged for one of the office staff to run an errand that would give Spuhn a lift back to the job site and his mother's car. Kenny and the others had left for the day. The sky still held some dwindling gray light and Spuhn had no class that evening, just some accounting problems and work on the marketing class assignment, the creation and presentation of a plan for a new business.

Not for the first time, he decided to drive home by way of the place.

It was an empty, one-story building, a yellow brick building that, briefly, had been the site of a pizza restaurant aimed at a community college classroom building that Scott County decided to postpone.

Spuhn turned into the empty, paved parking area – 17 spaces – and got out to look again through the front window at the empty area where chairs had been placed upside down, at rest on plain wooden tables in need of refinishing. Through an open door, with the help of the light from cars passing along River Drive and from the big, arched lamp at the edge of the property, Spuhn looked into the kitchen. He could see very little, just enough to tell that the kitchen still held on its counters boxes of cooking equipment.

In his mind, he could see the two of them, Spuhn and Jesus Hernandez, serving up food that would cram the parking lot with cars.

The sales agent still had his signs in windows on two sides of the building.

Spuhn worked with his numbers, and completed his plan for a chain he would call Spoon, a chain with well-made, down the middle fare for travelers and for locals. The quality would be consistent, the atmosphere welcoming without ostentation, the prices fair. Spuhn would make sure Spoon had fun as an element.

With Hernandez involved, adding his tasty wonders to the menu along with his upbeat way, how could it not? Spuhn knew Hernandez was available in Miami, was ready to be talked into the restaurant venture they had begun shaping at the Food Service training. Wasn't this the time to shit or get off the pot?

Even before the presentation to a small class made smaller by the howling beginning of a seven-inch February snowfall, Spuhn had his mind made up. He had gotten in touch with the sales agent, a retired high school chemistry teacher who quickly arranged a meeting. As they inspected the inside of the building on a day bright with sunshine reflecting from snow, the agent promised the readiness of the seller, First Security. The bank wanted to wrap things up. Make an offer.

The next time he was in the office and had the chance, Spuhn asked Mary for a time to meet with Mr. Klein. "Personal," he said when Mary asked the reason. He could tell how little he was hiding from her, even though she maintained her flat, efficient expression as she jotted the note on a small, ringed pad she kept tucked in a front pocket of her sweater.

Before the afternoon ended, as Mary and other office staff bundled themselves in heavy winter coats and varieties of scarves and hats for going to their cars, Mr. Klein called Spuhn inside.

"Well?" Mr. Klein said.

"I'm going to quit," Spuhn said. Before he could start on the script of thanks and acknowledgement of the training received from Mr. Klein and everyone else, Mr. Klein, in his usual way, went to the nub.

"What are you going to do?" Much later, Spuhn would realize the man meant "you and your family".

Spuhn erupted with an excited version of the presentation that had received a high mark in the Scott Community College class. He knew Hernandez would come aboard. All Spuhn had to do was call and make the suggestion.

Mr. Klein let Spuhn present his plan. As Spuhn slowed, Mr. Klein stood up, told Spuhn to keep seated where he was – anxiously forward on the heavy chair in front of the desk – and pulled one big roll from among the tubes of plans and drawings stored inside a metal cabinet.

When Mr. Klein cleared a space on the desk and unrolled the document, Spuhn stood to see a map of the Iowa side of the Quad Cities, one with platting of things that were more discussed than actual.

"Location, location, location," Mr. Klein said. He was enjoying Spuhn's quizzical expression.

"Spoon? Maybe so," Mr. Klein said. "But not there. No." He ran his finger north on the drawing, beyond the Davenport edge Spuhn knew and into an area of farms bordering Brady Street, labeled Highway 61 outside the city. "You want to be here."

Sure enough, Mr. Klein, whose business depended on interpretation of others' plans and anticipation of their interests even before the investors and planners recognized the interests, read the unrolled document with assurance that the area he pointed out would have an interstate highway. Mr. Klein put his finger on the spot where he said Highway 61 and the new road would intersect. "You go there, take a look, and you come back to talk to me," Mr. Klein said.

As Mr. Klein knew he would, Spuhn drove straight up Brady Street and then Highway 61 to the open space where barbed wire fencing showed the borders of cropland and pasture lying beneath half a foot of snow.

Evening had come with a clear sky, enough light for Spuhn to scan the snowy, level Iowa swath where the new highway would come. Where the Brady Street, Highway 61 interchange would be, the snow held some surveyors' sticks. Traffic moving to and from Davenport on Highway 61 illuminated footprints and tire tracks that gave evidence of attention to an area that, otherwise, looked no different than the next mile of roadway either north or south.

When work wrapped up at the apartment renovation the next afternoon, Spuhn drove to the Klein Construction office, where he was glad to see Mr. Klein's Caprice parked at the back entrance. Mary and a few others were completing tasks, getting ready to leave.

"He's here. I'll tell him," Mary said as soon as she saw Spuhn.

In the few moments before he heard Mr. Klein's summons, Spuhn combed at his hair with his fingers and worked at the plaster dust that coated his work jeans. The paint blobs on the cuffs of his blue work shirt had dried. Same for the smears on his fingertips and the backs of his hands: in Mr. Klein's office, he would not add to the marks made by Mr. Klein's stream of careless construction workers.

The change in Spuhn since the day before amused Mr. Klein.

Spuhn entered the office and accepted the chair across from the desk with a chastened air. Mr. Klein could see that his young fireball, the Marine veteran so impatient to rise, had arrived this time without his customary assurance. The look on Spuhn's smooth, intelligent face was perplexed. Spuhn was ready to be instructed.

Mr. Klein set about the task.

After unrolling the drawing of the platted area north of the Davenport limits, Mr. Klein had

Spuhn stand beside him for close study of the spot Mr. Klein had chosen for the new Spoon venture.

"This restaurant of yours, this Silverware. . ."

"Spoon."

". . . this Spoon of yours should be right here."

Spoon would have the southeast corner location at the new interchange.

But how? And with nothing there yet? No road.

Mr. Klein laid down his plan like a bridge player using a handful of trump. These weren't ideas or possibilities. These were the events that would transpire. His manner was brusque and sure, his normal style. "I've got a hand in this parcel," Mr. Klein said. "We'll put you here once we cook up some sort of partner arrangement. Forget that River Drive spot."

Mr. Klein had some people he wanted Spuhn to meet but not until Spuhn had his plans thought out, not until he was ready to answer every question these stingy little old ladies were going to ask him.

Spuhn's spirits, already sparkling in his green eyes, soared as Mr. Klein revealed what he had in mind.

Mr. Klein, prescient enough, informed enough, bold enough to own land surrounding the new interchange, would lease Spoon the needed property. Mr. Klein knew the vacated, failed restaurant on River Road was going to sit, and sit long enough that the bank would shit and go blind the moment someone made an offer. Mr.

Klein knew someone who could want the property but wouldn't have any use for the restaurant equipment. They'd buy all that, put it at the interchange spot.

In the meantime, Spuhn would hold his horses, would keep working at Klein Construction, at least through May.

"You get that plan ready," Mr. Klein said, setting the first of the coming week as a deadline. They'd go through it then. "And put me down for an interest in this. Twenty-five percent."

Spuhn's grin was ebullient when the appointment ended and he and Mr. Klein shook hands.

With clumsy, hurried movements, his mind on anything but the coat, Spuhn pushed his arms through the sleeves of his father's old Army jacket and began buttoning the front.

"By the way," Mr. Klein began. A mischievous, amused look had come over his face. "You any good at this cooking? Lots of problems we start poisoning folk."

Spuhn laughed in return. "Damn straight I am," he said.

Damn straight. Jesus Hernandez in that kitchen, Spoon would have people coming from all over.

Three blocks from the Klein Construction office, Spuhn pulled up to the payphone of a Shell station. The cold was still and intense under a sky full of stars. Spuhn touched the change in his pocket and hunched away from the cold as he dialed Hernandez in Miami and waited for the operator to tell him the cost.

"I'm fucked up," Hernandez said, beginning a matter-of-fact telling of the clumsy way he walked, even after all the rehab, even with the new orthotics since the round pierced his boot. "The government does send me a check every month, though. Uncle Sugar."

Hernandez was on his end of the phone like a malleable, compliant pet. Nothing else to do, just getting on everyone's nerves.

"Yeah, sure. Cook something, something people eat. Let me know," Hernandez told Spuhn.

Then the operator cut into the call. While Spuhn was dropping six quarters into the slot, Hernandez hung up.

CHAPTER 15

Ain't no use in lookin' down
Ain't no discharge on the ground

Even as the coke elevated her and held her in floating rapture, Anna Adamski gave her mind over to the stunning perfidy: Gunnar had sold her. Sold her!

Across the room, she saw him giddy and flushed, his silky shirt unbuttoned and wet from what he'd spilled on himself, one arm around sloppy drunk Barbara and his eyes aflame as he laughed at her babbling "I. Am. Bic. Pentameter." At the same time, along with the Beatles and the Stones, Anna felt waves of laughter and nonsense from the others in the room, the friends from General Mills, two busty sisters from the floor above theirs, some pals from the University of Minnesota, and a brooding, incongruously proper secretary Four had brought from some Center for Treatment of Preternatural Timidity.

"His name's Steve," Gunnar had said the first time he heard Anna call the tiny court jester "Four."

"The Four Stooges," she said. "Moe, Curly, Larry and Steve."

Steve probably knew the dismissive tag Anna had given him, but the earnest sycophant, always so happy to be with Gunnar and the circle of ex-jocks, never let on.

"You and your names. You advertising people," Gunnar said. Sure, you advertising people. But there had been a time, there had been times, many times, when Gunnar, the Northern Region Sales Manager for Jenson Electronics, had looked forward to the attention from Anna Adamski, then a Client Services Associate for Jenson's agency McGregor Stanton.

The jokes had come freely then. When does the client service begin and how's that for service?

"We might as well wear bunny tails," said Anna's friend Bonnie. Hired six months sooner than Anna came to the firm, Bonnie took delight in the New York City visits that helped her keep up the New York look she favored. The clients liked the way the red-haired woman with the good time huskiness in her voice touched them. She let them enjoy the sight and nearness of her breasts, her cleavage warmly visible in whatever East Coast fashion she wore.

But now the joke was over.

With foggy indifference, Anna watched Steve's clumsy attempt to comfort the frightened woman he had brought to the party. Pressing her legs rigidly together, she shrank from Steve, who alternately giggled and pushed his mouth against her ear. The beers, the drugs and the overheated, crowded room had him red-faced and dripping. The dark brown coils of his thinning hair were wet. Anna sat immobile, able to watch herself in cubist multiple dimensions, her warm body leaned back against the side of the black leather armchair with her legs extended so far, so far away from her navy miniskirt and so far away from the breasts that were being massaged by the bony-wristed man named Eric, the friend of Steve's who had been high bidder when maniacally madcap Steve began the game. She could feel Eric's stubbly beard. She could smell the cigarettes. She could feel. But she couldn't move against Eric's needy hands, against the realization that should have been rage except for the coke that made it just a point, just a flashing insight within the float

of the drug. Ash tray. Eric became Ash Tray. New and improved.
Ash Tray. Ash Hole.

Were others watching? Probably. She didn't care. Gunnar had
sold her.

Where the idea came from was unclear. All of a sudden, amid
the sounds and conversation, the Beatles and Stones, the flirting in
the crowded apartment, small, maniacal Steve was coaxing bids for
a bewildered, stoned, grinning woman who wore no bra under her
small pink t-shirt.

"C'mon. For the Gophers. For the alma mater," Steve shouted.

When the confused girl and a solid accountant with a sailor's
grin had made their way out of the living room into the apartment's
back bedroom, another friend of Gunnar's, someone they called
Mickey, auctioned off another woman, this one a brazen, intoxicated, midwinter-tanned stewardess who added a lap dancer
seduction while she played the room to Mickey's calls.

"Rah, rah, rah, ski-yu-ma." Steve led his audience in Gophers
cheering as the stewardess and her shy escort left for his second floor
apartment.

And then Gunnar was up, unsteadily up, the key speaker,
Gunnar Henning, the running back stirring a Gopher pep rally.

"This is your chance. Delta Delta Delta," Gunnar said.

"Who pays for that?" one of his friends catcalled.

"Yeah," said another. "Can't get laid? TriDelt."

"Do I hear $50? Fifty dollars for the University of Minnesota?"
Gunnar asked.

"Fifty."

"I've got fifty. I've got fifty. Do I hear. . . ?"

Anna heard Paul McCartney singing "Yesterday", heard Ringo
singing "Act Naturally", heard two men across the room making
plans for tennis.

Gunnar boomed, "Sold American. Eighty dollars for the pride of Iowa, Anna Henning."

Eric put his check on the little pile, got a beer, and dropped down heavily, beside Anna on the carpet.

She wished the winner had been Mark, Mark from General Mills marketing, polite Mark who had gone with some fraternity brothers to a weekend basketball game, Gophers versus Badgers, in Madison.

As she came down, as she pushed herself up in a narrow cove where a couch had been moved from the wall, she realized Gunnar was no longer in the room. The living room was shadowed, its curtains open on windows that faced the airless summer night in Minneapolis' Loring Park.

Then Anna slept, waking to know what was already apparent, had been apparent for at least a year. She pulled herself up from the carpet, stepped out of her skirt, and righted the lamp that was on its side near one end of the couch. A couple she didn't recognize slept there. A burly man in the rumpled pants of a good suit, probably a lawyer's suit, lay on his back, shirtless and unconscious on the softness of the carpet across the room. He wore one black wingtip shoe.

The room looked to Anna like her marriage. It looked askew, awful, desperate, wasted.

Gunnar would come back, would come back haggard and handsome, in need of a shower and quiet, an evening of dead man stare at the Ed Sullivan show, at a mystery, a war film, at whatever came after whatever came on. When the baby was asleep or going to sleep in the little room next to theirs, Gunnar might become bestially randy.

He was handsomely athletic, softly changed from the running back he'd been into the man who now counted calories, played regular sets of tennis, and, in his sales work, stood comfortably on the recognition that came from being Gunnar Henning, the former Big Ten running back.

They were more separate when coiled together than at other times. Anna remembered unfolded laundry while Gunnar, while Gunnar lunged.

She drank a glass of water and then lit one of the Marlboros from a pack left on the glass of the living room coffee table. She drew on the cigarette, felt the pain in her throat, drew in again. She felt an ache for Jan, for hugging him, for making the little 13-month old chortle as she made faces, raised her arms, and repeated over and over, "Yippee for Jan, yippee for Jan, so big." As keenly as she needed aspirin, she needed to hug her son, needed to be still with her nose pressed in the sweet baby odor in the soft, dark hair of Jan's head.

She wouldn't have the chance.

In mid-morning, before Gunnar returned, his parents appeared with the boy, took in the chaotic state of the apartment with dry, aristocratic distaste and withdrew with Jan to their large Edina home. Gunnar was the former Big Ten running back but his father, only an inch shorter and determinedly trim, was the father of the Big Ten running back. When Hendrik Henning - Anna titled him Heil Henning - spoke instruction in his rich, counselor tone, Gunnar as well as his brother and his sister, probably the dog as well, fell in line. Gunnar's mother, Heil Yes!, never seemed to need the guidance. Anna had never seen the dainty, handsomely attired woman in any posture except at the man's shoulder, always in line, always an instant second for whatever Heil put on the family table.

In the flush of his football celebrity, enjoying his easy rise at Jenson, Gunnar had been, by Henning family standards and general standards, a maverick. Then Heil and Heil Yes! began adding their pressure to the lifting force that came with life as a promising Minneapolis figure. Gunnar liked the club tennis courts.

He liked his business card. He liked American Express. He liked belonging.

And though Gunnar would never acknowledge what Anna could see, Gunnar was learning from the example of his physician brother Per's rewards for a lifestyle so pure, so closely hewed to the Henning line that Anna could not imagine the passive elder brother with the Henning good looks peeing in a woods or leaving his own impressive Edina house without a fresh handkerchief. For his wife, of course, Per had chosen the vacant soulmate Thea, quickly thought of by Anna as Trainee, trainee to Heil Yes!

Only for a short time was Gunnar tolerant of the cutting humor that made up the mother's milk of the free-spirited McGregor Stanton workplace Anna knew. Briefly, as Anna and Gunnar approached the date of the storybook wedding Mrs. Henning had put together, from the selection of the high-necked brown brides-maid's dresses setting off her own sunny yellow outfit to the floral decorations to the seating arrangements that placed Anna's own parents and sister Jenny in a partially obscured nave, Anna was able to make Gunnar a party to imagined rebellion.

"I'm going to convert," she told him. Gunnar had his arms around her as they kissed in his XKE.

Gunnar nuzzled her ear.

"Convert to what? What do you mean?"

"I'm going to join your parents' religion," Anna said.

They kissed for a long moment.

"They don't go to church," Gunnar said.

What he said was true, except for Christmas and Easter. On those days, crisp and beautiful in fine attire, high, wide and hand-some, the Henning family worshipped with a vengeance.

"I know." Anna couldn't help giggling. Gunnar had one hand between her legs. "I'm not going to be a fallen away Catholic any-more. I'll change and become a fallen away Lutheran."

Gunnar guffawed and reached into her crotch.

In no time, the marriage felt the harness of Henning super-vision. During Sunday evening dinners, Mrs. Henning, pert and graying, saw Anna's shape revealed in the most carefully chosen, most conservative outfits and was displeased. Anna learned that Senator Hubert Humphrey, widely popular, could not be ap-preciated or tolerated or mentioned. No discussion of events was safe. No area excursion or plan could enter or come near the North Minneapolis area where the city's four percent Negro population, with all its attendant crime, was concentrated.

Jan, the first grandson, cousin to two pretty blond girls showing up at everything in matching dresses and hairbows, became territory, a small, innocent, smiling territory to be shaped and governed exclusively by the parties. If Anna put the newborn in a wrap of blankets and went along the lake in Loring Park, Jan became exposed to sickness as well as the misfits found among others in the park. And if the Hennings cared for Jan, the boy came back later than promised, in deep sleep, and off his routine of nap-ping, eating, and playing. Worse, when Anna's parents visited and Anna and Gunnar gave up their bedroom for a living room bed made of couch cushions, they all felt the gimlet eye of the Hen-nings, who feared that Jan would learn Catholic worship from the two doting grandparents.

A few hours after the Hennings came and then went away with Jan that Sunday morning, Anna answered the phone call she thought would be Gunnar.

But it wasn't. Steve – Four – had worked himself up to a cheer-ful dialogue containing an invitation to let him buy her a drink. She wanted to know about Gunnar, wanted Gunnar to call. Steve wanted to have a drink. He persisted as she declined. She said good-by, Steve said good-by, and the apartment fell silent except for a movie with the excitement of Cary Grant hiding on a hotel balcony.

Anna called in sick Monday morning, the same morning Gunnar closed their bank accounts. She wouldn't see him for more than a month.

Shortly before noon, as she dozed through a quiz show contestant's audience-assisted consideration of answers and doors, another phone call sounded.

She didn't take in the name of the dry lawyer at first, but would come to know the name well: Jonas Tucker, calling her on behalf of Gunnar Henning, who was suing her for divorce. Anna wanted to know about Jan. "Is Jan with Gunnar?"

"Jan is fine," the lawyer said. "Your son is with his grandparents."

"They stole him. They don't have the right." Anna was excited and didn't care.

"Listen carefully," the lawyer said. "You have a very important decision to make."

"What decision?"

"Authorities will come to you and they will find evidence of your use of narcotics."

"What?"

"You have been very open. There are a number of witnesses."

"If there are, they can say plenty about my husband, too."
"Your husband is a witness."

Anna was in a fury. She began to sob.

"If the authorities find evidence of your narcotics use – and that seems to be the case – you are likely to have your son taken from you."

"He's my son. He's my son," Anna said. Her voice was shrill.

"There's an alternative."

Anna fought against her sobbing and didn't answer.

"Mr. and Mrs. Henning are very worried about you. The failure of your marriage is a great disappointment for them, a great sadness for them and for their son."

"Oh, I bet it is." Anna could picture the dour, flat, unblinking looks of the in-laws.

"It is. A great tragedy. Not what any parents would wish for their child or for their grandson." "Certainly spoils the next Christmas card," Anna said. She spoke haltingly.

"As that may be," the lawyer said. "The Hennings are concerned about you. They want you to have the chance to get better."

"What does that mean?"

"This is the alternative. You will voluntarily commit yourself for a one month program of psychiatric care and evaluation."

Anna made no answer. She was too enraged.

The lawyer waited.

"Or else what?"

"Or else you are very likely to have your son taken away from you."

"I'm not crazy."

"That may be the case. The psychiatric evaluation, the psychiatric help can establish that."

"I want my son. I. Am. Jan's. Mother."

The lawyer spoke with deliberate patience.

"One of the intake staff at St. Peter's State Hospital will call you this afternoon and tell you the arrangements. You will voluntarily admit yourself before two o'clock tomorrow afternoon."

When the phone call ended and Anna had cried herself dry, she called Bonnie.

"They're screwing you," Bonnie said. "They've got you in a box. The Hennings know everyone. There's no client stuff tonight. Don't cry, Anna. Don't cry. I've got an idea."

Anna showered, put on clean clothes, studied the image of Jan in the silver frame at the apartment door, and went to meet Bonnie.

Paying no heed to the sweaty hockey players who wanted to buy them a drink, left alone by their waiter friend John, Bonnie and Anna talked.

Bonnie was as angry as Anna, and also methodical.

With Gunnar in mind, the two women shared cold duck, ate salads with dressing served on the side, and toasted gruesome means of execution.

"Boiling in oil!"

"Drawn and quartered."

"Hot poker up the rectum!"

"Neutered!"

"Beheaded!"

"Hari kari!"

"Dripping blood in a shark pool."

"Gonorhea!"

That was fun, but Anna and Bonnie knew that Gunnar would escape undamaged, free of an encumbering marriage, attractively wounded by a love who had betrayed him, still good-looking, prosperous, related to Minneapolis aristocracy, and rising in his career. He – his family – would have Jan.

Anna would have trouble.

Bonnie had a friend at another agency. She also had a breakfast meeting the next morning with the new client from Boston Boxes. She had to go. Oh God, I feel bad for you. Bonnie would call. She would find a new job for Anna, a new place Anna could stay.

The next afternoon, Anna stepped out of the yellow taxi sent by the lawyer Jonas Tucker, sent by the Hennings, took her little green Samsonite case containing shorts, blouse, toothbrush, hairbrush, pair of flats, silver-framed photo of Jan, and went inside St. Peter's State Hospital.

CHAPTER 16

Hey, hey Captain Jack
Meet me down by the railroad track
with a bible in your hand
I'm gonna be a preaching man

"And what does Anna feel this morning?" Anna asked herself, moderating aloud the sardonic reflection of events while she drove to Harlan, Iowa from Des Moines.

Around her, in the white light, a keen wind hit the car head on in pulsing surges and drove scraps of stalk and brown leaf scudding away, across the thin, icy late winter snow. So early on this March Sunday, in this western Iowa so removed from anyone's wish to be outside and subject to the weather, the cars were few. Over the crests of the small, flat hills, the trucks came regularly and heavily toward her, making the car move frighteningly left or right a few inches as they delivered a walloping mass of air and loosened snow.

Anna passed through an Iowa drawn in, the black and white of dairy cattle gathered closely in feed pens, all else closed, shuttered, and quietly turned against the wind. The Burma shave signs shook and gleamed with ice. Except for the cows, and an occasional crow, there was nothing between the horizons but some farmhouses, silos and barns amid barriers of pines and Chinese elms. No deer showed on the flat fields. No pheasant moved from ditches at the edge of the highway.

"Anna feels. . . out of sorts," Anna said. She laughed aloud and edited herself. "Out of sorts. Now that's expressive, isn't it?"

"Oh, Anna, I'm sure we are all sorry to hear that on such a fine morning in Iowa. Isn't that right, Patrick?"

Slack-jawed Patrick would be twisted around himself, intent on the way his right foot was hooked under the rung of his chair.

"We are all very eager to help. Why don't you tell us, Anna? What has you out of sorts today?"

Anna paused, slackened her speed a little in fear of the ice that here and there waited in thin bands or collected in smooth, small pools where the roadway had fissured.

"Where to begin? Patrick is not listening."

"Yes, he is. He is, aren't you, Patrick? Rosemary, Darlene, Tom and I, we're all listening."

"And pigs are flying," Anna said.

The smile left her.

"And Anna is crazy. Crazy!"

What in the hell was Anna doing driving three hours from Des Moines – three hours if she could find the place, three hours if she didn't get blown into a snowdrift – on the recommendation of someone she hardly knew, Magda, who had heard from someone who heard from someone who was there?

Anna turned the radio on, heard "The Lord said unto. . . ", turned the radio off. She turned down the heat a notch. The little Falcon, her company car, had a good heater.

What the hell? Why not?

Life had gone to pot. Life had gone to rack and ruin. There had been the helpless ignomiiny of the St. Peter's confinement, the mean divorce with her unemployed, helpless again against the relentless power and sanctimonious scolding of her former in-laws, everything quickly resulting in the removal – forever – of Jan. Jan, the Jenning. Jan, the possession. Jan, her son. Jan, hers.

Anna's mother, her English perfect, her sense of the world still Estonian, came sadly and loyally to be with Anna, but Anna's mother, confused in the cutting courtroom environment, only sat in regal dignity, a satisfying counterpoint to the Jennings with her whitening hair and slim, delicate face. Jenny was young, engaged in her own cross country team and her launch into Iowa. Bob, Bob had gone East and begun being *not from Iowa* as soon as he found work with the bank. The Christmas cards, including the one posted to the old address in Loring Park, had long ago begun coming from The Robert & Linda Adamski family. Anna had not seen the house; its living room fireplace made a rich background for a photo of Robert and Linda in back, Tyler and Sarah smiling in the foreground.

At the end of the trial, there had been no Jan, no apartment, no job.

Bonnie had let Anna stay.

"What was it like there?"

"A 30-day party at McGregor Stanton, that's what it was like."

When Bonnie went to work the first morning, Anna had drunk coffee with artificial sweetener and looked out the window.

Then, only two days later, thanks to the loyalty, the generosity, even the bravery of sympathetic Daryl Devermore, of steady, friendly, good-natured butt of McGregor Stanton fun, DD, thanks to his good recommendation, Anna had found quickly her position as Western Iowa account coordinator for Woodson & Son in St. Paul. The tiny eight-person firm advised small agricultural clients, including those farm co-ops given to Anna.

"How wonderful. A new firm. A fresh start."

Anna sniffed and fought not to cry.

"Yes, a fresh start. A wonderful fresh start. And now, introducing the star of our show, will you welcome please. . . in the center ring . . . . Cancer!"

Quickly, she regarded her breasts, their form barely apparent under a heavy cream sweater, her camel coat and a long, red scarf.

"How do you like those apples, Patrick? Cancer!"

So why listen to Magda? Why confide in the motherly friend Anna had made in the course of her visits to the Proctor Creek Hog Growers Co-op?

Anna had to confide in someone. Life was too big to hold the news of the Wednesday medical appointment. As soon as Magda had the first sense, her kindly responses and the anguish in her own broad look had removed the cap from Anna's worry. Anna had gushed until both women were in tears in Magda's little office.

Now, in the car, Anna said angrily, with her hands tight on the car's wheel, "Damn it, damn it, damn it, damn it to hell."

The doctor didn't know yet, had sent the samples from the second test, was waiting, was not certain, could be wrong.

At McGregor Stanton, Anna had worked with another woman whose doctor didn't know yet, had sent the samples, was waiting, was not certain, could be wrong, wanted to confirm. And then the woman began to wear a headscarf, began to vomit the little food she could eat, and then she took her wasting form away. Anna had seen the woman small, still, horizontal with a tiny cross in her hands at the wake where a group from McGregor Stanton had gone to pay respects.

Anna imagined Dr. Allen listening at the edge of the group and making checks on his clipboard. He wouldn't care. Dr. Allen was never wrong in his diagnoses. Things just didn't turn out the way he expected each time. But what fun trying with all the new medications.

Magda had not been sure, either, but had offered the gleanings from a string of hearsay in an effort to raise Anna's spirits. That was enough for Anna, ready to seize anything. The maybe, the possibility, the hazy account of a holy man who was curing some of the people who came to him, that was enough to lift Anna.

She had to be one county east and north, in Carroll, Monday afternoon for a visit to a big hog producer, so jumping the schedule a day made sense. She took down what Magda knew of the place and the directions, then wavered about going until she was in the car and navigating the windy strip leading to the address in Harlan's vicinity.

"OK, everyone," Anna said, addressing the St. Peter's session about to wrap up in her car. "That's all the time we have this morning. Great contributions, everyone. Rosemary, yes, we will start with you next time, you have my word. Greg, you are always Tuesday. Tuesday. The next session will be Thursday. John, I know. Celery makes you sick. I will remind them."

For the next 30 minutes, she timed the 30-second script of a new radio spot for Cow-Care, the product Country Labs had developed against bovine diarrhea, and then practiced transitions she could use in a speech she was writing for John Drescher's address at the Northwest Iowa Agri-conference.

The day might be a wild goose chase, Anna thought wryly, but at least it was a billable wild goose chase. Certainly, nervous Woody Woodson would recognize this Sunday as one with religious observance in it.

Magda's directions turned out to be good once Anna determined that the vacant Russian church and the storage shed half lost in a drift of snow were unincorporated Navalny. She guessed correctly that the big red 'M' hanging from a long oak branch at the side of the road marked the Mattingly Farm. Counting houses from that point, she came to the windswept drive leading toward and then around a little house with blue, decorative wood trimming three small windows. There she found three cars pulled up to a decaying white barn with its door slightly ajar. A rude, three-foot high cross made of crossed branches confirmed Magda's directions: Anna had found the Knowing God Place.

For a short time, Anna's curiosity and the warmth built up from the Falcon's heat sustained her. Soon, as she waited on one of the hay bales organized into pews and and as she studied the others, she felt the cold. The space was windless but just as bitter as the air outside the barn.

Nine other people were already inside and waiting in the center space where another rude cross hung over a wooden chair from a support of the upper floor. Five of the people were a Mexican family: compact mother and father, a boy, two girls, all with shining black hair and eyes, the five quietly watching as they huddled together. The others were a young farm couple who had brought an elderly parent or friend. The ninth was Teddy, a grizzled, worn Patrick-type about forty years old with eyes set deep in pockets the color of weak tea. Rocking in his own world on a stump seat close to the cross, wearing no gloves in the cold, he stared at the bare barn floor and spoke to himself in low tones that seemed fiercely angry.

Another handful of people entered, several greeted by the young farm couple. A woman in an olive-colored coat with its hood snug around her face smiled each time as she circled the waiting group and handed each person a flyer titled "Will You Be Ready for God When God is Ready for You?"

"I have one," Teddy told the woman, apparently someone he knew. At least, when the woman finished distributing her flyers, she chose the end of a bale beside Teddy and began talking with him.

Anna accepted the tract and put it next to her on the bale. With nothing to do but wait, she kept her hands pushed into her pockets and her head pulled into her collar while she wondered at the text beneath an image of a stern, winged angel directing a crying couple toward the smoke rising from just around a bend down the hill.

Was this Jehovah's Witnesses? Anna wondered. Had Magda sent her to the same people who regularly knocked at the door in Des Moines?

Oh, well. In for a dime, in for a dollar. Anna kept her head drawn into her coat with only her eyes and a bit of her forehead exposed.

A man of college age came in, carrying a case with a guitar. His hair long enough to fall in his eyes and over his ears and neck, he wore round, wire-rimmed glasses that gave him a studious look. He made a seat of an overturned feed cannister, tuned the instrument, and began to pick quietly at pieces of tunes. Except when he tossed his head to throw his hair back from his eyes, he fixed his gaze on the floor ahead of him.

Their noise sounded inside when two cars of high school students arrived. Anna and the others waiting heard the voices of young people speaking loudly to one another, laughing, and then nine teenagers entered along with a fresh abundance of cold air. There were five boys in Harlan High letter jackets and four girls who tittered loudly when a large boy with a broad, flat nose and a square face said out loud, "God damn, it's cold in here."

He looked sheepish but also pleased when a shocked girl with caramel-colored hair and a womanly shape pulled his arm to shush him. Then, with another of the boys, he arranged a bench from some boards laid across a chair on one end and some upturned cans.

As she looked about over the edge of her collar, Anna remembered a Gospel story that had some lesson from a hodge podge of people attending a wedding. No wedding garments here, she thought to herself, assessing the guitar player in his jean jacket, the boys in their athletes' garb, the Mexican family bundled purely in warmth, and the women and girls dressed in their own variety of hoods, scarves, and one coat lined with lamb's wool.

Then a heavy step sounded, the big barn door rolled open, closed and a giant with wet, black hair and a face red from heat came to the center of the space. Over a blue workshirt, he wore an unbuttoned, farm-grimed lemon coat with tattered knit cuffs. Showing no awareness of the others with him in the barn, he had gray-blue eyes narrowed and unblinking as he began crossing himself and bowing multiple times.

In silence, Anna and the others watched.

Anna recognized the man. She knew him. Tank Vetrov! Tank Vetrov, the Iowa wrestling star, Tank Vetrov was the holy man, the healer, Magda had found?

No doubt about it, the Lord works in mysterious ways, Anna thought to herself. The ways couldn't get much more mysterious than what she was witnessing on this morning in this wreck of a barn.

The Knowing God Place? And every other place, she thought with bitter irreverence, the no!-ing God place everywhere.

Still alone within himself in their center, Tank Vetrov completed his silent prayers, took a black bible from his coat pocket and settled on the chair, a worn, paint-blotched relic that seemed inadequate to the size of the man.

Then the man raised his eyes and looked at those before him.

Even when Tank's gaze was on her, Anna felt that the man they addressed as "Reverend" or "Coach" or "Maestro" did not recognize her.

For the next hour and a half, she watched and listened as the little congregation bundled varieties of practices and concerns into a worship.

The disheveled, haunted Teddy Anna had dubbed Iowa Patrick kept up an angry, mumbled commentary that erupted two times into an assertive discourse with Tank Vetrov. Suddenly talking over the point the guitar player was making about a passage from a poem named "The Prophet", Iowa

Patrick demanded that the soft-voiced musician offer his own opinion of St. Anselm's proof for the existence of God. Later, Iowa Patrick launched into a loud complaint about the futility of the Goldman Conjecture, which, Iowa Patrick said with force, "Euler expressed: 'Every positive integer greater than or equal to four is the sum of two primes.'"

The agitated man was oblivious to the loud snickering of the high school students. "Big hairy deal," one of the boys said, before a look from Tank quieted the boy and his companions.

When Tank moved to comfort the man, Teddy twisted away and said loudly, "I'm not on your payroll. I don't work for you."

Tank opened the bible and read silently. Iowa Patrick resumed mumbling in a low voice.

Did that count? Anna wondered. Had Tank Vetrov cast out a devil? Would the man walk into Harlan, begin wearing a coat and tie, and marry the Mayor's daughter?

"This morning, I read the holy word of the almighty maker of all the earth and everything under heaven," Tank said, staring fixedly ahead. His warmth had subsided. Where his thick dark eyebrows and the shag of his hair did not cover his face, his skin was white and cold. Then he recounted a Gospel story Anna remembered from her own school days, the story of the woman caught in adultery and brought to Jesus by some Pharisees and Scribes.

"They wanted the Lord Jesus Christ to accuse the sinful woman, to condemn her. They wanted to stone her."

Tank fell silent. The look on his face made Anna and the others see a young, terrified woman pushed before the Almighty Son of God by a weaselly committee of ill-intentioned schemers such as the officious assistant administrator of Anna's client in Red Oak.

"But the Lord God is merciful. The Lord God loves the sinner," Tank said. He spoke with rising passion.

"'Let him who is without sin cast the first stone,' the Lord Jesus, Son of God, commanded. He wrote in the dirt. One by one, the Scribes and the Pharisees, they went away."

A look of anguish came on Tank's face.

"If God is for us, who can stand against us? If God is for us, who can stand against us?"

Tank fell silent again, his look so sad that Anna thought he might cry.

"I know that I have sinned mightily. Mightily. I stand in front of my Lord Jesus Christ same as that young woman. A adulterer. A sinner. A man who let the devil rule him. A man who shamed himself and shamed his mother and father, all his friends, with the evil he did all the times he was drunk. A man who is an alcoholic.

"In my mind, I see the Lord Jesus writing in the dirt, writing about me, about my evil, terrible sins. I see the Lord Jesus writing and writing. I see his hand getting tired. On and on, he goes. Writing."

Anna heard a sob in Tank's voice.

"'I do not condemn you,' said the Lord Jesus to that young woman. 'Go and sin no more.' If God is for us, who can be against us? Who?"

Near to crying, he began bowing and crossing himself, repeating a prayer in Russian.

"Holy God, Holy Mighty, Holy Immortal One, have mercy on us," exclaimed the woman in the olive coat, the woman who had distributed the flyers. "Hallelujah, bless the Lord God Almighty. Holy God, Holy Mighty, Holy Immortal One, have mercy on us."

The woman's exhilaration set the Mexican woman in action, too, and then the others in her family. "Gracias al Senor," the woman said.

Led by the young man with the guitar, most of the assembly swung into a spiritual as Tank fell still with his eyes closed:

Somebody's knocking at your door.
Somebody's knocking at your door.
O sinner, why don't you answer?
Somebody's knocking at your door.
Knocks like Jesus!
Somebody's knocking at your door.
Knocks like Jesus!
Somebody's knocking at your door.
O sinner, why don't you answer?
Somebody's knocking at your door.

When the song ended, the young farmer came forward with his own bible. In an even, sure voice, he announced two verses of Psalm 139 he would read, then proceeded.

Anna remembered hearing the Psalm before, probably at a funeral:

O Lord, thou hast searched me, and known me.
Thou knowest my downsitting and mine uprising,
thou understandest my thought afar off.
Thou compassest my path and my lying down,
and art acquainted with all my ways.

Then the man with the guitar raised his hands and began a prayer that soon became a plea for everyone – Everyone! - to pray to Almighty God for the healing of his grandfather's pneumonia.

The woman in the olive coat asked the same for her sister, who had terrible rheumatoid arthritis up in the Twin Cities.

A high school girl prayed for healing for her grandmother's bad heart. A second high school girl prayed for healing for an aunt in Omaha who was losing her sight.

Of a sudden, numbers of the people rose and began to assemble in a procession toward Tank.

"Now we have the healing line," the woman with the olive coat said when she saw the confusion in Anna's look.

Anna followed her into the little procession of people she took to be, like herself, in need of healing.

"She no more sick. No more sick," the excited, happy Mexican woman said, presenting her middle child, a shy, polite girl with long, lustrous black hair.

"I can hear now, Padre," the girl said as Tank gave the mother and the girl a soft embrace.

"Where do you hurt?" Tank asked the next in line, the woman holding tightly to the arm of her young husband, the man Anna felt was a farmer.

"It's my mother, Reverend," the woman said. "My mother's hip is painin' her, painin' her fierce."

"Let us ask God, lovin' God, for comfort," Tank said. He took the man, his wife and mother-in-law in a great, soft embrace.

At Anna's turn, as she looked into Tank Vetrov's face and expected to be recognized, she saw warmth and concern but no memory of someone who would have been a freshman that year, that year a decade in the past.

"Cancer," Anna said. "It looks like I have it. A tumor. Breast cancer."

She felt the light pressure of his large hands on her shoulders as he raised his eyes and prayed a quick, silent prayer.

Back at her place on the hay bale pew, while the little procession concluded, Anna assessed her own sensations. She felt nothing new, nothing good or bad, just the chill that had her longing for the Falcon's heater as she aimed it at some place she could thaw herself in Harlan.

Soon, once the woman in the olive coat had prayed loudly and rapturously with a punctuation of "Hallelujahs, Lord Jesus" and the young folk musician had led them in some verses of "Amazing Grace," the prayer meeting came to an end.

Same as with other Masses and worships Anna had attended in her time, some people left right away – the farm couple and mother-in-law were the first – while others lingered. Some – Iowa Patrick, in this case – seemed uncertain what to do next while others appeared caught up in savoring the feelings and thoughts sparked by the peculiar worship.

The nine high school students rushed to Tank and addressed him easily and familiarly as "Coach."

"My hand feels all squared away again, Coach," the large student said. "It was all tingly sort of after I went too high on the leg grab the match yesterday."

"We need to work on your pivot," Tank said. "You're lucky you could muscle him but that won't get it all the time."

A second wrestler, crewcut and thick-necked from bridges, was anxious to give his own report.

"Bruise on my leg's all healed up now."

Anna stood and shivered. She had nowhere to go, just a motel room to find in Carroll and a speech to smooth for her client.

She stayed for curiosity and then became fixed on another intent. She began waiting to speak with Tank Vetrov in hopes of something, something that would make her tumor wither into nothing more than a misread laboratory blot.

"You go in the sauna this morning, Coach? That why your hair was all wet at the start?" one boy asked.

"It's a banya. A banya," another corrected.

"The crick is froze, too," another boy said. "Go-d . . . " The large boy was about to swear. "Man, how can you stand it, to go in that crick in January?"

"In March."

"In April," said another.

Same as she would cut through a reception and reach a prospective account, Anna sidestepped Iowa Patrick and the woman in the olive coat.

"Is there something you can do for my cancer?" she asked.

Tank's face was still the face of a distracted, quiet holy man. He didn't show any sign of recognition.

"I ask God for that, I truly do," Tank said. "I will pray on that."

Anna felt he was about to say something, to explain, but he only said in a gentle voice, "We are the people of God and God has his plans for each one of us."

Then he put an arm around Iowa Patrick, who edged away.

"Did you ever read *Worlds in Collision*? It's by Immanuel Velikovsky. Very interesting. Venus came very close to Earth, very close, man, and the Earth began to spin in the other direction.

That's what he says. You should look at it."

"Thanks, Teddy. Thanks," Tank said.

Anna noticed that Tank did not promise to read what the man had recommended, maybe because the promise would have been a lie, a violation of the way this Tank Vetrov now strove to live.

The woman in the olive coat waited and then took Teddy in hand. On her way into town, she told him in Anna's hearing, the woman would drive him home to his mother's. Gently, she directed him.

Tank's body language now had turned impatient but he remained, smiling and polite, as the Mexican family first thanked him, then confirmed that next Sunday would be the same.

"My mother wants to know if next Sunday this will be church," the boy said.

As she left the barn behind Teddy and the woman in the olive coat, Anna felt no different than when she arrived. Without touching the spot under the coat, under the sweater and other garments that covered her breast, she didn't know. But she hadn't felt any sensation.

Still, she was full of feelings.

At Dolly's Cafe in Harlan, Anna mentioned Tank Vetrov to the friendly pair who stood with her while a waitress they called Sis cleared two tables. Solidly built but favoring an arthritic hip, the man now moved with his wife into town after a career of farming, knew everyone at every table.

The couple knew Tank Vetrov, knew all about him.

Anna accepted their invitation and joined Mr. and Mrs. Neustadt at their table. Very soon, Mrs. Neustadt asked "You have family, honey? A husband?"

They were curious about her, about what she was doing in Harlan this day.

"Nikolay, that's his name, Tank. Nikolay Vetrov. People say he's turned into a good preacher," Gerhard Neustadt said once Anna had answered in a reserved way the principal questions about her marital status and her Harlan business.

The Neustadts answered with authority once they began, and answered loudly. Neither of the pair enjoyed good hearing. In the other noise of the restaurant, with people greeting and waving good-by to one another, they spoke loudly and made her repeat most of what she said to them. Nikolay Vetrov was a champion wrestler, almost the best in the country one time. Then he began drinking back east, over in the Quad Cities. A couple years ago, he came back, stayed with his mother till she died, and now he stays on that farm by himself.

"Every morning, he chops a hole in Little Creek, jumps in all the way, right in that freezing water, and then scoots into the sauna thing he's got there, same as his father used to," said Val Neustadt. "Warms himself all up."

"Honey," she said. "You should find yourself a good husband here in Harlan. Lots of fine young fellows in Harlan." Turning to her husband, she raised her voice. "Said Anna should find herself a good husband in Harlan. Here. In Harlan."

Gerhard Neustadt began to name some.

CHAPTER 17

Stand up buckle up shuffle to the door
Jump right out and count to four

First there was shrieking at the creek and then the sound of someone bursting through the rooms.

"Who. . .?"called Tank Vetrov as he rose quickly from the wet plank in the steam room.

At nearly the same moment, he saw before him the woman. Naked, lovely and voluptuously shaped, the dripping intruder was gasping and swearing from the cold.

Quickly, Tank dropped back on the bench and covered his groin with a handful of birch branches. "What're you doing here?" he asked.

He knew her, recognized her from the Sunday worship, the remarkable woman who had seated herself off to the left and then came forward in the line with others seeking healing.

What did she have to lose?

Four days ago, the dry, methodical physician cleaned his silver-rimmed glasses with a tissue and cleared his throat before explaining Anna's hard facts and options to her. Curt and scientific, he smelled of Mennen and a new shave. His coat pocket held a pipe.

She would need surgery, and time to recover from surgery. She must alert him to signs of metastasis. Call one of his nurses immediately. And if the cancer did metastasize, if it could not be arrested, yes, that would be very serious. Yes, fatal. Not always. Not always.

He held his glasses at arm's length, then worked at one spot with another tissue.

What else? What else? Listerine, she wanted to say.

And if she had a minister – did she? - talking to someone like that, to a close friend. . . would be prudent, helpful.

For the rest of the week, Anna examined herself, soon arriving at an option as firm as the tightening mass in her breast.

What did she have to lose?

With a new set of client meetings as a cover and with clear weather forecast, Anna drove to Harlan the night before, right after work on Friday.

"Ah. . . ah. . . ah. . . ah. Freezing my bunnns off. Ah. . . ah. . . ah. . . ah. . . ah. . . " she said, bouncing on her toes and shivering, a living *Playboy* foldout throwing her own intense heat into the vaporous little space where Tank had been letting his thoughts roam among bits of Scripture and prayer and students he coached or taught. She spoke through chattering teeth. "Whewwwww,, that water is cold. You must be out of your ever-lovin' mind."

Holding the first branches across himself, Tank grabbed another leafy cluster and began striking the woman on her shoulders and then her legs. "Here," he said."Try this."

She took a branch from him and began whipping herself front and back, arms and legs. That and the scorching steam soon turned her pink. Her hair, brown and wet, reached almost to her shoulders. Her breasts, firm with fine nipples the color of deep mahogany, swung almost at Tank's face.

She was closer to Tank, more arousing than any stripper had been at the clubs in East Dubuque and Clinton.

"You went in the creek?" Tank asked.

"You're not kidding I went in the creek," she replied. The look on her face was fierce at first and then amused. Her full lips were losing their blue color. "Ohhhh, that is cold. Don't think I will be trying out for the run and jump in the frozen creek team. There's a plain clue when water has to have a hole cut in it before you can swim. It's goin' to be cold."

The hot, steamy space was warming her by this time. She stood still, naked, aware of the force she was exerting over the powerful man doing his best to hide an erection with a clutch of birch branches.

Looking him full in the eyes, making him focus his own gaze on her blue ones when his eyes and all his senses were tingling from the awareness of her whole body, she asked "Is that a banana in your pocket or are you glad to see me?"

She laughed when Tank answered with a surprised, choking sound.

"Why are you doing this?" Tank managed to say.

"I wanted you to look at my breast."

He grunted in indistinct confirmation. Even in the warmth of the steaming room, Anna saw his face color.

"I want you to pray on it. I have cancer."

The smile stayed on her face as the look of confusion grew on his.

With care that the branches remained over him, Tank stood up, went into the central room for a towel, and returned with it wound around him.

Anna continued to menace him with her nakedness, amusing herself with the way he moved away and maintained the small separation between her body and his as the steam heated them.

From memory, in an effort to gain control of himself, his tone urgent and plaintive, Tank began to recite from a psalm:

"Hide thy face from my sins,
and blot out all mine iniquities."

"This is not a joke," Anna said. "Can you cure me? I have cancer." Moving her breast near his face, she placed a finger at the spot of the tumor.

Tank averted his face.

"You're a lot more shy than you were the last time we were like this."

Tank looked up.

"You don't remember pulling my blouse off? You ripped it."

Tank's look became anguished. Knowing the wildness and the libertine wrongs in his debauched past, he tried to remember encountering. . . hurting the woman before he saw her seated on the hay bale in the barn the Sunday before.

Closing his eyes, he began to cross himself and to repeat the Russian prayer Anna had heard during the barn service.

"At Iowa. Your senior year. My freshman year. Your fraternity invited us Tri Delts to a party. . . "

"And I was drunk." Tank had his hands clasped, his eyes averted on her knees.

"Everyone had a crush on you. I couldn't get over it, that you would notice me, that you would, you know, dance with me."

"I got drunk, didn't I?" Tank asked.

"Blind. Drunk as a skunk. I was a freshman. Boys were always getting drunk, at least pretending to get drunk. I was drinking. We girls liked drinking, too."

Tank clasped his hands together hard.

"What's your name?"

"Anna Adamski."

Tank looked up. "Did I do something? After I got plastered?"

"You went all the way."

After a beat of silence, with his hands clasped and his head lowered, Tank fairly moaned, "*If thou, Lord, shouldest mark iniquities, O Lord, who shall stand?*"

"We began making out and it was nice but then you wouldn't stop and you did it and then you got sick all over me."

Neither spoke. The room had sounds of steam hissing from the heated stove, of condensing water dripping onto the floor.

Anna's own eyes were moist. Intending a joke, she picked up a choke in her voice when she said, "So maybe I've got a healing comin' to me?"

"*He that sitteth in the heavens shall laugh: the Lord shall have them in derision,*" Tank recited. When Anna put a consoling hand on his shoulder, he shrank quickly away.

Sadly and softly, Tank continued to recite the Scripture he pored over regularly as he dwelt on the arrogance and privilege that had caused hurt to his mother and to him.

For thou hadst cast me into the deep, in the midst of the seas; and the floods compassed me about: all thy billows and thy waves passed over me.

Then I said, I am cast out of thy sight; yet I will look again toward thy holy temple.

Anna took a seat next to Tank on the bench. Immediately, he tried to avoid the touch of her leg and arm against him but the bulk of him left no room for escaping the pleasurable feeling of her warmth, the tickle of her damp hair.

"Have you memorized the whole Bible?" Anna asked.

Tank tried to continue his praying.

"You didn't used to be like this."

"I was a drunk. I am an alcoholic."

Her time at McGregor Stanton, her years living had made Anna familiar with at least three co-workers and an Iowa sorority sister in

Tank's condition. Many client dinners had more drinking than eating, too. At McGregor Stanton, she remembered, there had been jubilation when the agency landed Minnesota's largest liquor distributor.

"You don't drink anymore?"

"By the grace of my savior, the Lord Jesus Christ, yesterday I was sober 46 days." After more than 13 months of sobriety, he had collapsed into a mean abandonment of his teaching, coaching, studying, praying and hoping. With patient empathy and the telling of his own failings, Tank's sponsor, a shift foreman taking time off from his own work at Schaefer Castings, found Tank holed up at the motel and coaxed the foggy, depressed giant, coaxed him like a beast from a log back into the routine of the program.

Shaky and haggard a night later, Tank had watched his wrestlers defeat an Atlantic team hurt by the loss of two boys ill with winter flu.

"How did you change? What made you religious the way you are?"

Without looking at Anna, Tank explained the effect of his mother's example, something he had seen his entire childhood but only noticed when, low and with nowhere to go, he had come back to the farm from the mental hospital in Wapello near Muscatine.

Without looking at Anna, Tank explained the effect of his mother's example, something he had seen his entire childhood but only noticed when, low and with nowhere to go, he had come back to the farm from the mental hospital in Wapello near Muscatine.

"My mom, my dad, they knew God. They felt God. They were happy. My mom did know the Bible. She read it. She thought about it. She had the Lord Jesus Christ with her. Just no doubt about it. Hands down. She had him with her. My dad, too."

The water vaporized. The steamy heat surrounded them.

Galina's memories and stories were acquainting him with the comfort, the purpose, the happiness their parents had found in knowing God as surely as they did.

"Now I study the Bible, too. I try to know God." Settled in the small house amid the familiar fence, trees, structures, country quiet and horizons of the farm, Tank held to a stabilizing routine of meetings, teaching, coaching, exercising to exhaustion, studying to penitent repair, and reflecting in the heat of his banya. Most Sundays, he appeared at the worship of one of the Harlan churches.

"And you started your own church?"

"No. People just show up. They want to know God, too."

"And they want to be cured," Anna said.

"Yes."

"Do they get cured?"

Still looking at the floor, Tank said. "I don't know. *How unsearchable are his judgments, and his ways past finding out!* I pray on it. We all pray. The Lord Jesus Christ is almighty."

"Will the almighty Lord Jesus Christ cure my cancer if you ask him?"

"I am an alcoholic. I am a sinner. Who am I that the Savior of the world listens to me?"

Just outside the small structure, on a branch next to the banya wall, a bird emitted a long trill.

"A cardinal," Tank said.

Anna increased the pressure of her arm and leg against him.

"This is the day the Lord has made. Let us be glad and rejoice in it," she said. She slid her hip into him and rested a hand on his knee.

Tank kept his eyes down, shifted and began to bless himself again.

Anna moved against him and, again, he tried to shrink away.

She twisted around on the bench. "God helps those who help themselves," Anna said into his ear as she pulled the towel from around him and settled on him.

In the midst of it, she thought about speaking in tongues, in intermingling of tongues.

Then she didn't think.

CHAPTER 18

Honey, honey
You get a line and I'll get a pole
Baby, baby
You get a line and I'll get a pole
We'll go down to the fishin' hole

When the uproar occurred two years later, the *Morning Democrat*'s Seed Corn columnist Jim Seid would identify them as "the gams of a pinup goddess." This June afternoon, when Dennis Spuhn first caught sight of Jenny Adamski bent into the pale blue Fairlane, reaching for something left on the passenger seat, he had an equally powerful impression of the legs. Jenny's extended in long, tanned grace from bright yellow hotpants exactly fit to the curve of her bottom.

"Holy shit," said Jesus Hernandez as he stared out the front window from the dining area where he and Spuhn were cleaning cooking equipment in the little pullman style building Mr. Klein had found and brought from the vicinity of Sterling in Illinois. The two men were shirtless, dripping in the premature summer humidity and filthy with dust and old grease. Spuhn wore a pair of cutoff fatigues. Hernandez had on old, paint-spattered madras shorts secured with a white plastic belt. Both wore jungle boots blotched with droppings of paint and dirt.

Jenny Adamski had grown used to her beauty. After two years of college, she bore her looks now as something mixed with everything else she was and aspired to be. Her older sister Anna was remembered for her rich figure, full lips, and dark, brunette beauty. Jenny had the graceful, athletic form of a runner filling to young maturity, a delicate nose and thin lips turned in a bright, friendly shape, the yellow to her sister's brunette. Set for her sales call, Jenny came through the open door of the diner, took in the sight of the fans and parts and boxes of cookware placed in what would be the dining area, and, with a smile, asked Spuhn and Hernandez "Mr. Spuhn?"

"That's me. Dennis Spuhn." Spuhn placed a screwdriver on the serving counter and wiped his hand on his cutoffs before reaching to shake Jenny's. Her fingers felt delicate and warm in his. "This is Jesus Hernandez."

"Hi," said Hernandez.

"I'm Jenny Adamski."

They would remember. She stood, unrushed, her eyes dark and large, chipmunk alert. She let the flustered Spuhn come to the realization that they should find a place to have whatever conversation had brought her to the site where he and Hernandez were preparing for the opening of Spoon. She could tell he recognized "Adamski," had realized her as the younger sister to Anna. Nearly five eight, not far below Spuhn's six foot one eye level, Jenny wore her thick hair in a ponytail fastened with a dark plastic clip. She held a folder at her front, an easy posture that framed her athletic figure with bare, tanned arms. The sleeveless white blouse she wore tightened across her bosom when she moved her arms or turned.

They went outside, where Spuhn and Hernandez had two folding chairs in the thin shade outside the back door of the building.

"Want a pop? We have beer," Spuhn said.

She took a 7-Up.

"You have a big grease smear on your forehead," Jenny said. "Here." She took a paper napkin from her small black purse and made him sit still as she rubbed at the grime. Spuhn's hair had grown civilian again, long enough for him to have it combed back in brown waves. Compared to Clayton's Beatles style and Szabo's neglected one, Spuhn still kept the look of a barbershop customer, someone who maintained his ears and the back of his neck in respectful form. Jenny used her fingers to comb a lock back from his forehead.

Spuhn smelled her perfume, noticed that the tan lobes of her ears were pierced, that short golden hairs grew free of the clip that held her ponytail. On her nose and along her cheekbones she had a soft dusting of some freckles.

When Jenny finished her work, she studied the effect for a moment before the arch of her dark eyebrows relaxed and she took a sip from the can of 7-Up.

Hernandez brought a stepladder from the diner, his numb left foot landing heavily as he worked his way outside. Before he sat down, while still behind Jenny, he caught Spuhn's eye and gave him a silent "Hoorah."

Jenny saw the response in Spuhn's green eyes and turned to look at Hernandez. She knew the macho look of the two young workers, each with his military tattoo showing above the inside wrist of his right hand.

She also knew a lot about Spoon, that the restaurant would open in three months, weeks after the I-80 entrance and exit ramps would go into use. In the meantime, the lanes were a scene of graded, dark earth with stakes and forms and construction planners in hardhats gathering for a look at plans unrolled on the tail of one of the pickup trucks. The well-prepared visitor knew of Dennis Spuhn and knew of Mr. Klein's backing for the venture.

"We have boards you'll need," Jenny told Spuhn and Hernandez. She was speaking of the company her father represented, Iowa Outdoor. Thrilling Spuhn with her light nearness, she drew a sheet from the packet Spuhn held on his lap and pointed to locations along Brady Street and areas near the high schools St. Sebastian and Central. "Look. We can supply up to 12 boards right along I-80 as soon as the road opens. Eleven are lighted boards, 24 hours of visibility, east and west.

"This is Spoon's demographic. It is, isn't it?" she asked. "You're going to need reach with frequency at manageable cost. You're going to need to build demand in town before you begin getting traffic from the interstate." She drew three sheets from the packet on Spuhn's lap. "These are some arrays. We're flexible, nothing in stone. Painted boards. Lighted."

Spuhn was willing to listen, willing to slow the accomplishment of the tasks he had set for Hernandez and himself on this Friday, one of the three days each week Mr. Klein left him free for what the restaurant required. In the distance, where crews of workers were setting forms and graders were shaping the yellow and tan, hard-baked, clay tracks of ramp paths, Spuhn could already see children and women moving toward the workers from cars parked at the edge of the construction site. The humid air of mid-afternoon was still under a blue sky without clouds. A few crows picked at lunch leavings. The sun blazed, glinting here and there on car mirrors, tools and the buckles of workers' clothes.

"What are the kids doing?" Jenny asked.

"Friday's payday," Hernandez said. "Momma wants to make sure the old man doesn't beat feet with her grocery money."

"They go to the taverns," Spuhn said. "The money disappears."
He liked the sweet, thoughtful expression on Jenny's face.

"That stinks," she said. "That happens? They spend it all?"

"Some of them do," Spuhn said. He thought of Kenny's crew,
how quick Lee's girlfriend was to pounce on him each payday. Was
that the big, broad-shouldered woman standing with a couple of
others near a parked yellow bulldozer? Kenny's crew was at work on
the south entrance ramp.

Spuhn was torn. He didn't want Jenny to leave but he didn't
want to slip on completion of the schedule he'd set for himself.
Hernandez lived in the moment but Spuhn pulsed with things he
wanted done, always with yesterday as his personal deadline. In the
second floor apartment he and Hernandez rented from a stern
woman who kept two cats and a "decent" house, her summation of
the edict forbidding female visitors after nine o'clock, Spuhn had
his restaurant plans spread across a big desk under a bulletin board
full of pinned task notes.

Now Jenny helped him. She asked to be shown around the diner
Spuhn and Hernandez were turning into Spoon restaurant.

Spuhn flooded her with his enthusiasm. They would install the
equipment from the Riverside location here and here once he and
Hernandez finished cleaning it. This area would be the kitchen,
with the main grill here and work counters there. There would be
six counter seats and eight tables.

Spuhn explained the design as if he were rolling back the door of
a secret laboratory.

"What's your logo look like?" Jenny asked.

Spuhn didn't have one yet. Nor did Spoon have stationery. He
didn't have a business card ready to give her.

"And you're going to open?"

"Columbus Day weekend," Spuhn answered.

In reply, she fixed her eyes on him. Her smile was a challenge.
"That's three and a half months," Spuhn said.

"Yes, October." She emphasized the point with a glance around her, at the counter stacked with tools and paint rollers, color swatches and a dish of bolts removed from something waiting to be reassembled and installed. The diner had arrived from Sterling with its fragile structure tarnished from more than a year of emptiness. Since then, a Klein crew guided by Spuhn had opened the front for addition of a space for tables. Sheets of plastic formed the temporary wall.

Jenny, who seemed to know the schedule Mr. Klein allowed Spuhn, returned the following Tuesday with a folder of drawings and designs she called Spoon's corporate identity. Spuhn, who had been prying old flooring loose from the cleared dining area, wiped his dripping face with an old shirt, and pulled a table near the open front door. Hernandez came from the bathroom, where he had been connecting the pipes of a washbowl. Once seated with Jenny and Spuhn, Hernandez stomped his foot a few times and reached down to awaken the pad of it with his fingers.

"Yellow and black are Hawkeye colors, Iowa colors," she said. Her manner indicated that the designs she spread on the table for stationery, business cards, menus, the side of the diner and billboards were for adoption, not conversation. The spoon character that would represent the restaurant was smiling, friendly, and animated.

"These are compliments of Iowa Outdoors," Jenny said, not telling Spuhn and Hernandez that she had completed the designs herself, with help from one of her father's staff.

They were fine with Spuhn, everything clean, professional, and without cost. In his mind, he transferred that part of Spoon's budget to a reserve.

Before she left, Jenny held Spuhn's arm in a thrilling, authoritative squeeze at the tattoo and leaned toward him. "Dennis, Columbus Day is in 15 weeks."

Spuhn had gained a partner, maybe a supervisor. The remarkable beauty with the practical way, with legs and curves that pulled his thoughts from counter tops and menu plans, had made the restaurant her project, too.

In the slanting afternoon rays of the hot sun, Spuhn and Hernandez stood at the front window for sight of Jenny pulling keys from her purse and getting into her car.

"Number one all the way," Hernandez said. "I'd lowcrawl over a mile of broken glass just to kiss the tires of the truck that takes her panties to the cleaners. Damn sure."

Spuhn laughed as he kept his gaze on Jenny's car. "Drill Instructor Monroe."

Drill Instructor Monroe said it about everything, every girl, every woman.

"She's got buku hots for you, man," said Hernandez.

That was all Spuhn needed, the insertion of Jenny, the pull of her away from the work he had to complete each day, each night until Spoon was not only open, but succeeding and expanding. "You don't just start a business," a guest speaker from Des Moines had told the marketing class. "You marry it. Remember the first time you went off a high dive? You either went or you didn't. Went or you didn't. And once you were away from the board, there was no getting back on. You were married to being off that safe, steady board. There's no half way."

That evening, like all eves of his return to the Klein Construction force, Spuhn pushed himself into early morning hours as he worked on the plans for Spoon. The move into the apartment with Hernandez had reduced the distractions of his parents' curiosity. It gave him distance from the mornings disturbed by bad cards the night before. At the apartment, he didn't have Mike, Veronica and their friends spoiling his concentration with their comings and goings, their fascination with the notes they saw him marking and arranging on the schedule board he had created. Here, the phone, except for the times Hernandez spoke with Coral Gables or talked love blather with one of the Davenport women from his growing circle, was for business, for Spoon.

Delicate, distant heat lightning flashed in a sky that remained dry, without relief of the heat that was gathering perspiration on Spuhn's face and in his eyes. At the stove in the small kitchen, moving rhythmically and happily with the Latin music coming from a cream-colored GE radio, Hernandez cooked hamburgers, each one flavored with ingredients and spices Hernandez remembered his grandmother using.

Spuhn saw Hernandez's rhapsodic face and realized that Jesus had toked up, probably while out and about for some of his cooking items. How stupid Hernandez was to add such risk to the starting of the business. Spuhn had tried grass a few times and formed a low opinion of it. Like getting bombed, getting high was for Spuhn a time-wasting distortion of reality. Why have a false reality when he was so anxious to control the real one?

Whenever Spuhn's anxiety boiled over, Hernandez only answered with a big placid smile and then a penitent tilt of his face. "Fuck it. What're they goin' to do, send me to Vietnam?" he said.

"Yes, maybe," Spuhn replied. Hernandez's kitchen talent came with a maddening need for sensible oversight.

At least, Hernandez was making progress at the stove.

Spuhn tweaked numbers on the spreadsheet Klein Construction had printed for him, checked the index and read articles from three trade magazine collections he had to return to the community college library, tweaked the plan again, and then bore down on the report he would give Mr. Klein at the end of the next day.

There was buku needing to be done. After work at Klein Construction the next day, he would go to the diner with Hernandez and get locations marked for the shelving the carpenters would install. The electricians would need to know about the new connections for some switches and lighting. Hernandez needed to settle on the menu, on portion sizes and ingredients, at least for the main items.

And, damn, with all that Spoon needed from him, Jenny's scent was with him, the feel of her fingers on his forearm, the grace of her curving movements, the tone of her legs. Damn!

She was exceptional. She was near. And he had no time, no money. That is, he had no spare money, only what he saved up and carefully husbanded for the months before Spoon began to generate enough revenues for a salary. Too often that balance dipped when he saw the look on his mother's face and stopped her with "Mom, here" before he left the house.

"You have to be in love with your plan," the man from Des Moines had told them. "Because you are going to suffer."

Spuhn took a yellow card and printed with a black marker what he had underlined and circled in *Think and Grow Rich*, "You are the master of your destiny." He pinned the card at the center of the board he faced from his desk, next to "Quitters never win. Winners never quit."

He didn't need a card to be reminded of Jenny Adamski. Her directness and her warmth bolstered her striking loveliness in a way that Spuhn had not known before: she seemed approachable but neither submissive nor desperate. Without being haughty or vain, she was sure of herself.

On Saturday morning, still damp from running at the riverfront, she came up the outside stairs of Spuhn and Hernandez's apartment, knocked loudly and tried to see through the screen. A trickle of pre-dawn rain had cooled the air. The morning had sunshine and blue sky with clean formations of cumulus clouds.

"Dennis. Hey, Dennis," she called into the apartment.

"Coming, coming," Spuhn said, pulling on a pair of jeans and an olive t-shirt. He had worked until two a.m. Hernandez was gone, absent with an Augustana nursing professor he knew from Clayton's introduction.

As soon as Spuhn unhooked the screen door, Jenny opened it and came right into the little kitchen.

"Good morning, glory. I want to show you some boards," she said. Always firm, today she was insistent. "My dad said I could hold them for you. But he's got other companies asking for them. You need to see them."

What could Spuhn do? What did he want to do, his mind so often on her?

While he shaved and used the bathroom, Jenny washed out yesterday's coffee grounds, found the container, and made a fresh pot. As the pot bubbled, she moved into the little living room-bedroom, the space where Spuhn slept on a couch across from his desk and the board of pinned notes. A door beyond the couch opened to a bedroom used by Jesus. Jenny placed her hands on her hips and began twisting her upper body in slow turns.

"Make yourself at home," Spuhn said.

She answered with a smile.

"We're painting all weekend," Spuhn said, taking the coffee cup Jenny handed him.

"Don't worry," she said. "It won't take long to show you this."

By then, Spuhn had noticed the damp of her hair and of the yellow and black running outfit she wore. "You went for a run?" he asked.

"Not far. Three miles," she said. Holding onto the back of a wooden kitchen chair, she reached back to pull first her left leg, then her right, in a stretch.

Taking their coffee with them, they went down the steps to Jenny's car.

Spuhn had been going for runs, too. He liked the military feel of being athletic and valued the chance to sort through plans as he moved around a park or along the riverfront. Maybe they could run together. But the starting of a business had suffering in it. The card on the board had Spuhn's promise about being master of his destiny. Being married to the new business. Being firm. He kept the running idea to himself as Jenny began a tour of the board locations she had selected for Spoon.

Her hair, pinned in a ponytail, had dried and now fell richly one way or another as she talked, as the breeze passed into the car and around her. The straps and the sides of her bra showed at the edges of her yellow Iowa tank top. Her legs were long, graceful, remarkable, in full view.

She drove along the river until they reached the bridge where Rte. 6 came across the Mississippi into Iowa. Then she followed Rte. 6 in its curve around the northern edge of Davenport, west toward Brady Street and north again toward the location of Spoon. In between pauses at the board locations, Spuhn and Jenny learned about each other.

Spuhn told of the Marine Corps, of Hernandez, Clayton, Szabo and his other friends, of what Spoon would be. Jenny learned from him of his father and mother, of Michael and Veronica, of the lucky bridge play during the flight to Vietnam. He said nothing about Lauren. He still thought about her, but not with the ache or regularity of that time.

From Jenny, Spuhn heard about her choice of fine arts for a major, of Marjorie, of people remembering Anna, of her brother

Bob living with his wife and children near New York, of classmates
and courses she liked at Iowa, classmates and courses and professors
she didn't. She didn't tell of Marjorie getting pregnant, leaving
school for a semester. She didn't tell of Val, of her falling away from
him more than a year ago. She didn't tell of others, the boy from
Mason City, the quiet hurdler from Kappa Alpha Psi who could
not be at ease with a white girlfriend.

"Maybe, sometime, we could go for a run together," Spuhn said.
He fiddled with the tilt of the side vent as he said it, then turned to
catch her looking at him.

"That would be nice," she said.

A beat later, she said, "I try to keep under six minutes."

Under six minutes. He'd have to di di mau. He'd have to go for
some runs before they went together. "That's fast," Spuhn said.

In his mind, Spuhn fastened a card to his schedule for the next
day: run. Run hard.

When they reached the construction site where the interstate
ramps and Spoon were coming into being, Jenny continued driving
north along Rte. 61. A quarter mile past the roadwork, she turned
east on a gravel road gullied in one spot by a storm that left fingers
of caramel-colored clay amid the white stones. Then, at a stand of
oak trees, she picked her way along a narrow dirt road and stopped
with the car facing east so that Spuhn could look out from the trees
onto the track cleared for the new interstate. In the distance, trucks
were moving with loads of scraped fill.

"Look there," Jenny told him. "Look where that twisted little
tree is all by itself there, on this side of the road."

Spuhn saw numbers of saplings growing on their side of the
interstate track.

"There," Jenny said, "That one." She had moved across the seat
and, with her right hand holding his shoulder, was extending her

left arm across him as she pointed at the tree she meant. "That one."

Her hair was against his nose and mouth, her breasts pushed against him, her weight rested against him with her leg touched to his.

Spuhn turned toward her and drawing her to him, kissed her with as much passion as he felt for Spoon, for a grand house, for being rich. He felt her push into the kiss.

"I need to take a shower. I smell," she said, remaining with her face close to Spuhn's, her fingers combing the hair at the base of his neck.

They kissed again. When they broke, Jenny drew away. The driver of a big dirt hauler had stopped to watch.

Jenny started the car as Spuhn gave the laughing driver the finger. "Asshole."

During the ride back to Spuhn's apartment, Spuhn sat against Jenny with his arm around her and his fingers stroking her bare arm. When she could, she rested her hand on his knee and squeezed it.

"That last place, you have to have that," Jenny said. "Pay attention," she said, pushing his hand away from her knee. "Everyone is going to see that board, right before the exit. Right before. That has to be a Spoon Restaurant board."

Spuhn had become business serious again. By the time they arrived at the apartment, he knew the costs and the deadlines. He promised to recommend the plan to Mr. Klein. And he promised to pick Jenny up for a run after the Klein Construction work on Monday.

At midweek, he still had the feeling in his calves as a reminder of the work it required to keep pace with Jenny on that run. For her, the exercise was a chance to be loose, to enjoy the store of energy that moved her in long strides along the riverfront sidewalk and let her determine for herself when the run was ended. Spuhn kept up out of competitive fire, his face red and his pale t-shirt plastered to his back. He didn't know the end spot of the run, and, even if he had been able, he couldn't husband energy for a distance. He simply willed himself to the pace, and only answered Jenny with nods and grunts when she said, "This is about halfway" or "Lucky the rain is holding off."

The feeling in his calves was pleasurable as Spuhn waited on a chair in the Klein reception area. No pain, no gain. The muscles were healing and strengthening, becoming ready for Jenny's pace when they met again on Saturday morning. Spuhn didn't intend to follow. He knew that Jenny had tested him with a soft pace, almost six and a half minute miles.

The storm had been building from the week's heat. Lightning, then thunder began moments after Mr. Klein came into the building and called for Spuhn to go ahead into the office. "Just have to stop in the john," he said, spreading his fingers to show dirt from whatever he'd been doing or checking.

Heavy rain was sounding against the windows of the office as Mr. Klein heard Spuhn's presentation in the company of a friend introduced with only a name, "Mr. Soukup."

Mr. Soukup had a sure way about him. During the presentation, he had nodded at certain points as Spuhn presented the current work calendar and once let a small smile show. Younger than Mr. Klein, he had graying hair worked in a spread across the baldness of his round head. He wore a navy sportcoat and well-tended brown shoes, no tie.

His questions showed he was familiar with Spoon's likely competition as well as the plans of the major businesses. Spuhn began to realize that Mr. Soukup's questions about menu, hours, staffing, market demand, marketing were instructions about menu, hours, staffing, market demand, marketing.

At the end, Mr. Soukup looked at Mr. Klein and rose to shake Spuhn's hand. "I give you a lot of credit, young man," he said. "You have plenty of backbone. You just may pull this off. You just may."

Then he gave Spuhn a card with Food Services Group, Cargill, Omaha on it. "Your friend Fred Klein will let me know when I can help."

"Goddamn right, George," Mr. Klein said before walking the other man toward his car. The force of Mr. Klein's five foot eight height landed in heavy, rapid steps along the hallway from the office.

When Mr. Klein returned to Spuhn, Spuhn was glad to see, but didn't understand, the pleased look showing on the man's broad face. Whatever had happened in the meeting, Mr. Klein had seen things unfold for the good.

Now, the business of Spuhn's progress report. Mr. Klein had paid attention. He'd get the electricians to work and he'd have the architect sit down with Spuhn about the need to improve the blocking of noise from the kitchen area.

Then, with a smile, Mr. Klein stood up and grabbed a roll of plans from the small barrel in the corner of his office.

"Take a look at this," he said, spreading the roll across the layer of papers and magazines on his desk.

The map showed the route of a completed Interstate 80 reaching from the Mississippi River to the Missouri River and Omaha. Mr. Klein indicated blue checks at points on the map, each check at an area where the interstate would have exit and entrance ramps.

He didn't need to explain. Spuhn understood that Mr. Klein meant for Spoon to expand across Iowa. The locations? Each check mark meant that Mr. Klein either controlled or knew how to control the spot. All Dennis Spuhn needed to do was be smart, work like a demon, and make Spoon succeed.

Obedient and thrilled, Spuhn followed Mr. Klein as he rested a finger at one or other of the checked sites. Carried on the back of the construction president's hand, the American flag tattoo from Mr. Klein's military service rode across the Iowa map, paused, pressed, moved to the next location.

All Spuhn had to do was make Spoon succeed. *You ain't done yet?* Mr. Klein and those DIs had a lot in common.

When Spuhn arrived at the empty apartment, he sat at his desk and stared at the notes pinned to the board before him. Then he took a dark marker and, on a fresh card, he printed "You ain't done yet?"

Once the card was pinned at the board's center, Spuhn turned to the evening's work. Once Spoon was going along in Davenport, they would put one in Iowa City, right smack at the exit nearest to the University of Iowa.

CHAPTER 19

Everywhere we go,
people want to know...
Who we are,
so we tell em...

Whatever had brought traffic to a near stop mid-river was out of Spuhn and Hernandez's sight, hidden by the truckload of steers a few feet ahead of Spuhn's car. Hernandez, mildly contrite, mostly just happily stoned and tired from his hours in his Augustana girl-friend's little bedroom, was just sitting as he let Spuhn cross the Mississippi, go anywhere at whatever pace Spuhn chose. Beneath them, a long, cream-colored motorboat was emerging, headed somewhere upriver to the east. Through the car's open windows, Hernandez took in the even throb of the boat's two engines and vacantly tracked the red, green and white running lights. The river gave the air, lightly sweetened with the country smell of the cattle truck, a pleasing bit of cool under a sky pretty with stars.

Spuhn, though, wanted to get back to bed, wanted to get a few more hours of sleep before he rose and plowed into the things needing attention. With Spoon's Columbus weekend opening now barely three weeks away, sleep was as carefully scheduled as every-thing else. Hernandez had explained why his car wouldn't work and why he had to call Spuhn for the ride, but Spuhn was preoccupied and only anxious to get back to their apartment. Spuhn supposed the Augustana woman, a nursing professor, had a husband due home. Hernandez once said the two worked at different schools in different cities.

The truck inched ahead a few feet, set its brakes with a hiss, inched ahead, set its brakes. The lurching unsteadied the cattle each time.

Spuhn set his emergency brake, and got out of the Chevy, the '55 that had been his mother's, for a look. The straw and manure smells of the truck were strong as he passed the patient animals, who were sending ripples across their shoulders against the gnats and flies traveling with them. Off to the sides, the river was dark at midstream and mostly empty as it ran between the downtown lights of Davenport and Rock Island.

"Some jackasses up there with too much liquor and too little sense," the truck driver said. Burly and set at his wheel, the sandy-haired man about ten years older than Spuhn, all country, was pleasant and conversational. "I guess they gave the toll collector some lip and he called the cops on them."

"Just what we need," Spuhn said. Four cars ahead, a squad car had its doors open as two policemen dealt with whatever four men had been doing at two a.m. on the Quad Cities' Centennial Bridge.

"Get back in your car, troop," one of the policemen said to Spuhn when Spuhn approached. The flasher atop the squad car washed the scene with bands of soft blue light. Up at the top of a street lamp, a couple of moths and a small swarm of gnats played against the globe.

"Sure," said Spuhn. "How long you think it'll be before we can move?"

"Long it takes to get these knuckleheads squared away," the young policeman answered. "We have to wait for another car.

"They have the idea walking on your hands across the Centennial Bridge is a fun thing to do in the middle of the night. Well, one of 'em does. His friends are just keeping him company."

Recognizing his signal in the stream of noise from his car's radio, the officer climbed back inside and spoke into the microphone.

With the officer distracted, Spuhn moved ahead. He could see four men, two of them very intoxicated, in argumentative discussion with the senior police officer, a thick-bodied man in a uniform that had grown tight.

"Settle down, settle down," the officer said. He was patiently firm.

"We're walking across," one man repeated. He had a flat face and small teeth in a wide mouth. Like the others, he was dressed in factory garb. Unsteady on their feet, a couple of the men were leaning for support against the railing of the bridge. Spuhn recognized one skeletally thin man from dances where students from all the schools mixed. Because of their age and the shortness of their haircuts – one of the very drunk ones was losing his – Spuhn took them for men not so long out of the military.

"Is there a law against walking?" one of the men asked. He had a loud, rasping, crow call of a voice that sounded over the engine noises on the bridge. "I'm asking you: is there a law against walking?"

"There's a law against public disturbance, and a law that says you have to pay the toll when you use this bridge." The officer spoke in an even tone.

Spuhn supposed the four had gotten off the swing shift at Alcoa or International Harvester and had too much to drink in one of the Rock Island taverns.

Intoxicated to the point of certainty, a long-necked man with overalls and a blue workshirt hanging loosely on his frame, guffawed. "But what if you're walking on your hands? What if your feet ain't touching the ground? Just your hands. That walking?" The man laughed so hard that a string of snot jetted from his nose.

Someone was walking on his hands across the Centennial Bridge? Who? Spuhn judged the handwalker was the silent, round-faced man who was regarding everything around him with a big, giddy smile on his face. The man was flushed, probably from being upside down and laboring at his progress to that point on the bridge.

A man who had been listening to jazz in a white Mustang at the second spot in the stopped line came up beside Spuhn. Spuhn had glimpsed Ohio plates and a back seat full of sales catalogs and a large box of a briefcase.

"The four of them were right in the lane, hoggin' the whole road. That kid with the big shoulders, the red-haired one with the shit-eatin' grin there, he walked on his hands the whole way, till the cops showed up."

"Why?"

"Drunk. Somethin' to do, suppose."

Spuhn studied the pink-faced man whose stunt had been the cause of the bridge jam. Somewhere around 25 years of age, sturdily built under a soft, faintly pink form, with his shoulders squared in a white T-shirt, the man was thinking his own easy thoughts as his agitated, long-necked friend tried to influence the inflexible police officer. When something amused the handwalker all of a sudden, Spuhn heard the man's laugh, a true and infectious, slightly boyish eruption that came with a rosy flush and a broadened grin.

Not sure why, Spuhn dwelt on the impression of the ruddy-faced man against the bridge rail. The paddy wagon pulled up against traffic on the Davenport side. Soon, the four revelers were inside, the wagon was turned around, and traffic resumed. When Spuhn and Hernandez exited the bridge and passed the stopped squad car, Hernandez had come down enough that he shrank from a direct stare in that direction.

Spuhn slept until 6:15, rising without enough time for full preparation of the ideas he would discuss at eleven with Mr. Klein and the second investor, Mr. Klein's friend George Soukup.

Worse, when he did wake, more than an hour off his pace, Spuhn woke consumed with a new plan that couldn't be set aside.

A few minutes ahead of eight o'clock, Spuhn drove to the Scott County Jail a little west of downtown and north of the river on 4th Street.

"You don't have to post bail for him," the tiny clerk told Spuhn. "They're letting him go this morning -" she looked back at the clock on the office wall- "in about a half hour."

"They're letting him out?"

"Less he turns up wanted for something, and I don't see that here. Once they sober up, they let these types out, most times. They keep showin' up, that's a different thing. But this Ronald Tonti – that how you say it? Tawnteee? He's a first offender."

Ronald Tonti. Ronald Tonti. Reacting to Spuhn's polite questioning and his near-military grooming, his curling hair kept neatly long enough to part, the efficient woman wrote down Ronald Tonti's address of record before turning to the next person in line, an anxious young black woman trying to keep a baby soothed.

The address on the note was less than half a mile away, close enough that Spuhn could stick a message through a mail slot and arrive on time at the Klein Construction meeting. Fortunately, he still had a young man's beard and he had shaved just before noon the day before. Mr. Klein and Mr. Soukup would notice, but they wouldn't complain. The plans, the status, the next steps, energy and confidence, that's what interested Spoon's two backers. Spuhn would have pleasing news for them, possibly extraordinary news for them if they liked what he had in mind for Ronald Tonti.

Mr. Klein and Mr. Soukup had approved, even delighted in, the arrangement Spuhn had made – after Jenny's encouragement – with Big Jimmy Cooper and Owen Williams, who wrestled as the popular Justice Dispensers tag team. The two wrestlers would be present and would sign autographs the afternoon Spoon opened. The *Morning Democrat* notice Jenny had gotten into the hands of her father's reporter friend was already stirring interest among the high school and college students, as well as many men and some women who loyally attended all Justice Dispensers combat. Jenny felt right away as Spuhn felt: the Justice Dispensers, the defenders of the Free World against a succession of devious opponents bent on the ruin of democracy, would get the freshly renovated Spoon restaurant full of talkative, exhilarated patrons ready to know where Spoon was, what it was, and what it provided: the imaginative, tasty burgers and sides that no other place could provide because no other place had Jesus Hernandez.

Hearing of Spuhn's Justice Dispensers idea, Jenny had championed the plan so ardently that she and Spuhn were soon out of their clothes and paying no attention to the demanding column of task notes pinned above the desk in the little apartment. Spuhn, otherwise so exactly planned, couldn't help himself. Without studying or facing the realization, he knew that, although he had had sex – not as much as Hernandez and Clayton, who would jump anything - he had never made love with anyone. Now, wherever things were going, he was making love with Jenny, and, with more struggle than he liked, holding to his Spoon schedule, too.

Spuhn veered to the right and stopped on 4th Street, right next to Ronald Tonti.

Through the open window, Spuhn shouted something that brought the man around, his face first startled and then coloring with amusement.

"Shouldn't you be on your hands? What you doin' on your feet?"

Ronnie Tonti smiled and bent to squint at Spuhn.

"I'm not a homo," Spuhn said. "That's not what I want."

Spuhn introduced himself and offered a ride.

Tonti got in the car and reached to shake Spuhn's hand. "Ronnie Tonti."

As he had appeared the night before, Ronald Tonti, though tired, was comfortable and calm. The sunshine and humidity of a day that would hit the eighties had already made Tonti flushed and sweaty.

Right away, Spuhn felt certain about the likable passenger. Ready to answer any question, Tonti diverged when he needed to get Spuhn to the blistering Queen Anne with half a dozen mailboxes in two rows at a heavy front door. There, in front of the house where Tonti said he was shackin' up with a nice little girl named Dottie, they talked until a busty, sandy-haired woman in a big bra and white underpants came onto the porch and called to Tonti.

"You goin' to the plant today?" She patted at the loose pile of her beehive.

"Lo, dumplin'," Tonti said to her. "Be a minute."

The woman, Dottie, went inside.

"Ol' lady's fussy this mawnin," Tonti said to Spuhn, and then in answer to Spuhn's question, replied, "N'Awlins," Tonti said. "Nawth 'n east. Slahdell."

"Slahdell?" Spuhn repeated.

"Unhuh. S-l-i-d-e-l-l. Slahdell."

What hadn't Tonti done for work, for work with those short, thick fingers and wide hands? The Army, most of it in Germany. Dishwasher, construction in St. Louis, carnival crew member assembling, disassembling and running rides all that summer as the enterprise worked county fairs and church festivals up the Mississippi Valley from St. Louis. Then, a buddy learned Alcoa was hiring. Tonti had gotten a job in the plate mill.

He yawned and turned back to face Spuhn. "Gonna be hard to stay awake this afternoon's shift."

Still, his grin was wide and his expression showed no concern. His eyes, faintly blue, had reddish lashes. In the light pink of Tonti's round, boyish face, there were occasional, barely discernible freckles.

"I saw you get arrested last night," Spuhn said. "On the bridge."

"Whoo-eeee." Tonti shook his head and grinned. "Unhuh, ol' Mr. Policeman didn't like that one."

"You walked on your hands all the way to there?" Spuhn asked.

"Unhuh."

"Why?"

"Some boys at the bar got arguin' about I could do it or not, started makin' some bets, and. . . " Tonti grinned.

"The cops spoiled your bet."

Tonti laughed. "No, didn't have a bet. Was just seein' I could do it."

"Your friends payin' you?"

"No. I was just feelin' good, decided to just go ahead and do it."

"For nothing?"

Tonti shrugged.

"For free?"

Tonti shrugged again.

"Would you have made it all the way across?"

"Yeahl. It was goin' all right."

"All the way across, from Rock Island to Davenport."

Tonti just smiled.

"That is outstanding. Hands down outstanding," Spuhn said.

Tonti yawned. He stretched his arms and smiled, then opened the door and began to get out.

"Pick you up again at one ?" Spuhn asked. "I'll give you a ride to Alcoa and I'll pay you to walk on your hands a little ways for my friend."

Spuhn showed a twenty dollar bill.

When Spuhn completed his meeting with the investors and returned for Tonti again, he had Jenny with him. She waited in the car and examined markings she had made on a university course catalog while Spuhn went onto the porch and entered the house in search of the apartment marked 2E.

"Ronnie, it's the man who drove you here. Ron-nie," Dottie called into an apartment that smelled of breakfast cooking, cigarettes and piled laundry. Barely over five feet tall, Dottie was wearing a purple halter top that showed the cleavage of her breasts as well as a small roll of stomach. She hadn't worked the new day's makeup yet; dark flecks of mascara showed in lines beneath her small, dark eyes.

While Ronnie made rushing sounds in a bedroom, she studied Spuhn, liking his looks. The summer had tanned him. Spuhn was used to, and used, the way his Marine, long-lashed, mannered appearance warmed clerks, investors, and girlfriends. By inclination and by design, he kept himself cleanly removed from the shaggy look of the Vietniks and folksingers who discomfited so many adults the age of Spuhn's father and mother, adults the age of Mr. Klein and Mr. Soukup.

During the few minutes of waiting for Tonti, Spuhn rubbed the back of the gray cat that had come to press his ankles. Dottie lit a cigarette and settled, facing Spuhn, at a table with an open

National Enquirer.

When Tonti saw Jenny, his normal, broad smile took on a brief, revealing look of interest. He let Jenny slide to the middle of the seat, close against Spuhn, before Tonti took his place with a tiny, deferential space between his own leg and the long legs Jenny troubled to keep fitted over the hump in the center of the floor. Wearing jeans and a sleeveless lime-colored blouse, smelling of fresh shower and a little cologne, she was ready for driving to Iowa City for the next day's morning of classes. Pressing against Spuhn as they rode, she fanned fingers along his thigh in a familiar way that excited both men.

"My car's over there in Rock Island," Tonti said. He had an arm along the back of the seat, just barely out of contact with Jenny.

Before going to Tonti's car, Spuhn drove them to the riverfront strip where he and Jenny jogged.

Affably, easily, Tonti handwalked along the path as Spuhn and Jenny accompanied him.

"How far can you go? How long can you walk on your hands like this?" Spuhn wanted to know.

Tonti was having no trouble talking.

Spuhn was amazed and pleased. Seeing the same, approving look on Jenny, Spuhn began talking about the restaurant opening as the three of them, Tonti on his hands, moved forward.

A hundred yards along, at Spuhn's decision, they stopped and Tonti righted himself. When he stood up, Tonti had some drops of perspiration on his forehead, which had reddened like his cheeks. "Next show in a hour," he said, accepting the twenty dollars Spuhn gave him.

You want a job?" Spuhn asked. "I want to hire you. I want to pay you for walking on your hands like this the day we open our restaurant. "We're opening the Friday before Columbus Day. You do it?"

If Jenny were involved, if Jenny would be nearby in a close-fitting shirt, her fingers playing at the silky hair falling over her ears, and her long legs bearing the whole of her in a way that made his dick so hard he could chip it, damn! Tonti would handwalk over broken glass through hot grease. Reading the feeling on Tonti's face, Spuhn added to the opening day arrangement.

"Jenny will come get you that morning. Right? That okay?"

Jenny nodded.

Tonti wouldn't have to be at Alcoa till his three-o'clock shift. He was agreeable to everything Spuhn laid out, especially the antici-pation of Jenny's company.

"Outstanding," said Spuhn. "Outstanding."

They'd have to decide a route, maybe have Tonti start with an inaugural handwalk somewhere around St. Sebastian's or St. Ambrose like a Pied Piper and then ride in a caravan of cars up Brady Street toward I-80 and Spoon. Walking on his hands, Tonti could circle the Spoon site at regular times, with trips inside Spoon on a route among the tables and the patrons. Spuhn was full of ideas. Maybe they could have the Justice Dispensers flank Tonti in their purple tights and gold capes. Even if the October day were cold – early October could be anything in the Quad Cities – the muscular wrestlers surely could tolerate being outside Spoon long enough for photos and even television recording of their bare-chested appearance on the restaurant's opening day.

Hands down, the opening was going to be outstanding. Hoo-rah!

By the Friday of the opening, a light jacket day of sunshine, things were so much in place that Spuhn in his excitement couldn't sleep past four. After showering, shaving, and sorting through the checklists and notecards on his desk, he drove to Spoon. There, he flicked the lights and admired the gleam of the restaurant, all ready for the customers brought by billboards, two features in the *Daven-*

port Morning Democrat and its sister paper, the *Davenport Evening Times*, an appearance he and Hernandez had made on Adrianne Smith's "What's happening in the Quad Cities" morning radio program, and the attractions of the Justice Dispensers and hand-walker Ronnie Tonti.

Had Mr. Soukup been right about the expansion that gave the dining area room for four booths and an additional four tables? In hours, they would know.

Hernandez, nearly as excited as Spuhn, had carefully arranged everything in the kitchen the night before. Nervous that he had miscounted his inventory of meat, fries and condiments, he repeated the placement of everything just so in the refrigerator and freezer as well as the shelves and cabinets within reach of his own station. At the apartment, he remained awake, lazily studying a *Look* magazine as he listened to an Otis Redding album. Before going to sleep, Hernandez hung his cream-colored Spoon uniform shirt and other fresh clothes on a kitchen chair and wrote a reminder for Spuhn to make sure and wake him at six-thirty.

Hoo-rah!

Hernandez, a serious look on his face, had the kitchen sizzling by ten o'clock. In his new Spoon shirt, one showing the folds of first wearing, and with his dark hair shining in the neat discipline of his interview haircut, Hernandez was the striking, clean-shaven embodiment of an inspired young chef. He was moving with sure concentration as Marcie Malone from TV station KQRI arrived and began taking b-roll before positioning Spuhn outside for an interview at 10 a.m. right in front of the Spoon logo beside the entrance. She would miss the Justice Dispensers, not due until 11:30 but, no matter. Jenny drove up in mid-interview with Tonti, who wore his own Spoon uniform shirt as he commenced walking on his hands.

Tonti was flawless on his hands and lightly flirtatious in his accommodation of the red-haired reporter. Marcie Moore, just turned twenty-three and ambitious for a rise into a major market such as Chicago, was in a race to cover a Garfield Elementary School science fair at 11 and after that, the arrival of a new fire engine equipped with an hydraulic turntable ladder she planned to climb for an interview with one of the men from the Central Fire Station on Scott Street. KQRI was assigning a camera man for that interview. She meant to smuggle a stuffed kitten doll aloft, then discover it desperate on the edge of the roof as the spot concluded.

Despite her rush, with Tonti playfully moving, almost gamboling, about the restaurant, and all the while responding to her in a New Orleans accent, she spent an extra five minutes following him on his path from the tables area into the kitchen and among the feet of the laughing Hernandez and his busy pair of young cooks.

Just after 11:30, making a *Morning Democrat* photographer and John Roswell, a seen-it-all reporter with a flaking pink face and a short, gray flattop, wait only seven minutes behind schedule, Councilman Horace Williams, a friend of Mr. Klein's, arrived to stand with Mr. Klein, Spuhn and Hernandez for the cutting of a thick purple velvet rope held at each end by a Justice Dispenser. In front of it all, big smile on his round face, Tonti stood on his hands, sure as a column.

After shaking hands and accepting the plate of hamburger and fries Hernandez had prepared with his Spoon seasonings, the councilman left for return to City Hall.

From then on, until the ten o'clock close, Spoon boomed. Just as hoped, I-80 eastbound travelers appeared in numbers that forecast significant patronage once the new Mississippi River bridge came into being and began adding westbound vehicles. When the ribbon-cutting concluded, a surge of high school students taking advantage of their teachers' professional development afternoon followed the handwalking Tonti and the powerful Justice Dispensers inside. The noise became intense and festive: high school students called to each other and to the celebrities dispensing autographs. Hernandez and his crew announced ready orders to the busy young Spoon waitresses Spuhn and Hernandez had trained in preceding weeks. At the tables, friends recognized friends, including Spuhn's parents and two couples from the bridge group.

Mr. Soukup's plan called for Spoon to cover its costs locally and prosper from the Interstate travelers. Spuhn saw many of both.

"Remember. It's quick food. Good food, quick food," he shouted at times into the kitchen. "Roger that," Hernandez replied. He was busy, happy amid his two young assistants and the waitresses who were pulling orders together as the food came from the grill.

When she had eaten, Spuhn's mother came to him and kissed his cheek. "You should be proud," she said. "Everyone is raving. Congratulations."

Veronica hugged Spuhn's waist and Mike rubbed his own sated belly just before the family left, on the way to drop Mike at a practice. "Bye, Denny," Veronica called.

In between handstands and handwalking, Tonti settled at booths, mostly at those where high school girls had pressed shoulder to shoulder, hip to hip across from other excited girls and one or two loud-talking boys.

As Spuhn visited the tables and simultaneously kept an eye on the line of customers waiting for take-out orders, a line made up of a couple of truckers, a crew from a construction site, and some students in performance level conversation with friends seated nearby, he asked, "Who is having a birthday this month? Anyone?"

"She is. Maureen, you are."

Maureen, Joan, Debbie, Greg, Dan, they all, especially the high school girls, reacted happily at the recognition from Dennis Spuhn, the young, confident Marine Corps veteran and owner who had been interviewed by the reporter from station KQRI. On the inside of his right wrist, they saw, he had the Semper Fi tattoo, a small one like those of one girl's father and one boy's uncle.

"Happy birthday, Maureen," Spuhn said, writing his name on a coupon and handing it to her. "This will give you an extra dollar off on your birthday. Write down your address and your birthday and we'll do it next year, too."

Maureen, Joan, Debbie, they all flushed, aware of the young owner's smile and the envy of the friends pressed around her.

They all - girls, boys, two clerks from Jenner's Hardware, a trucker, a salesman from up the river in Dubuque, it turned out - most of them at every table, wanted their birthdays known, too.

Spuhn took Becky aside, split her tables with Kathy and Janice, then set the college student to recording all the information in careful script on a notepad Spuhn took from the cashier's station.

"Are you married?" one bold girl asked, to the amusement of those crowded with her in the booth. They giggled at Spuhn's surprise.

"Do you have a girlfriend?" a second asked.

"My brother was in your class. He went to St. Sebastian's same time you did. His name's Randy Hartmann," another girl said.Spuhn remembered her brother, recognized in the girl a resemblance to her brother's freckled forehead.

"What's Randy doin' now?"

"He's in the Army. They sent him to Vietnam last month."

"Hope that's goin' all right for him," Spuhn said.

"He gets extra pay," the girl said. "He's savin' up for school again."

Later, a girl whose L&M filter had flecks of her red lipstick, asked, "Do you curl your hair?"

Spuhn laughed. The pace had heated him, intensified the way his damp hair showed waves. "Do you have a need to know? You're getting' personal here."

To the admiration of her table, the girl stayed coy. "Maybe," she said.

In groups, students came and went, sometimes returned. Travelers and curious business neighbors kept the lunch hour popping.

When Jenny came into the dining area and found Spuhn, the tables of students stared in voyeuristic awe.

Smelling of light perfume and dressed in a brown skirt that only came to mid-thigh, she interrupted Spuhn's circling of the crowded restaurant for a kiss on his cheek and, into his ear, a promise to be back in the evening, after attending her afternoon class. On the way to class, she would take Tonti back to his car.

"Whoo-eeee, Jim," Tonti said to Spuhn, giving Spuhn's hand a big pump. "Whole town's here."

"Bye, Ronnie, bye," called some of the students.

Spuhn gave Tonti a fistful of spoon-shaped coupons for opening celebration meal offers and told him to pass them around at Alcoa."That's a rog." After pressing the coupons into the pocket of his pants, Tonti pleased the restaurant crowd by flipping onto his hands and letting Jenny hold the door for him as he exited.

"See you tomorrow," Spuhn said. Tonti would come to the restaurant Saturday, Sunday and then Monday, an engagement that would keep the opening excitement at a high level through the fall holiday.

Mr. Klein, who had come in and out a couple of times during the afternoon, was excited and smiling when he came up to Spuhn in the middle of a dinnertime rush. He looked around the restaurant.

"George's tying up three more locations for us, Denny," said Mr. Klein. "We're going west."

CHAPTER 20

Down by the river
Down by the river
We took a little walk
We took a little walk
Ran into Charlie
Ran into Charlie
And we had a little talk
And we had a little talk
We pushed 'em
Hey!
We shoved 'em
Hey!
We threw 'em in the river
We threw 'em in the river

Ninety-one days before Joe Yoder became one of three casualties in his infantry platoon's standoff with a small NVA unit north of Pleiku, he poked at Jim Clayton and badgered him for a cigarette.

"C'mon, you damn beatnik," Yoder said. "Support your neighborhood GI. Unless you want to walk home from here."

"Here" was the table at Spoon, in a mid-afternoon Saturday lull at the end of February, 1969, and the ride would be in the screaming yellow Plymouth Duster Yoder had bought in Alexandria, Louisiana as soon as he completed his advanced infantry training. During the remaining days of leave, Yoder planned to drain the fluids and leave the car on blocks in a farm shed till he returned from Vietnam.

Clayton, at home preparing for a law school exam, was cashing in the Spoon Party Bring-a-Friend birthday card he had received at the end of 1968.

Now he grinned and pulled a pack of Winston's from the pocket of the black vest he wore over a white, button-down shirt. In deference to style, he had the sleeves rolled almost to his elbows.

After lighting the cigarette and taking a long draw, Yoder said, "And get yourself a haircut, too, troop. Don't you e-e-e-ven let Sergeant Major Johnson catch you walking around with all this – " Here he snatched the shiny black bangs falling to Clayton's eyes and gave a yank.

Tony Szabo laughed as Clayton smoothed the mussed hair with a motion that continued over his ears and through the dark waves at the back of his neck.

"What're you laughin' about, Szabo?" Yoder asked, running his fingers lightly against the stiff bristles of his own light brown cut. A widow's peak was beginning to show. "General Hershey'll be sendin' you one of those 'Greetings' letters of his pretty soon."

Szabo, who was working to sport sideburns along cheeks damaged by some blots of old acne problems, had his own dark hair at a helter skelter length that made Clayton's even Beatle playboy look seem reserved.

"When I get out, I'm goin' to grow my hair down to my ass," Yoder said.

"If you have any," said Clayton.

Spuhn was too busy to sit with the trio but he kept track as he came and went from the kitchen area, where he was using the phone in the small office area he had made at the end of a work table.

The numbers now were good and promised to rise once the spring weather came, not only in Davenport but in Iowa City, and Williamsburg near the Amana Colonies. But Spuhn worried. Nothing was certain. January, when wet snow came in mid-month and then unusual warmth at the end, had met the forecast but with a trough that made Spuhn nervous. For Mr. Soukup and Mr. Klein, the roller coaster had been a good exercise in staffing, something to experience soon and while small. Spuhn, though, had nothing but Spoon, unlike the two investors with all their other enterprises and income streams.

The good weeks pleased Spuhn and also made him anxious about the ability to match staff recruiting, training, scheduling and materials management with the growth. Any hint of a flattening pace or, worse, a slowing one, absorbed Spuhn in working and reworking of solutions.

"You need to relax," Jenny said when she came home to see him of a weekend or when he stayed over in Iowa City after business at that location. With a push of her hip into his, a bite of his ear, she easily took him from the matters making him distant. Often, each time bringing notebooks, sketchbooks, pens and texts in her dark green, cloth book bag, she joined him for drives to whatever needed attention in Williamsburg and Grinnell. The four Spoon locations, once Grinnell's opened July 1st, would span 125 miles, nearly the whole eastern part of Iowa.

Tonti's handwalking had been successful in drawing attention to each opening. In addition, Spoon had begun offering the performance at private parties when orders of Spoon's food were sizable.

Despite Jenny's chiding at Spuhn about his working pace, whenever she herself sat, she worked. Wherever she was, she sketched. At times she was without her sketchbook, Spuhn still saw her studying something in front of her as she committed a patch of light, the motion of a bird, the shape of a chin, the angles and colors of crops to memory.

Spuhn was aware and irritated that when they ran together, Jenny dropped her pace a notch so that he could stay with her for the first three miles before she accelerated, even over stretches of slick path, for the remaining two. Maintaining the pace of that first three miles, however, put Spuhn at his limit and momentarily cleansed his mind of whatever Spoon issue festered. More than once, as he caught his breath at the end of a run and returned to thought of Spoon, he also found some answer firmly settled.

One wouldn't go away, though. Spuhn could run to the moon and that one would be waiting for him: his unease about Hernandez.

The big, likable Cuban, such a cog in the restaurant's appeal, was too good to be true. Unconcerned, disinterested each time Spuhn began to talk about any business aspect of the restaurants, Hernandez took his delight in experimentation with Spoon's fare. The basic hamburgers, sides and salads that began with Hernandez's memory of a grandmother's cooking had broadened into a series of new offerings – mixes of relish, pork, breakfast fare - that crossed Hernandez's Cuban recipes with others he discovered or just invented.

Thanks to Hernandez, this day training kitchen workers in Grinnell, Spoon was serving food that people could find only at the Interstate locations Mr. Klein and Mr. Soukup obtained. Hernandez was important when Spuhn began planning the restaurant. He was vital now.

No one worked harder than Spuhn but Hernandez, with a fifteen percent interest, didn't lag by much. The little salary Spuhn allowed the two of them was enough for their modest costs: the apartment, gas, Hernandez's grass. They lived simply.

For Spuhn, the satisfaction, the reward came from the restaurant's growing footprint. Already at three locations with a fourth in progress, Spoon was visible, increasing, and associated with Spuhn, the founder.

But for Hernandez, a fifteen percent interest or no interest or an eighty-nine percent interest seemed equally unimportant. The little upstairs apartment he and Spuhn shared or a fine Bettendorf crown of the bluff house, both were the same for Hernandez, who made no complaint and took no evident notice.

Hernandez's relationship with the professor from Augustana College had gone on for a long enough time that Spuhn was startled when Hernandez reverted to his old pattern. The two women he had dated since had large, showy bosoms and a freewheeling manner of talking and touching. One wore a wedding band.

One or another came into the restaurants at times, usually just before closing but, beyond a wave and a big, white smile of hello, the curvy women didn't get much from Hernandez when he was involved with his kitchen and his cooking.

But what if Spoon lost Hernandez or if Hernandez lost interest in Spoon? And what if Hernandez got caught smoking grass or, with his new girlfriend, tripping on acid?

Szabo looked into his glass and poked at some crushed ice with a straw as Spuhn passed the table. "This is so far out."

"What is?" Clayton asked.

"Spuhn. Spuhn, you're turning into a capitalist pig."

Spuhn's sour look made the others laugh.

"Hands down," Clayton said. "Spuhn is living the American dream."

"Just look at him," Szabo said. "You look like you're goin' to a funeral."

Ready to attend another session as a non-voting board member of Klein Incorporated, the umbrella organization of Mr. Klein's construction and development firms, Spuhn was wearing a navy blue sport coat and a tie with a bright orange paisley pattern. Mr. Klein had created the board position as a way for Spuhn to hone executive skills as well as familiarity with the entire enterprise.

"Fuckin' A," said Yoder.

"This is a family restaurant," Spuhn said. At the three other occupied tables, no one was paying attention. "You can't talk like that in here."

"What're you goin' to do? Send me to Vietnam?"

Spuhn laughed, too.

Then Yoder, Clayton and Szabo got up and went to kill the rest of the afternoon at Stubby's Pool Paradise, still their leisure time haunt.

Their unconcern about time made Spuhn feel separate, wiser than the three friends even though Szabo and Clayton had earned college degrees. Clayton was in law school. Szabo was just spinning, consumed with thinking about problems he would never solve: racial prejudice, nuclear weapons, war, the draft. Yoder was on the conveyor belt that would move Szabo someday, too: military service, work, marriage to someone, resumption of work to earn a college degree.

But Szabo was feeling the workings of other gears, they learned. Stirred by the first CBS news report that US military deaths in Vietnam were approaching the figure for the Korean War, Szabo and his father had an explosive argument that left Szabo's mother crying and Szabo set on being at a protest in Chicago. After spending the night in his girlfriend's apartment, Szabo, his small, quiet girlfriend and two other St. Ambrose acquaintances drove to Chicago in Szabo's touch-and-go Corvair. One of the others making the trip had a friend at the University of Chicago. They could stay in his Hyde Park apartment.

Within 24 hours, Szabo was arrested as he burned his draft card.

No one could miss the images and reports coming from Chicago. They were a narcotic that flowed through conversations and thoughts in Iowa as well as everywhere else. With Dr. Martin Luther King, Jr. and Presidential candidate Robert Kennedy assassinated the year before, deaths occurring in Vietnam, inner cities enraged, even in the sun-bathed quiet of the Quad Cities, unease was rampant.

Spuhn, like everyone else, was drawn to the news but not so much that he took his mind off Spoon and its needs. In regard to national policy and Vietnam commitment, what bearing could his opinions have on any of it? Glimpsing a news photo of Greg Benson engaged in an activity of the Richard M. Nixon Iowa campaign the previous fall further diminished Spuhn's interest. Young lawyers for Nixon? Benson was barely in law school at the time, that brown-nosing shit-for-brains.

Spuhn could see Benson taking on the distorted shape of the bodybuilder. His neck had thickened so that Benson's face in the photo seemed almost at rest on his shoulders.

In the meantime, whether Benson blew up or blew away, whether the astronauts reached the moon or not, Spoon needed a new manager found and trained for Newton, needed a rollout of two new sandwiches Hernandez had designed, needed a plan for the one year anniversary of Spoon, and needed the reports required for each meeting with Spoon's forty percent partners, Mr. Klein and Mr. Soukup.

And he needed Jenny. In the beginning, she had interfered with his plan, had drawn him from a pure focus on establishing and growing Spoon.

But not now. Spuhn slept less, ate more quickly, worked hard and long on Spoon – around the times Jenny was free for a phone call, for a run, for resting against him, for kissing and touching that would bring the two of them to a throbbing, gasping legs and arms-wound one.

A need to visit the other Spoon locations, to be in Iowa City on the way back?

He had no retort, just a grin, when Hernandez said, "You are pussy-whipped, man. I'm hearin' wedding bells."

If it wasn't Spuhn, if he sat on his hands, plenty of others were available. Jenny's friendly way and her head-turning loveliness would give her no lack of chances. She drew looks wherever she and Spuhn traveled. Tonti, whose randy thoughts brightened his pink, freckled face whenever anyone in a blouse was nearby, treated Jenny with unusual respect. Her self-assurance and her beauty cowed him as much as her association with Spuhn. Not so Clayton, who took the striking, athletic woman as only a date the first time Jenny appeared with Spuhn at a campus party. In the manner of a campus playboy working a catch and release stream, Clayton went to work on her with talk and dimpled smiles that made her lastingly wary of him. Even in the midst of that attempt, she caught him glancing beyond her, once for a study of Marjorie's bosom. As Jenny learned about Clayton, she wondered, too, about the knee problem that seemed no impediment to anything but his eligibility for the draft.

With increasing frequency, about once a month, Spuhn's schedule included a speech or an interview marking and expanding his reputation as a young Iowa businessman. The newspaper articles amused Mr. Klein, who had his own mixed history with reporters, and stirred no comment at all from Mr. Soukup.

"What do you know?" Mr. Klein said, pointedly folding the *Evening Times* for a reading of "At Work with Successful Young

Business Founder", an article complete with photos taken of Spuhn during a day. "I didn't know you shit roses."

Curiosity and notoriety also brought former St. Sebastian classmates for their own sampling of Spuhn's enterprise. In the company of another Iowa couple and a tall, blond-haired Iowa athlete who kept his arm around her, Mary Siemons came within weeks of Spoon's opening. The man, same age as Spuhn, shook hands with a strong grip and smiled when Mary introduced Spuhn as her "classmate from St. Sebastian."

All four at the table signed up for Spoon's birthday list. Mary returned with her friend Fran Hasenburg and the birthday mailing in mid-February, a day Jenny had come to visit and help. The restaurant was busy and, in addition, Spuhn had a two o'clock meeting with Mr. Klein, so conversation beyond hello was spare. Mary admired Spoon and Spuhn congratulated his former girlfriend on the position she had accepted with an accounting firm in Mason City. Whether Mary had come with any specific hope beyond the fanning of an old flame, Spuhn could tell she knew what she needed from the sight of Jenny close to him, their eyes on one another, their conversations spoken sometimes into an ear.

Mr. Hayes, always friendly, warmly enthusiastic about Spuhn and the busy restaurant, came with another St. Sebastian teacher or two whenever an assembly or other school event put a hole in the midday schedule.

In late January, on a day of icicles growing and snowcover shrinking in a sunny thaw, Greg Benson, on the other hand, planted himself at a table like the government authority he meant to be. From the kitchen, Spuhn saw Benson pivot his broad-shouldered form and take stock of the restaurant. To the amusement of another man and the embarrassment of a stiff young woman, Benson struck a dismissive air as he put sweet, hardworking Bonnie through her waitress paces. From the buttons the three wore, everyone knew they were supporting the Republican gubernatorial candidate Robert D. Ray. Benson still had a button supporting the newly inaugurated Richard M. Nixon.

Spuhn's duties made it impossible for him to avoid moving among the tables, so Benson, in the haughty role of a customer, was able to pounce. Would Spuhn get a clean water glass for him? Where did Spoon buy its beef? Looking meaningfully at the glass in his hand, Benson asked about the cleanliness of Spoon's kitchen.

Pretending that they were catching up, Benson confirmed that Spuhn had no degree beyond high school while Benson himself was studying law at Iowa.

Holding Spuhn in conversation, Benson said loudly he had heard that the majority – was it sixty percent? – of restaurants fail. Was Spuhn going to go back to school if that happened at his restaurant?

Spuhn excused himself, not before firing through a radiant smile, "You know, I hear law school's not so easy, either. A whole lot of people flunk out, don't they?"

Benson sent his meal back with a complaint about temperature, bothered the young waitress for ice and napkins, for uncreased birthday celebration forms in place of some he had smudged with ketchup, and left her coins for a tip.

In contrast to what he said about Spoon and its food, Benson began visiting with regularity, most often showing up with other campaign workers in tow. Sometimes, he removed his jacket and hung it over the chair back with a movement that exaggerated the show of his exposed arms.

Annoyed as he was when Benson appeared, Spuhn became practical. He used Benson as a training aid and rewarded waitresses who coolly took proper care of "a big asshole of a customer."

Each time Benson finished and left, they all checked and then laughed about the pittance Benson put down that day for a tip.

On the day Benson appeared with a stylish date for claiming of his birthday celebration benefit, Spuhn saw that Bonnie sat Benson and the well-dressed young woman with the streaked blond hair right next to a table of three westbound New Yorkers who had made their own table a stick-in-the eye forward camp of granny glasses, mutton chops, mustaches and beads. Their entire presence a sneer at Benson and his politics, the long-haired travelers giggled while ordering and eating three of Hernandez's Banana Splitacular creations.

The laughter sounded through the table area: psychotic screeching to Benson, music to Spuhn, Bonnie, Hernandez and the others.

Along the interstate, the positions were reversed. To be in a car along an Iowa highway was to be in Benson's contentious world, full of debates and claims that held small interest for Spuhn. The fury and hardness in the signs for the Republican Ray or the Democrat Robert D. Fulton or for any candidate brought to mind red-haired, weights-muscled Benson, always appearing in Spuhn's thoughts with eyes aflame, arms waving, and his round mouth hissing with one accusation or platitude after another.

The more talk, the less action Spuhn expected.

Absorbed in his schedule of appointments and his thoughts, busily leaving and entering the road for pay phone calls, Spuhn passed among the boards without much reflection on the images beyond the distaste of their association with Benson.

Fortunately, the end of the national election made boards available for Spoon's needs, including the restaurant's one year anniversary in seven months. Early on a morning before the restaurants opened, Spuhn met with Mr. Klein for discussion of celebration plans. During Columbus Day weekend, Tonti would handwalk through a gauntlet of dignitaries – and news reporters, TV camera crews – into each restaurant. Special meals and pricing would attract children and families. Free coffee and Hernandez's straw-berry-rhubarb pie dabbed with fresh, whipped cream would coax interstate travelers.

And each quarter after that, Spoon would open at a new inter-state location on a path to Omaha.

"Your friend Ronnie is goin' to have some busy hands," Mr. Soukup said over the phone.

Busy hands were fine. Without telling Tonti or explaining to Hernandez, Mr. Klein and Mr. Soukup, Spuhn had become careful about Tonti's readiness to do more than walk with his busy hands. The entertaining, friendly handwalker was good for business but his unfettered impulses also veered toward actions that could put Spoon in the news and then in decline. Spuhn could imagine Tonti doing more than flirt with the women - and, too often, the teen-aged girls - who liked provoking him in return.

At every event, Spuhn kept Tonti in sight of himself or a sensible Spoon employee such as the level-headed young waitress Claire. At the end of Tonti's part, the watchful Claire or one of the men immediately drove Tonti somewhere away from the temptation of the women. If Tonti found one or another of them later, at least none of it would be official restaurant business.

Fortunately, the transient Tonti acted wed to his role with the restaurant group. The showman in him looked forward to Spuhn's requests for appearances at stores and events. Among his Alcoa friends, Tonti's appearances in the news gave him a celebrity that let him slip the traces of the plate mill's schedule. The supervisor found ways of accommodating his amusing, likable worker as the restaurant group drew him close.

For a reason Spuhn couldn't fathom, Jenny tolerated in Tonti or Hernandez what disgusted her in Clayton.

"Tonti's just as horny as Clayton is," Spuhn said.

Jenny called Tonti a puppy; Clayton, a wolf.

"Tonti is what he is," Jenny said. "Clayton is just full of himself."

At a later time, the conversation came into Jenny's mind with the realization that Clayton bothered her for the way he assumed other lives, even Spuhn's life, without the work of being Spuhn. Strip Clayton of his dimple and good looks and self-assurance and nothing remained, just a chameleon's ability to take on whatever hue he needed for satisfaction of a want. Slice Tonti or Hernandez or Spuhn and they were uniform up down and sideways.

On that evening, Spuhn didn't care about Tonti or Clayton. First quarter results, even with the January dip, surpassed plan, Jenny and her father had held the boards Spoon needed, and Spuhn was with Jenny in the apartment she shared with Marjorie Haas near the west side of campus. Hoo-rah!

He would wake early for reading of the packet Mr. Klein wanted him to study before the next afternoon's meeting of the Klein Incorporated board.

While the majority of the meeting concerned the status of present developments and discussion of two new ones, first, a mixed-use hotel and retail and apartments project at a Bettendorf site near I-80 and then construction of a 110,000 square foot distribution facility in Cedar Rapids, Mr. Klein touched quickly on Spoon and the plans for new locations reaching to the border at Omaha before the end of 1971: There would be ten, maybe eleven operating if the folks in Earlham got sensible about their price: here (Newton), here (Des Moines), here (West Des Moines), here (Lorah), here (Yorkshire), here (Council Bluffs).

The map on the easel showing Spoon's cross-Iowa path hung in Spuhn's attention as he shook hands and talked with the other five board members: a sensible, calm lawyer who had long been Mr. Klein's adviser and was now engaged in securing the Bettendorf

site, an owner of an engineering firm associated with Klein Construction in many projects, the chief operating officer of St. Luke's
Hospital, and two private investors who were frequent golf partners
of Mr. Klein.

Spuhn was anxious to leave but waited at Mr. Klein's signal
while all the good-byes concluded.

Immediately, as they stood in the hallway at the exit from Klein
Construction, Mr. Klein, excited and happy, gripped Spuhn at the
elbow and said as if telling a confidence, "Nels Benson called about
Spoon catering the big party he's throwing at his house for the
Republican muckety-mucks. They're from all over the state, the
backers of the Robert D. Ray campaign."

Spuhn answered with only a smile as thoughts came: Nels
Benson, Greg Benson's dad. Greg Benson's home. Greg Benson.

"He wants Tonti to walk on his hands."

Benson, Benson, Benson. That shitbag. A thousand, pesty
phone calls and Benson at the end of every one of them.

"The impression I get from Nels is that there will be a number
of these, for the Republican legislative candidates, too. They like
the way Spoon is growing, the way Spoon is Iowa."

"Sounds good. Outstanding," Spuhn said, accepting Mr. Klein's
strong, pleased handshake.

"You have the number. Call Benson at the bank tomorrow and
he'll give you the details."

The map of Iowa, the six, maybe seven new locations, pressed
over the Benson news in Spuhn's mind the rest of the evening.

As Hernandez, mildly high, played happily with some frying
meat and potatoes mixed with other vegetables and they both
listened to Janice Joplin, Spuhn grew excited about his plan: Tonti
would walk on his hands across Iowa, from the Mississippi River to
the Missouri.

Spuhn couldn't wait to tell Jenny the idea.

CHAPTER 21

I had a girl, looked good in blue
Honey, honey
I had a girl, looked good in blue
Baby, baby
I had a girl, looked good in blue
She could make a fool out of you

At the top of the crest, behind the onlookers, Dennis Spuhn could have been watching a Kentucky Derby horse, his horse, as it smoothly, splendidly carried itself and its rider toward glory. Solidly hands down, his feet bobbing over his flushed head, Ron Tonti, Spuhn's horse, was rhythmically mounting the cleanly swept sidewalk on the west side of Brady Street toward the finish of Day 2 at Palmer College of Chiropractic.

Just in front of Spuhn was a crowd of merry college students.

Encouraging Tonti at the edge of the street was Jesus Hernandez, excitedly extending his arms and using his bulk as protection against the happy young crowd.

"Wowie zowie, man, you're almost there. Almost." Hernandez's voice rang above the other calls. Pulling his numb left foot into place with swings of his hip, Hernandez moved up the hill to check arrangements at the finish, then returned to Tonti and resumed guardianship of Tonti's path.

Could Tonti's three year hands down journey across Iowa have begun with more success than it had this day and the day before?

Sweetening the start for Spuhn was the satisfaction of thwarting the obstruction that good for nothing waste of space Benson had tried to create – as usual, with the influence of his father on a John Birch ally somewhere in the upper ranks of the Midwest region of the U.S. Department of Transportation. A handwalk across the Mississippi River and then along the Brady Street sidewalk constituting interference with interstate commerce because Brady Street was also U.S. Highway 61?

"Sit tight, don't get your shorts in a knot," Mr. Klein had said to his agitated young partner.

Calmly enjoying the ceremony of it, Mr. Klein then called the Mayor's office, pulled the official from a meeting, and set in motion a pair of phone calls that, within the hour, brought word that Benson's hope had been squelched. With a chuckle, Mr. Klein commented that "They might vote with old man Benson, but they don't much like the bossy son of a bitch. That helps."

Spuhn hadn't caught sight of Benson at any time, so maybe Benson was in Iowa City and attending his law classes. He could be on the moon, Spuhn knew, and still be buffeted by all the attention generated by the beginning of Spoon's promotion, a three year walk on hands, from the Rock Island bank of the Mississippi River to the Omaha side 313 miles away, depending on decisions they would make about the exact route. Turn on a radio, watch a TV, read papers as varied as the *Des Moines Register* and the *Rock Island Argus* this second day and Tonti's image, all the association with the expanding group of Spoon restaurants, would be inescapable. Repeatedly, happily, transfixingly inescapable.

Mr. Klein was hearing from friends everywhere. That morning, lucky to catch his son spending a night in the apartment, Mr. Hernandez had called Jesus from Coral Gables after hearing something on CBS radio. Each time Spuhn returned to the restaurant or the Klein Construction office, he found new messages that Jenny had called between her classes. Drawn to class, needed at the restaurant, Spuhn and Jenny held each call, ended them reluctantly. Spuhn would go to Iowa City that evening.

The April weather, too, was propitious with sunny temperatures in the fifties and sometimes into the sixties, the kind of weather that brought winter weary Iowans outside. The students delighting in the handwalk were delighting, too, in sunshine fit for the discarding of winter gear and gloom. Trees had begun to bud, yellow forsythia and crocus and daffodils had appeared. The dawn found fishermen working the Mississippi from their silvery boats or from the levee wall containing the so far unthreatening rise of all the water flowing from the northern snow melt.

All around, there was a mood of cleansing. The Presidential election had ended, most of the campaign signs and billboards had gone away, and the ongoing demonstrations about Vietnam had become routine enough that, along with the daily actions of new President Nixon and his advisers, the coming and going, the battling and dying of soldiers as well as the outbursts in segregated cities had retreated in a consciousness of spring and restoration.

The air was clean to breathe, the sun pleasant to feel on him while Spuhn watched the preparations unfolding into a success. Making the handwalk a second day news event at the Palmer stop, approximately 1.7 miles along the route, there were two news photographers and a tall young cameraman setting up for KDRI-TV. In front of them, along a path between lines of high-spirited college and high school students, some curious city workers and passers-by soaking up spring sun, Tonti had a determined, pink face as he worked the last couple of hundred feet toward the day's finish.

At the finish mark, indicated with a low-hanging red crepe ribbon suspended between two Spoon logo placards, Spuhn waited with a welcoming committee of four Spoon customers celebrating their birthdays. They were two high school students, a St. Ambrose College junior, and a dark-haired young mother in a tight beige skirt and a short black coat.

Hernandez came up beside the woman. After watching her as she attempted to comfort the troubled newborn raising its red, pained face from the diaper on the mother's shoulder, Hernandez took the baby, rewrapped the little pink-gowned girl in her blanket and settled her against his own shoulder. Bouncing lightly, he talked to the child, massaged her back and laughed with the young mother when the girl suddenly released a loud, milky burp into the diaper Hernandez had moved to his shoulder.

"Hey, Jesus," Spuhn called to him. "Are they coming with the food?"

Hernandez handed the bundled girl back to the woman. "That's a rog. I called and talked to Mary. Ten minutes ago. They were putting it all in Chet's car."

Spuhn pictured the reliable high school student and the '53 Chevy with its lumpy applications of Black Magic where Chet was repairing quarter panels thinned and pocked by winters of salt. They'd know when Chet was coming near: if Chet went to as much trouble with his engine as he did with the sound of it, the Chevy's hot tires would be melting ruts in Brady Street.

Another trio from the restaurant would follow, equipped for handing out discount coupons along with forms for registration of birthdays.

With Jesus responsible for watching over Tonti when the day's walk concluded, Spuhn would be free to pull away from the Palmer College marker as soon as the *Morning Democrat* and *Evening*

Times writers obtained the quotations they needed from him and as soon as the KDRI-TV cameraman had his gear disassembled. Even with the extra time they had given Tonti when he rested at the five-sixths mark, even with the slope of Brady Street's rise from downtown, Tonti was arriving at the Palmer Chiropractic mark nearly 15 minutes ahead of plan.

To Spuhn's relief, the cameras were ready in time to record the steady, red-faced Tonti breaking the day two tape and righting himself as the four Spoon birthday celebrants, joined by boisterous college students, encircled him. The cameras went to work again as the Spoon delivery arrived and the four-person crew equipped Tonti with a perfect tray of Spoon's most popular order: hamburger, onion rings, and choice of soda. Tonti took swigs of his Coke and remembered to hold the cup with Spoon logo visible as the cameras worked. Just as on the day before, Tonti was remembering the instructions Jenny had given him. He had exasperated her with his inattention, his gazing around the Spoon dining room at all the young women eating or working there, but he had done what Jenny said to do.

Amid the happy press of those congratulating and calling Tonti's name, Spuhn saw Tonti catching his breath and showing the crowd a grin that could have been used for a dental chart. Tonti took a swig of the Coke and then, to the applause of the students, as the young *Evening Times* and *Morning Democrat* reporters began asking questions, he took a dramatic bite of an onion ring.

Spuhn worked his way to Tonti's side.

"You going to be able to go across the whole state?"

Tonti's happy gaze flicked across the *Times* reporter's big gold hoop earrings and fixed on her eyes.

"With bells on, chére'. Get youself to Omaha," he replied. "You just watch."

"What do you think about while you're walking on your hands?" *The Morning Democrat* writer asked.

"All kinds of things," Tonti said. "I wonder whether this little darlin' is goin' to be there in Omaha to meet me."

The students pressing around them laughed.

"Mr. Spuhn, what thoughts come to you as you watch Mr. Tonti?"

Was Jenny passing questions to the intent young writer with the twisted paisley tie? Spuhn lunged into the promotional opportunity.

"I think about how fast we're opening new Spoon restaurants all the way across Iowa, so we are ready for Ronnie Tonti and all our customers when he gets there."

The TV cameraman spoke. "Mr. Tonti, can I get a shot of your hands? Just hold them toward me."

When Tonti obliged, showing the flat of his hands toward the lense, the *Times* writer said, "They're filthy."

"That's good Iowa dirt, chère," Tonti answered, turning the display of his blackened palms and fingers directly toward her. "A man's got to get his hands dirty if he's goin' to go anywhere in this world."

"Rich Iowa dirt, that's what Spoon is sitting on," Spuhn said. "All across Iowa by 1971."

Afterward, delighted by the course of the interview and a schedule with twenty minutes suddenly available, Spuhn elected to stop at his family's home on his way to the Brady Street Spoon.

Spuhn's father was away on his schedule of calls. Spuhn saw no evidence of triumph at cards, nor evidence of any play: no new stereo or other living room prize. Michael and Veronica were at school. Spuhn found only his mother – and three loaves of newly baked bread – at the house.

"Go ahead, there's one for us. This one," his mother said, indicating the loaf she considered imperfect, the one with a fold in the crust along its top. "The other ones are going to Mrs. Kelly. She has family staying with her."Spuhn settled on a stool at the counter in front of the loaves and watched his mother cut slices for him. He remembered Mrs. Kelly, the widow who had always bought magazine subscriptions, raffle tickets and whatever else the schools and baseball teams sent for selling by neighborhood children.

"We need this recipe for the restaurant," Spuhn said.

"I told Jesus he can have it," she said. "Remind him to come over for a lesson."

Spuhn looked at the clock over the sink, saw that the noontime news program was underway.

Taking the plate of buttered bread, he said "Thanks" around a first mouthful and moved into the living room, where his mother had been working on a new numbered painting of a mare with a colt.

After showing Tonti at his handwalking a couple of times, the KDRI-TV news announcer arrived at the story of the Day 2 walk. As he watched, Tonti remarked the elements: display of the Spoon logo on the cup in Tonti's hand, name "Spoon" once, twice.

"What's the matter?" Spuhn's mother asked. Spuhn's expression had soured.

The news report had made Spoon and the handwalk a platform for a mischievous consideration of Iowa's sidewalk and roadway surfaces. Over the slowed image of Tonti's extended hands came the sure voice of a St. Ambrose biologist fulfilling a life's dream as he opined about the composition of Iowa's surface. "And that's the dirt on that one," newsman Charles Fletcher concluded.

"Go to hell," Spuhn said to the television. Just the same, a thank you letter wrapped around Spoon coupons would go to the newsman and the assignment editor the next morning.

"What?" Spuhn's mother asked.

"Nothing. I've got to go." Spuhn stood up, kissed his mother's cheek and thanked her again for the bread.

While she wrapped two more buttered slices for him, Spuhn slipped a roll of bills, enough for two weeks of groceries, into the purse his mother kept on a chair near the back door. Used to the practice now, neither would mention the help Spuhn had begun to supply each month. For Spuhn, the contribution was a satisfying confirmation of the success that was separating him from so many others.

So was the used yellow Corvette convertible he had bought from one of the Klein board members, an easy-going insurance agent who traded cars each year and now wanted a Porsche.

While driving the short distance to stop at the restaurant, Spuhn twice pulled around and passed cars holding to the speed limit. Along the way, a WOC radio news report at the half hour made conventional, pleasing note of the second day of the handwalk "sponsored by the restaurant chain Spoon".

What he saw and heard at the restaurant maintained the lift in Spuhn's spirits. The tables were full, with other customers waiting in line and amiably visiting with those they knew among the patrons and the staff. Recognizing Spuhn, many greeted him on his way toward the office at the back of the kitchen. As he passed through the customer area, Spuhn saw the displays, everything properly mounted, with a map of the Iowa handwalk route, the present and future Spoon locations, and some photographs of Spoon customers greeting Ronnie Tonti on the Iowa side of the bridge.

The phone messages Spuhn found, mostly congratulations from Klein board members and his parents, were calls he could sort through and return from Iowa City.

Top down, enjoying the sun on his face and the wind tousling his hair, Spuhn drove to Iowa City in the left lane.

He found in Iowa City what he had seen in Davenport: the sunny weather, the handwalk news reports, Hernandez's popular recipes, everything had the restaurant busy. The manager, an all-business twenty-two year old who had worked three years for Howard Johnson's before pouncing on the rumor of Spoon's expansion, had seen to the same handwalk display as the one in Davenport. As earnestly as Spuhn wanted Tonti's handwalk to succeed, Susan Walters wanted it to succeed on schedule. Spuhn was careful when he talked dates with her: the drill instructor of a manager would expect Tonti, bright-eyed and bushy-tailed, punctually leading a column of customers into the restaurant on whatever date that lodged in her mind.

Business concluded, Spuhn said to the manager, "You know where to reach me."

"Yes. Your girlfriend's."

Yes. "Yes. Your girlfriend's."

Yes.

"I thought maybe your car broke down," Jenny said. Marjorie had arranged to be out of the way: at class and then with a friend at the library.

Enjoying the tease, Jenny continued as she moved toward him and put her arms around his neck. "Or maybe you forgot the directions." Mischief in her big brown eyes, she looked into his.

Spuhn laughed, pulled her against him, and kissed her. Her hair on the side of his face smelled richly of her soap, of her. Her gold hoop earrings were cool. She was wearing jeans and the old Marine fatigue shirt she had taken from him for a painting smock.

"Not now," Jenny said, reaching behind to push his hands down.

Reluctantly, he kept his arms around her, but relaxed them.

"Why?"

"I have something I want you to see."

"I have something I want to see, too," Spuhn said.

"I know you do, but you have to wait. This is important."

First, Spuhn had calls to make from the phone in the small living room, nearly twenty minutes of just-checking-in contacts with each of the four Spoon locations. With Spuhn's fingers on her knee, one of her hands on his, Jenny settled in a big, cream-colored easy chair near the ottoman Spuhn was using and resumed reading the assigned chapters in Abraham Maslow's *Theory of Human Motivation*.

Spuhn pressed in his conversations, conducted them with opening warmth, a mutual delight in the handwalk or the response to an offering, and then moved into a curt I'm talking, you're listening, you're doing set of commands that made Jenny wonder. That was Spuhn: busy, moving, looking ahead, and still a Marine in the way he gave instructions as orders. A couple of calls were parallel: Jenny heard him tell the Brady Street manager the same task he had just given to the manager of the restaurant in the Amana Colonies.

Spuhn's wavy brown hair was no longer quite Marine Corps, though. She had made him alter his haircuts so that he met expectations his business associates had for a groomed young executive but still pleased her with the way his hair grew in long curls and the way it passed over the tops of his ears. Standing up, she combed his hair from his forehead and moved his phone calling to a conclusion.

"No, let's go," she said, pushing his hands away from her waist. "I want to show you."

He relented and went with her down the squeaking stairs and out to the street.

A spurt of Corvette power, enough to make her hair fly and her face light up, and the two of them were at the Fine Arts building, on their way up the stairs to the studio space where Jenny kept her work.Spuhn's delight at being in Jenny's company was fierce but, still, thoughts of Spoon and the handwalk flickered in his mind. Tonti should wash his hands at the end of each portion of each day's walk, never eat anything before they were clean: Spuhn would tell Hernandez in a phone call that evening. Was the weather forecast holding? Spuhn would have that checked.

"Here's the first one," Jenny said, turning a canvas so it faced Spuhn.

He would have done cartwheels over a stick drawing but he didn't need to pretend. What Jenny had done was not completely intelligible to him, an arrangement of the Eiffel Tower posing on a stool for an artist at work on a canvas of the Empire State Building, but he could see in the composition of artist's hand and brush and palette in the foreground, the canvas in the middle and the posing tower in the background a skilled execution. He knew from watching Jenny work and knew from teachers and other art students that she had talent.

The intensity of Spuhn's examination pleased Jenny, who began turning other canvases toward him.

He had seen Jenny poking at, adding to a canvas while she concentrated on a shadow or a shape, a color in the arrangement of fruit or a bouquet of flowers. In the paintings she showed Spuhn now, the near image was of the fingers of an artist with a palette in them. The tip of a brush worked at the near canvas and, beyond that, the posed model sat. But, in each case, the canvas taking shape did not relate to the painting modeling on an easel or to a person posed on a stool. In Jenny's paintings, Adolph Hitler posed for Josef Stalin; the Mona Lisa posed for the President's wife Pat Nixon; Bob Dylan filled a canvas in front of . . .

"That's Rembrandt," Jenny said, seeing how the image of a young man in a plumed hat puzzled Spuhn. "One of his self-portraits."

Spuhn knew as he looked from one painting to the next that Jenny had a legitimate claim on space amid the work considered "art." His own experience of art was small and accidental: a family trip to Chicago, one that indulged his mother with a visit to the Art Institute before they went to Comiskey Park for a White Sox game against the Senators. On television, he saw scenes set in museums or saw bits of programs about artists and works. In magazines and in textbooks, he saw images of the Mona Lisa, even some that made Jenny's Rembrandt look familiar.

"I like these," he said. "Man."

"You don't think they're too far out?" she asked.

The question puzzled him; wasn't she the artist? Wasn't she the one who determined? "No," he said. "The Eiffel Tower like someone modeling, that's a funny idea."

"They're going to put these in the student show. I have to finish two more before May fifteenth," Jenny said. "They're called 'Compare and Contrast', like the exams all the English profs give: 'Compare and contrast Shakespeare to Mark Twain, compare and contrast *Oliver Twist* to *Moby Dick*."

With that assistance, Spuhn could continue. "So compare and contrast the Eiffel Tower to the Empire State Building."

"And Pat Nixon to the Mona Lisa."

They both laughed, their eyes on Jenny's work as if they were young parents admiring their sleeping child.

"Cool. Really cool.'

Their hips touched, then pressed. Spuhn's arm went over Jenny's shoulder. His fingers played in her hair.

"The next one's going to be Elvis Presley and Frank Sinatra, maybe a hound dog."

Spuhn laughed, kissed her ear.

She pulled her head away. "Then I still need one. It's going to be like Mayor Daley and someone. I'm not sure. Abe Lincoln, that Gilbert painting of George Washington. I'm not sure. Like Abby Hoffman, for some reason."

"Man, that would be like crazy, like just buku crazy."

In the car, no matter the top was down, spilling over with excitement about one another, their beauty, the upward slopes of their futures, they made out before Jenny convinced Spuhn, "Not here."

With Marjorie generously absent, Jenny's apartment was "here" for making love and then being in love, naked and caressing one another as they spoke their plans.

Beyond the series of canvasses she was preparing for the student show, Jenny had ideas, ideas about how art should be and how artists could use their talent so that everyone could draw on art for empathy and inspiration in the whole community, like in everything.

Spoon was growing, would be across the state in three years, maybe go beyond, into Nebraska, one coast to the other. Without speaking the thought, unable to articulate the feeling, Spuhn savored the satisfying awareness of the relationships forming with Mr. Klein and the business community he knew. At the age of 23, Spuhn was beginning to arrive in offices and meetings and events with his introduction already made – by Mr. Klein, by interviews, by comments during golf games and dinners about someone, about this kid going somewhere. Mr. Klein made sure that Spuhn appeared with him at Chamber of Commerce breakfasts and other business gatherings where one civic official or business leader after another came to say hello.

While Jenny showered, Spuhn made short, checking on things calls. When they went out for the rice and some vegetables Jenny needed for a Chinese dish, the night sky was clear as the warmth of the April day fell into the crease of winter and spring.

At the checkout counter, a smiling woman still given to wearing her fading red hair in pigtails made conversation. "I like Chinese food, too. Do you and your husband have that a lot?"

"Yes, sometimes," Jenny answered.

"It's very healthy."

Spuhn felt proud, proud again when some passing students, loudly together but each dismally single, stared at Jenny holding his hand and then looked enviously at him before averting their eyes.

"Peace," said one, quickly making the gesture with two fingers up.

Jenny smiled. Spuhn nodded. Together, Spuhn's arm over her shoulder, their conversation merry with school, Spoon, reasons to smile, laugh, touch, they returned to Jenny's apartment.

The next morning, awake before his travel alarm would ring at 4 a.m., Spuhn showered, shaved, kissed Jenny on the ear, shaped her blanket on her, and hurried toward the meetings and handwalking activities awaiting him in Davenport. Less than two miles along the way, before reaching I-80, he pulled into the empty parking lot of a Kroger's, made a tight circle and sped back.

"Spuhn?" Jenny said, not opening her eyes or turning toward him.

He sat next to her and lifted her toward him.

"Jenny, I want to marry you," he said.

She woke.

"I want to marry you, too," she said, as Spuhn began to kiss her. "Oh, I need to brush my teeth."

He kissed her, then stood up.

"I need to get to the restaurant. Go back to sleep."

"Spuhn?"

Jenny kicked free of her blanket but Spuhn was already leaving the apartment before she was wrapped in a robe and at the door.

She left messages for him twice during the morning, missed one from him, but they didn't talk until the restaurant had finished a noon rush heightened by the promotion of Tonti's handwalking.

In the meantime, just before Spuhn left to meet Tonti and Hernandez and Tonti's excited followers at the 2.4 mile rest stop, a pleased Mr. Klein had called for his own midday check.

Mr. Klein had read the newspaper articles, seen the photos, heard about the TV report.

"Hell with it. You're telling me, they said the name right."

Mr. Klein paused. When he spoke, Spuhn heard a chuckle in his tone – along with a caution.

"We got a lot of miles to go yet, a lot of time. Think Mr. Ronnie Tonti's goin' to be able to keep his pecker in his pants all the way across Iowa?"

CHAPTER 22

He'll hug you and he'll kiss you,
And treat you like a queen.
There is no better Fighting Man:
The United States Marine!

Jesus Hernandez had met Joe Yoder, had met him among many
others who had been Dennis Spuhn's schoolmates and teammates.
Hernandez's likable manner made him a welcome newcomer
among the friends whose histories reached back to Boy Scout
campouts and Mr. Hayes' freshman math class, to seeing Spuhn
riding a bike with his sister Veronica or brother Mike on the handle-
bars, to surprising some coy St. Sebastian's girls with cannonballs at
Lake Herman. Among all those, Joe Yoder was one handshake and
one familiar face as Hernandez joined the founding and growing of
Spoon.

Just the same, when the bachelor party moved from Stubby's
Pool Paradise to cool, dark, pinball game-pinging Town Tap and
then to a middle of the night assembly at Joe Yoder's gravesite,
Hernandez endorsed Jim Clayton's idea with the insistent force of
someone who could have been Yoder's best friend.

"Yesss. Fuck, yes," he roared, putting a fist in the air and then
washing everyone else with a grin that was all merriment and

272 – BY TOM FIGEL

coaxing. His black hair shone in the lights of the cemetery. His smile was white and luminous.

His eyes were brilliant from the grass he and Szabo had been sharing. The two of them had the giddy, bright-eyed look of things plugged into the Scott County power grid. Their faces set and reset according to the amusing, disconnected thoughts they enjoyed and Spuhn abhorred. The willingness to let go of plan and control for lost hours of careening insights from marijuana or acid was, in Spuhn's eyes, not much different from letting money float away on a Mississippi current.

"Fuckin' A, as Yoder would say." Szabo, too, was in favor.

So was Clayton's law school friend Slick.

Rolly and Lee had to be at a Klein Construction site in less than six hours. They would, but they couldn't.

The rest of them then – Spuhn, Hernandez, Szabo, Clayton and Slick – would drive to Chicago, follow Clayton to the forty-first floor observation level of the Prudential Building, and, in memory of Joe Yoder, moon Vietnam. They'd moon Vietnam and the horse it rode in on. From the height of the Prudential Building, they'd give the finger to Vietnam, the war, the draft, and all the sadness of Yoder's death.

Then they'd drive back to Davenport in time for the wedding rehearsal and the dinner.

"You promise to get me back? No screwing around?" Spuhn demanded.

With Hernandez organizing the complicity of Spoon's staff and then assisting Clayton and Szabo, the bachelor party group had snatched Spuhn from the Brady Street location. All evening, Spuhn had been restless and painfully unproductive. Now his jaw set and his face clouded as he listened to silly plans being made by drunks.

"Spuhn, you're not scheduled to be here the rest of this week. You're getting married," Rick answered to Spuhn's protests at the start of the outing. Efficient and responsible, Rick liked chances to show the owners how he could manage, same as the way he once showed his father he could raise a champion calf. Each time Spuhn added something to his posted mantras of instruction and encouragement, Rick took the phrase to heart and did his best to adopt in his own manner the determination shown in "Make dust or eat dust," "How badly do you want it?" and, two days before, "You get what you work for, not what you wish for."

Spuhn had anticipated the kidnapping and planned for it. With phone calls over the time of the wedding and honeymoon, he'd be able to monitor Spoon as well as Tonti's handwalking, now taking advantage of summer warmth and the entire state's encouragement.

"We'll be back. I have to go to work at five," said Slick.

"Fuckin' A" Spuhn heard from all around. Yoder's reflexive answer was the night's mantra.

They had the use of the new blue Camaro Clayton had borrowed from his older brother. Spuhn, who had spent the evening drinking Tab while Clayton drank some beer and the others drank too much beer, did the driving while giggly, excited Hernandez homed in on radio stations, Slick dozed, Clayton talked, and Szabo said at times, "This is so far out. This is insane."

When they stopped at a gas station near Princeton for the use of a restroom, Hernandez and Szabo, agiggle and ravenous, bought candy bars and capsules of Pez candies.

As he drove, Spuhn let his own thoughts flow, many of Jenny, languorous and lovely, close. Marty Tomczak, the burly officer, the Saigon patron so deft with military process, was due the next night. Now a captain assigned to Pentagon duty, Tomczak was certain to show up with hopes of a bridge game and a delight in introducing his own wife and their young children, a boy and a girl, the four on a cross-country vacation drive. Spuhn imagined the droll banter, the absent look the cagey Tomczak would throw over a mind locking on the combinations in the cards. In the black, country quiet over queues of silvery, grinding semis, mileage markers made Spuhn think of Tonti and the handwalk, now past Williamsburg, almost one-third of the way across Iowa. Heavy rain had only taken out two days of the handwalking, less of a delay than Spuhn had budgeted. Most of all, Tonti had caught fire, even had to be dissuaded from surpassing one day's progress with an astonishing distance the next day.

For Ronnie Tonti, the handwalk was a gymnastic event.

Spuhn, though, was attentive to choreography. Tonti had to be seen. He had to arrive on main streets and, most of all, at Spoon locations when patrons and reporters were most likely to assemble, celebrate and act. And Spoon, soon operating in Newton as well as Grinnell, Williamsburg, Iowa City and Davenport, had to keep the westward pace that would give Tonti places to arrive.

The honor guard of college students on summer vacation, Jenny's idea, worked. Tonti enjoyed the companionship of the pairs of students staying with him, giving him company and protecting him as, red-faced and determined, he made his way, approximately 87 hundredths of a mile per day, six hours a day. Now richly tanned and attuned to perils, the mildly starstruck students known as Tonti Tenders positioned themselves so that Tonti had some protection from passing cars and even from farm dogs roaring out to the roadway from rutted drives between rows of oak or maple.

The students Jenny had chosen took seriously, too, their evening stewardship. When the day ended in late afternoon, a driver returned Tonti to Dottie's Davenport apartment and sometimes went with the two of them for settling in at a small tavern where Tonti's open merriness and celebrity gave him an admiring court. The bartenders had Spuhn's number. Except for one night in early May, Tonti's flirting and philandering had been within the loose bounds of his understanding with Dottie. On that night, Spuhn was able to retrieve Tonti from two agreeable young policemen and then keep watch over him as Tonti slept and sobered up on the couch in Spuhn's apartment.

They were within 70 miles of Chicago's Loop when Spuhn and his sleeping passengers pulled into a rest stop close to Morris, Illinois. There, Spuhn and the others slept until, at dawn light, the nearby sound of a semi's diesel engine and the hiss of its setting brakes woke them.

Spuhn wanted to call Jenny, just wanted to hear her, but wouldn't do that so early in the day. Jenny was in a house astir with happy activity: on Wednesday evening, Jenny had met Anna's train in Burlington, IA, the first visit of the sisters in more than a year. Neither cured of cancer nor suffering from it, five pounds more voluptuous and with brown hair dulled more than the last time, Anna arrived showing nothing in the quiet set of her smile and the attentive look of her blue eyes but the effects of the long ride from Omaha. She moved her body carefully. Anna was the beauty she had been at Iowa and then in Minnesota, but without the same center of things manner. Anna called him Tank. Tank made her happy, Jenny could see.

Then an Iowa friend arrived with her husband and infant son. The newborn stirred Anna's sadness about Jan and also put her parents to proving their mettle as grandparents-in-waiting for the family Jenny and Spuhn would begin. The Adamski house had people sleeping in every bedroom and on the living room couch. Jenny, Anna and their parents still hoped. If her brother Bob was able to re-organize his appointments and get to the wedding, he'd have to put himself in a motel, but they'd have the first full-family visit in more than four years.

Jenny, Spuhn knew, was busy, beautiful and immensely happy.

Clayton knew the Chicago route from weekends spent with a United stewardess. He drove then, sure of their Camaro's place in a morning commute that brought them along the south side lakefront and then, traffic light by traffic light through the Loop, into a parking garage a couple of blocks west of the Prudential Building, 41 stories in height.

By nine-fifteen, they had ridden the elevator to the observation deck, gone to the window line overlooking the city, and let Hernandez lead them in a fast, bold mooning of everything beneath and in front of them, everything connected to Vietnam.

Before a wondering young woman in a security uniform could get to them, they had their pants up and were laughing as they rushed to the elevator.

"Wowie zowie," Szabo said on the way down. "That was so far out."

While the others went out to the street, Spuhn used a lobby pay phone for calls to Rick and to two other managers.

By the time he came up to Clayton and the rest, Spuhn found they had made a plan. Before starting the drive back to Davenport at noon, they'd walk through Grant Park to see Chicago's Buckingham Fountain and then follow Clayton into the nearby Art Institute, where Clayton assured them, the place was crawling with girls.

Clayton was right. The girls were present and were the lookers he described. The young women were also rebuffed by the manic, up-all-night craziness of the laughing bachelor party pack. The more Clayton, Slick and everyone called attention to themselves with loud talk and joking, the more intent the university students and tourists became in studying the brush strokes and compositions of the art. Entry of the Davenport group quickly thinned the crowd in each gallery.

Spuhn had been eager from the first moment. He burned to be back in the car and driving toward Davenport for the initiation and completion of all the wedding events.

Clayton, though, separated himself from the others and adopted a blank, expectant look in front of a door leading into the Art Institute's galleries of impressionist work.

His air of authority brought him two graying women on a visit from Peoria, and then a mother and two children from the Chicago suburb of Wheaton. Grown to five, the group in front of Clayton added new members very fast as Slick and the others enjoyed what was afoot.

"Let's begin here," Clayton said, leading the group to stand before a painting of an adolescent ballerina.

Spuhn and the others could see Clayton taking note of the painter's name.

"Notice what Degas has accomplished here," Clayton said. "He saw, and magnificently recorded, the light, magical, yet powerful verticality of the young dancer's pose. With his choice of colors, he made a powerful statement about the rigidity of the life this girl led and the life she faced. See how these elements, these strokes, add tension, the conflict with the hopes she has for herself and the crushing expectations imposed on her by a demanding society."

Clayton's rapt audience did not hear the bachelor party group.

"Clayton is so full of shit," Slick said.

Even Spuhn was laughing.

"Clayton is insane," Szabo said.

"Notice the framing of this piece," Clayton said at another painting, this one of haystacks in moonlight.

Fifteen minutes later, after sending his group into the next gallery, Clayton rejoined his own group for a rollicking walk back to their parked car.

"You're goin' to be one hell of a lawyer, Clayton," Spuhn said.

"Where did you get all that crap?" Hernandez asked.

Clayton smirked. His satisfaction with the stunt showed in a dimpled grin and some dashboard drumming the whole time he was at the wheel and moving them along in the Chicago traffic toward Joliet. There, they stopped for hamburgers at a tollway oasis with a restaurant bridging the lanes of east and westbound traffic.

The sun reflected warmly off the silver roofs of passing semis. The sky was blue with occasional formations of cottony white clouds.

Lazy as the clouds, the rest of them could have lingered at the table but Spuhn came back from making calls and hurried them along. He drove without stopping the rest of the way into Davenport.

At the restaurant, once the others dropped him there, Spuhn called Jenny and told her they had returned from Chicago.

Relieved, she laughed. "What a bunch of assholes you are," she said. "Wow. All the way to Chicago and back for that."

Spuhn agreed.

"Hernandez, too? Same as Szabo?" Jenny asked.

"All of us."

Yes, Hernandez, Szabo. Spuhn knew that the friendship did not surprise Jenny, either. Hernandez's friendliness was unbounded, large enough that it encompassed Szabo, so determined to be distinct and separate from everything military, everything straight, everything down the middle American. If the soldier who had wounded him ever turned up, Hernandez probably would end up shooting pool and sharing pot. The big, good-looking, unworried Cuban friend came without rules. Nor did he impose any. Valuable as he was to Spoon, Hernandez was more puppy dog than partner. Just having him in the wedding party, present at the wedding, would make the events turn out well for all the family and friends.

"Fuck it. What are they going to do, send me to Vietnam?" That statement summed up the man.

Less than an hour later, Jenny called back to remind Spuhn of the time. This time, she had news that excited her.

"Bob came."

Spuhn would meet Jenny's brother, the Bob who had left Iowa for New York and Connecticut, the Adamski family royal whose handsomeness, intelligence, banking knowledge and success gave his distant family a bedrock of pride.

For Jenny's sake, Spuhn liked Bob when he was introduced to Robert Adamski at the start of the wedding rehearsal in St. Anthony's church. Then, for his own sake, Spuhn liked Robert Adamski during the private supper at the Blackhawk Hotel. A couple inches taller than Spuhn, with handsome maturity showing in some white sideburn hairs and in lines where his forehead pursed and where his smile surrounded even, white teeth, the investment banker shook hands and conversed gracefully. Jenny had chosen Spuhn's light slacks and plaid sport coat but Spuhn wished she had found the runway look of Robert's blue sport coat and creased gray pants. When Robert listened to Spuhn and spoke with him, Jenny's brother showed an admiration and a knowledge of Spoon that suggested familiarity with Spoon's level of business and with levels much beyond anything in Davenport.

Robert had begun to work with leveraged buyouts, different from what Spoon would need, but he wished to hear from Dennis when Spoon's own plan anticipated a liquidity event. He gave Spuhn a crisp white business card with address and name in un-adorned lines of black type.

"I can put you in touch with some people," Robert said, before he let his mother lead him on a charming re-introduction to two good friends who remembered Robert from years ago, when he and Anna went to St. Anthony's school.

The next day, in a wash of joy and pride at about three-thirty, Spuhn drew Jenny to him and kissed his wife with the fierceness of someone being pulled aboard from a cold sea. They kept their arms around each other and kissed a second time as the people watching from the pews and from the altar clapped.

"I love you, Dennis Spuhn, I love you," Jenny said. She kept her brown eyes open as she readied to kiss again.

"I love you, Mrs. Dennis Spuhn."

From there, everything went according to expectation, if not to script. The open bar at the Outing Club succeeded with Hernandez and Szabo as well as the rest of the wedding party. Spuhn saw his sister Veronica check a few times on Mike, who had become red-faced and high school stupid quickly, not long after Hernandez began helping Spuhn's brother get beers.

Shyly to the side, staying near the entrance to the set up hall that led to the kitchen, several of the staff took turns viewing the grown-up Dennis Spuhn with his wife, pretty as a movie star. When Spuhn came to greet them, the women pressed his hands and a couple patted his cheek. One pressed an envelope with a card from the group and twenty-five dollars into Spuhn's hand before she snugged her apron back in place and returned to her stove.

The Tomczaks sat with Mr. Klein and his wife at a table that included other Klein board members and spouses, while Robert was the ornament of his parents' table. When the dancing began, after Jenny's father had wished his daughter and Spuhn an eternity of love and happiness, after tipsy, mildly toked up best man Hernandez reminisced about getting to know Spuhn in the Marine Corps and then getting to know Jenny, who was perfect for Dennis, Robert followed his father in a smooth foxtrot with his proud mother.

Clayton, pleased with the notice of young women who included Mike's girlfriend and a number of wives, moved about with a deferential woman whose pretty face was alert to signs of anything Clayton wanted to do, from dancing to meeting a seated couple.

Clayton wore a fitted beige Nehru jacket and, mostly for appearance, gold wire-rimmed glasses.

By now, the bachelor party trip to Chicago was known and amusing. Even the rigid veteran who worked with Spuhn's father let the thing pass and joined his wife in talking about the house their son and daughter-in-law were building in Decorah.

"Sit down, Spuhn," Mr. Klein said, indicating with his look that Jenny should move on among the tables while he had a business word with the woman's new husband.

Two other Klein board members at the table, Mr. Klein's good friend the lawyer John W. Diebold and a stiff George Soukup, pressed in for the announcement.

"We're making you a voting member," Mr. Klein said.

"Wow," Spuhn said.

"Don't go gettin' a puffed head about it," Mr. Klein said. "We're still gonna work your ass hard. Your shit will still stink. My office will have the papers ready when you get back from your honeymoon. The board thinks you should have some extra stock, too."

With that, Spuhn was encircled with hands reaching for a shake or a rough squeeze of his shoulder.

"Thank you. Thank you," he said to Mr. Klein, to each congratulation. Spuhn felt his grin just barely held back in the territory of a business meeting exchange, just barely held back from the swearing whoop of a fan watching a score.

"How's our circus fellow doing?" Mr. Klein asked.

Mr. Klein knew full well the state of the handwalk, the choreography of the stops, the heartrate of Spoon's representative Ronnie Tonti. Mr. Klein also knew the rest of Ronnie Tonti's situation.

"Getting towards Grinnell now," Spuhn said.

"Let's hope that he behaves himself out there."

"Yes." Spuhn's look turned serious, the way the burly, sure contractor intended. Spuhn said thanks again and went to link his arm with Jenny's as they moved among their friends.

Ronnie Tonti. Spuhn had argued for Tonti's presence at the wedding, for Tonti's signature handwalking as the upturned man led Spuhn and Jenny down the aisle after the ceremony, but Jenny didn't even want Tonti attending. He was the little Louisiana boy with the curl: when he was good, he was all grins and charm but when he was bad, he could ruin the whole wedding. If Dottie came with him and if Dottie had too much access to the drinks, anything could happen. Dottie liked Spuhn but she could just as well drop onto any man's lap. When Dottie was bombed, she thought she was Ann-Margret with a sandy beehive.

Between the cutting of the wedding cake and Spuhn and Jenny's departure for a couple of nights of honeymooning in Chicago, sometime while Jenny was throwing the bouquet that an Iowa classmate took out of the air just above Marjorie's raised hands or while Spuhn was flipping Jenny's garter over his shoulder for Mike to catch with an accidental reflex, Robert got into his rented Mustang and hurried to Chicago, where he would golf at the suburban Exmoor Club with a client early the next morning.

Mr. Klein had arranged for Spuhn to have Mr. Klein's own price for two nights at the Drake Hotel, where Jenny's striking looks together with her friendliness kept hotel staff forever noticing the newlywed couple. In the hotel and out on the city walks amid shoppers and business people, Spuhn drew some looks for his own features but, otherwise, he was anonymous.

The valet parker who admired the yellow Corvette and, furtively, Jenny's legs didn't know Spuhn. At the desk, the clerk pronounced the name "Mr. and Mrs. Spun."

The feeling made Spuhn notice what he took for granted in Davenport and the other places Spoon existed: in Iowa he stood out. Away from Iowa, he did not. At least, he did not stand out for his own sake. Hand in hand with Jenny, seated with her at a lakefront bench or anywhere else as her brown eyes happily took in all the wonder of her Chicago surroundings, he did command attention, but only the visible, common curiosity about the man who could talk with, sit with and be with a woman as remarkable as Jenny. At the hotel, Spuhn had deference; lovely, open, magnetic Jenny had an audience.

Spuhn loved having Jenny as Mrs. Dennis Spuhn. He loved having her, having Spoon, having Jenny plus the breeze and the wave sounds from Lake Michigan when they walked and jogged. Spuhn loved the times coming, the times that were certain to include the spread of recognition and deference from Davenport to Chicago and beyond Chicago.

On the way back to Davenport, as Spuhn talked about the manager they'd found for the Newton restaurant and about the things he was learning from the graduate student who had introduced himself at the Iowa City Spoon that spring, Jenny played her fingers along his neck and shoulder. She smiled, listened, and, from time to time, rested her head against him.

The top of the Corvette was down, the sky away from Chicago was starry. A mellow DJ played Beatles, Stones and Blood, Sweat and Tears in between advertisements for bedding and banking services.

Familiar with the way Spuhn organized his own impressions and plans by presenting them to her, Jenny enjoyed the happiness without focusing on the words themselves. She didn't care that the truck drivers they passed could look down into the vette for sight of her and of the way she rested against the animated man at the wheel. The breeze moved her yellow hair in a caressing wave over the skin of Spuhn's neck and his shoulder. The light coat she wore and the feel of Spuhn's warmth were enough for the evening September cool.

In the stream of Spuhn's talking and the other night sounds, Jenny caught tiny islands of recognizable content: the opening of the next Spoon west of Newton in Des Moines, then West Des Moines, what the leasing broker needed to straighten out with the Cedar Rapids distribution center, a recipe Hernandez was developing with peppers.

With concentration, Jenny remembered Randy Isaacs. The short, slender grad student wore heavy glasses that rested in a pair of red pits dug into a bony nose. Even though his voice cracked and rose in excited torrents of information with few recognizable parts, Randy Isaacs had gotten Spuhn's trust. The file cards of Spoon birthday registrants were a growing packet of Fortran cards that could be read in myriad ways by the University of Iowa's IBM mainframe. With the ease and love of a concert pianist beginning a performance, the bright little teaching assistant with the careless shave and haphazard dress could set the machine to working.

"You should see," Spuhn said. "Randy makes the thing kick ass and take names."

The two of them, Dennis and Randy, were exulting in the data relationships appearing in the Spoon data. They were also imagining other grand applications for Randy's programs.

Jenny listened with her head on Spuhn's shoulder. She had heard Spuhn tell of the things before and would hear them again. Now she exalted in his happiness and in their prospects.

By the time Spuhn and Jenny were crossing the Mississippi into Iowa, Spuhn was quiet. Under the dark, starry sky and the arched lights of the bridge, Jenny was teasing him with bites on the lobe of his ear and stroking his crotch.

On the door of the apartment, they found the same note Mr. Klein had left at the Davenport and Iowa City Spoons: "Call me. I don't care what time. - K."

Hernandez was in jail.

One of the college kids would have wiped his face with a towel, but Ronnie Tonti didn't bother, just closed his eyes tightly when the salty dribbles bothered him and continued forward. Around him, amid the grass and some milkweed and tree sprouts, he caught sight of grasshoppers moving from his path. He could feel his face red and could see pink on the backs of his hands and his forearms as he moved. Under the sound of the three college kids, his escorts, talking, he could hear his own deep breaths.

Two farm boys in a dull brown pickup truck slowed as they overtook the group, mostly for a look at Kathy, the small Iowa sophomore. For her sake, to attract her notice, the boys called to Tonti but got nothing in reply, only the sight of a flushed, broad-backed, determined man moving ahead with three college kids carrying a Spoon sign.

In the increasing warmth approaching noontime, Tonti was alone in his task of crossing this line of fence, this intersection of county road with Route 6, this oak-shaded picnic stop. He moved forward, hands down, keeping his balance.

Most of the time, he just moved with no thoughts, nothing important enough to carry into the next day or the next segment of the cross-Iowa path.

For Tonti, the handwalking had become his job. He had held other jobs, work washing dishes or sweeping floors or digging trenches, jobs that gave him rent money and paydays, enough for fun at the tavern, for whatever food Dottie or another chère didn't put in front of him. This time, he needed no blackhat Airborne instructor harassing him around a three-mile run, no coach, no harsh Franky, no pouting chère

suggesting where he could work or move and threatening what he wasn't getting if he didn't.

Hands down, Dennis Spuhn had set out a good path.

Dennis Spuhn could say what he wanted, promise what he wanted, plan what he wanted.

Up ahead, within .87 miles every day, there were people to cheer Ronnie Tonti, girls to flirt with him, touch him, faces showing admiration and wonder that he, Ronnie Tonti, was doing something no one but Ronnie Tonti could do. Hands down, because he could, because he meant to do it, he was crossing the whole state of Iowa. Listening to his own breath, he pushed forward.

CHAPTER 23

Everywhere I go
There's a Black hat there
Everywhere I go
There's a Black hat there
Black hat
Black hat
Why don't you leave me alone
And let me go back home

As a furiously silent Spuhn watched him early the next morning, Hernandez put on his belt and scooped his coins and keys from the counter in a corridor of the Scott County jail on Fourth Street. Spuhn's hard green look made Hernandez drop his own gaze to the centering of his belt buckle. Thanks to the two calls Mr. Klein had made first thing, the arrest never occurred: stubble-faced and groggy, sheepishly grinning in Spuhn's scolding presence, Hernandez was free to accompany his partner as they headed to Spuhn's car and then to the apartment.

Arcs of lightning had begun to flash and thunder had begun to rumble in a darkening western sky.

With another call, this one to the *Morning Democrat*'s publisher, Mr. Klein quashed the appearance of Hernandez's name in the police report.

As soon as Mr. Klein finished with the publisher, he called Spuhn at the apartment and told him to get his ass down to the office.

"You better tear that jackass partner of yours a new asshole," Spuhn heard as soon as he was facing Mr. Klein across the desk.

"I will," Spuhn said.

Mr. Klein looked hard at him. "You damn well better."

"I know."

Damn it, damn it, damn it. As soon as he and Jenny crossed the bridge into Iowa the night before, news of Hernandez's arrest vaporized Spuhn's euphoria. A threat to Spoon, a possible loss of everything accumulated through months and years of work, large and dangerous enough to overshadow the joy of the union with beautiful, smart, head-turning, precious Jenny, Hernandez's impetuous vulnerability to grass, acid and everything except common sense attention to the needs of the restaurant was from that moment no longer a private worry of Spuhn and a few other Hernandez friends. Mr. Klein knew – had known, had known. Now, but for Mr. Klein's influence that morning, Hernandez in cuffs and maybe on the way to prison could have shamed the whole fragile business.

Even the sight of Jenny in the kitchen of the apartment when Spuhn returned with Hernandez didn't lift Spuhn's gloom. Outside, heavy rain beat on the house and pushed cool air inside. West of Iowa City, there would be rain heavy enough to sideline Ronnie Tonti's handwalking shy of Grinnell, almost a third of the way across the state.

Jenny could see the preoccupation in the way Spuhn played with a fork as he heard the rain and inside, the sounds of Hernandez showering in the bathroom next to the kitchen.

Jenny put a hand on Spuhn's shoulder, kissed him on the ear. "It will be okay," she said. She had dressed for class but really for him, in a navy miniskirt and a sleeveless blouse. A bit of her black bra, lacy and light, showed when she raised an arm.

"Mr. Klein is ticked off," Spuhn said.

She didn't answer.

"This crap doesn't cut it."

Jenny had arranged the table with a stalk of black-eyed susan cut from the yard. "Are you very hungry? I'm making French toast."

Doing his best to coax Spuhn back into good humor with a broad smile and the optimistic sunniness that was his natural disposition, Hernandez settled before his own plate. "Far out. French toast. Number one, Marine," he said. In deference to Spuhn as they ate, he was careful not to let his gaze linger on Jenny when she placed and removed things from the table.

Hernandez went ahead to the car while Jenny put her arms around Spuhn's neck and pressed the shape of herself hard against him. "I love you, Dennis Spuhn," she said.

"I love you," he said, smelling the perfume she had dabbed behind her ears, letting his spirits rise.

"You'll be quick?" Jenny asked. "I have class at two."

"I'll be here," he promised, meeting her kiss, a hard one they both nursed.

"This is a bummer way to start the week," Hernandez said, running a hand through his wet, dark hair. His smile was large, his manner deliberately loose in his attempt to repair the tension as Spuhn turned on the wipers and pulled from the curb.

"No shit," Spuhn said. He looked steadily where he was driving and said nothing more. Along the roadway, rainwater carrying twigs and paper scraps ran toward drains too small for the flow.

Spuhn was angry about the behavior that jeopardized the business he and Hernandez had begun but, in a way that he would only comprehend through additional hours and days of brooding, Spuhn was angry that friendship, that affection for Jesus, made obvious decisions terrifying. Spuhn knew what Mr. Klein wanted, knew what a CEO did, knew it the way he knew when he did something like climb the steps of the diving platform at Lake Herman and then pause, waver, reflect before pushing weakly forward. Then it had been experienced seventh and eighth graders hurrying him from the queue on the ladder, girls such as Mary Siemons and friends such as Szabo and Clayton watching from the lake. This time, it was Mr. Klein, the board, everyone tied to Spoon.

In the silence, Hernandez turned on the car radio, already set to Chicago's WLS.

Spuhn turned the radio off. When they arrived at Spoon, he turned and stopped abruptly at a spot near the rear entrance. With Hernandez working hard to speed his heavy-footed limp, Spuhn led the way into the kitchen.

Shedding Hernandez in the kitchen, noticing with additional displeasure the sounds of others greeting Hernandez, many looking to him for attention, Spuhn made his way into the front of the restaurant. The size of the midmorning crowd showed the lunchtime would be solid. With orderly haste, the two young waitresses were keeping the tables of interstate travelers, Davenport regulars and students served.

At the moment, no one needed Spuhn. In the respite, he took in the smooth workings of the business he had designed: the people were eager and trained, smooth in the execution of whatever tasks they had been given. Except for a couple of tables being bussed, the restaurant was clean and displays were in order. Spuhn noted the progress marked on the big poster of Tonti and his handwalk across the state. Soon there would be a new poster with additional Spoon locations in in Des Moines and West Des Moines.

There would also be posters of the new sandwich plate, the pork sandwich offering Hernandez had developed from memory of the spices used by the mother of a Cuban friend.

But would there be a Jesus Hernandez presenting the new item, something now being tested in Grinnell and in Williamsburg?

Getting nothing done, Spuhn fussed at the mail that had accumulated during the time of his wedding and honeymoon. When he arrived at the apartment for the drive to Iowa City with Jenny, his agitated state smothered the love-making she had in mind. In the car, she tried to settle him with light touching of her fingers on his thigh and with news she had received from the graduate student curating the fall show of student and faculty work: the curator, a sculptor, praised the compare and contrast series and told Jenny the two new pieces she was completing would be part of the show.

Her happiness raised Spuhn's spirits enough that he could sort through Hernandez with her.

"I like Jesus," she said.

"Yes, so do I."

Spuhn hesitated, felt her fingers on his thigh as he recognized the decision he could not avoid.

"I have to fire him," Spuhn said.

Jenny's fingers stayed.

"Hernandez can't work for us."

They were passing a farm with a herd of Herefords. Until she could control her tearing, Jenny studied the cattle. Only a couple were lying down. The heavy rain that had fallen on eastern Iowa during the morning was over for now.

"That will be rough for him," Jenny said. Her voice was soft, sad as she resumed the circles on Spuhn's thigh.

"I know."

"Is it from Vietnam? The way he is? The way he likes to get high?"

'I don't know."

"What will he do?"

Spuhn finished passing a trailer hauling new, multi-colored Ford Mustangs before he answered.

"He'll have money. We have to buy his stock back. His dad has all kinds of money, too. "

They talked then in spurts about ways they should have interfered with Hernandez, tendencies they had let develop. Several times, her fingers moving on Spuhn's thigh, Jenny said, "I am sorry you have to do this. What a bummer this is for you."

"Thanks," he said each time. Once he glanced left so Jenny would not see the water at the edges of his own eyes.

"I heard the rain was three inches in Iowa City," she said.

From the beginning, Spuhn had taken to Hernandez, had paired with the likable recruit whose easy way was so unlike his own deliberate conduct. Two years older than Spuhn, liked even by the DIs, wise and uninhibited in his enjoyment of a world he found full of attractions and adventures, empty of anyone but friends, Hernandez generously introduced everyone around him to whatever he discovered. Learning of a drill, being told of an inspection, he shared the advantage of foreknowledge with the other members of the squad. Able to buy a beer, he shared it. Everlastingly at ease with women, with pretty, flashy women drawn to his big, white smile, his accented English and his easy way, Hernandez had the women include pretty women they knew, other lively, stirring, curvy and leggy women so that Hernandez and his friends could all have dates. Maybe Jenny, attracted to Spuhn when she found

Spuhn and Hernandez working that hot afternoon on preparations for the first restaurant, could have turned from Spuhn to the fun-loving, exotically Cuban Hernandez. Hernandez wanted Jenny more for Spuhn than for himself; Hernandez curbed any impulse, always respected Jenny as Spuhn's.

Vietnam. Spuhn tried not to think about the wound that left Hernandez with his limp. Out of affection for Spuhn, indifference to his own Marine Corps fate, Jesus had joined Spuhn in training for the Food Technician Specialist MOS. From there, Vietnam. In Vietnam, on patrol, in danger, wounded, Medivacked, discharged with a lifetime disability. But how many Marines did not go to Vietnam? Any? Spuhn had not been accountable for Hernandez in country. Hernandez was the one who enlisted, who extended. Semper Fi, semper Vietnam. All Corps roads led to Vietnam. Step on the yellow prints, arrive in country.

Marine or no, Spuhn or no, Hernandez was Hernandez, impulsive and unthinking in his habits, creative and adventuresome in his role at Spoon. He came that way, nothing to do with the Marines or with Spuhn.

"Don't worry. It will turn out all right. Don't get uptight," Jenny said, kissing Spuhn on the ear before she got out of the Corvette at the Art Building.

"Meet you here when you're done."

During the hour Jenny attended her drawing class, Spuhn went to a pay phone in the Memorial Union, put the Grinnell manager in charge of the next day's staffing meeting for Newton, and then called Hernandez at the Davenport Spoon.

"Jesus, you around tomorrow morning, nine at the apartment?"

Hernandez was upbeat, perfect. "Roger that. Spuhn, you talk with them in Williamsburg and over in Grinnell? We're putting chives, very fine, in the pork. Man, wait till you have a taste. Wowie zowie."

"Yeah, that's good news. Number one," Spuhn said. "Jesus, I got to go. See you tomorrow. I'll be at Marjorie's with Jenny."

With that, Spuhn took hold of himself. The Hernandez fat now in the fire, he drove back to the Art Building and thought about replacements for Hernandez, maybe the eager, serious Drake graduate who had been writing about an interview; at the end of the summer, having earned her own college costs, having finished in less than three and a half years, she would graduate from the agriculture program with a degree in nutrition. Or Spoon could replace Hernandez with a team culled from all the restaurants. Spuhn could think of a quick, hardworking Mexican cook they had added to the Williamsburg staff; his English would improve, his cooperative manner only needed to hold steady. There was an unlikely candidate, too, a precocious high school senior who had no hesitation about proposing seasonings and whole meals she had learned from her Italian grandmother.

His mood improved, Spuhn was ready to go with Jenny to Marjorie's apartment and exhaust himself before going to meet Randy Isaacs at about seven.

Finding Marjorie uncomfortably present in the apartment, at work in the small living room on a spread of notes and open texts for a morning education theory exam, Spuhn and Jenny only kissed and pressed against each other while Marjorie talked to them through the closed bedroom door. After changing into clothes for a run, they left Marjorie to worry over her exam preparation.

"Just be patient, horndog," Jenny told Spuhn, pushing his hand from her waist as they arrived at a grassy, riverside spot for stretching. The hard morning rain had raised the Iowa River where it passed through the campus. Near Spuhn and Jenny, the water foamed over some driftwood snagged against the trunks of cottonwood saplings growing from a sandstrip hidden this day in the stream's shallow edge.

Spuhn was ready for a purging run but, even with the need to pound his Hernandez and Spoon worries into one of his orderly plans, he could only keep up with Jenny, not lead her. She ran happily, lightly, able to talk if she wished, to note trees and buildings and people as they passed through the campus. Spuhn judged the route to be three miles in length. When Jenny forgot herself and drew ahead, Spuhn enjoyed the bounce of her yellow ponytail and her athletic, long-legged form as he pressed to increase his own pace. He had married the prettiest, most stirring woman he could know.

At the end of the run, they settled on another grassy spot, one not so moist as other parts of the lawn, and rested with Spuhn's back against a maple tree. Jenny lay back against him as they watched the river pass in eddies and foam before them. At the Iowa's intersection with a tiny creek, the river was undercutting a thin point bearing a cottonwood already far tipped toward the water. The roiled water worked at the base of the bank while, a couple of feet above, the tree shook in cool, after rain breeze.

Contented, relaxed from the run, enjoying the feel of each other, Spuhn and Jenny were quiet.

Artist that she was, Jenny unconsciously added the river, the collapsing bank, and the imperiled tree to the catalog of images she would draw upon when she designed one of her works. She could tell that within a short time, maybe by the next afternoon, the point would be gone, its clay, sand and pebbles distributed, the river greater in width and, with the new material added, more shallow than she saw before her now.

Jenny let Spuhn nuzzle her ear, asked him not to worry, not to get uptight.

"I won't," he said.

With her head and shoulders pressing back against him, with her hands stroking his arms, Spuhn felt held by her will from acting meanly, vengefully, rashly. Spoon? She was proud of the restaurant, happy with it but not in the defining way Spuhn was proud of it, happy with it. Optimistic always, sure of enough, Jenny only loved Spoon for its importance to him, not for the sake of the prosperity and importance and freedom an established business, this business, would mean for them.

Jenny went from there to her studio while Spuhn went to learn the new insights Randy Isaacs had culled from analysis of the cards supplied from Spoon locations in Grinnell and Williamsburg. Randy would have talked all night about the common characteristics and the regional ones in the data. Spuhn, though pleased about the insights, no longer needed proof that Randy could tease them from the coded customer information Spoon was gathering. At most times, Spuhn delighted in the far-ranging consideration of possibilities the smart, voluble programmer could pull from a mainframe such as the one in the University's center. Tonight, though, Spuhn wanted to learn about costs, just that, and then go back to meet Jenny at her studio. With effort, he turned the spigot of Randy's conversation toward the calculation of mainframe leasing costs and programming requirements.

In less than an hour and a half, Spuhn was at Jenny's studio. Ignoring his eagerness to go, she made him wait, told him to go use the phone beside the stairwell while she worked another ten minutes. Her attention was on the jaw of Charles de Gaulle, the French leader supposedly drawn from Mahatma Ghandi, shown modeling for the composition.

Following her wish, Spuhn made an unnecessary call to the apartment, where Hernandez did not answer. At the Grinnell Spoon, the manager, efficient Jeff Tompkins, reported that the morning's rain had held Tonti's handwalk to sixth-tenths of a mile. But Tonti hadn't wanted to quit and was going to catch up before Thursday.

Only 22 years old himself and younger than that in appearance, the manager said, "Those college kids thought they were all goin' to get hit by lightnin' for a little while there. They said Ronnie just didn't care."

"That's it," Spuhn told himself. "How badly do you want it? How badly do you want it?"

Then he made the manager go quickly through the arrangements for the Thursday arrival of the handwalk. After applauding the preparations and Jeff's attention to them, Spuhn said thank you and returned to Jenny in her studio. With her smock removed, she was studying a completed composition, an arrangement of the well-known Iowa painting, artist Grant Wood's American Gothic farm couple posing in the background for the work taking place in the foreground, a reproduction of a photograph from the wedding of David Eisenhower and Julie Nixon.

"Wow," Spuhn said.

"You think it works?"

"This will be the hit of the show."

Jenny smiled at him and let him help her gather her brushes. Her drawing pad, he saw, was open to a sketch he recognized as the Iowa River tearing at the fragile bank they had seen at the end of their run.

"How was Randy?"

"Same. He is a hundred miles an hour."

"Same as you."

"Clayton's going to help us set up a new company."

"Clayton? He's still in law school."

"He says he can do it."

At Marjorie's apartment, they lingered a moment out of polite sympathy for Marjorie's fear of the next day's test, and then went to bed in the room that was still Jenny's. During the night, close and naked after making love, they woke twice when Jenny felt Spuhn start.

"What's wrong? You were jumping around."

She rested her face under his chin and held him each time as Spuhn quickly fell back to sleep.

In the dark the next morning, Spuhn pulled from the bed and showered and shaved for the return to Davenport. Before leaving the apartment, he ran a hand lightly over the curve of Jenny's hip and the side of her arm . She didn't wake as he drew the sheet over her and smoothed it around her neck.

He dreaded the day the way he had dreaded looming PT tests, Vietnam, some of his meetings with Mr. Klein, even as he knew he would surmount each of the challenges. He would not have chosen the situation with Jesus. Jesus had made the situation what it was. He had forced Spuhn to make the decision he was going to reveal that morning.

The apartment was empty and straightened up, the LPs all sheathed in jackets and slotted at rest against the base of a book-shelf, the kitchen floor swept, only a cup in the sink, when Spuhn arrived before seven-thirty. As far as Spuhn could tell, Hernandez had vacuumed and cleaned the apartment of his grass. Spuhn supposed Hernandez had gone to spend the night with a nurse named Gisa.

Spuhn settled at his desk, moved a couple of notecards to a new column and got nothing done before he heard Hernandez coming up the outside stairs. Hernandez's left foot, numbly distant from the rest of him and turned slightly out, bore his weight with a heavy sound.

"Hey, man," Hernandez said. He smiled uncomfortably.

"Hi," Spuhn said. Hernandez had shown up in time for the nine o'clock appointment – ten minutes early, in fact.

Spuhn began.

"Jesus, this isn't working."

He saw Hernandez's eyes begin to water. Agitated, unsurprised, Hernandez combed his fingers through his hair and stood gazing at a point in the rusty pattern of the room's linoleum floor.

"The business can't take a chance on you. We have to break it up, you and me. No one knows how you're going to behave, what you're going to do. It isn't working."

Hernandez's breathing had a choke in it. He looked at Spuhn. "I'm fucking up. It's such a bummer, such a bummer, man. I don't want to fuck things up for everyone. Not for you, Spuhn. Man."

In the pause of their own conversation, Spuhn and Hernandez could hear a car and then a delivery truck pass on the street. A small dog down the block barked at something.

"Look, Jesus, stay at the apartment the rest of the month. Get your stuff squared away. I'll talk to Mr. Klein about your stock. We'll get it valued, and we'll do what the partner agreement says."

Tearing and showing an amused, frustrated smile, Hernandez shook his head. "I don't give a fuck about the stock. Fuck the stock."

"This is all between you and me," Spuhn said. "No one needs to know what's going on. You're just leaving, that's all."

Hernandez's smile broadened in amusement. He thought his own thoughts and said with spirit, "That's fucking big of you, man. Out fucking standing."

"People think a lot of you. They know what you've made happen. They just don't need to know the whole thing, that's all."

"Yeah. What are they goin' to do? Send me to Vietnam?"

No longer fighting the tearing in his eyes or the sadness in his look, Hernandez picked up the paper bag holding his overnight gear, moved into his bedroom and closed the door.

Spuhn left. At a Sinclair gas station along the way to the Brady Street Spoon, he stopped and called Jenny.

She began to cry.

"Don't cry."

"I feel so bad for Jesus."

"He's the one made this happen."

"I know."

"Everything will be okay."

"We're not all like you."

The sight of customer cars filling more than half the lot of the Brady Street Spoon would have pleased Spuhn on most days, but this time the activity made him wonder how much of the traffic was attributable to Hernandez. Would Spoon be able to continue Hernandez's inventive ways? And with Hernandez suddenly gone, how should Spoon explain the departure?

After some restless time in the office, unable to reach Clayton about the new company with Randy, not ready to call Jenny a second time, Spuhn drove to Klein Incorporated, where he waited for Mr. Klein to return from a meeting with the hotel architects at the Bettendorf project site.

"You look like somethin' the cat dragged in," Mr. Klein said by way of greeting. He led Spuhn into the office and closed the door.

The session with the hotel group must have gone well. Mr. Klein was having a good time with the unhappy Spuhn.

"I've got five minutes," he said. "What can I do for you?"

"I told Hernandez he's fired."

"That's good." Mr. Klein rocked in his chair, kept his eyes on Spuhn and waited.Spuhn had nothing to add.

"Is he gone?"

"Yes, he's gone from Spoon. I told him he can stay in the apartment till the end of the month."

"I see."

Mr. Klein studied Spuhn's face for another beat, then stopped rocking and sat forward to meet Spuhn's eyes.

"You don't run the show till you draw some blood," he said. "You want to run the show, you got to be able to do that."

"Yes, sir," Spuhn said.

Buying out Hernandez's interest wouldn't be a problem. Mr. Klein thought Spuhn should take over that share. The board, he thought, would go along. If Spuhn couldn't come up with the funds himself, Mr. Klein would lend Spuhn what he needed. Had Spuhn given any thought to it?

Spuhn answered that he had nearly nine thousand dollars put away and could get some more from the bank.

"Never mind the bank," Mr. Klein said. "Make this deal with Hernandez, if you can: give him the nine thousand now, pay him $500 a month for the next two years, and then make a balloon payment for settlement of the balance. You'll be buying the cow with the cow's own milk."

"That should work."

Mr. Klein rose to shake hands and move Spuhn from the office.

Before releasing his grip, Mr. Klein said, "Spuhn, somedays you eat the bear, and somedays the bear eats you."

"I guess so."

Less than two weeks later, just after the brisk, burly developer started his freshly waxed Caprice for the drive home, no one around him to notice, the bear ate Mr. Klein. He fell to the side, dead of a heart attack.

CHAPTER 24

Dress it right and cover down
Forty inches all around
Nine to the front, six to the rear
That's the way we do it here

Spuhn had only begun reading the first few paragraphs in the large stack of documents when the lawyer, Jack Diebold, John W. Diebold, interrupted him.

"Dennis, here's what all that boils down to," he said, pausing until he had Spuhn's attention. As always, the big man's voice was radio host rich and his manner was calm: whatever was in the documents would end up causing no harm, not while the affair was under the management of the affable, prominent Davenport lawyer with JWD monogrammed on the pocket of his shirt. Mr. Diebold hesitated long enough to fix the sit of his jacket sleeve with the right amount of stiff white cuff and a silver cuff link showing. His tailored suit was dark navy with thin, cream-colored lines. In the pocket of his jacket was a handkerchief folded to show a quarter inch of clean white.

When he had made Spuhn wait long enough, Mr. Diebold said again, "What all that boils down to is one entity, Klein Enterprises Incorporated, jointly owned by Fred Klein and his spouse Jeanine

Klein. Underneath that are lots of other entities. For liability reasons, for tax reasons, for segregation of capital. Your own Spoon restaurants, for example."

He paused and straightened the angle of the pens resting in a desktop holder with a white marble base.

Mr. Diebold's measured presentation reminded Spuhn of Mr. Klein's manner, the way Mr. Klein used to pace himself and emphasize things when he meant his words as a tutelage.

The look on Mr. Diebold's wide face was patient and deliberate. The lawyer's peppery hair, now worn slightly long with a suggestion of sideburns, was freshly cut with a sheen of oil along a high part. Spuhn could smell bath powder and skin lotion scent in the office.

Jack Diebold waited again, long enough for his matronly secretary to enter and, with quiet efficiency, place a fan of some documents at the lawyer's side for his signature. Accustomed to days of placing and removing, placing and removing documents, she was exact and impassive, with a manner that suggested the habits of a good milkman's horse paying attention to nothing except the stops along a daily route.

The office held so many Hawkeye and Iowa team photographs and emblems the room could have been an anteroom of the university itself.

Along a wall to Spuhn's left, a display of framed photographs showed Mr. Diebold shaking hands or in groups with Iowa officials. In one, he was with Richard Nixon, who was not yet President. In another, the lawyer was part of a group watching Governor Harold Hughes sign a document. In a photo framed next to a headline reading "Number 11 Buckeyes Fall to Hawkeyes", a young Mr. Diebold and two Iowa players had written their signatures with the game date "October 9 '48". Behind Mr. Diebold's wide, orderly desk was a window giving a view over three downtown blocks of buildings smaller than the law firm's First National Bank building and then the river, where Spuhn saw a tugboat managing a line of barges heading downstream.

"That light too strong?" Having signed the papers for his secretary to take, Mr. Diebold stood and was about to adjust the tilt of the big man, more than six feet, with the softening of almost forty-three years masked by the careful fit of his clothes around him. From the breadth of Mr. Diebold's face and form to the paneling of the room, everything was solid, expressive of Mr. Diebold's substantial legal partnership as well as, from a selection of photos and mementos, his own Davenport patrimony. The city had sprinklings of the Diebold name: a park, a street at the height of one bluff, and the law firm Diebold & Harper.

"No, this is fine for me," Spuhn replied. He shifted his chair slightly to his right.

Twenty minutes later, Spuhn's thoughts, already whirling since his dismissal of Hernandez early in the month and then Mr. Klein's death the evening before, were twisting in a hurricane of information and possibilities.

Spuhn had been in a hurry before Mr. Klein died. Now, his rush to settle everything with Hernandez, to secure the funds and the ownership transfer, seemed like a slow walk to the starting line of a race. Spuhn would have to accelerate.

In a matter-of-fact tone that still revealed no apprehension of trouble and disorder, Mr. Diebold explained the competing interests of the parties, including Dennis Spuhn.

George Soukup wanted to gain control and was already talking with two of the board members. That was for openers. There was also a group being put together by the Bettendorf banker Spuhn knew, Nels Benson.

Since the Kleins had the Diocese of Davenport in their estate plan, the diocese would be watching. What Mr. Klein was leaving the Annie Wittenmeyer Home would be paid directly from an insurance policy, so the home would not be a party. Mrs. Klein would remain a donor, but not through the company.

Spuhn knew of his mother's admiration for Mrs. Klein and her husband, whose daughter, born with Downs Syndrome, only lived until age 14.

"And there's you. Dennis Spuhn. Mrs. Klein wants me to help you. The long and short of it is, Dennis, Mr. Klein had you in mind as his successor. And Mrs. Klein has the same feeling."

There were no flies settling on Mr. Diebold.

"Jeanine, Mrs. Klein, knows she should liquidate some of her interest. If you can find a backer. . . backers. . . Mrs. Klein will accept you as an owner. She doesn't feel that way about the others. Besides, they all want her out of the company."

Giving Spuhn a sharp look, he said, "You don't like these people, do you?"

Spuhn realized his reaction to mention of Benson showed.

"Mr. Soukup I only know a little. Mr. Benson, his son was in my class at St. Sebastian's. He's a loser."

Mr. Diebold smiled.

"George Soukup, George Soukup, you know, don't you, that he's been trying for a long time to talk Mr. Klein into divesting Spoon?"

He smiled when he saw that the news surprised Spuhn. "Divest you really."

Mr. Diebold went on.

"They're types. Soukup still has his first nickel. Your classmate's father has a good opinion of himself, that's for sure. Nels Benson's a bully."

Spuhn remained silent while he waited for advice. He felt stupidly surprised, as if he were watching a bridge opponent run trump. Spuhn had to rouse himself, had to get hold of the lead and use his own cards.

"Have you talked with Mrs. Klein?"

"Not about any of this," Spuhn said.

Right after receiving the call from Mr. Klein's weeping office manager Mary the night before, Spuhn had spoken with another woman at Mrs. Klein's house. That morning, he had gone to the Klein Enterprises office and talked with other stunned, confused workers but, except for the message he gave the woman at Mrs. Klein's home and except for the floral bouquet that would be delivered from Jenny and him within the next two hours, he had not spoken with Mrs. Klein.

From the office manager's second call, Spuhn had learned of Mrs. Klein's wish that he be one of the bearers of her husband's casket. Mr. Diebold would be another.

"All right, I'll say something. " The decisive tone of the statement signaled the end of the appointment. As he rose, Mr. Diebold looked at his watch.

Spuhn was slow to rise.

"What's the matter?" Mr. Diebold asked.

"I don't know how much money I can get my hands on. What's all this going to take?"

"Everything goes the right way, don't worry. You'll be buying the cow with its own milk."

This time, Mr. Diebold was ending the meeting. "I've got a couple of things I have to do here. We'll see each other at the wake."

Before then, Spuhn went to the Brady Street restaurant, where the staff members' general unawareness of Spoon's connection to the deceased Fred Klein kept familiar procedures in place. Spuhn could see friendships in the banter, hear the instructions and answers of a cohesive group getting food made and served, getting the job done. Working hard now, they would go home, go to school, do whatever they did when they were not in their Spoon uniforms and their Spoon roles.

Accustomed to seeing Spuhn dressed for business appointments or for one of his speeches to a Chamber, a Rotary, a business school class, they did not pay much attention to the formality of Spuhn's dress this early afternoon: a wide tie with a paisley pattern of purple and cranberry and fresh white shirt, a dark, slim suit with modestly belled pant cuffs and shined black wingtip shoes.

At the apartment, Spuhn studied himself in the hallway mirror and asked Jenny, "Does this look okay?"

Jenny came close, picked a bit of something white from the shoulder of Spuhn's coat, pulled the coat into place with the shirt collar showing and said, "You're fine. What you're wearing is fine."

She turned a circle in front of him. "Now me. How am I?"

She was wearing a black dress with a ruffled white trim that would have opened to show cleavage except for the gold pin drawing the dress together above the shape of her breasts. The dress fit her smoothly down her body from her shoulders to its stop a couple of inches above her knees. She wore nylons and black high heels.

"You look like a million dollars."

She scowled at him and turned to fix her hair, woven today into a French braid that she pulled around in front for her inspection.

"I don't want to look like a million dollars. I need to look respectful."

"You look respectful," Spuhn said. "And you look like a million dollars."

As Jenny leaned back against him and they looked at themselves in the mirror, Spuhn suddenly realized the potential of his cards in the competition with Soukup, the Bensons and any other suitor.

Mrs. Klein would decide for all of them, yes. But Spuhn now thought he had a way to improve his hand.

"It's time. We need to go," Jenny said.

"I need to call someone," Spuhn said.

"You always need to call someone."

From under a paperweight at the corner of his desk, a silver dollar encased in plexiglass, Spuhn pulled a page with a half dozen names and phone numbers.

First, he called the office of Hernandez's father and, after identifying himself, asked for Mr. Antonio Hernandez.

"Ah, the friend of Jesus," the woman said. No, Mr. Hernandez was not there but he would be back that afternoon. She would tell Mr. Hernandez. Mr. Spuhn should call at five.

Spuhn thanked her and promised to call. He would do so at four his time, five in Coral Gables.

Then, with no hesitation, Spuhn called George N. Forrest II in New York. Spuhn heard the same efficiency as before, this time in a proper Eastern tone instead of a proper Spanish-accented one. "Madison Alberts Investments, Mr. George Forrest's office."

A moment later, Mr. George Forrest was on the line.

"Well, Marine, what's the good word from out there on the prairie?"

"We have running water and inside toilets now," Spuhn said.

Mr. Forrest laughed.

Spuhn began to tell about Spoon and what the business was becoming.

Mr. Forrest cut him short. "I know, I know. I see those chest-thumping communications you mail us. Congratulations. What do you have now? Seven restaurants?"

"Just about," said Spuhn. "Before the end of 1971, we'll have them all the way to Omaha."

"Then what? A vacation home in Minnesota? A shiny Remington and a silky pointer named Rex?"

This time Spuhn laughed.

"Not yet, not yet." As he launched into the circumstances with Spoon and with Klein Enterprises Incorporated, with the intention of joining Mr. Klein's widow in control of the collection of companies, Mr. Forrest listened, asked a few questions about revenues and then about the board. Abruptly, he asked "What is today, Tuesday? Can you be here Thursday afternoon? Come at one. We'll have lunch and then meet with some of my partners. We'll need income statements, all the financials."

As he put the phone down, Spuhn became aware of Jenny watching him with impatience.

"Whoever that was, you sure seem to be in a better mood than you were. We need to go," she said.

If she had any doubts about the improvement of his spirits, Spuhn's assured manner at the wake dispersed all uncertainty. Spuhn smiled, touched, greeted, responded like the heir Fred Klein had created. Through Mr. Klein's introductions, Spuhn knew a circle extending beyond the board of Klein Incorporated, knew city officials and business owners, even the manager of the Davenport Country Club and members of the Rotary and Elks Clubs. With Jenny beside him, handsome and successful in his own right with his trim looks, his modish brown hair, bell-bottomed dark suit and the reputation burnished by numbers of articles celebrating the progress of Spoon, Dennis Spuhn pleased the room of business leaders with his youthful deference even as some obsequiously approached him.

Spuhn's sadness was real as he and Jenny knelt and prayed beside Mr. Klein's open casket. Jenny wept quietly, with a tissue at her eyes. Spuhn took in the arrested, besuited form of the patron lying with his eyes closed, his customary, solid chin forward expression frozen in a wash of applied color and preservative. Affixed to the lapel of the brown suit coat was a ribbon with what Spuhn recognized as a bronze star. Mr. Klein's strong hands with the American flag on the back of one now held the beads of a black rosary. Unabashed by anything in life, he seemed equally unfazed, equally sure in his coffin.

At Jenny's prodding tug, Spuhn stood, the awareness coming to him of the finality, the removal of his patron. But knowing that feeling, what would Mr. Klein have done? Briefly, Spuhn felt amused. Mr. Klein would have belittled the uncertainty, would have said something gruff but steadying. "Get your head out of your ass, quit playin' with yourself, look where the work is, it's in front of you," something of that sort.

Spuhn noticed that, while he and Jenny were at the bier, the banker Nels Benson had arrived and had begun gladhanding among some men his age, people Spuhn didn't know well but recognized from Chamber and United Way meetings. Let Greg Benson's father, overweight and loud, prosperous and porcine with a thin, reddish scruff circling his bald, perspiring scalp, move where he wished. Spuhn hardened his gaze when he saw George Soukup standing right beside Mrs. Jeanine Klein in the receiving line of family and close friends.

As Spuhn hesitated with Jenny, the choreography of the line abruptly changed, thanks to the deft intrusion of the former Iowa linesman Big Jack Diebold, who spoke loudly and used his large body to block Mr. Soukup's sight of Spuhn, Jenny and Mrs. Klein, a small, gracious woman whose rings and bracelet and necklace sparkled with diamonds. Mrs. Klein seemed just as aware and grateful for the buffering as Spuhn was. After acknowledging the condolences of Spuhn and the wet-cheeked Jenny, Mrs. Klein said in a soft, sure voice to Spuhn, "My husband had very high regard for you, Dennis. He called you his Marine." With affection, a kind queen with two subjects, she squeezed Spuhn's hand and one of Jenny's in her own. "Mr. Diebold is going to help us settle these complicated affairs. I understand we are meeting with him next Monday morning."

Then Mrs. Klein, moving her hand to Spuhn's elbow, turned him toward her sister Irene for an introduction.

"That was slick, Mr. Diebold," Spuhn said, when the lawyer caught up to Jenny and Spuhn in another part of the room.

The lawyer kept his look blank.

"Oh, George Soukup. We haven't seen each other lately and I just wanted to say hi." Then he winked and smiled. "Mrs. Klein would like the two of us to meet her at her house Monday morning at nine. Come to my office at eight and we'll drive together."

With that, Spuhn left Jenny visiting with one of her St. Sebastian's classmates, a smiling woman dividing her attention between a delighted Jenny and a newborn stirring in a tight wrap of pink blanket. In a quiet corner of a neighboring building's lobby, Spuhn found a pay phone and dialed Mr. Antonio Hernandez, Jesus' father.

Under Mr. Hernandez's cordiality, Spuhn could recognize what he had expected: caution in speaking with the business partner who had jettisoned Mr. Hernandez's difficult son. But Spuhn also detected sadness, the exasperation of a parent who had hoped and now felt confronted with the reality of his son's destructive arc.

They did not talk of the Marines, of Vietnam, of Jesus' impulsive conduct.

Mr. Hernandez was sympathetic, understanding of the need for his son's removal from Spoon.

In an even voice, Spoon told of the plan he expected to complete with Jesus for purchase of Jesus' interest in Spoon.

"I am glad to hear this," Mr. Hernandez said.

At the operator's instruction, Spuhn took coins from the pile in front of him and paid the additional sixty-five cents.

Then, doing his best to control his voice, to keep his tone calmly informative, Spoon went on to another plan.

According to this one, a new company would form, one that would employ Jesus as a contracted provider of menu development assistance to the sister company, Spoon. By implication, Jesus would remain in Iowa; he would not return to Coral Gables. Spuhn would provide the oversight for Jesus' work and again, by implication, Spuhn would provide oversight of the erratic son.

"I see. And this gives the restaurant protection in case. . . ." Mr. Hernandez stopped.

"Hands down, this protects the restaurant, Mr. Hernandez. Same with Jesus. Hands down, this will be good," Spuhn said.

Taken with Spuhn from the time Jesus and Spuhn, two Marines vacationing before Vietnam service, stayed with him in Coral Gables, Mr. Hernandez let Spuhn advance another hope, this one for investment in accelerated expansion of Spoon.

"Estas atrevido, amigo," Mr. Hernandez said. "You are very courageous, very courageous. I do not say no."

Spuhn inserted additional coins.

The numbers Spuhn had thought about were bold but tolerable, consistent with the impression Mr. Hernandez had formed from the mail announcing Spoon accomplishments and from phone calls with Jesus.

"Some of the board want Jesus to go. If some other groups get control of Klein, it won't be good for the restaurant. If I have backing for Spoon, then, hands down, we can form the new company and do a lot of other things."

Spuhn listened as Mr. Hernandez considered the request.

"Are there other investors?"

Spuhn answered yes. When he met with George Forrest on Thursday, Mr. Forrest was sure to back Spuhn's plan. Spuhn knew it.

Saying neither yes nor no, Mr. Hernandez turned the conversation. "How are you doing with the man on his hands, the man walking from one restaurant to the next one?"

"We are almost 100 miles now, a third," Spuhn said. Mr. Hernandez didn't need to ask. He would know the same from the mailing of the previous week, one containing a copy of an article with Ron Tonti's photo from the *Iowa City Press-Citizen*.

After inquiring about Spuhn's health, about his wife and his parents, Mr. Hernandez returned to the investment proposal.

"This is something I am willing to think about," he said. "Of course, I can not answer you tonight."

Spuhn agreed. "I will mail you a copy of the financials early next week, maybe Monday," he promised.

After scheduling a second phone call for Saturday afternoon, they ended the call.

The two conversations had taken long enough that Jenny was at first irritated when Spuhn rejoined her amid the people attending Mr. Klein's wake. Then, in response to Spuhn's visibly improved spirits, Jenny let her own spirits lighten. In the line now were Klein Enterprises managers and other employees who saw Spuhn and nodded or said hello to him while they moved up the queue of mourners.

If Spuhn had been playing bridge, he would have been taking heart from the cross ruff of Mr. Diebold guiding Mrs. Klein, Mrs. Klein favoring whatever reasonable proposal Spuhn could bring, and now two prospective backers mulling participation. Spuhn looked around the room and, with Jenny at his side, went to stand with the group of Klein Enterprise managers a few moments before

Father Jim Flaherty from the diocesan office began leading the praying of a rosary.

During the prayer, Spuhn gave way to the confidence he felt after the two phone calls. Not far from Jenny and him, Mrs. Klein seemed to have drawn away from Mr. Soukup; through reading glasses she wore with a silver chain around her neck, she was giving complete attention to a small prayer book held in both hands.

Around the room, Spuhn saw some men noticing Jenny, some women noticing him. Without looking, he could feel his wife's loveliness, a beauty enhanced by her simple acceptance of it, unlike buxom Marjorie and other pretty friends who seemed always taken up with tweaking of their makeup, the choice of their clothes and little else except being pretty. Jenny's steadiness contrasted with the giddiness and shortsightedness of many otherwise pretty women Spuhn knew from Jenny's university life and from the likes of Clayton, Hernandez and Tonti. Why did someone like Marjorie – smart, loyal in all her friendships, attractive – or even the undergrad Clayton dated during the spring, the curly-haired Zeta Tau from Council Bluffs, why did they let their potential go unused, obscured by unimportant, immediate worries and impulses? Currently, Marjorie, often bouncing from one fancy to another, was growing excited about an application she so far only talked about, an application to become a United Airlines stewardess at the end of the next school year.

Long before Father Flaherty concluded the rosary with a prayer for the poor souls in Purgatory, Spuhn was planning his departure from the wake. He had to make an airline reservation for the next day or the following morning, as soon as he could get to Chicago from Mr. Klein's funeral. And he had to look in on everything at the restaurants, including the progress of Tonti's handwalking. Jenny wouldn't want to miss her Thursday and Friday classes; if she didn't want Spuhn to arrange a ride with the kids in the Tonti escort, she could catch a ride from one of the friends who commuted or Jenny could use her mother's old '53 Ford.

Because the funeral Mass went long next day, concelebrated at Sacred Heart Cathedral by Bishop Franz Keller, Father Flaherty and the pastor of the Kleins' parish, Father Joseph Nolan, the day was long for Spuhn, torn between honoring Mr. Klein and making a timely drive across Illinois to catch a plane at O'Hare Airport. Holding Jenny's hand as he listened, Spuhn did learn from the scholarly Bishop Keller, a former professor of history at Loras College in Dubuque, that the scar running below Mr. Klein's eye had come from Marine combat on a scrap of island named Saipan toward the end of World War II. Referring familiarly to Jeanine, the bishop lauded the Kleins' faith during the difficult years they spent caring for their daughter Angela and, through Mr. Klein's life, the generosity of Fred and Jeanine to work of Catholic Charities and of Wittenmeyer Home, where Angela had found happiness with the home's training.

Led by two Marines who would remove a United States flag from Mr. Klein's casket, fold the cloth and present it to Mrs. Klein after a third Marine blew taps, Spuhn and the others were equally stiff and sober as they bore Mr. Klein's weight. Gracious and strong, Mrs. Klein came to each man at the end of the gravesite prayers and thanked him.

"He was a very nice man," Jenny said as she and Spuhn drove from the cemetery to the reception at the Outing Club.

"Yes. Hands down, he was," Spuhn said. He was, with no ceremony about any of it. Even the decision to stop doing business with Wally Meadows Chevrolet came as offhand news, a remark as Mr. Klein made desk room by brushing aside the brochures from an Outing Club friend's Ford dealership.

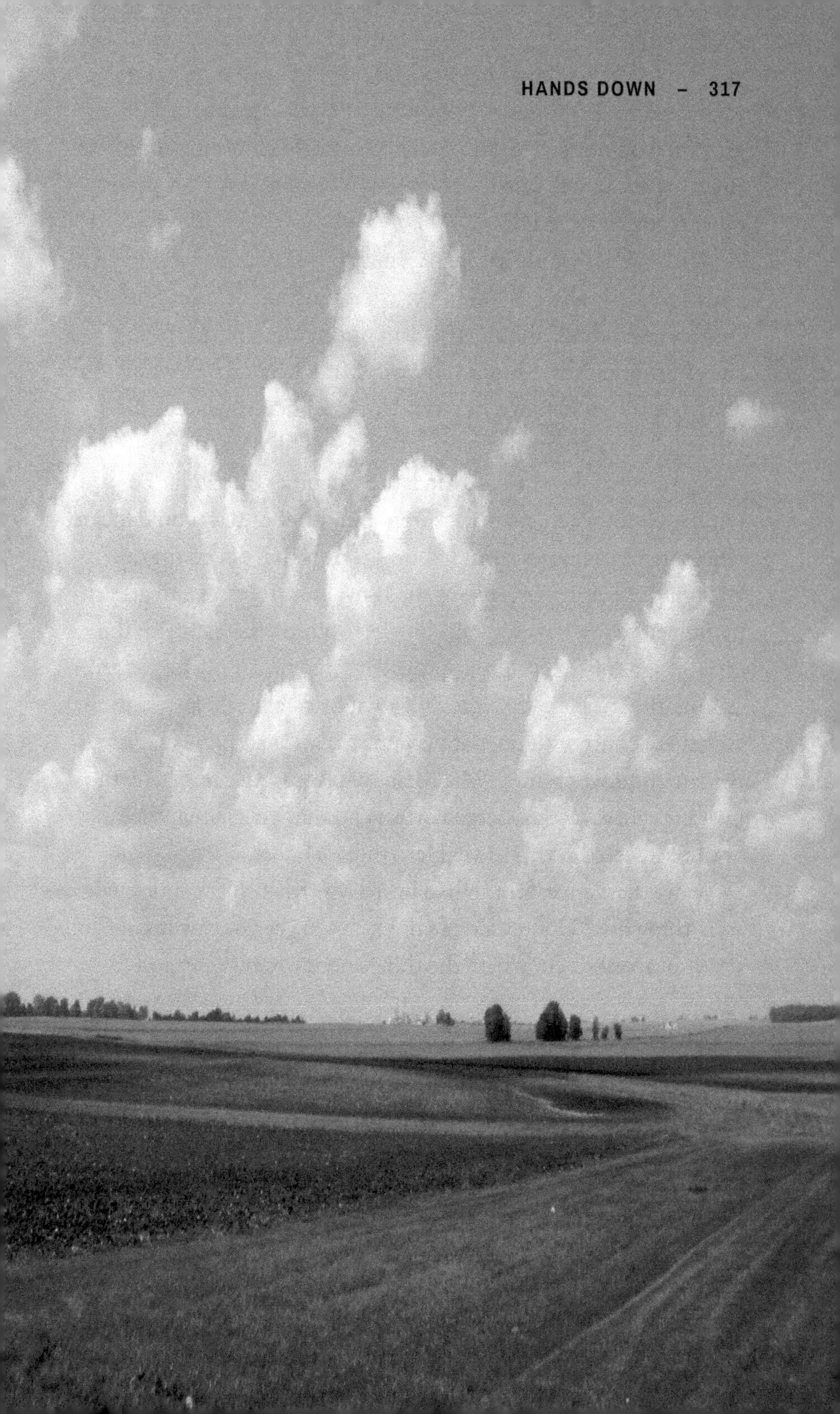

"Did you notice?" Spuhn said to Jenny. "The bishop didn't say anything about Mr. Klein's company. Nothing. It was all about other things they did."

With the car windows open a crack and the country odors of grass and cattle and growth in the wind mussing his hair, Spuhn continued to think about Mr. Klein during the solitude of the late afternoon drive toward Chicago. Mr. Klein himself would not be sad. In all probability, he would look confidently out at the warm fields where rows of corn plants head high were showing under the blue sky of the day in late September. Mentally, he would remark places where manufacturers and warehousers would locate, where strips of homes would fit on the outskirts of certain towns emerging as centers because of roadways, courthouses and government facilities. He would take in what Spuhn was taking in: the distant sight of small communities gathered under bowers of green around the steeple of a white or brown brick church, an occasional basketball court with boys at play, the games as serious and rich as the late summer evening. Mr. Klein would approve the drive, the meetings ahead with George Forrest and the others, including, Spuhn expected, a trip to see Hernandez's father.

More than once, Spuhn had heard Mr. Klein spark action with something like "Goddamit, it's not goin' to get done by itself. Quit screwin' around. Go where the things need to get done, and do 'em."

That's what Spuhn would do.

Straight from LaGuardia Airport the next morning, by cab in time for the one o'clock meeting with Mr. Forrest, Spuhn went ready for a forceful assault, one he found unnecessary. Once they settled down to conversation over the plates of salmon Mr. Forrest had provided, the banker soon unfurled proposals well-steeped in his firm's careful system. He knew Klein Enterprises Incorporated financials and projects and opportunities to the comma.

Mr. Forrest had changed only slightly since 1965. Wearing a tailored suit and vest of silky charcoal, he sat tall and powerfully in a display of regular exercise and careful diet. Hardly any additional white had appeared in his trim, Van Dyke beard.

Spuhn saw that the little impassive woman hearing nothing, seeing nothing while she cleared the meal took from Mr. Forrest a plate with about half the salmon, none of the almonds or seasoned potato eaten.

"Your timing is impeccable," Mr. Forrest said, after introducing Spuhn to his partner Spencer Sherman, a proper, attentive man with long English teeth and a mild tic when he blinked. His eyebrows and lashes, the same color as his hair, were on the verge of white, as pale as autumn corn husks. His slenderness made him seem tall; that plus his precisely erect posture gave the impression that he was seeing everything with mild trepidation, down the angle of his nose. About ten years junior to Mr. Forrest, the partner smiled and sat ready to answer and engage but could not mask completely his wish to leave the conference room and be active with other work.

"Thanks to Mr. Sherman and his astute recognition of an opportunity. . . what, eighteen months ago?"

Mr. Sherman, flushing slightly and smiling, moved to protest.

Mr. Forrest continued. "We have had a very nice payday and, as a result, well, let me explain."

He took two wire-bound booklets from his partner and handed one to Spuhn.

With an evenness that showed comfort with large numbers, speaking with the center-of-the-stage voice Spuhn first heard at the Stuckey's restaurant in northern Florida, Mr. Forrest explained a proposal that would have Madison Alberts taking a thirty-one percent interest in a Klein Enterprises Incorporated entity headed by Dennis Spuhn, who would also have an interest, a voting one.

Twenty percent of Madison Albert's stock would be preferred, with, of course, the agreed-upon dividend and the option of forcing repurchase of the holding or a part of it at set times after the first year, and with an agreed-upon premium. The individual Madison Alberts partners, including George Forrest and Spencer Sherman, would have a senior opportunity for personal investment in any partnerships formed by Klein Enterprises Incorporated for its development and property ownership activities. Mr. Forrest's firm would keep a minority interest in Spoon, the restaurant entity, with the right of first refusal in the event Dennis Spuhn chose to reduce his own percentage of ownership. Madison Alberts would have a seat on the Klein Enterprises Incorporated board.

With a prescience that made Spuhn imagine ways Mr. Forrest could be monitoring plans forming with Randy Isaacs for a new company, the banker promised that Madison Alberts would be paying attention to maximization of Spoon's process for gathering information about customers.

"That is a competitive advantage, a true, important one. Mr. Sherman has a very apt explanation."

Pleased at the cue, Mr. Forrest's partner said, "A business needs to know the texture of its transactions," he said. "It's no longer binary, yes sale or no sale. There is advantage in texture.

"To be perfectly candid. . . "

"When are you not?" Mr. Spencer said boldly.

Mr. Forrest smiled and continued. "To be perfectly candid, it is your clubs and such things that made us begin taking more than casual interest in your little reports from the front."

In the spirit of the moment, Spuhn told the two bankers about the intentions with the University of Iowa computing center student. Mr. Forrest nodded and twice slapped the table.

"Top of the list. Yes. No delay," Mr. Forrest said.

Assuming no hitches during due diligence and assuming the

present majority owner Jeanine Klein's willingness to sell no less than half of her own stake at the price Madison Alberts proposed, Madison Alberts would expect to complete the transaction within sixty days.

Spuhn could not hide the thoughts playing in his own expression. The staggering numbers and features had him leaving the immediate conversation and floating into Spoon and board meetings and the running of Klein Enterprises, then returning to the conference table of Madison Alberts with alternating seriousness and escapes of quick smiles. Spuhn saw Mr. Forrest's amusement.

In the high-ceilinged castle atmosphere of Madison Alberts, amid the antiquities and references to stolid ancestry, Spuhn was a squire in a surprise knighting.

With deft skill, the banker guided the discussion through the next tasks, the things both parties would do. Next Monday morning, or very soon, Spuhn would arrange a meeting with Mrs. Klein and her attorney for Madison Alberts. Possibly, Mr. Forrest himself would make the trip, unless Mrs. Klein and Mr. Diebold would be willing to come to New York.

Before ending the meeting, once the junior partner Mr. Sherman had left them, Mr. Forrest politely took up personal subjects, as if he had no other activities, no other business awaiting him before the afternoon ran out and the weekend began.

"Do you come to Florida anymore? Edward and I now have a place, a modest one, in Palm Beach. You remember Edward. "

Yes, Spuhn remembered the muscular, smartly dressed companion who had been with Mr. Forrest at the Stuckey's. Spuhn remembered their poodle, too, the frisky dog that had been the cause of the Stuckey's stop.

"Argent? Argent has gone the way of all flesh. Edward and I and our friends grieved appropriately and sent Argent on to the next world, where he surely is enjoying the licking of his own testicles in paradise. Lady Jane is now three years of age. Lady Jane is hardly a lady. She's a Pembroke Corgi, sassy and right in fashion. In Palm Beach and everywhere, the times they are a'changin'."

On the plane back to Chicago, Spuhn mulled Madison Alberts' packet and the things Mr. Forrest had said. Anticipating a free hand with the restaurant, Spuhn was beginning to recognize the drag of Mr. Soukup's questions and body language during discussions with the board.

If everything were a bridge game, Spuhn was beginning to run the play. If Mrs. Klein favored him the way Mr. Diebold said she did, the purchase offer from Madison Albert or something close to it, should be acceptable. She'd have a bucket of cash for her own needs and for her contributions to Annie Wittenmeyer home, where counselors were assiduously looking after, training children who reminded Mrs. Klein of her own Angela.

But what about the mop up of the present Klein board, the need to buy out George Soukup's seven percent and the small interests of two other board members?

The problem didn't perplex Mr. Diebold when Spuhn found him that Saturday afternoon at the end of eighteen holes played at Davenport Country Club.

"If your friends in New York come through and if you are the CEO, the others won't have the taste for second tier status. Think you can lock down the backing from Mr. Hernandez? Make a deal with Mr. Hernandez and then buy out the Soukup group."

Mr. Diebold was already looking away, catching the eye of a waiting friend near the entrance to the men's lounge.

"What's the matter?"

"I'll owe so many people so much money I won't know what to do."

The lawyer laughed. He signaled for his friend to go ahead and then said, "No, you owe so much money, they won't know what to do."

A beat later, he said with his eyes exactly on Spuhn's, "Tell you one thing. You own all of it or some of it, they won't let you run Klein unless you can run Spoon. You prove that you are making something of those restaurants and they'll let you sit up high and mighty at the whole company. But first you got to make it hum at Spoon."

Calmed by the lawyer's calm, Spuhn gave in to anticipation of the meeting with Mrs. Klein on Monday, the trip to gain Mr. Hernandez's backing after that, and, in the meantime, the normal weekend touching and leading of Spoon. Spoon was going to hum and Spuhn would make sure it was his when it did. Running hard beside Jenny Sunday evening as a long summer day drew down under a golden sky, Spuhn felt excited.

How badly did he want it? He could taste it, taste it, taste it. The hand hadn't become a laydown but it was moving that way. Hoorah!

Ronnie Tonti's dick was so hard he could flat chip it.

"Over here, darlin'," he called to Dottie, who was holding a white, fringed jacket and reaching for a hanger in the jumbled closet across the bedroom. She had returned from her job with a cloud on her: the groom's cousins had just plain gone to town on that unit eleven. The room all full of pizza mess and vomit and bottles one end to the other.

"Over here." Tonti patted the bed beside where he lay.

Dottie knew what he wanted, what she had under her skinny strip of red underwear, and she was using her advantage.

Kathy's little sister again.

Tonti put on the most innocent, little boy with the curl expression he could muster and told Dottie, "Oh, darlin', don't be like that. She wasn't nothin', don't mean nothin'."

Dottie shot him a look and turned to straighten other clothes hanging in the small closet space. "She's one started it," Tonti said. The walk had gone easily that day and he was feeling full of honey and sass during the drive back to Davenport from near Iowa City. The girl, a new high school graduate who had wheedled a chance to join Kathy that day on the Tonti escort, was eager to start on life. She laughed at everything, let her bare leg move against his in the back seat, and moved so the nipples of her breasts pressed out against her small t-shirt. That evening, the frisky little thing came along Third Street on a one-way circuit, and took Tonti, the handwalking celebrity, into the car.

"I'm not talkin' about that one, that little slut that one time," Dottie said.

Tonti fell silent while he thought of a new way.

Resting on one elbow, he patted the bed. "Oooee, mama, you're makin' me crazy tonight with those little red panties. You know you are. Get yourself over here. Tonight I've got a eight inch dick and a pile-drivin' ass."

Dottie let herself move too close to the bed, close enough that Tonti could take her wrist and guide her down onto the mattress.

After they were done, Dottie's irritated expression returned. Rising up against his chest and the hold of his arms, she fixed her eyes on him.

"That Spuhn is swindlin' you, you know."

"How's that?"

"You know how's that. You go out every day and you go workin' your way across Iowa like a . . . a trick dog and he's a one gets all the good from it. Not you."

Tonti liked the handwalk. He liked the strength he felt from one muscular arm to the other across the breadth of his shoulders, the fun he had with the college kids spending time with him each day, the pictures and the TV shows and the people who wanted autographs when he arrived at one of the restaurants. He flat out liked it. Hands down.

"*That boy is gettin' rich from you. I don't see you drivin' any yellow sports car.*"

Tonti was used to other people having more than he did. He didn't think about such things the way Spuhn and other people, now Dottie, too, thought about it. Tonti had his smile, his way, his handwalking. He had enough. The world was always full of open doors and spread legs.

"*Oh, darlin',*" *Tonti said, putting an arm around her again.*

Dottie wasn't done. This time she got up from the bed and pulled the sheet away from Tonti.

"*Time you get done goin' three hundred miles, you're gonna be all lopsided,*" *she said.* "*You'll be all upside down. You'll be all strong up top and your legs like the itty bitty arms of a polliwog.*"

And he'd be walkin' on his hands, all high, wide and handsome across the bridge into Omaha. Tonti imagined the crowd greeting him that day.

CHAPTER 25

The prettiest girl
I ever saw
Was sippin' bourbon
through a straw

Dennis' absence frustrated Jenny but didn't surprise her. Her husband's preparation for the October marathon in Chicago, plus his habit of pre-dawn work, made her accustomed to waking alone in the small, forest green trailer home she and Dennis rented from a retired couple living in the nextdoor bungalow. A terse note waited on the kitchen table: "Had to go to Newton. Solving a cluster fuck. Love, D."

They would meet in Iowa City, where Jenny had class and Marjorie allowed them the run of her apartment.

Jenny had expected something to pop. The rhythm of business – businesses, really – had become at once exhilarating for Spuhn and for her, and also consuming. Meanwhile, the losses from her father-in-law's card games were a manageable subsidy for Spuhn but also a constant worry for him and his family. His father's passive suffering of the bullying sales manager, of his dishonest card friends baffled Spuhn, who was himself so determined to be head of his own business. Jenny didn't know but she could guess what would happen that morning in Newton. Jenny was glad, one way or the other, for the decision to go, to get the distracting issue settled. She didn't want to think about the speed Spuhn was driving.

The matter was a small thing: the ignored, disorderly state of a big refrigerator smelling of sour milk at the Newton restaurant, nothing as serious as the three days of fierce April rain that had put Tonti's handwalking almost three miles off the Des Moines-on-July 4th pace. The corn was making up for lost time but out among the cornfields Tonti was off schedule. The delay pushed Spuhn to make the daily handwalk a seven-hour matter, a hair more than a mile each day, at least until July 4th.

For Spuhn, the pebble-in-the path disharmony of the Newton refrigerator with the plans and ambitions he had for the restaurants was the crushing straw on a back already carrying too much else. Klein's new summer, 1970 construction season was beginning with the addition of a warehouse center project in West Des Moines and a Holiday Inn near Spoon's Brady Street location. A joint venture with a Des Moines investment group was coming into existence under the management of Jack Diebold and Clint Graham, the methodical chief operating officer and former Army medic recruited from a South Dakota company of about Klein's size. The data company was succeeding rapidly, with Randy Isaac's ability to tease patterns from business records benefiting Spoon as well as two or three new clients each month; the staff now numbered seven, including the professor whose reputation had first lured Randy to leave New York for Iowa.

Spuhn expected push and drive and determination in everyone, most of all, in himself and in Jenny.

When they could, Spuhn and Jenny went to look at the five-acre home site they had chosen in the Klein Residential Development property named Oakcrest north of Davenport.

"Four bedrooms?" Jenny's father asked in amusement. Jenny knew her parents looked forward to grandchildren. Even before Anna lost Jan to the Hennings, the Adamskis seldom had any access to the boy. Bob's children Tyler and Sarah never came to the Midwest from their Connecticut home. Eight bedrooms would not be enough for Jenny's parents.

Certainly, while Dennis descended on his Newton restaurant like a motivating – and maybe an avenging – angel, Jenny had plenty to occupy her. She would graduate from Iowa in less than four weeks, soon after the Davenport Municipal Art Gallery show would include three of her Compare and Contrast paintings among the works of other rising Iowa painters and sculptors. With modest help from Dennis, she had found a former dress shop in a strip mall and completed a lease: by the first of September, Jenny would begin art classes for Quad City children in a bright space with a view of Rock Island Arsenal across a channel of the Mississippi River.

Before anyone else showed for work that day in Newton, Spuhn entered the restaurant, took the refrigerator apart, scrubbed it, and replaced the contents in Germanic order.

As he cleaned, his anger grew, his mind looping with "Who is in charge of this mob?"

He was waiting for the disconcerted manager when the man arrived, the fourth staff member to appear, Spuhn noticed. Awareness of his own neglect added to Spuhn's anger: when Jeff Tomkins left for a California position with the Montgomery Restaurant Group, Spuhn had trusted Tomkin's recommendation of the replacement.

Make dust or eat dust. If it's not done well, it's not done. The only direction is up. The signs were up at all the Spoon restaurants and also in the office and locker room of Klein Enterprises.

"See this?" Spuhn said, after throwing open the refrigerator door. "This is squared away. The whole restaurant. This place better be standing tall. A-sap."

Then, scrubbing his early plan to check on Tonti, at the time handwalking less than two hours west, Spuhn got back in the yellow Corvette and drove east to Iowa City. As he knew it would and just as he intended, the shuddering news of his morning's work and his venting traveled through Spoon. He didn't have to look: to the bottom of the Iowa City refrigerator, everything was strac, perfectly clean and in place.

By the end of the week, the Newton restaurant had a new manager as well as gleaming order.

When Spuhn caught up to Jenny at Marjorie's apartment, there were shadows of exhaustion under his green eyes, but his mood was elevated from the release of his Newton pressure as well as the phone conversations with people in the business offices of Klein and SI Data. Jenny had a termpaper and an exam looming but Spuhn was there, Marjorie was discreetly absent, and they had the chance for lovemaking.

Jenny left Spuhn asleep and went on foot to the art building for additional work on a painting she had in mind for the Davenport show. This one had the Third Reich's Swastika-adorned Heinrich Himmler in the forefront of a Ku Klux Klansman whose white covering emphasized the hard set of the young man's brown eyes.

Paying no attention as she went, enjoying the bloom of a large bed of red and yellow tulips, Jenny blundered into the path of Greg Benson, who was coming the other way with two law school companions. Benson moved to block the path and force Jenny to see him.

Her discomfort pleased him.

"Look out," Benson said to his amused classmates. "Don't get in the way of the University's famous nude model."

Jenny moved to the right, onto the lawn next to the path, and passed the trio with her eyes averted and her step quickened.

"Say hi to your husband for me," Benson said. "Tell him I'll be a lawyer in another year and will be able to sue him for all those people he's making sick with his food."

One of the two students with Benson whistled at Jenny's legs. All three turned to watch her as she hurried away.

The encounter broke Jenny's spirit for painting. Fuming, her mind wandering away from the work she had in mind, she puzzled over Benson's insult and the laugh from the two other law students. Why did Benson suddenly call her the University's famous nude model? In fact, she was more than ordinarily covered up, dressed as she was for her studio work in a long-sleeved old shirt of Dennis' and a splotched pair of faded jeans.

When she returned to the apartment, little accomplished at her studio, Jenny said nothing to Dennis about seeing Greg Benson.

The news came to Spuhn, and then to Jenny, in another way: in a phone call the former St. Sebastian's classmate made to the Iowa City Spoon, Greg Benson's message a congratulations to Spuhn on being married to someone becoming so famous for her art.

Spuhn had nothing to say.

"You know about the big show she's in at the Art Gallery, the Davenport museum? It's pretty controversial. That's what my dad says."

"Controversial how?"

"Let's just say the board is talking about it."

"Okay, thanks. That it? I've got to go."

"We should have lunch sometime, Dennis. We never see each other anymore."

"Yeah, sometime."

A big deal exhibit grabbing the attention of Benson's father and the rest of the Art Gallery board?

Spuhn was too busy to indulge curiosity about the facts of Benson's smug warning or even the fact of his call. What wasn't Benson's father hot and bothered about? Seemingly always upset, with warmth showing on a large head fringed with a scruff of rusty hair, the powerful banker was always ready to assert the force of the family's place in the economic and cultural fabric of Bettendorf and neighboring Davenport. Piss on him. Spuhn had his own concerns.

Jenny was not so sanguine. She took Marjorie into her confidence.

As soon as the exhibit space was available to the exhibiting artists, Jenny and Marjorie drove to Davenport. Ostensibly, Jenny wanted to be certain of the hanging of her three works. Marjorie, soon to begin training as a United stewardess, was on a lark, glad to have a day without a schedule.

She had no trouble identifying the painting.

"Jenny. Oh, God, Jenny," Marjorie said. "Come look at this."

There on its own prominent wall across from the show entrance was the painting the artist had titled "The Legs That Prove the Existence of God." Faithfully executed, the long legs – Jenny's legs – angled up the large canvas to a luminescent vaginal opening at the exact center. Beyond that thrusting vulva, like a neighboring range of peaks, were the perfect, nippled breasts of a yellow-haired woman whose head - Jenny's head - was thrown back in eyes-closed ecstasy.

Jenny looked at her legs, her vulva, her breasts, her face. She looked at herself.

Then she looked around to see if anyone else in the space was looking.

"What are you going to do?" Marjorie asked.

Jenny didn't know. With Marjorie following, she went in search of the graduate student, the sculptor who had been given responsibility for curation of the show. He wouldn't be there until the next day.

That was too late for Jenny. She and Marjorie went to the offices of the museum and, on the second try early that afternoon, were able to talk with the administrator, an inattentive man whose dramatic brown muttonchop sideburns were a failing anchor for the crown of hair slipping rearward from his high forehead.

"This is a student show, an adventuresome exploration of new ideas and new talent," the man said. He spoke in practiced phrases and pride, an administrator whose young career would elevate from the show. Controversy? Bless controversy. Nourish controversy, his manner said. Use controversy.

"An art museum can't be static. It has to probe. It has to provoke. It has to excite," he said to Jenny, who by then was speaking with interruptions of sobbing.

If the controversy of the painting was a satisfaction for the administrator, it was ecstasy for the quiet painter neither Jenny nor Marjorie remembered from the time they modeled. Shy and uncomfortable in conversation, the delicate artist named Craig Owens looked downward through wire-framed glasses. Jenny and Marjorie understood well enough from his evasive mumbles and head shakes: the painting was in the show because it was shocking. The shock could spur a career that was up to this moment unnoticed. After Davenport, there would be another exhibition in Des Moines, and then representation by a gallery in Cedar Rapids.

"How much do you want for it?" Spuhn asked when he learned of the painting, talked his way into the space and found the artist.

What price notoriety? The quiet, uncomfortable artist was as inflexible as the museum administrator. Craig Owens would not sell the work, would not withdraw it from exhibition.

Unable to dislodge the painting from the show, Spuhn and Jenny thought of passing up the preview cocktail party. But Jenny wanted to know the reaction to her three Compare and Contrast works and, in addition, hoped that the location of the Legs painting in another room would protect her from recognition. For his part, Spuhn wanted the chance to mix with the business and community heads who were on the museum's guest list.

Before mixing with any of those, however, Spuhn had to mix with Greg Benson and his unctuous attention. Attending the show with an excited Iowa student who would begin her junior year in the fall, Benson and his date Pammy were in a group led by Nels Benson. While his father sought out his own prospects and cronies, Greg Benson and Pammy hovered near Craig Owens' work, The Legs That Prove the Existence of God.

From neck bridges and weights, Benson had picked up the stolidity and muscular shoulder hump of a grown steer. The heft and the thinning of his hair was making him physically as well as temperamentally his father's slightly shorter understudy.

"When did you model for this, Jenny?" Benson asked, loud enough that others turned to regard the painting and Jenny together.

Jenny had dressed more conservatively than fashion required, in a blouse and jacket that came to the throat and a straight tan skirt that came almost to her knees.

Later, from among guests standing and talking near other works, Spuhn and Jenny watched Benson call attention to the Owens work. "The model is also an artist, Jenny Adamski. She's married to Dennis Spuhn, the restaurant guy."

Married to Dennis Spuhn. The restaurant guy. Nude model for the art classes. Nude. Getting ready to open her own art school for children.

Like a salesman pulling wanderers from the aisle of a trade show, Benson had his patter ready when he recognized the *Morning Democrat* writer Jim Seid in the room. As Spuhn monitored the

Seed Corn columnist's visit from a far doorway, he could hear the
carefully offhand descriptions Benson was offering in his rising
voice and the questions Seid was asking in a smoker's rasp. Seid was
taking notes in a small spiral pad. Beside them as they talked,
Pammy, too young to drink and over-served with the party's
champagne, looked increasingly unmoored and merrily flushed.

Spuhn called two other *Morning Democrat* writers but could
only reach one, a business writer who said Jim Seid was so popular
that he was left free to write whatever he wished. His column sold
papers. Spuhn could draw his own conclusions. Spuhn did. The
man was what he seemed to be: popular and godly in print, crusty
and opportunistic in person.

The next morning's column justified Spuhn and Jenny's unease.

Jenny's maiden and married names appeared throughout,
thoroughly associated with the Spoon restaurants. The "Legs"
painting sparked the poet in the columnist: "the gams of a pin-up
goddess", "like a temptress from the shadows of a Lautrec", "Iowa's
own answer to the painted ladies of Carl Sandburg". But most
alarming to Spuhn and Jenny was the open warning in Seid's report
of Jenny's intention to teach young Quad City children at her new
art school studio on Riverside Drive. In addition to Benson's
ingenuous damnations, Seid had included comments from a
professional educator friend, an Iowa Wesleyan faculty member
who had not seen the painting or the show.

Benson had accomplished his purpose: virtually a community
alert that Jenny's art school would be the core of a red light district
meant for cherubic innocents. With Seid's column as a reference,
the villagers would know exactly where to assemble for the torching
of Jenny's school.

Normally contained, Spuhn seethed as he went about the work
of Spoon and the other companies. His short patience plus the
Newton story made all of Spoon edgy. When he looked, Spuhn saw

unusual cleanliness in restaurants where managers and everyone else were circumspect, preternaturally quiet and occupied. The supervisors and managers at Klein stayed out of his path.

At SI Data, Randy was so immersed in algorithms that he had no capacity for the show, let alone the match of any shirt with whatever pair of pants he pulled from a laundry pile.

The head of *Davenport Morning Democrat* and *Evening Times* advertising sought Spuhn out and apologized. Except for when Spuhn himself began to joke at Benson's expense, except for when Spuhn opened the subject with derisive slurs on the painter and the "best of Iowa" show, the Seed Corn column and the other articles were verboten subjects in Spuhn's presence.

For Jenny, the debacle could have been a race. After the crying and frustration of the show night, she became gathered and decisive, same as she was when she increased her painful speed in the final part of a track competition. Rather than begin the art school in September, she and Spuhn would delay the opening for an additional 30 or 60 days. The extra days would give Jenny a chance to visit art schools that interested her in Chicago, St. Louis and Omaha. When the term ended and she graduated, Jenny began with the Omaha trip, a chance to spend time with Anna in Harlan.

Anna, still weak and recovering, cheerfully settled with the former Iowa classmate, the wrestler, wanted to talk with Jenny about news of something happening with Bob's family in Connecticut.

While she was away, Spuhn and Jenny continued to benefit from an unintended effect of Greg Benson's mischief. Among the young patrons of Spoon and among business associates who had been observing the progress of Dennis Spuhn's career, the notorious painting increased curiosity about the athletic, youthful entrepreneur and his movie star wife.

At the same time awareness of the painting raised some interest in Dennis Spoon, his wife and Spoon, awareness of the show soon collapsed it: An angry museum patron, Nels Benson, first managed to gather board support for placement of the "Legs" painting in a limited-access exhibition room and then succeeded in dimming the Davenport career of the museum administrator. By the time Jenny's art school opened, the executive had taken a position on the East Coast.

Ronnie Tonti woke to a knocking that had the door of his rooming house space slamming in the loose fit of its frame.

As soon as he unlatched the door, Mrs. Fink rammed it open, enough that she was able to stick her head inside and confirm Tonti's danger to the standards of her home.

"You have woman in room?" Mrs. Fink pressed to enter the room, one with barely enough room for Tonti, the single bed, and the dresser scratched with the initials of some previous boarders.

"Alohrs pas, mamere," said Tonti, setting his round, boyish face in a practiced look of innocence as he let the determined, birdlike woman scan the disheveled space where Tonti had begun staying at the beginning of June, as soon as nightly return to Davenport became impractical.

"You have woman in room," Mrs. Fink said. "Thursday. Woman in room."

"No, Nana," Tonti said. Thursday, was it? That was Thursday, the wild little chère who had attached to him as soon as she settled him with a menu at the Newton Spoon? An acne sore flamed red along one side of her nose but she shook and brushed against him with the spark of a woman. The way they went at each other when they reached the rooming house, it's a wonder the whole rickety place didn't collapse.

"You no good," Mrs. Fink said. "You no stay more."

Groggy, knowing there would be no sleep, Tonti agreed and kept agreeing until Mrs. Fink gave him "hour", enough time for him to wash, shave, throw his things in a gym bag and go to the diner down the street for coffee and flirting with a cautious waitress named Susie. Already, the handwalking had progressed nearly ten miles past Mrs. Fink's rooming house in Newton, almost to Colfax. He had seen enough of Mrs. Fink, upside down at first as he worked along First Street, the Rte. 6 path in front of the gray house with the line of chairs on its aging cream porch, and then during the week and some days he had been staying there.

No woman? Spuhn had bumped the pay and accelerated the pace at the beginning of May. The extra hour each day, and the distance, made the trip back to Davenport long. Dottie had only driven to see him those two times and, when he was with her in Newton or in Davenport, she pouted and scolded about the way he was letting Dennis Spuhn horse him around.

Tonti didn't want to hear it, didn't want to think about it. He just wanted to get upside down, and get moving deliberately, rhythmically, hands down toward Omaha. Seven hours, a mile a day? Maybe he'd just keep going. There was a lot of room on the other side of Omaha.

CHAPTER 26

I know a girl out in the east, Oly Oly Anna
She's the one I like the least, Oly Oly Anna
I know a girl out in the west, Oly Oly Anna
She's the one I like the best, Oly Oly Anna

By now, there had been enough handwalk arrivals at Spoons that a procedure had developed for all of them, including this day's July 4th event. With a college student staying at his side - Donna this time - Ronnie Tonti completed the last stretch at a pace that let the clapping, shouting onlookers savor the sight of him and of excited photographers and two television crews maintaining position for their own documentation. Following immediately behind Tonti were two athletic young men carrying a Spoon banner and wearing Spoon restaurant attire, same as Tonti.

The warmth of the day was already undoing the hosing of the parking area's new asphalt. The spraying plus the brooming of the path were improvements on some other arrivals, when the heat and the bits of gravel burned into Tonti's hands.

For the sake of timing, the first part of the morning's handwalk ended close enough to the finish that Tonti could arrive flushed from being upside down but still fresh for photos and for the banter Spuhn allowed with customers as well as reporters.

This holiday as always, Tonti warmed to the audience and the pageantry. Upside down, grinning as he took everything in from his angle, he responded to calls from children and teenagers along both sides of the stanchioned route. When a high school band sweating in heavy fall uniforms began to play, he added a bounce and a sway to his movement along the path.

A Marine color guard led the way to the front of the new Spoon, then took a position in front of a contingent of veterans from the American Legion.

At the completion of the walk, upon a large white "170" that exaggerated the walk's progress by a few miles, Dennis Spuhn took over Donna's stage manager role. While the mayor of West Des Moines saluted the national holiday and the opening of a fine new restaurant, while the band played the National Anthem, Spuhn attended to the positioning of Tonti, the public officials, himself and the Spoon banner in the line of sight for camera crews and photographers.

For the next two hours, with Donna and other summer crew members close by, Tonti mingled and signed autographs. Some had Kodak and 35mm cameras with flashes. The restaurant was jammed to fire safety limits and noisy with celebration, fragrant with the smell of hamburgers, fries and all the Spoon fare. Additional Spoon staff moved about with registration forms for the Spoon birthday and promotions database.

By the time the two Iowa students who were his drivers brought Tonti to his boarding house in the small cluster of buildings named Colfax, the western sky was turning gray with flat clouds.

In his room before he went to the tavern nearby, Tonti watched his image and then the weather forecast on a black-and-white Zenith television. Briefly, before two giggling women at the bar became brave enough to feel the muscle of his arm, Tonti gave sour thought to the television report: Ronnie Tonti, sweaty and clownish, made the crowd applaud while Dennis Spuhn, turned out in his fitted sport coat and his Rolex watch, had the part of respected Rex, monarch of the prairie Mardi Gras. Was Dottie seeing the same in Davenport? Tonti knew what Dottie would say.

Spuhn saw the grandeur of the home in the look that escaped from Bob as they turned into the long driveway. Stakes and ruts of dried clay and topsoil were everywhere. The sound of hammering and sawing came from other parts of the Oakcrest development as well as from the three-story wealth display where Spuhn and Jenny had taken up residence about two weeks before, at the end of August.

Spuhn moved some sawhorses a little to their right, and led the way across the long front porch into the paneled foyer.

With the windows open, and with the heat of the previous weeks replaced by air that was only warm, the big living room was a good place for hearing Bob's presentation and going over his firm's proposal for sale of most of Klein Enterprises. Except for the electricians wiring the rest of the kitchen and the carpenters finishing the cherry wood moldings and cornices and other woodwork in the combination office and library overlooking what would be a flower garden, Spuhn and Bob had the home to themselves. Jenny would be working at her school until late.

Bob was proud of the work of the analysts who had studied Klein's financials since mid-summer and constructed scenarios for a number of purchasers and economic environments.

"This is a good time, people optimistic, wallets coming open. The smart money thinks the recession has run its course," Bob said.

When Spuhn met Bob that afternoon at the airport in Moline, Jenny's brother seemed distracted and unprotected. That passed quickly, before Spuhn knew what he was sensing. In a blink, Bob set his handsome features for corporate engagement and hewed to the smooth niceties of concentrated interest in Spuhn, Jenny, the businesses and what could be noticed in the familiar, but progressing, Quad Cities. In the living room, with his perfect summer weight khaki suit coat hung on the back of a chair and his starched French cuffs rolled two flips up his forearms, Bob had no apparent concern except the ferreting out of the most beneficial way for Spuhn to effect the sale of most of Klein Enterprises, all but the parts related to Spoon.

"You've got revenues from a good leasing portfolio, and the rest is attractive, too, but look at this. Here, right here, midway down the column on this page."

The Klein pension funds, in the aggregate, were over-funded by as much as twenty-four percent.

"Twenty-four percent." Bob emphasized the number again. "Get the thing structured right, and your buyer can buy cash. And, for the privilege of doing that, pay you and other owners a big multiple."

With care during the next two hours, Bob then presented buyer scenarios, each with possibilities for amount and timing of payment, risks, and rewards to each shareholder, mostly to Mrs. Klein, to Spuhn, and to some managers who were small holders.

Under any scenario, before taking into account any tax consequences, Spuhn and Jenny came out multi-millionaires able to sparkle with jewels and to waste steak. In Spuhn's judgment, the most appealing were those possibilities that freed money for investment in SI Data and in other data ventures Randy Isaacs was touting. The sale would give Spuhn money for investments in the data management category and additional time for Spoon, a restaurant enterprise he had begun imagining as a coast-to-coast entity.

The prospect also permitted Spuhn to think about a plan known only to himself: the idea of investing in, maybe owning, a trucking firm that could employ his father as a manager, probably head of sales.

Bob and his firm felt they knew the financial aspects of the proposed deal. Spuhn would have to convince Mrs. Klein and the other owners, enough of them that Spuhn would be able to proceed with his interest and theirs constituting a majority.

"I think they'll like it," Spuhn said.

Money would be the trick. Spuhn hadn't seen anyone put off by the chance to have money. Even quiet, steady Mrs. Klein, Spuhn felt, was as susceptible to money as anyone else. In her case, except for the cost of the cruises she took once in awhile with her sister or her pilgrimage to the Holy Land with her parish group, she just liked shoving it all toward the Annie Wittenmeyer Home unless some other charity had caught her ear. Who else, except Jenny, perhaps, was like that? Jenny could love him rich or poor, she said to him. But poor? What would there be of him for her to love?

The carpenters and electricians finished before Bob looked at his watch and gathered his documents into the slots of his briefcase.

Bob had chosen to stay this time at the Blackhawk Hotel, convenient to Jack Diebold's office and some other appointments, not with his parents or with Jenny and Spuhn.

Before they met Jack Diebold for dinner, Spuhn drove his brother-in-law to the Blackhawk, then went to Klein Enterprises for an hour of phone calls.

From then on, as the sale progressed through presentations to the Klein board, through visits to investors George Forrest in New York and to Antonio Hernandez in Coral Gables, through the time of due diligence, Robert Adamski's appearances became regular. By the middle of October, the Oakcrest house was finished enough that Jenny's brother had the use of a second floor guest bedroom with a phone and, down the hall, a second bathroom. Anticipating a daughter when she and Dennis began to have children, Jenny had chosen a delicately pink wallpaper with a shepherd girl and lambs pattern.

After presenting sale options in a way that persuaded the Klein board, Spuhn's brother-in-law fashioned a second presentation that informed Mrs. Klein of the sale's good effect on her ability to fund Annie Wittenmeyer Home programs.

At first blush, Mrs. Klein favored an Omaha contractor on Robert Adamski's list of prospective acquirers. Her husband had known the father of the present owner. Also, Mrs. Klein knew of the firm's involvement with Creighton University and its contributions to the expansion of the city's St. Joseph Hospital.

A Chicago firm the investment banker found attractive for its strong financials and the likely fit of that company's government contracting expertise with Klein's experience in commercial development, including hotels and bank branches, held no interest for Mrs. Klein. The firm had been the lead in a venture with Klein and a St. Louis civil engineering firm at one time, a project that ended with negligible revenues, litigation and bad blood. She remembered her husband reading the obituary of a former CEO and remarking, "Francis X. Shannon died. Son of a bitch's probably halfway to hell by now."

Ordinarily pressed, perfect and possessed, the investment banker arrived with an exact calendar, new and old tidbits of business information that included first names and nicknames, and an Eastern wardrobe well-matched to his disciplined, handsome form. When a sudden trip caught Spuhn wrapped in West Des Moines meetings Jack Diebold and Clint Graham had scheduled with their partner in a new community of 250 homes, Jenny went to Moline Airport and met her brother.

They hugged at the airport and talked lightly during the drive across the river into Iowa and Davenport. Jenny saw her brother looking tired and unusually distracted. An easterner, he snickered at

Jenny's impatience with bridge traffic: someone ahead was slowed for a look at the Mississippi. In proper form, Jenny's brother asked about and shared his own information about Anna's cancer, about their parents, about the way Davenport had changed since Bob graduated from Iowa in 1956. Then, after two slow years of Army duty with a unit assigned to peace-keeping in Korea, he had let a connected GI friend guide him into New York banking.

Happy herself, excited about the progress of her art school space, glad of the chance to be in a car under a sunny, blue October sky with her admirable brother, Jenny found herself working to hold his attention, to keep his expression from turning slack and troubled.

Maybe Bob knew something about Anna and Tank.

Tank puzzled Spuhn as much as he did Jenny. "What do you think of Anna living with him while she gets her cancer treatment?"

Bob ignored her and answered a question she hadn't asked.

"Sarah is giving us a rough time," he said.

Jenny could not remember Bob thrown off stride by anything. Twelve years her senior, long departed from Davenport, he was moved away, moved East, mannered and familiar and successful in realms of the prosperous east coast, a place of fashion, clubs, luncheons with white gloves, celebrities and famous universities. "Sarah. . . rough time": the soft admission was like the ripping away of a bandage.

Before they arrived at the Oakcrest development, Jenny knew the wound was large and painful. Freshman year at the good high school was a triumph for Sarah. Good grades. New friends. A part in a play. The discovery that Sarah liked art and had talent. On and on. Fine reports, liked by teachers.

Then, during the summer, things changed. Sarah became testy, very quiet, completely averse to any rules about anything: a time to go to bed, chores, mealtimes. She cried about nothing. She sketched and painted in her room. She played music at top volume. One day in July, when Linda had taken time from her own charity obligations and made lots of plans for an outing to the Met in the city with Sarah and Tyler, Sarah wouldn't get out of bed, just wouldn't go. While Linda called Bob, Sarah got up and went out. Some girls from another high school, girls the family did not know, picked Sarah up and they all went somewhere till almost eleven that night. Sarah wasn't drunk when she came home but she smelled like she'd had some beer and been around lots of cigarette smoking. After Sarah fell asleep, Linda looked in Sarah's purse and found those Zigzag papers that go with marijuana.

As troubling as Sarah's transformation was for Bob and for Linda, Sarah's unhappiness was a mystery, too. Already a pretty child with her mother's dark hair and eyes, the promise of her mother's figure, Sarah was maturing into a young woman as attractive as someone who would become a model. People always recognized her as Linda's daughter. No one ever guessed she was only 15.

What could the girl lack for happiness? She was doing well in the area's best school. Her house was not the ten-acre estate of the Gibbons but Bob and Linda were making plans for a pool. Certainly, Sarah had fine clothes and means. The family had spent a week in Ft. Lauderdale, right on the beach, at Christmastime and would take a similar trip this Christmas. Linda had bought Sarah a bracelet with pearls in it. Sarah didn't even need braces; the dentist couldn't get over the perfection of her bite.

Bob and Linda and Sarah's brother Tyler never knew what would happen anytime: when they ran into a neighbor, at school, anywhere. Bob couldn't risk having Sarah around if he would see a client at the club.

Just keeping Sarah at the high school was precarious. Bob and Linda worried constantly that a teacher or an administrator would notice Sarah's change and begin a process that would lead to separation from normal classes and maybe from the school altogether.

Pushed to it at last, Bob confided in a doctor he knew at the gym and received a recommendation. The first three visits to the psychiatrist in the city were expensive and baffling, with no apparent effect, but Bob and Linda would continue. Jenny's brother didn't know what else to do. Nor did Jenny. The niece Jenny remembered from a Thanksgiving visit two years before and from Christmas card photos was a fashionable, dark-eyed, city-knowledgeable girl who gave off a sweet sense of promise.

At the house, Bob took over Spuhn's upstairs office. A clock from the home of Jenny's Estonian grandfather ticked in the living room. At times, Bob's voice and the sound of laughter came down the stairs and into the sun room, where Jenny had set up an easel.

Bob's revelation had put shadows into the afternoon. Jenny stretched, looked at her canvas with no confidence for working on it, wrote two small checks for small art school bills, and thought about her niece. Jenny went for a three-mile run, half within the muddy development and half on the graveled road past the cattle pasture and cornfields of farms to the north. Deep in the distance, a green combine followed by an open-topped grain truck worked at harvesting soybeans.

Spuhn arrived home in good spirits further raised by what Bob reported about his discussions with interested buyers.

"Outstanding. Hoorah!" Jenny heard. When she came to the office room with water for Spuhn, Tab for Bob, her brother had returned to Robert Adamski, his manners and sure voice fully obscuring the wound he had shown his sister.

By the next evening, the banker and Spuhn had their business wrapped up. Jenny's brother would manage the communications with George Forrest, Antonio Hernandez and their advisors and partners. Spuhn would present everything to Mrs. Klein before Bob returned for a meeting with the Klein board. Bob expected the completion of due diligence and the accomplishment of the sale before the end of 1970.

"Hoorah!" Straight from a phone call with Randy Isaacs, Spuhn found Jenny at her easel and hectored her with biting of her neck and nibbling of her ear until they moved to the bedroom.

CHAPTER 27

Few more days and we'll be through
I won't have to look at you
So, I'll be glad and so will you

Only two days into the situation with Joe Szabo, Jim Clayton wasn't even trying to mask his unhappiness. Szabo, Clayton's roommate Slick and anyone else could read on Clayton's dimpled face the sour thought in Clayton's mind: "What a pain in the ass."

But what could the hunted, haunted Szabo do? And how could Clayton get out of the same predicament? Just knowing Szabo, let alone sheltering him, could upset the whole law career applecart.

Now in his second year of law school, taking to the levers and tricks of legal argument, feeling the power of the lawyer's life that would be his, Clayton was safe in his 1-Y world, deferred from the draft and from real consideration of Vietnam because of the fall from that rodeo horse. But now, here was Szabo, nutty and dismal and unfocused, seemingly ready to cower indefinitely with the dusty, lopsided venetian blinds drawn down against sighting by anyone interested enough to look in from an apartment in the neighboring 50-unit building.

"Hey, man. . . " Slick had begun saying, his smile and shrug a clear indication that Clayton needed to clear things up, to get his fugitive high school friend settled someplace else.

"I know," Clayton said each time. "I know. Don't get up tight about it."

Clayton's apartment mate, Gerald Schlichter whose family farmed near Estherville not far from Minnesota, was losing patience with the refugee who had planted himself on the old wine-colored couch. No war hero himself, a draftee clerk at two U.S. posts during his service, the normally easy-going Slick was paying for law school with the GI Bill.

Hapless and confused, Szabo was dragging Clayton into all the problems of Vietnam. Szabo's presence was also troubling to the psychology student who had become skittish about using the apartment for sex.

Szabo knew of the University of Iowa War Resisters and the draft counseling available from them.

"So go there. Talk to them," Clayton said.

But Szabo, so frightened he was frozen, wouldn't risk it. Would Clayton go for him?

"The pigs will be watching everyone there," Szabo said. "And the FBI must have people working undercover."

There was no advising Szabo. Sallow from weeks, months of uneasy sleep and too many cigarettes, Szabo was only beginning to have his thinning black hair grown back in a semblance of civilian style. For all his effort and for all his touching and combing, a black Fu Manchu mustache still appeared as a weak, uneven string of black hairs.

"I need a lawyer," Szabo had announced as soon as Clayton answered the two in the morning knocking at the apartment door.

A lawyer? Clayton was less than halfway through law school.

"You're smart. You know how to look things up. You know how to read the regulations," Szabo said.

Szabo's arrival wasn't a complete surprise, not for anyone who knew Szabo. A month before, in mid-October, the FBI had begun looking in earnest. Not only Clayton but Szabo's parents and a roster of St. Sebastian's classmates had been called or visited by an agent looking for the military deserter who had left midway through basic training at Ft. Polk, Louisiana.

"You had your head shaved. You were wearing Army clothes. How did you get away from the Army base?" Clayton asked.

Szabo smiled and drew in on the last of one cigarette. After exhaling, he said, "Everything is FTA. Fuck the Army. No one wants to be in. No one. A second lieutenant gave me a ride off the post and then I just started hitchhiking wherever anyone was going. The Army is a heavy thing, man. You know the spirit of the bayonet? Kill. You don't shout that, you don't shout 'kill', one of the grit sergeants makes you do pushups till your arms fall off."

Clayton didn't have to ask why Szabo showed up at the apartment Clayton shared with Slick. But Clayton asked.

"I figured the pigs wouldn't look here. You're not the type gets so involved."

Spuhn? Had Szabo called Spuhn, gone to see him?

"Spuhn's straight, way too straight," Szabo said. "I like him but Spuhn is so American now, you know? So uptight. He's got all his businesses and everything now."

True, just that week, a *Des Moines Register* writer who had easily succumbed to Spuhn's charm quoted the restaurant owner in an article about co-promotion marketing trends. Contrary to his intentions, curiosity made Clayton open each of the envelopes that came from Spoon.

Szabo laughed. "I just remembered Hayes, what he said that time at St. Sebastian's about the color of Spuhn's eyes. What color would they be if money were some other color? Remember that?"

Clayton did remember. "Before you know the law, know the facts," Clayton had heard and written in his notes that same week. The fact was, Szabo could have Spuhn, this Spuhn, pegged. Clayton knew where that left him.

Thanksgiving break began in three days. Clayton would risk it. He'd go and talk with a law student involved with the War Resisters. There would be no mention of Szabo. And when Clayton and Slick came back from the break, Szabo would be gone.

Nodding to Janis Joplin and "Ball and Chain", giving Clayton half his attention, Szabo agreed.

"Looookin' at the rain," Szabo sang badly, miserably over Janis Joplin and Big Brother and the Holding Company.

Flakes of snow were making the apartment steps slippery when Clayton left to attend class and find the War Resisters classmate.

When he came to the area of the library where the former paratrooper in his mid-20s had his face turned down and his medium-long blond hair falling forward as he studied, Clayton didn't interrupt. He settled himself at a table on the same floor and took stock of anyone able to see or hear. Twice, Clayton got up and moved toward the draft counselor's spot before noticing another student within hearing. In the end, Clayton gave up the chance to have the draft counselor's advice. Sure that revealing Szabo, even without Szabo's name, would risk something too great for a law student with a 1-Y and an intention of having a prosperous practice, Clayton cleared his study desk and left. Szabo's waste of the time disgusted Clayton.

When he returned to the apartment, the snow had deepened. Wind curving hard around the building had sculpted the steps into a mound with nothing solid until Clayton's weight punched holes more than half a foot deep. Inside, as he stamped, he saw Szabo, inert, asleep on his back with his jaw slack, his near arm hanging to the floor amid the debris of his stay: an ash tray ringed by by over-flow, a crumpled Winston pack, a book Clayton had been given by a girlfriend and read that fall, *Soul on Ice* by the Black Panther Eldridge Cleaver.

CHAPTER 28

Somewhere there's a mother
She's crying for her boy
He's an Airborne Ranger
With his orders to deploy

After postponing once in deference to Spuhn's schedule and
also knowing that Anna's brother Bob could not leave a deal, Tank
Vetrov and Anna Adamski went ahead with their wedding.

In the end, the delay was propitious. Jenny and the others who
came for the ceremony missed the six degree high of the original
date in January. By comparison, as Jenny heard all day, besides
falling on Valentine's Day, the wedding now luckily fell on a day of
relative warmth, almost 19 degrees forecast for western Iowa by the
time Tank and Anna would be wed.

The delay also allowed time for Railway Express to deliver the
gift package from Bob and Linda, an elaborately wrapped fondue
set and five-piece mixing bowl assortment. Anna had put the
accompanying note of congratulations on the mantel, where Jenny
saw photographs of other family members, including one of Anna's
son Jan.

Jenny regretted Spuhn's inability to pull away from Spoon and
from Klein long enough to be with her this day but she, Anna and

Tank knew the wedding could not have taken place at all if Spuhn hadn't arranged for Jack Diebold's law firm to straighten up the loose ends of Tank's short marriage to Angie. "Tell Dennis thanks, tell Spuhn thanks," Jenny heard from all sides.

In the warmth of Tank and Anna's home, before following Tank's friend, the retired wrestler Hurtin' Henry, across the open space of the yard into the Place for Knowing God, Jenny kept at Anna's side, ready to help with the adjustment of a collar, the combing of a curl, the catching of a fall. The chemotherapy regimen plus the previous year's mastectomy of her cancerous right breast and her left one made Anna, despite her lively eyes and the lustrous regrowth of her brown hair, wan and vulnerable.

"Why don't we drive you right from the house to the barn?" Anna's mother asked. "Your father can drive you."

"Mom," Anna said. "The car would get stuck in the snow. I'll be all right. Don't worry."

"You look beautiful," Nina Bjornson said, placing her big body in front of Anna and reaching to adjust a fold of the cream-colored dress. Anna's dress was simple and made her happy, just as Nina's own purple one made Tank's childhood schoolmate feel elegant.

"I'm a bride. I'm supposed to be beautiful," Anna said. "That's the script. You know, rolling, tight on the bride."

Nina's smile made ridges of chins. "I don't know what you're talking about, Anna, but you look beautiful, I am saying that."

The appearance of one of Tank's burly high school wrestlers at the kitchen door started the procession. Pretending he was not cold, the boy drew his thick neck into the collar of a Harlan letter jacket, pushed his reddened hands into the front pockets and endured the cold breeze fluttering the sandy mop of his hair.

"Everyone's ready now, Mrs. Vetrov," the boy said when someone opened the door.

Galina, a stickler, was about to correct him.

"I'm ready, too," Anna called out in amusement and happiness. "Let's go. I'm ready to become Mrs. Vetrov."

The hazy white sunlight on the snow of the yard was enough that Jenny had to squint before she and the rest of the wedding party entered the barn's darkness. They moved toward the beamed space where a string of weak lights hung over the waiting Tank Vetrov, his best man Galina's husband Jim Casper and the burly former wrestler, Pastor Henry. As she had been doing since the day before, Jenny studied the University of Iowa wrestler so famous for powerful, abandoned chaos before the change that transformed Tank into an equally determined, reckless penitent. The small town, the plain house on the scrap of farm, the fierce pondering of Scripture, everything about Tank clashed with the sorority darling life Anna had led at Iowa and then in her advertising jobs.

Anna's boyfriends had been stylish men who knew fashion and where to show it.

Now, here was Tank, about to marry Anna, who had been living in every other sense as his wife for more than a year. That morning, Jenny had wondered at seeing him coming in the kitchen door with his skin pink and his hair matted back wet.

The surprise had made Anna laugh.

"He jumps in the creek naked most days and then cooks himself and beats himself with branches for a while in his banya. Don't you and Dennis do that?"

He could heal? Why didn't he heal Anna?

Tank's own form more massive than the minister's, Tank wore the same tan plaid sport coat his students saw at the high school, along with a red tie patterned with small pheasants. As best he could, Tank had drawn the knot high against the shirt collars pulling away, unable to close at his thick neck. A new haircut left his hair too thick and too short for combing; the dark shock of it pushed down on his forehead, over heavy eyebrows. Gathered into himself, Tank had the somber, frightening expression he once showed moments before a match.

Anna leaned against him and the warmth still showing on his cheeks and neck.

A respectful young Klein worker stood at the edge of the room, in position to watch over the generator and the three space heaters Spuhn had sent on a Klein Construction pickup truck. Anna was to stand close to the heater the worker had placed in the center of the worship area.

Tank's sister Galina and Nina sat close enough in front that they could join Jenny in straightening a fold of Anna's dress, adjusting her bouquet. Beside Galina sat her children Anton, Mike and Pam, shy around the beautiful Jenny.

Like the patrons and business associates who saw Jenny at times, the powerful near-men who had come to see their coach married stared furtively at the blond, movie star wife whose husband owned all those Spoon restaurants.

Everyone waited, listening to an intense guitar player whose eyes were closed and whose silky hair moved with the rhythm of his thunderous strumming. He accompanied the ardent singing of a young woman who threw her long, flaxen hair about as the two performed her own composition, a sweet prayer about water into wine, sinners into holy followers.

Half a dozen of the 40 or so people stood. The rest were seated on makeshift benches, rickety chairs and overturned buckets.

The eyes of two barn cats glimmered as they advanced and retreated in shadows at the peeling back wall.

When the song ended, broad-shouldered Hurtin' Henry, now Pastor Henry with his own small church, a cross-bedecked, tar-paper covered basement in an unincorporated area close to Mason City, stood silently. Majestically, he swept his gaze from one side to the other of the assembly of high school students, neighbors and Knowing God congregants before turning to the work of the wedding.

In front of him were Jenny and Anna's parents on two chairs brought from the house, members of Tank's wrestling squad, Tank's sponsor Greg Beutel from AA, other high school students, a Mexican couple who had found work after the harvest season, and various people Tank knew from the high school, the Ten O'Clock Club and from being Tank, the preacher, the healer. Among those were the mumbling, lost young man who moved about in a tight space and a miserable young woman with most of her face hidden in the gathered collar of an oversize coat with black and red checks.

Behind her as she faced the pastor, Jenny heard one of Tank's congregants, a woman, shushing a man whose mumbling threatened to rise into the ceremony.

"Praise the Lord Jesus Christ," said Pastor Henry.

"Amen" came from around the space.

"Praise him the one true loving God in all his majesty and in all his powers."

"Amen."

"Brothers and sisters, I feel like prayin'. Pray with me."

"Amen."

Anna squeezed Tank's hand with her small one. Jenny saw her sister's eyes bright and happy as she held herself upright against the stolidity of Tank.

"I feel like saying thank you to my almighty God for this day, this day when the love and the blessings of heaven will float down on these children of the Lord God, these Nikolay Vetrov and Anna Adamski.

"I feel like raisin' my arms to heaven and sayin', Lord, we are here. In your sight. In your house. "Because we believe."

"Amen."

"Because we believe that you have the words we need for eternal life."

"Amen."

"Because we believe you see us, Lord. Because we believe you walk with us. Because we believe you protect us. And love us. And because we believe we have salvation in the name of the Lord Jesus Christ."

"Amen."

The tempo now set, the "amens" coming to cue, Pastor Henry settled into a familiar track, a sermon that soon showed hallmarks of use with all types of worships and ceremonies.

"Brothers and sisters, I used to rassle. I used to do awful things. Terrible things. I used to hurt people. In the ring. In my sinful, vile, evil way of living.

"People who knew me then, they say to me, 'You're a Jesus freak. When did you become a Jesus freak?'" Pausing to sweep his close-cropped, glowering look slowly over the group, Pastor Henry stilled even the agitated, young man with the long, vacant face. Suddenly, the minister took on an expression of enraptured certainty. The veins and tendons corded in his thick neck.

"When did I become a Jesus freak? I-became-a-Jesus-freak-when-I-knew-in-my-heart-my-savior-was-a-Pastor Henry-freak. That is the moment I became a Jesus freak."

"Amen, Jesus."

The barn cats and some of the congregation shrank back from Pastor Henry's booming voice.

"There are those who mock us, brothers and sisters. There are those who make fun of us. There are those who feel sorry for us because we are Jesus freaks."

"Yes."

"Tank and me, I admit it. We were confused. We were lost. We were rasslin' and runnin' around and doin' all kinds of things that the devil put in our minds. And then our Lord and Savior Jesus Christ put us in a good, big headlock and he made us think straight. He made us see the way to be saved in the grace of Jesus Christ almighty. And when Tank was seein' everything straight, almighty God put Anna Adamski right there in front of him. Jesus made Tank understand: this is a godly woman for you. And Anna, almighty God showed you: this is a man who's all washed and clean in the blood of the lamb. This is a godly man."

Continuing the theme, the minister brought the service around to a barn-shaking wedding service joining Jesus freak Nikolay Vetrov to Jesus freak Anna Adamski. With Jenny, Nina and Galina at the ready, Anna, visibly tiring, pushed herself up into the hold of Tank's arms and met his kiss with all the force she could muster. Her wan face was all rapturous smile as she hung on Tank's arm and let him move the two of them in a procession through the friends reaching to touch and congratulate.

In the house, Anna clutched at Jenny for help and went straight to the bathroom, where Anna vomited, washed and fixed her make-up.

"Well, they sure don't put that part in the fairytale wedding stories, do they?" Anna said to her sister.

"They don't put cancer in them, either," Jenny said.

"It is what it is," Anna said, checking her dress, gathering herself for return to the group crowded into the house. Pastor Henry's loud voice layered the sound of all conversation.

In answer to Jenny's silence, Anna repeated what she said often, "I tell Tank too bad I wasn't a horse or a sick calf 'cause he'd of healed me in nothin' flat."

To the delight of his Harlan wrestler guests, Tank and Pastor Henry went from reminiscing to re-enacting old moves on the snowy front yard in sight of the house.

Tank ducked under the other man's arm and raised Pastor Henry into the air.

"You've gained some weight," Tank said, bending so that the big minister could get back on the ground and regain his footing.

"This is when Hurtin' Henry would start the hurtin'," the other man said, trying to catch Tank's wrist.

"Not if Hurtin' Henry was supposed to get whupped," Tank said. "Not if . . . " Here, Tank caught Pastor Henry's own hand, twisted the man around, gripped his arm and made as if to deliver a powerful shot against the ribs with an elbow. ". . . Hurtin' Henry was gettin' his title taken away again."

Laughing and pink, sweaty, wet from the snow, the two men with the high school wrestlers in tow returned to the house, there to be dried off and fussed over by the women.

"It's fifteen degrees," Galina said.

"About twenty," said the young woman who had sung at the ceremony. She had just looked at the thermometer outside the window over the kitchen sink.

After the wedding, Jenny stayed longer than she intended, three days longer than her mother and father, who began the drive back to Davenport on Sunday afternoon, after Tank's morning service. Making herself useful, Jenny molded her habits to Anna's schedule, one punctuated with spurts of conversation and hot tea and bits of Scripture amid sitting that turned into napping. Jenny's nearby chair gave her a view of the white fields and dark lines of barren hardwoods outside while she sketched or read and kept company with her sleeping sister.

When he returned from his morning meeting before driving back into Harlan for his day of teaching and coaching and when he returned Monday evening, Tank came to kiss Anna and hold her hand.

Jenny could see they were absorbed in each other. Paying no attention to anything Jenny served him, Tank ate quickly with his eyes on Anna. Until she dozed, they talked with her hand in his. Then, keeping her hand in his, Tank read to himself from the Bible.

The rest did its work. Jenny saw her sister rally.

By Tuesday afternoon, Anna had caught up on sleep. Nina, who visited on most afternoons and stood ready to drive on any day Tank couldn't take Anna to a doctor's appointment, left her coat on when she saw Anna enjoying a visit with Jenny.

"You're goin' to need some eggs," Nina said before she left. "I'll stop with some tomorrow morning."

Color had come back into Anna's face and warmth back to her hands. The kitchen radio had come back on, too, with rock'n'roll during the day, until the time Anna settled before a small color television for the Huntley-Brinkley Report of news. Like their father, Anna added her own voice. A terse general angered her. Advertisements, she mocked and remade. Then, when the main stories concluded, she unwrapped the new fondue set, cut a small steak into pieces, heated vegetables left over from the wedding, and set the pot of hot oil where Jenny and she could cook chunks of meat and squares of potato as they caught up.

Tank was with the team at a match in Carroll, so the sisters had time for bundling in two quilts, drinking tea, and listening to each other. Anna made Jenny laugh with accounts of her experiences in Harlan. "Bob Dylan with a sore throat," she said about a spiritual, serious man who couldn't sing and yet wanted to lead a choir. "Except it's not the blind leading the blind. It's the tone deaf leading the one hundred percent, just plain tone deaf. Tank prayed for guidance and the man found work over near Logan, west of here. The Lord heard Tank's prayer. The spirit guided the guy right out of town."

They talked of Bob, Bob and Linda, Spuhn, Iowa, the Compare and Contrast work. Bob's daughter Sarah, womanly already at age 15, her dark hair worn long in the Adamski family photograph received at Christmastime, was attending a new high school. As Anna repeated the report that concerned their mother, Jenny remembered noticing the distance in Sarah's deep, dark-eyed expression and in the small separation from the other three family members.

"When are you and the Emperor going to start the royal family? You planning to have a kid anytime?" Anna asked.

Yes, when? "I couldn't do anything like that while I was getting my degree, and then I had work to complete for the show. Now, we want to get the business more steady," Jenny said.

"It's hard to plan," Anna said, looking at Jenny, who understood the import. "You never know what's going to happen."

As if to wrap herself back up in the protection of her humor, Anna glanced out the window and got a twinkle back in her blue eyes. She drew her quilt around her.

"Mom made this when I was in the hospital," Anna said. "Kids, you, too, can have one of these magnificent Estonian Sympathy Cloaks. Just collect the boxtop everytime you have a double mastectomy."

Jenny showed an uncomfortable smile.

"And in case you're bothered by it, you get one of these mastectomy dealies and all that 'built like a brick shithouse' stuff, you don't hear that anymore. "

Because Anna expected it, Jenny answered with a short laugh.

Anna softened her tone when, a moment later, Tank's big Pontiac sounded on the frozen drive. "Jenny, if the cancer hadn't come, there wouldn't be Tank. He is given to me by my loving Jesus, my Lord and Savior, he truly is."

What Jenny saw confirmed what Anna said.

Tank was too large to enter delicately and too excited about finding Anna, anyway. After wiping his shoes on the small rug inside the kitchen door, he came respectfully into the living room, recognized that Anna and Jenny had stopped their conversation, and wrapped Anna up into a long kiss that made Jenny homesick for Spuhn.

When Spuhn and she embraced, Jenny experienced passion, pleasure, a thrill of the moment that contained expectation of the same for all the years she would be alive. In the tenderness and the gratitude Tank and Anna showed, Jenny sensed appreciation for a joy enhanced by its precariousness.

Quickly, the day came to an end. Tank did not need to eat. Anna was tired. In the house sounding with small night noises of the refrigerator fan, a kitchen drip, the periodic knock of the pipes connected to the basement furnace, Jenny had the living room and the couch – her guest bed – to herself.

Before she fell asleep, she returned to the idea that had begun forming at the sight of baby Jan on the mantel. What if Anna did not survive the cancer? What if she never again saw Jan?

When Nina came early the next morning with a bowl of eggs just collected from her hens, Jenny asked discreetly about the state of Anna's health.

"She's doin' way better'n everyone thought but it's hard. It's hard," Nina said with uncharacteristic worry in her answer. "No one tells me right out but I always hear the doctor talking about new tests, new things they can try. That can't be good, can it? We just keep prayin'."

By the time Jenny reached Davenport that afternoon, the idea had passed from a possibility into an imperative: she and Spuhn would contrive for Anna to see her son Jan. She and Spuhn would give Anna and Tank a honeymoon trip to the Twin Cities as a wedding gift. They could go in the spring, as soon as Tank's wrestling season ended and as soon as Anna was through with all the follow-up to her surgery. The rest Jenny would leave to Spuhn: he would pull strings, get Jack Diebold to work out the law part, do whatever had to be done so that Anna had a chance to see Jan.

Then Jenny kissed Spuhn with a feeling that made him wish she had wanted that help long before this bleak midwinter day.

Jenny remembered. She did not let Spuhn forget the Twin Cities while he managed the activities of the entire organization, including the new SI Data Incorporated that was now a 12-person venture operating out of a small space leased from an Iowa City windows fabricator.

The meetings that kept Dennis from attending Anna's wedding had gone well: he and Mr. Diebold had found three good additions to the management group that already included the responsible Susan Walters, the young woman doing such a good job with the Iowa City and Grinnell Spoon locations, and two of Klein's experienced project supervisors. They had hired the undergraduate Randy wanted for SI Data.

Before Spuhn could act, though, without making his plan completely clear to Anna herself, Tank began feeling certain of the need to take Anna to Jan.

Jan was her son and he was as captive with the Henning grandparents as the Israelites had been those years in Egypt. Tank felt the call of the Lord, felt bringing Anna together with her son and praying would loosen something. Tank didn't know what it would be but, ever since the thought first occurred to him, clues kept poking through the pages as he read Scripture each day.

Psalm 10 had jumped at him as he thought about himself and then about Jan: "Why standest thou afar off, O Lord? Why hidest thou thyself in times of trouble?"

Then, in Ecclesiastes he saw what was said of the newborn Moses: "And the daughter of Pharaoh came down to wash herself at the river; and her maidens walked along by the river's side; and when she saw the ark among the flags, she sent her maid to fetch it. And when she had opened it, she saw the child: and, behold, the babe wept. And she had compassion on him, and said, This is one of the Hebrews' children."

The same week, when Tank attended the meeting of his AA group, he also heard something profound in a young member's recollection of his squad leader's habitual instruction: "You do it by doin' it, simple as that."

So convinced, Tank acted on his intention as soon as Anna had enough energy and as soon as his coaching schedule broke for sufficient time. On a clean March day when bare fields were being crossed by a first light blowing of a new season's wind, Tank made sandwiches for the trip and set out with Anna for Mason City. After a night there with Pastor Henry and his wife, Tank and Anna would reach Minneapolis.

Happy and unusually vigorous, wearing jeans and a ribbed gold turtleneck sweater under a hooded winter coat, Anna thought of Jan as she hurried the day through constant tapping of the radio that kept losing its weak hold on signals when the car bumped or swayed. Harlan Principal Tom Daniels, the previous owner of the car, had shown Tank how to firm the connection but Tank's size and his liking for prayer time during drives made Tank reluctant to push his big body into position for poking beneath the dashboard.

Out of politeness, Anna kept her impatience hidden the next morning when Pastor Henry led them off the highway and a short distance along a county road to the spot where he and his congregation had their worship. Funding was just enough ahead of construction that the minister and his congregation had achieved a basement level roofed with tarpaper. Inside, Pastor Henry flicked a light that illuminated a room organized into spaces for worship and for small study groups. Before long, the Lord would guide them to completion of the plan for an upper church space and then to a companion building for Bible study.

Eventually, to Anna's relief, the Lord sent Pastor Henry back up the stairs and outside, where he prayed over the three of them before leading Tank and Anna back to the highway.

Tank was no less eager to complete the trip. At times, he spoke about a passage that came to mind or remembered being in one of the towns for a match but, most of the time, with Anna happy beside him, he bore down on the driving. The road was straight and wet at places from sunshine melting ice at the road edges.

As both Tank and Anna hoped, they were in Minneapolis, near to the neighborhood of Jan's Henning grandparents, soon after noon.

Before she met the man she followed to Atlanta the summer before, Bonnie told Anna of seeing the Hennings' Cadillac many mornings and afternoons at the L'il Farm daycare.

Now, Tank and Anna went there but, not finding sign of the Hennings, Tank and Anna parked and watched from a spot across the street. Fifteen minutes passed with no sign of children, no sign of parents arriving to retrieve anyone, no sign of Jan emerging from the buff-colored, flat-roofed school that had most of its long windows pasted with artwork.

Anna teared. Tank stroked her shoulder as he watched and prayed aloud. He thought of Joshua and Caleb, scouts sent by Moses into Canaan. They came back trusting in God's promise, were rewarded when God fulfilled it.

Then cars arrived and children with thick coats and many bundles of new art emerged under the supervision of some attentive young teachers.

Anna did not see the Hennings. Nor Jan.

"Let's go to the Hennings," Anna said. Only speaking to give the grim Tank directions into the neighborhood of curving streets and large, gracious homes, Anna guided them to a stop across from the big, crenelated home of her former in-laws. Up the driveway, at the side entrance just beyond a dry, winter garden of evergreen shrubs, brown vegetation, birdbaths and, for the sake of art, some large boulders striated in waves of black, Mrs. Henning's white Cadillac sat parked.

Anna didn't need to explain. Tank followed her as she exited the car, crossed the street, and moved up the driveway toward the house.

Before she reached the steps, the door opened violently and Mrs. Henning emerged with her long face set in stiff, aristocratic rage.

"Go away," she shouted. "This is private property and you're trespassing. You know the judge barred you from this."

"Mrs. Henning, I just want to see Jan."

"Anna just wants to see Jan," Tank said. "That's all."

"You can't."

"Just for a moment," Anna said.

"I'm going in, out of the cold," Mrs. Henning said. "Now, you go away. I've already called the police."

A moment later, a squad car pulled into the driveway, came close to Tank and Anna and stopped. Two solid young policemen emerged.

"One at a time," the older of the two policemen, said.

"She's a horrible mother, an addict," Mrs. Henning said. "She is not allowed to be near my grandson."

Quickly, the dispute turned into an admonition to leave.

"You're on the Hennings' property," the senior policeman said. "Sir, you have about two seconds to leave this neighborhood. Or you'll be leaving in handcuffs."

Tank's face took on the dark stare that had preceded eruptions in the ring.

Methodically, indifferent to the presence of the two policemen and the shouting of Mrs. Henning, Tank moved into the dry garden, reached down and strained until he had dislodged the nearest of the decorative boulders. Then he rolled the heavy stone onto the driveway, within inches of the rear bumper of the squad car.

Breathing hard, Tank said to the protesting policeman, "We came to see Anna's son."

Suddenly, catching sight of her son looking curious at the glass of the storm door, Anna avoided Mrs. Henning and went up the stairs to the house. She pulled the door open, reached down for Jan and lifted him into the air.

"Jan, it's Mommy. Hush," Anna said, her own tears coming as she squeezed and kissed her son.

The boy, terrified by the policeman and the angry adults, called for his grandmother. Realizing the boy's fright, Anna put the boy down and let him go to Mrs. Henning.

Another squad car arrived. Jan, crying, watched from the protection of his grandmother. Not the policemen, but the wet March cold making Anna shake was what broke Tank's determination. He moved the stone from behind the car and accepted the cuffs while Anna hastened to a phone for a call to Jenny.

In his own call to the Iowa Attorney General who had his staff call the Minnesota counterpart, Jack Diebold learned that the police only wanted to remove the fearsome Tank from the Henning property and then from Minneapolis.

"One of the cops knew you," the lawyer told Spuhn. "He has family in Des Moines, eats at the restaurants all the time."

Anna had cried herself dry by the time Tank was freed. They drove home as quietly vanquished as the Israelites forestalled from entering Canaan.

CHAPTER 29

I had a pig
And his name was Sam.
Sunday he was bacon
And Monday he was ham.

Much as he tried, even though he took Jack Diebold's counsel and did not head across the state, Dennis Spuhn could not remove Spoon and himself from the standoff at Tank and Anna's. There Joe Szabo, exhausted from more than a year of jumping at sudden sounds and vacating one place or another seemingly steps ahead of a pursuing FBI posse, simply joined two other deserters encamped in full sight at the small farm owned by Nikolay Vetrov and Anna. A political hound in full cry, Greg Benson in his role as a member of the staff of the ardently anti-Soviet Congressman representing a western district, was making sure that the excitement about a strange preacher harboring cult members and Communists always included references to the family ties of entrepreneur Dennis Spuhn and Tank Vetrov.

Able to secure the Congressman's position through the fortuitous joining of an Army Reserve unit headed by one of the politician's supporters, Benson had begun a one-semester hiatus in his law studies. As far as Jenny and Spuhn could tell, almost more than he wanted a career-shaping hand in the re-election of a Republican governor and Republican president, the former St. Sebastian's classmate intended to harm Spuhn while bringing about the imprisonment of three young men being called the Navalny Three.

For the sake of family and loyalty to someone who had been her husband's friend since childhood, Jenny argued for whatever influence Spuhn could bring to bear. In her gentle way, her inclination to empathy, she gave no consideration to the public consequences that Spuhn and his lawyer recognized as immense.

Spuhn, though, wouldn't ignore them. Benson had drawn the restaurants into the confrontation.

As for family and loyalty to a friend, Joe Szabo had gone another way, become different, years before. Anna was the sister of Jenny, known to Spuhn through lustful high school awareness, and now through a small number of family celebrations and events. Anna came with the wedding band on Jenny's finger. Anna, in turn, brought her husband, the wrestling star turned holy man. Nikolay, Tank Vetrov, was just a loose canon, a real tank grinding into and over everything on the way to some destination only the giant man and God knew. Should so much of Spoon, so much of Spuhn's business accomplishment be risked for the sake of any of them?

Neither Spuhn nor Jenny thought deeply about the connections. Spuhn reacted to the threats against the restaurants as well as everything good or bad in regard to Greg Benson. Jenny worried about her sister and Tank as well as the old St. Sebastian's classmate who, just because he had spent years in the same classrooms with Dennis, just because Szabo had cheered the same baskets, the same touchdowns and pins, the Army deserter was more meaningful than a stray name in a stray newspaper. At the same time, Jenny worried most about Dennis Spuhn.

Why, for that matter, should Benson be having any success with the fox hunt he was turning into a discrediting of Dennis Spuhn and the most known of Spuhn's business interests, the restaurant chain now reaching almost to Omaha?

The whole country, Iowa included, was weary of the Vietnam war. Even the Secretary of Defense was predicting the removal of U.S. troops by the summer of 1971, in about six months. By now, who besides Greg Benson cared about the dark matter so depressingly present in the country? The discharged forces, the war veteran young men with the GI bill and the pent-up libidos of 19 and 20 year olds who had come face to face with things never imagined in Iowa or California or Arkansas, were returning home to grow sideburns and hair to their asses. They were enrolling in the community colleges and universities where they would assimilate into classes and settings where cheerful, open young women who had begun to know their own bodies would come close in t-shirts and blouses inviting exploration. By now, from grandmothers to the man who refilled the candy bar machines in the Alcoa plant, everyone had an opinion about the war. Most shared one opinion about it: discussion was tiresome and without purpose. Ignore the dark matter pervading everything.

Instead, the country could woolgather through the images of politicians debating inflation solutions, revenue sharing plans, and disarmament agreements. With the Southeast Asia news cleared away, evening audiences could become steeped in the trial of the bizarre women attempting to sacrifice themselves for Charles Manson or, passing up the nightly news altogether, could guffaw about Archie Bunker and the other All in the Family members as they bulled their way in laughable ignorance through days of turmoil and trepidation.

Even the FBI had better things to do than Vietnam. There were the Weathermen and the Black Panthers set on violent revolution, groups far more alarming than a meditative pothead fantasizing about universal tranquility and brotherhood. Those were the problems of California, New York, Boston and Chicago. Who but Greg Benson cared about Joe Szabo and his threat to a surrounding world of crops, cattle-raising, birthing, dying and Des Moines traffic congestion?

In Iowa, though, the Iowa of interest to Dennis Spoon and the Spoon restaurants, Greg Benson was having success attracting news attention, and Spuhn feared, with fomenting of concern and anger about Joe Szabo and two other deserters living openly and easily under the care of an unusual preacher, all in this January, 1971 time of Charles Manson cult awareness.

When Benson and the Szabo alarm first poked up through the news, Spuhn noticed but was too busy with Randy Isaacs and the shaping of a grand agreement with a Texas retailing group, too busy with the normal monitoring of the restaurant group, and too heavily engaged in preparation for an approaching Des Moines marathon. Spuhn threw Ron Tonti at the issue; Spuhn dispatched one of his corporate managers for arrangement of a mid-winter burst of a Ronnie Tonti appearance in Des Moines and then in a circling of the court during the halftime of a basketball game between a West Des Moines team and the team from Audubon, situated between West Des Moines and Harlan. As instructed, the manager made sure the *Harlan Tribune* received photographs and sent a reporter.

Figuratively and once in reality, Spuhn had Diebold's big, restraining hand on his shoulder. Spuhn knew enough not to act on his instinct, the urge to drive pell-mell across Iowa, straight through the storm then roaring eastward along an Interstate 80 thinned down to crawling semis, a handful of cars, and some heavy plow trucks with flashing yellow lights. Jack Diebold didn't have to labor the point: Dennis Spuhn in person, Dennis Spuhn, head of the Spoon chain at the side of Communist, draft-dodging, peacenik Joe Szabo would change Greg Benson's Chicken Little performance from a bleat in the back area of a stage into a full-scale orchestra performance.

But then, a day later, as the same storm howled into Scott County and the Quad Cities, Spuhn and everyone else saw the newspaper photo that tipped Spuhn's cart and sent him rushing to his lawyer's office.

In the end, Spuhn could have been in the middle of acquiring McDonald's, Burger King and Howard Johnson's. To choke Benson, to cut the microphone and pound the round-faced, thick-necked antagonist and his sanctimonious keening into the ground, Spuhn would have left anything in limbo.

In a photo taken before the storm, Greg Benson stood at the edge of Tank and Anna's property with a cluster of Spoon takeout bags pulled, Benson said, from the little community's trash. Benson, all innocent indignation, a member of the staff of a dedicated Congressmen protecting all Americans from Communist domination, charged that the three deserters were receiving meals sent by the Spoon restaurant chain, owned by the family of the sheltering minister. For the sake of the *Harlan Tribune* photographer, Benson held the bags so that the Spoon logo on the one in front was in full display.

"Yes, you can sue," Jack Diebold said, explaining what Spuhn already knew. "Here are some reasons you don't want to do that."

Spuhn knew without the need of hearing. "What then?"

"Sit tight, You're not goin' to win a pissing contest with a skunk," the lawyer said. He didn't need the big roll-a-dex ring on his desk for the phone numbers he was about to dial. First, he sent Spuhn from the office, told him to go about his business while Diebold talked things over with some folks.

For the next two days, the storm smothered all else. Photos of cars encased in drifts, sad steers huddled as shivering vectors in windblown barnyards, repairmen at work on power lines, these plus illustrations of national and regional weather left no room for anything except sports and syndicated columns of recipes, Peanuts, and political opinion. For radio, the storm was a day long chewing of cud. Interviews with emergency workers, school administrators, and men in the street filled gaps around repeated news of weather conditions and cancellations of school and sporting events.

During that time, Diebold was able to learn government plans and affect them. Szabo would get his wish for an end to his flight. The arrival of the Federal agents on Tank's property would occur as soon as the county roads were cleared. The arrest would take place quickly, without notice, and at a time inconvenient for any media. Once in custody, the three deserters would go to St. Paul, away from the influence of Benson and his Congressman. The whole affair would be done and over while the storm remained the state's most interesting news event.

"What your friend Benson's been doing is bothering Republican Party people," Diebold said. "Benson's boss has a safe seat. But lots of others are antsy this time around. You know how they are, anyway. The politicians are always on edge. They might agree with Benson, but they don't want him setting the whole barn on fire while he's chasing mice."

But then the storm lifted from the news without the smooth arrest Diebold had predicted. Sunshine shone brightly on snowbanks shrinking in crusty mounds as the thaw began sending rivulets across roadways and bringing people outside.

If the FBI was coming for Szabo and the others, the authorities were in no rush. Diebold made new calls and came to the conclusion that something was going on between Benson's Congressman

Pat "Patriot" Sawyer and the officials managing President Nixon's run for a second presidential term.

At the small farm where Joe Szabo had taken up residence with Tank and Anna, the change from storm to sun brought relief and then new anticipation of resolution. When the roads cleared, everyone believed, the FBI or other law enforcement officials would arrive for the resolute deserters.

Not that Joe Szabo, and the two other deserters who had taken shelter on the farm gave evidence of any regret for their refusal to serve

Early on the morning the thaw began, Tank completed his banya sweat and a prayerful meditation that coursed from Scripture to Anna to sobriety to the wrestlers he was preparing for that weekend's match against teams from nearby Carroll and Ames. Pink-faced and warm, intent on the exercise session he would complete with the set of weights he had contrived from pieces of machinery and tubs of concrete, Tank paused, struck as he came to the doorway and looked into the dimly lit barn at the three young men taking shelter there.

Joe Szabo and another, an ebullient Kansas City native named Lev, were having a meandering conversation in low voices as they paced in a tight circle amid the snow melt dripping from several spots in the roof. Lev spoke with his whole, small, energetic form, with exaggerated gestures and looks, same as he must have performed in the University of Kansas classroom where he was a grad student teaching one of the freshman English requirements. Artie, the third man, so slender of build that his long skeleton seemed chicken-like, had his head down and his eyes closed as he worked at a tune on a reddish brown guitar with a braided green strap.

As he looked in from the brightness behind him to the dark of the barn space, Tank suddenly felt an emotion so strong his eyes watered. The vision of the trio became intense as Tank dwelt on three Israelites in a Babylonian king's furnace. Could Shadrach, Meshach and Abednego have been so much at ease, so young and confident as the three resolute deserters? Betraying only small signs of nervousness in a laugh or in combing of their beards and mustaches as they paced and picked, the three were awaiting whatever event would bring their individual opposition directly against the beliefs that compelled many others to accept military enlistment, and perhaps combat.

In addition to the story of Daniel, Tank thought about verses he had read that week in Wisdom. In his first break between classes, he found the chapter and read again of the way the righteousness of a just one disturbed others: "If the righteous really are God's children, God will save them from their enemies. So let's put them to the test. We'll be cruel to them, and torment them; then we'll find out how calm and reasonable they are! We'll find out just how much they can stand!"

What would Harold Voigt from the Ten O'Clock Club, a Lutheran, see in the barn?

"Tank," he had said the evening he came to express his worries. "This is reckless. Reckless. Good Christians can not make trouble like this. These boys, they are breaking the law."

The three men as Shadrach, Meshach and Abednego stuck in Tank's mind. They were young, yes, courageous, yes, and full of righteousness.

The three young men at ease in the shadowy space of the barn, Tank felt, were of Godly mind, maybe God's children. But if the comparison held, where was the fourth, the angel who had come to join the three Israelites in the Babylonian king's furnace?

From the first, always respectful of whatever God wonder brought any of the people who assembled for the barn gatherings that had become services, Tank and Anna took the men's sincerity for granted. Tank and Anna both understood the absence of some Mexicans who feared the law enforcement officials who drifted along the road, who gave Tank and Anna's property more scrutiny than the area had ever had. A few of Tank's Ten O'Clock friends came one Sunday. They gave the three deserters a looking over and, once outside, spoke with Tank in indirect ways.

"Bitten off a lot here, Tank," loyal Greg Beutel, Tank's AA sponsor, said. "You handle it?"

"With help of God."

More than Tank, who was occupied with his routine of prayer, banya, teaching and wrestling, Anna sat listening and commiserating many days in the kitchen as the three ardent men talked and helped with the cooking of meals or the boiling of water for tea. During the warm months, the three deserters had placed her on a chair in the shade of a lilac bush or the broad-leafed catalpa tree as they carried out Anna's instructions for tending of the big vegetable garden she had begun her first summer with Tank.

They amused her. Lev, who shared her liking for Walt Whitman and encouraged her to read Eric Hoffer, called Tank the Big Yawp after a phrase from a Whitman poem about an unrestrained, barbaric shout.

Soon, they all began calling Anna's serious husband "Yawp".

Keeping Anna at ease in the summer shade, watching for times she needed her gray blanket about her and for times she needed the blanket drawn away, the three men set to work on scraping and then painting the house. Artie, clever with carpentry, pulled back shingles from the roof above the dining room and replaced some soft boards where a leak had developed. By the time cold weather interfered with the work, all the trim of the eaves and windows had been completed with fresh coats of shiny, richly blue paint. Only the barn side of the house lacked fresh painting with a nearly flat white color.

Reading, dozing, calling out admiration and thanks, Anna kept the men company in the sweet smells of summer and the warm days of fall as they worked and talked.

The advance of her cancer tired her and made her lose concentration at times but the men, one or another or several in midspeech, never seemed to notice the sudden tightening of her lips or the wash of gray before her eyes became blue and concerned once more. Anna wanted to understand, wanted to see ahead with them the way she had assisted her advertising clients.

All the conversation made Anna sure of her guests' conviction but unsure of the exact reasonings that led Szabo to his pacifism, Lev to his equating of Peace Corps service to the Army or any other part of the military-industrial complex, and the other man, long-fingered Artie, to a shrug each time as he looked into the distance and explained how he was unwilling to fuck up a world so unbelievably fucked up already. Anna didn't care.

The deserters made friends of the neighbors who turned up for weekend worship and gave respectful attention to the non-sequitur ramblings of mentally ill Teddy. On their clothes, Anna noticed, the three deserters wore their own emblems of military opposition: Szabo had buttons from groups named Sane and C.O.R.E. Lev had the same Sane button along with End the Draft. Artie wore a single button, Draft Beer not Students. They spoke of drill sergeants, of Gandhi, Tolstoy and Dorothy Day (Szabo), of Camus (Lev), of Bob Dylan, Country Joe and the Fish (Artie).

From the school principal Tom Daniels, Tank learned that his three Israelites were being joined by angels, not just an angel.

Shortly before noon that day, small groups of Drake University students began showing up in support of the men they called the Navalny Three.

When Tank called Anna, he heard that, in the pamphlets the members of the Drake Committee for Non-Violence had ready for handing to anyone near, they referred to Tank and Anna's land, the Place for Knowing God, as a "sanctuary."

People were coming and going. The kitchen table was filling with casseroles and baked goods delivered by Nina and some other friends.

Then Dennis Spuhn called the high school.

"Tank," he said, "what the hell is Hernandez doing there?"

"Hernandez?"

"Jesus! What the hell is Jesus doing there? Jenny saw him on TV."

Tom Daniels let Tank turn his remaining afternoon class into library research time.

When Tank came to his home, he found the driveway blocked by a combine driven there by a burly neighbor whose son had been on the Harlan team the first year Tank coached. Sent to Vietnam the year before, the boy had been missing since late October.

Tank walked up the driveway, past fired up, threatening Greg Benson, and found Jesus Hernandez in the company of the three deserters and the half dozen Drake students. For all Tank could tell, they could have been a group of friends talking and laughing as they waited for a class to begin. Joe Szabo agreed to go into the house and call Spuhn.

Spuhn had so many questions, Szabo calmly interrupted and began answering what he knew Spuhn would want to learn.

"Jesus is here."

"I know," Spuhn shouted. "What for?"

"He wants to drive us somewhere, to get us away from here."

"Shit."

"Jesus is more worried than we are, man. It's just time.""What about Clayton? Have you talked with him?"

Szabo laughed.

"What's funny?"

"How do you think the FBI knew I was at Iowa?"

"Clayton?"

"Benson made one of his goofy little remarks at class one day and Jim got worried. Mostly, it was his roommate, I think. Anyway, the draft counselor warned me and I split."

"Clayton," Spuhn said.

"Don't sweat it, man. It's no big deal. It's time for this to be over."

"Tell Jesus to call me."

"Okay."

"You need money? A lawyer?"

"None of that. Thanks, man."

"They're taking you to Minnesota. St. Paul. Getting you away from that Congressional district you're in. Keep your head down."

"Peace."

At about nine o'clock that evening, two trim men with FBI credentials came to a stop in the front of the house.

"The pigs are here", an unnecessary announcement, sounded from a Drake student.

Anna welcomed the polite agents at the door and led them across the living room into the kitchen. When the first of the agents, a man with the red signs of a developing cold showing in his eyes and at the end of his nose, spoke, his voice was husky.

Deferential to Anna, appearing ill at ease as they watched, the agents let Anna present packages of sandwiches, cookies and apples while she softly cried and accepted kisses from the three deserters. Szabo offered the near agent his apple and one of Anna's oatmeal cookies.

Before the three men went with the agents, Tank opened the bible that had belonged to his mother and turned to the Psalms. Then he prayed from memory. With the extension of his arms over the group and the sweep of his glance, he took in the young men,

Anna and the two agents together as he first asked the Lord's blessing and then recited from the Psalm: "Blessed is the man that walketh not in the counsel of the ungodly, nor standeth in the way of sinners, nor sitteth in the seat of the scornful."

Pausing for the briefest of moments, as if taking on a new load of grace, Tank raised his view above those before him and concluded: "May we be right in your eyes, Lord God, Jesus Christ, as Peter was when he said the words of David, 'For David speaketh concerning him, I foresaw the Lord always before my face, for he is on my right hand, that I should not be moved' and 'Thou hast made known to me the ways of life; thou shalt make me full of joy with thy countenance.' Amen."

One of the agents blessed himself in the quiet that followed. Anna gave both of them jars of hot tea and a bag of cookies.

"This will make your throat feel better," Anna said.

"Let Tank pray over you," Joe Szabo said. "He can heal."

The man coughed and pulled back. "We need to go," he said.

"This will make your throat feel better," Anna said.

"Let Tank pray over you," Joe Szabo said. "He can heal."

The man coughed and pulled back. "We need to go," he said.

Joe Szabo, Lev and Artie, smiles on their faces, Artie foolish with the marijuana he and Hernandez had smoked with some of the Drake students, moved with the agents along a watching line of students and some regular members of the Sunday congregation. Jesus Hernandez returned their peace signs as the car drove away.

Untroubled, ready, the men turned and called good-byes. "Bye, Anna. Yawp."

Greg Benson, flexed in futile readiness, his thick neck pulled down in the breadth of his shoulders and his face hard, watched alone from the other side of the road. *The Harlan Tribune* had gone to bed.

When Ronnie Tonti came from the bathroom, he saw Dottie sitting on the bed with a letter in her right hand as she worked with the other hand at tucking a sandy loop of her hair back into a beehive. The white slip she wore was taut over the fullness of her hips and her breasts.

"Who is Melinda?" Dottie asked.

Tonti had seen her accusing look many times.

"Melinda? I don't know any Melinda," he said.

Dottie flipped the letter so she could read the signature. "Melinda Beasley."

Dottie fixed her look on Tonti. "She says she knows you. You two met in the Quarter. Where's the Quarter?"

"The Quawta? That's N'Awlins. Anyplace you go there, dumplin', you meet people. That's how N'Awlins is. Bons temps rouler."

Tonti came to the bed and sat beside Dottie, who went back to studying the letter as she ignored the touch of his thigh against hers.

"She's almost a doctor. This lady's a college girl."

"A doctor?"

"'I am almost done with my doctorate in history, concentration on Louisiana history, from Louisiana State University', that's what she says."

Tonti could speak honestly. The day had been long. He was tired. He didn't remember a Melinda. And why had Dottie become upset about that letter among the others that came to him at Spoon?

"'You probably don't remember me. I was with my brother Daniel and our friends Owen and Bill the weekend before Owen and Bill went to Ft. Benning for jump school'", Dottie read.

Tonti knew right away that an image of a college student with bright black eyes, black bangs and a one-piece white shorts outfit showing her tan legs had come to him and revealed itself in the look Dottie saw. In the same instant, visible to Dottie, he calibrated the girl become the woman.

"*I know you know her,*" Dottie said, pulling completely away from him. The look on her face moved between crying and anger.

"*Darlin',*" Tonti said.

"*I don't want none of your bullshit, Ronnie. Why do you always lie to me?*" Dottie pressed her face against his shoulder and allowed him to stroke her arm.

"*She was a chère with her brother in the Quawta. They got tricked by some col'd boys workin' the tourists, and they saw me watchin' it all.*"

"*You don't know her, why's she wantin' you to come see her in Illinois?*"

This time, Tonti stiffened with surprise.

"*What for?*"

"*You're Tonti family and she is studyin' Tontis, that's what she says in the letter.*"

Tonti's face was blank.

"*For my Tonti family book, I am going to Peoria, Illinois next summer and working at a place where Henri de Tonti buried some things. That's right next to Iowa. Will you let me interview you?*"

"*Huh.*"

"*She probably had your baby, that's what I think. She found out you're famous now. She thinks you're rich.*"

Tonti stroked Dottie's soft arm as he thought.

No baby, he knew that. Hands down, no baby. And not rich. But Tonti, yes. And that sweet Melinda wanted buku Tonti, buku.

CHAPTER 30

Here we go!
Here we go!
On the move!
In the groove!
In the groove!
Here we go!
All the way!
Every day!

Hovering at the open front door, just beyond the edge of the sunshine warming the porch and the first few feet of gleaming wooden floor, Jenny gripped her right leg at the ankle and stretched her hamstring again. That leg done, she did the same with her left leg and then circled through a truncated repetition of the hip twists and arm sweeps that loosened her for a run. She knelt and tightened the lace of her right shoe. Something more than a normal hesitation before abandoning her relaxed ready-to-run mood for the willing-to-run state slowed her. Then she left the house, breathed in the smell of the nearby lilacs along with the last of a warm day's damp morning cool, looked at her watch, and started her run.

Behind her, the house was quiet. Room upon room, it exuded the dismal sullenness of a sleeping teen-aged girl.

Dennis and Jenny's brother Bob were long gone, headed for a break of dawn breakfast with Randy Isaacs in Iowa City. Bob's daughter Sarah had not come downstairs and probably was hewing to the same schedule of isolation she had brought with her two days before. Jenny feared this would be the summer, an uncomfortable cohabitation with a seething, distrustful 15 year old girl woman angry at being brought for a summer stay, maybe a long stay, with a young aunt and her husband.

Jenny still meant to gain the girl's trust and friendship while Sarah assisted with the work of the art classes. The need, but no solution except persistence, filled Jenny's thoughts as she ran.

Sarah had a talent Jenny could appreciate in the sketches and in the canvas Sarah had begun the day before. But how dark she was. Jenny knew she herself became absorbed when she worked on her paintings but was that concentration as much a retreat and a rebuff as the palpable hostility Sarah manifested?

The oak grove that kept the lawns of some new homes near the entrance of the Oakcrest development in morning shadow held air cooler than the sunny area where former meadowland and cropland now held Oakcrest Avenue. Branching cul-de-sacs held other homes, some under construction, others with sodded lawns, plantings of maple, fruit trees and sometimes borders of marigolds. In the shadows beneath the high trees, filtering sunlight made wet, dewy grass shimmer. Along the black, fresh asphalt of Oakcrest Avenue, along with homes of grand size, Jenny came upon occasional crows picking at something dropped or crushed, and, at other spots, ridges of hard clay fallen from the treads of construction equipment.

Usually, Jenny began her run and completed most of it while the ground was dewy and the air was near daybreak fresh with the sun of a clear day still low and brightly yellow. As she moved along on those mornings, with cardinals and songbirds trilling, feeling cool morning air on her legs and arms, she savored the privacy, a chance to lose herself in anticipation of the day's events, both hers and Dennis', in review of large and small deadlines, and in ideas for improvement or creation of a painting.

Ronnie Tonti's handwalk had reached far to the west, sixty-five miles beyond Des Moines on the way to Omaha. In a week, Spuhn would have all of them, Sarah included, wound into the June 21st Hoorah for Summer plans of Spoon: Tonti would appear at the midday opening of the Anita restaurant on Friday, and, on Saturday, at the two Des Moines area locations, at Iowa City and then at the original restaurant in Davenport. Usually, just for the sake of scheduling her own life and her own weekend packing, Jenny would give the back of her mind over to faces she would need to recognize at the celebrations.

The run today was work, a labored exercise that was not elevating into a pleasurable, fast, top form rhythm of long strides and full lungs.

"I want one, too," Dennis had said when Jenny spoke her wish for a baby, and then nothing. The new car was a new model yellow Corvette, not a station wagon or even a big Buick or Oldsmobile with copious trunk space. She kept it secret from Dennis when her period, usually regular, did not come, did not come after she forgot – left? - her pills home the three days Dennis was meeting with George Forrest in New York. Then the bleeding came just before April, just as forsythia and crocus began forecasting warmth, sunshine and, Jenny hoped, hoped, hoped, her own place among the young mothers stopping to comfort and take pride in the passengers of buggies and strollers.

Until that day, maybe Bob's request for help with Sarah would be a placeholder, a happy mentoring friendship with a teen-aged niece whose shared artistic bent presaged a relationship more mother-daughter than aunt-child. Upon agreement to take Sarah for the summer, to employ her in the art school, to know her and to listen to her in ways that her exasperated Connecticut mother could not tolerate, Jenny imagined the fruition of all that Bob had predicted: "You're both artists, you and Sarah. Aren't there things she can learn from you while she helps you with your little school?" Jenny and Dennis also understood what was not stated: "You and Spuhn are young people, modern people."

"And you are not Linda, the mother whose distress and disappointment have become open contempt for a daughter whose unhappy face and distance return the same loathing."

Sarah had not called home and announced her safe arrival. Linda had not called to check on Sarah.

Only Bob called, Sarah barely replying to him, even when her father spoke of a car for the girl's sixteenth birthday in August.

By now, Jenny had come to the half-mile stretch of Rte. 61 she hated for the way clods driving semis, pick-ups and cars loaded with product samples, high school boys joyriding to school, even fathers with school children, slowed for inspection of her. This bright morning she wore very little. Drivers could view her legs, the working of her breasts, the yellow hair she had gathered and tied at the back of her neck. Warm weather brought catcalls; she heard one this time before she came to the county road where she left the highway and entered the long path cows had worn along the fence of a farm.

In her myopic anticipation of Sarah's arrival, Jenny had taken for granted an immediate high school social life guided by Dennis' brother Mike. But then the reality became apparent at the home of Spuhn's family the evening Bob and Sarah arrived in the Quad Cities. Unfamiliar with her Iowa family, angry about her parents' summer plan for her, Sarah was as quiet as Mike was shy in the presence of a cousin grown to womanly form while he, troubled with a large, red acne boil along his nose and with an adolescent voice, cowed from her on the other side of an age chasm.

If Anna had been healthy, if Sarah had gone to stay with Anna and Tank, there might have been understanding. Anna would appreciate the frustration of being a woman before finishing with being a girl. Like Anna at the same age, Sarah had a body blooming into magazine cover form, the appearance of a haunted model composed in a Manhattan setting. Sarah had her mother Linda's delicate, pretty face and dramatic black eyebrows, with an aloof mystery in her expression and the set of her pouty lips. Hair dark and rich as Linda's moved in rich abundance on and off her shoulders when Sarah raised or lowered her face. Mostly, Sarah let her hair obstruct any long study of her expression. Seated on the floor or drawn into an arm of the couch, the girl kept her long legs tucked, folded as much as they could be from view.

Veronica's happy 13 year old chatter had underscored the dashing of Jenny's hope.

"You look wayyyy more than 15," Veronica told Sarah, Mike and the whole family group.

Jenny made the entrance of the Oakcrest development and started the sprint that would conclude at the end of her driveway. She pushed her stride, ignored the need for breath, ignored the workers who looked at her from the muddy lot where they were framing a two-story home, ignored her wish to slacken, and finished.

Sure that she would make trust and friendship emerge with her niece, Jenny had looked forward to Sarah's presence. The unhappiness that came with the womanly girl could be solved with patience and with distance from whatever had been wrong in Connecticut.

Along the way to the art school at midday, Sarah was polite but quiet, with her face turned always uncaringly toward a view of everything along the route. Jenny pushed at the silence with cheerful conversation, with questions about artists Sarah admired and things she wished to do that summer. Jenny would show Sarah the Iowa campus and the art school when they had time Memorial Day weekend.

"Yeah, maybe," Sarah answered.

At the school, Sarah remained far from gregarious but was patient with the small children who populated afternoon sessions of finger-painting, water color painting, and composition with found and natural materials. Much taken with her soft, dark hair and her confusing, near-adult looks, two of the boldest girls probed Sarah with "How old are you?" and "Are you a movie star?"

She let some hold tresses of her hair and comb it.

"I'm four," a boy told Sarah.

"I'm this many," a girl said, showing three fingers.

"Ooh, you're big," Sarah replied, giving the boy or the girl a smile that really did make Sarah seem as perfect as a young Hollywood starlet.

To Jenny, the girl seemed content to be much the same age as the admiring children around her. Among the young members of the art class, Sarah was at ease, quick to follow what the children said, a little girl among little girls and boys.

The mothers who sat and visited with one another or who came for the children at the end of a class were also confused. "Is Sarah one of your sisters?" a few asked as they noticed the good looks of both long-legged art instructors.

"Where do you go to college?" others asked Sarah.

"What art school are you in?" the mother of a ten year old boy asked. The woman seemed skeptical when Jenny answered for her niece.

For the children, Sarah was an apparition, a touchable young goddess dropped among them. The afternoon sessions that day and all the days sounded with "Sarah, Sarah, Sarah" and "What do you need, Larry?" or "Just a minute, Diane" as the children pressed Jenny's patient niece for help and attention.

The evening sessions brought Jenny the disturbing sight of two modishly sideburned, flop-haired fathers flirting lightly with Sarah, mostly for the sake of entertaining one another. To Jenny's relief, the embarrassing questions and comments put to Sarah brought her adolescent nervousness to the fore. Her look darkened. She shrank from eye contact. Ignoring the self-satisfied men twice her age, Sarah bent and helped one child or another as they gathered work for showing at home.

Spuhn, full of his own ideas and business matters, only half-listened to Jenny's worries about their niece's withdrawn nature.

"She's only been here a few days," he said.

Always absorbed in Spoon, SI Data, investments he had made with George Forrest in startups that were storing or applying many types of purchase data, Spuhn's expression was happy, an indication that his schedule with all its phone calls, conferences and opportunities was playing out just right for the hard-working, ambitious entrepreneur. The stakes he retained in three of the Klein ventures were approaching a value almost a quarter of what he had gained from the sale of the whole company. The data company investments being found by George Forrest's firm were begetting rewards from sales and new formations. Spoon was within sight of reaching Omaha.

Whether the investment proved sound or just became another flow of subsidy, Jenny knew that a plan Spuhn was making with his father was already raising the spirit of Spuhn's family. In a private investment, Spuhn would become co-owner of the small, well-regarded Holstein Trucking with the founder's son. Dennis' father, his mind at play in the possibilities of the business he would expand with his rail transport knowledge, was showing himself too busy for cards with men he finally knew were using him for sport.

Just finished with a run, Spuhn rested on a cushioned porch swing with a light blue t-shirt pulled slighty up over a belly that was, like the rest of him, athletically lean. The brown waves of his hair were wet. His green eyes were full of satisfaction as he looked out over the handsome surroundings of his home.

By the time he showered and returned in bermuda shorts and a white t-shirt, Spuhn had made a decision, a pleasing one, about Sarah. At the Anita store opening the following week, on the Saturday of the Hoorah for Summer weekend, Sarah would join the two coeds escorting Ron Tonti during all the performance hand-walking of the event, from leading the high school band and dignitaries to the ribbon that would be cut, to the mingling of an upright Tonti with autograph seekers of all ages.

"She'll be on television," Spuhn told Jenny.

After eating quickly, he worked in his office for two hours and, still in fine humor, came to Jenny in their bedroom.

"Your nails are a mess," he said, as she played her fingers along his chest and stomach. With his own fingertips, he stroked along the silver band of the Cartier watch he had given her for her birthday in February.

"I was planting all the marigolds," she said. "I had to weed around a whole bunch of the iris, too." "She'll be on television," Spuhn told Jenny.

She heard no more about the nails, which she had filed and painted with clear polish before she and Sarah left for the weekend in Jenny's three year old Mustang, a green car with manual transmission she and Spuhn had bought from one of the Iowa Outdoors salesmen. For the sake of event preparation and also because Spuhn preferred his yellow Corvette, Spuhn was already overseeing everything at the new restaurant.

Sarah was used to sleeping until after 10 a.m. and, even then, rose groggily. On this day of the Spoon celebration, Sarah was white-faced and slow as she and Jenny left the house in darkness. The Anita tape-cutting and opening would occur at 11:30 a.m. For most of the drive, as the sun warmed cattle, tilled soil and young crops under a nearly cloudless blue sky, the girl slept in the back seat, then woke, asked where they were, slumbered briefly, and moved into the front seat when Jenny stopped for gas. In West Des Moines, they stopped at Spoon for a takeout meal of Papa Pows, the potato offering that Jesus had developed, along with two small hamburgers and bottles of cold milk. An anxious manager and some staff who recognized Jenny as Spuhn's wife greeted her and watched her warily as they directed the set up of some stanchions and displays for Tonti's appearance the next day. The remainder of the trip, Sarah sketched in a notebook with its cover raised against Jenny's view.

They arrived early at the Anita restaurant, early enough that they were ahead of Spuhn, who was coming from a stop at the Des Moines apartment building he owned with George Forrest.

Jenny felt sorry for the nervous Anita manager. The slender man with "Chuck" stitched on his Spoon shirt pocket, veteran of two other Spoon restaurant openings, was a "yes, sir, yes, ma'am" type who had the flattop haircut as well as the bearing of a young highway patrolman. He recognized Jenny at once and pulled away from the little group who had been receiving his instructions about some arrangement at the front of the new building. Among them, Jenny saw, was Jim Clayton, who was holding a tan poplin suit coat over his left arm.

Clayton arrived at Jenny and Sarah a couple of strides behind the manager.

"Nothing's going to get goin' for more than an hour, Mrs. Spuhn," the man said. "Would you like to wait inside, out of the sun?"

"Jenny, how's it goin'?" Clayton said. He wore a snugly knotted, wide tie, its silken cloth brightly patterned in rust, yellow and green. After showing Jenny a klieg light of a dimpled grin, he gave in to his instinct and studied Sarah, with obvious liking for the way the girl's bosom and hips appeared in a short, light green, leg-displaying dress.

"You're Sarah?" Clayton asked her. "Your father is Robert Adamski? Our firm has represented parties in some deals with him."

Taking a welcome for granted, Clayton once again gave Jenny the sense of savoring an internal view of the good looks he was presenting to all around him. In his own inner mirror, the handsome new lawyer reviewed with satisfaction the whole Clayton image, from the modish length of his hair to the aviator style sunglasses he held in the hand with his coat. Certainly, he knew others were observing him in the company of Jenny and Sarah. Spuhn's former schoolmate, Jenny saw, was elevating his importance by rooting himself in a public visit with the wife and niece of Dennis Spuhn. Clayton was ready to smile and laugh with appreciation for anything said to him.

For a moment, appreciating Clayton's discomfort at being suffered company, at being unable to get Sarah's heart stirred under Jenny's eye, Jenny suddenly reflected on Clayton and Dennis together. Longtime friends, both were handsome, comfortable, sure of themselves. Yet the men were not alike, Dennis so determined, so planned, so here I am the way I am. But Clayton repulsed her with his eternal expectation of advantage from his charm. What pretty young woman, what adult, what parent or professor could he not woo with his long lashes, dimpled smile, and clever conversation?

And at bottom, what friendship, what patron, what girlfriend could endure if self-interest challenged Clayton's unctuous fidelity? Was Clayton aware that Spuhn had learned of Clayton's Szabo betrayal? She guessed Clayton was, and also guessed that, if Clayton proved himself an advantage to the businesses, Spuhn's own practicality would make something close to the old ease develop. Always a good student, Clayton had finished with a high place in his class. He had the brains and the sycophantic cleverness for the work the big Des Moines firm would give him.

"Holler out if you need anything, Mrs. Spuhn," the manager said. Once off the dusty white apron of stone that gave the new restaurant an auxiliary parking lot, the man knelt quickly and used his handkerchief for repair of the shine on his black shoes.

The brightness of the morning sun made Jenny, Sarah and Clayton turn away, toward a sight of the just-finished restaurant and its new black, asphalt parking lot atop a low hill surrounded by farmland vista: a few distant white homes, silos and barns; planted and tilled fields, cattle gathered in a green expanse. A warm breeze stirred across the place. Anita itself sat a couple of miles south, its existence at the interstate barely more than the new Spoon restaurant, a nearby Shell gas station, and two sun-faded homes, one with a shadowed porch and uneven porch swing. A couple of farm dogs, mixes of collie and shepherd, rested in a sunny spot before the same house.

A good stream of trucks and cars, justification for the Anita location, moved north and south, to and from the new I-80 roadway.

Seeing two local officials arriving in a tan Cadillac with a soft beige interior, Clayton left Jenny and Sarah in order to join the manager in greeting them. Two of the parents from the band group hustled across the parking lot toward the arrivals. Jenny saw a beaming man whose green sport coat fit too tightly for the way he stretched a big hand toward the pair: an official he called "John" and an equally pleased woman wearing a bright jewelry disk pinned to the front of her blue coat. Clayton introduced himself and presented one of his Cutler & Mattingly cards as soon as he had the chance.

Once she was able to move with Sarah into the restaurant, out of the way of the people placing stanchions, posting a flag, stretching a wide red ribbon, and readying a table of water and pop, Jenny was grateful for Jesus Hernandez. Always without guile, happy, Hernandez was at the center of a party that he had already begun to enjoy for its gathering of friends he knew and friends he would make. Leaving the kitchen, his smile white and broad under a thick new mustache, he met Sarah graciously and immediately added her to the excited young helpers he was putting to the morning's tasks. Under his care soon after, Sarah met Ronnie Tonti and Ellen and Barb, the two University of Iowa students serving as Tonti's handwalk attendants.

While Barb, a blue-eyed, primary education major with the confidence of an older sister, found Sarah a Spuhn t-shirt in her size, a bemused Ronnie Tonti watched Sarah thread the hoops of her earrings through the shirt's neck.

"Whoo-eee, chère, you got more jangles on you than a Nawlins' gypsy girl," he said. "Maybe you tell me my fawtune."

After Tonti stepped away from them for the taking of a photo with two town officers, Jenny saw Sarah becoming comfortable, drawn into the following of Barb's instructions and lead.

"New York?" Jenny heard. "I bet that is one busy place out there."

"Have you seen the Statue of Liberty?" Ellen asked. "My aunt went there."

In the background, she and everyone else heard Spuhn enter. His appearance, his recognition of staff seeking his look, his banter and encouragements elevated the effort of the whole group. "Gotta take care of some things real fast here," Spuhn said, hugging Jenny and then quickly kissing her. He was full of energy, ready to be off for spreading of his entrepreneur pixie dust.

"Outstanding, outstanding. Donna, you and Marie, you're right here when things start. Okay, good. Here, Greg, Al, c'mon. You two studs. Let's move this cutter and all this gear to the other end of that counter." Spuhn picked up one end of the big machine. "All the meat arrive?" Jenny heard him asking questions, whirling around, touching, just so each recognized person could delight in his motivating warmth.

Jenny stayed out of the way near the restaurant entrance, where she skimmed through the first two of a line of Spoon articles framed along the wall. Handsome and energetic, principal representative of the Spoon chain, Dennis Spuhn himself gestured and smiled amid platters of Spoon fare or among freshly uniformed young staff members or in the company of some happy customers. One article had a photo of Tonti being applauded as he moved toward the entrance of the Des Moines Spoon, opened the year before.

An amused Hernandez came up behind Jenny as she read. "Walks on water, doesn't he?"

Noticing the tone, Jenny turned.

"Notice the war record? Whoever wrote that one turned Spuhn into the Marines' answer to Sergeant Rock," Hernandez said. "He's got the gift."

Jenny didn't answer. What Hernandez pointed out was true of that article and some others on the wall. In several, Spuhn's marathon runs were becoming those of an elite competitor. As Hernandez's tone showed, the big man knew he no longer had a place in the framed clippings.

Jenny went outside, into the bright sunshine where a high school band in long-sleeved, orange uniforms was organizing itself and beginning the jitter flurries of horn sounds and drumming.

Now wearing a tailored, golden wheat-colored silk jacket over a starched white shirt open at the collar, Spuhn was talking with a gray-haired man who was patiently cleaning his glass lenses and often stopping to call hello or accept a handshake. When she came up to the pair, kissed Spuhn and received his kiss and squeeze in return, Jenny learned that the other man, ready to welcome the new restaurant with ceremony remarks, was a Cass County Commissioner.

After the cutting of the ribbon, the Star-Spangled banner, the congratulatory remarks by the mayor and by the county commissioner, the photographs and the Tonti handwalk that led the whole group inside the new restaurant, Jenny gave her car to another Spoon staff member headed to the next event in West Des Moines. Sarah joined Ronnie Tonti, Barb and Ellen in the car driven by a 17 year old boy, a serious Anita employee assigned to a day of chauffeuring in the manager's new white Chevrolet Camaro.

In their car, Spuhn's yellow Corvette, Spuhn was relaxed and appearing pleased with the ceremony just completed. Still, he pressed on the road and kept a hand on Jenny's leg except when he flicked around an overtaken car or truck.

"Looked like it all went well," she said.

"Hands down,"Spuhn said. "Hands down. Outstanding. Be in Yorkshire end of July, Omaha in September. Hoorah!" he said to Jenny and to the cattle and farms spread out on both sides of the interstate as well as the heavens above the open top of the car. Aviator glasses sat on the ridge of his nose. Breezes combed through the wavy length of his hair.

Jenny hoped their children would have Dennis' nose, straight and firm, not so delicately boned as hers.

"Sarah likes those two girls," Jenny said. "The Tonti tenders."

"Yeah," Spuhn said. His mind was on other things.

"Linda hasn't written to her."

"Yeah, no love lost there. Bob said Linda was all over Sarah all the time about some doofus boyfriend, a college student there. Bob is just as bad. He was afraid the loser was going to knock her up. That's the main reason we have her, to keep her away from that waste of space."

Jenny almost said what she was thinking: "And now away from Clayton."

Out loud, she said, "Clayton lives in Des Moines now, is that right?"

She thought for a moment of herself, what she did with that boyfriend Val the months of freshman year when she was smitten enough that she ignored what she overheard in the snickers of the roommates about Val and his under-the-stairs PP, the close room she found out all the roommates called the Poon Palace.

"Yeah, he's taking the bar exam pretty soon."

Reaching out, Sarah combed Dennis' hair back from his forehead and brought her hand down to rest on his thigh. He put his fingers on hers.

When they caught up to Sarah and the other crew members at the Spoon in West Des Moines, Sarah was transformed.

"Those college people sure are funny," Sarah said.

"Like what?" Jenny asked.

"A boy in Barb's class stripped naked and got up and ran around the room right in the middle of an exam."

"A streaker. That's streaking."

"Did he get a good grade?" Spuhn asked.

"Barb said he was already flunking. He was going in the Army."

"College can be pretty crazy."

"Ronnie Tonti, he told all kind of funny stories. Like once, they got an old lady's cat drunk and put it back in her house. This boy named Ken, he told about stuff they make the new kids do when they come to join a fraternity: say stupid things like 'Hi yo Silver' every time they talk in class, paint their toenails, count all the cans of dog food at the grocery store, stuff like that. Oh, and things they eat in Louisiana. You wouldn't believe. We were laughing the whole time we were coming over here."

Jenny knew a reason for Sarah's high spirits was not only the expectation of joining the group for other Tonti appearances during the coming months. The main reason came from Barb and Ellen's invitation to be of college student age, to eat pizza with the rest of them and then visit in one of the rooms being used by crew members. Jenny gave permission, and an 11 p.m. deadline for returning to the Holiday Inn room Spuhn had booked, one with a small connected bedroom.

That night, Jenny listened and became enthusiastic, too, during Spuhn's exuberant telling of the progress with SI Data, slated in Bob's plan for an initial public offering after 12 to 18 months. Soon, she rubbed her chin against his hair as she drew his heated face into her breasts.

CHAPTER 31

Fired up!
Feeling good!
Motivated!
Dedicated!
All right!
Out of sight!
Dynamite!

If Nikolay Vetrov had withstood the grip of Oklahoma's Sam Elwin with the same determination that Tank and all his AA patrons threw into keeping him sober the week Anna took her downturn and died, the University of Iowa letter would have reached the hands of a former Olympic champion. As it was, the letter rested amid tissues and reading glasses and some uplifting books on the chair where Tank had sat with Anna's hand in his own.

"Anna was so proud of you, so close to getting your three year pin," Nina reminded him. "When she talked about you, she had the happiest look on her face."

Tank didn't have to close the bedroom door in order to turn his back on it. He left the house and everything else in the hands of Nina, his sister Galina and the other good Samaritans who managed

Anna's funeral, her burial in the Navalny cemetery and then the winnowing from the house of all the detritus of Anna's care. Her compression stockings, her bottles of medications, the bandages and pillows and hot water bottle went. The bedding and curtains disappeared, then came back with only a suggestion of Anna smell left from washing at Nina's house.

Galina let her own tears flow as she worked in the house the weekends she came with her family. While the three children roamed along the creek and about the property, Jim, happily immersed in the familiar things of farming, strung new wiring through new conduit for new fluorescent lighting over the front rows of seating in the barn Tank's Sunday visitors called the Place for Knowing God. Galina gathered the get well cards and the sympathy cards into a scrapbook she placed on a living room table under the bible Tank and Anna used in their bedroom.

A photograph from their wedding day, a photo Anna kept on the bedroom dresser, went onto the mantel in the living room, beside the photo Galina had put in a silver frame years before, the photo of her mother, a serious, dark-eyed teen among a group of equally serious bearded young men and some women standing close to a seated, smiling man with deepset eyes and a long beard. Galina held one framed photo, then the other as she gave in to a cry.

The women worried about Tank in the evenings, asked him often if he would be all right, if he would like to come to one of their homes for a good meal, a chance to visit. In the end, they accepted his gray-faced look, his softly spoken thanks before they left him seated with his bible in one hand and his eyes staring out the front window at the countryside changing from late afternoon to shadowy evening. On a table beside him, they left a plate of dinner made by Nina or Carol or one of the other women according to a schedule they had organized. Windows opened fully on sunny days, lowered when rain threatened, kept the air of the house in sync with whatever cool was available in the July temperatures.

On Tuesday and Thursday nights, his AA sponsor either came for Tank or arranged for a ride with another group member.

The well-intentioned women could have taken the house down to the studs and Anna would remain present.

Tank sat. If he had been nothing more than dust or a tuft of cottonwood fluff, any force, any light breeze would have picked him up with ease. Instead, burly, distant and uncaring, misery in human form, he sat, with an expression showing concentration on people and things not in the room or in the house.

Again and again, Tank roamed through thoughts of Anna, of her naked press and her encouraging faith in all that he attempted and would do, even if neither of them could know what was coming around their bend. The boys on the wrestling team loved her, would push themselves whenever they knew she was watching and clapping in the stands. Unable to travel, less and less able to sustain telephone conversations of any duration, she sent her spirit, her hopes to them in the calls she had with Bob and with Jenny. She only spoke praise and patience for Sarah, so troubled and troubling as a young woman. Tank saw Anna in his mind, heard her finding and encouraging goodness in everyone around her.

Instead of shaking Tank's faith, Anna's death firmed it.

Blessed are the peacemakers, for they shall be called children of God. Anna, peacemaker, child of God, his Anna, child of God. Patient patroness of the three boys accepting what came from the great gears their war resistance obstructed.

"Keep on trucking, Yawp," Lev wrote from Oakland, where he was teaching in a ghetto Freedom School and feeling Anna's spirit in the magic of the whole universe. "Peace and justice, Lev" he signed the letter.

After two weeks of noticing the almost complete withdrawal of Tank from the few summer activities bringing him to Harlan,

Tank's high school principal Tom Daniels grew impatient. Characteristically sure of himself, he added his own speculations to the things he heard in the community conversation, the news Nina and the others shared from their Navalny visits. His wrestling coach, his social studies teacher, his fellow Ten O'Clock member and neighbor, the principal knew without a doubt, was just sitting and falling apart in a rumpled, unkempt mass in a chair probably too flimsy for his settled weight. On top of that, Daniels didn't need to speculate about Tank's reaction to the University of Iowa letter. Lou Girard, who covered college football as the main part of his sports beat for the *Harlan Tribune*, confirmed at the week's Ten O'Clock get-together that the absent Tank had sent no answer to the University of Iowa Department of Athletics.

"Any the rest of us'd give our left nut for a chance to appear at a halftime ceremony but Nikolay is not so much as sayin' 'Thanks and maybe.' God almighty. You know who else Iowa is getting there for that ceremony?" Girard, Iowa class of 1961, bottom of the baseball team's roster his last two years, proceeded to name a string of Iowa sports stars, record holders and champions from the previous fifty years. "Nikolay is just sittin' out at his place and doing nothin' about the invitation. He hasn't said 'boo' to the university yet, and he won't talk to the paper about it."

"That would be a good thing for sure, hands down a good thing for Harlan, for Harlan High School," Daniels said.

"Damn straight it would."

Damned if Daniels would let such an opportunity get away from Harlan, his school and from Tank himself. The principal put together a delegation of three muscular, straight arrow please and thank you wrestlers Tank had coached. They were already making names on their college teams. The brothers Val and Donny Stronmeyer plus their friend Marty Cavendish were working on a construction crew rebuilding a long strip of Rte. 59 south of

Harlan. Val, immediately a star of the University of Iowa team, and Donny, who had been recruited for the freshman team, were staying in shape for the coming season. Marty had hopes of rejoining the Iowa State team once the mid-season ligament tear in his shoulder healed. With quiet respect, the three joined the high school principal in his antique green-colored Oldsmobile 98, a car washed each weekend and, so far, only driven 2300 miles.

In the elegance of the car, the three Harlan graduates deferred to conversation topics chosen by the school administrator known as Knobby for his buckeye of an Adam's apple: summer weather, family news, the invitation their former coach was not answering.

When they arrived at Tank's house and found him flushed red and wet-haired from his banya, now reading psalms in his living room, the other young men let Val lead them inside. They arrayed themselves with Tom Daniels in a semi-circle close before Tank.

A morning drizzle had become steady enough that the supervisor had called work for the day. Muddied from moving tools and barrels as they waited for starting work or ending it, the thick-necked young men gave off warm, rank, dirt smell from their damp work shirts and jeans.

Tank's expression warmed at the sight of them. He rose and shook each wrestler's hand firmly, gave his face a good study and greeted each one before the delegation sat in chairs pulled together.

"Who's coaching the freshmen now?" Tank asked Donny from the kitchen. Tank was studying the refrigerator for ice tea or juice or milk he could offer the guests.

Donny and Val both answered.

"He's good," Tank said. "He'll have you boys ready to kick ass and take names."

"Not at Iowa State," Marty said. "The Cyclones will flatten those pussies."

"Like hell," Donny said.

"We'll see about that next fall," Daniels said. "Tank, we want to talk to you about something else."

The wrestlers became serious.

"Yeah, Coach," Val said. Beside him, Donny and Marty froze as they awaited Tank's reaction. "What's the deal with the halftime of the Penn game? You should go."

Tank looked down at the floor as Val, then Donny and Marty talked.

"You're the best there was, Coach. Everyone famous is goin' to be there."

"Bud Elliott." "Walter Jones."

"That pitcher for St. Louis."

"Jack Meyer."

"Say yes, Coach."

"Tell them yes."

"All the grapplers, they know you, Coach. Everyone wants to meet you in person."

Already in a tearful mood when the visitors arrived, Tank rubbed his eyes and remembered himself, full of himself, taker of anything, of anyone in the Iowa years he held his strength and ability as his own properties, independent of anyone's generosity and genes, of any divine blessing. How lost he had been while feeling so elevated among thousands who were making their own life routes with individual mixtures of purpose and grace. Distant from his Lord Jesus Christ, he had used his wrestling for sinning. All praise had been deserved truth. All submission from coeds and classmates had been earned tribute. How could he go back? How could he stand at midfield and be cheered by thousands for the years he had adored himself instead of his heavenly maker?

Tank tried to voice his feeling.

"I wasn't good then."

"Bull fucking shit, Coach. You pinned the Michigan State guy, the state high school champ in one and a half minutes."

Val's coarse, blunt words made Donny and Marty shoot glances at Daniels.

"And the wrestler from Drake your sophomore year."

"Bunches of 'em."

"No, I wasn't good then. I was proud. I just did anything I wanted."

The three former Harlan teammates, confused, fell silent. At the same time, an idea came to Daniels, who picked up the bible Tank had placed on the table. Quickly, he turned pages until he found what he wanted and gained Tank's attention.

"Tank, listen," he said. "This was the text of our Sunday worship other day. It's about you."

Then, in the voice of the ministry student he had been before veering into education, Daniels read: "Ye are the light of the world. A city that is set on an hill cannot be hid. Neither do men light a candle, and put it under a bushel, but on a candlestick; and it giveth light unto all that are in the house. Let your light so shine before men, that they may see your good works, and glorify your Father which is in heaven."

The principal closed the book. With conviction, he set about explaining what he had just read.

"Tank, you are the light of the world here. You get out on that field and you are going to be the city set on a hill. Everyone will see you. You can let your light shine. You can show everyone that you are glorifying your Father which is in heaven, hands down you can."

Tank recognized the scripture as Matthew and remembered the other words around it, the sermon Anna took so to heart, the rousing descriptions of the poor in spirit, the peacemakers, the meek, the pure in heart. . . and they that mourn. Mourning had not been Anna's worry. Taking cheer from everything at hand, from the blooming of morning glories, the trilling of a bird, the clearing of the sky, the smell of loam, the arrival of Tank from school, she was pure of heart, peacemaker, advocate of the ministry that had grown around Tank's scripture reflections.

The text Tom Daniels read and the earnestness of the college wrestlers joined Tank's thoughts about Anna the rest of that day and the next morning. More than the difficulty of sobriety, he felt the prod of Anna's will. Certainly, she, lovely, generous child of God, had sent Tom Daniels and his three former wrestlers the previous afternoon. Who but Anna had put the memory of his Sunday worship in the principal's mind, had led his fingers to the words in Matthew and then to understanding of the tie to the letter sent by the University of Iowa athletic department?

As he sat in the heat of the banya with the morning light growing and glinting outside in the fragile morning cool that would give way to July humidity, with the thin creekside woods full of trilling birds, Tank calmly and then happily returned to a realization that was suddenly turning from wisps to substance.

Before the agents came for Joe Szabo, Lev, and Artie, the worried deacon had described Tank and Anna's tolerance as "reckless Christianity."

Anna, ever the advertising person, the copywriter, had liked the phrase, one she began applying in her own wry sense of their relationship with the Harlan community, the world, and the God Tank was thinking about at so many times.

"Greater love than this hath no man but that he would give his life for his friends," Anna said once as they talked about scripture Tank would discuss on a Sunday morning. "Beautiful copy. Lofty. But it's just copy, isn't it, until something sells? Until the thing is right there, and a person has to give life for a friend, or not give life.

A campaign maybe wins a prize but if the product doesn't move, what good's the campaign?"

Long before it happened, Anna knew that it would happen. Tank's feeling had changed. Without consciousness of the change, his need to know God had gone beyond the questions of yes, no, is there, isn't there and arrived at consequences.

Restless and excited from the nearness of clarity, Tank dressed, praised Jesus, and moved to the barn, where he cleared benches away from an area he needed for exercise. As he lifted and pushed the rocks and buckets and engine parts that sufficed for his weights, as he pinkened and sweat, and, most of all, as he worked back and forth through the Bible and through Anna's memories, he began feeling the power that had sent the Old Testament figures and then the New Testament personalities into action. Moses, knowing, had put one foot ahead of the other for 40 years. Isaiah, Jonah, the Apostle Paul, they had gone right into the marketplace, right into the face of the not-godly, and recklessly made havoc.

Tank heaved the iron bar with the concrete blocks up, up in an effortless fling, then did it again, again, again. He had hesitated, a blink, weighing things, riding the one point advantage, not hearing what the coach was screaming. In the blink, Sam Elwin, the Oklahoma star who would go on to the Olympics, saw Tank about to shoot for a leg and took advantage.

Paul, Peter, James, the rest of them, they had acted with no preparation, no laying aside of monies and winter coats, just boarded whatever vessel was going that way, set out on any suitable path and took what they had come to know into every place they could reach. Recklessly, they let the hands of God encircle and lead them.

Thinking such thoughts, Tank lifted and pulled his weights, let his grunts emerge in loud, determined series, and let himself redden and perspire. He thought and, thinking, tried to exhaust himself.

Reckless Christianity, Anna's Christianity. Shoot for the leg, for the takedown.

He wished it were September. He wished that the light was on the mountain, that he was at midfield, that he was telling the thousands around him of his repentance.

From the first, she reminded Ronnie Tonti of Melinda Beasley as Melinda looked that sunny afternoon she bent to touch the Mississippi River.

If her hair, dark like Melinda's, had not been so fragrant, her breasts had not shown against her light blouse and in the unbuttoned part reaching from her throat well down between them, if she weren't pressing herself ready and willing against him as soon as they entered the little bedroom, Ronnie Tonti might have remembered that small Iowa towns like Shelby had the same dangerous illusion as little towns like Slidell, Louisiana. The empty streets and shadowed porches on airless days intensely hot were no protection. Neighbors knew, strangers had eyes upon them, every secret oozed from one house to the next.

Tonti felt her leading him, having him with a quickness and an assurance he had not expected from a girl with the forlorn air she had. In the hot room with the thin white curtains hanging still at the single window, she shaped herself to him, pushed and let him feel her teeth and her tongue as she moved her face down the front of him. He held her head between his hands, each index finger pressing lightly on her through a hoop of her earrings.

As if sensing a husband's tread at the end of the block, as if she were in a porn film pulled through a projector set on "stampede", the girl opened her legs and let her breath become little cries. She kept her eyes closed, let Tonti see her seeing someone else.

When they were done, Tonti became furtive. He looked to see that the curtains, though thin, hung down over the bedroom window.

"Little darlin', boilin's where you start and then you light the fire, you flat do," he said. "They bottle a little bit of you in one of those spaceships, they get to the moon right now. Hands down. Bam."

After that, they didn't talk until they had come quietly through the house and were in the car on the way to the meeting with the other Tonti tenders.

CHAPTER 32

Left right alay oh
Left right alay oh
At a double time!
Left right alay oh
At a double time!

Jenny was about to leave the house and catch up with Sarah for the mid-afternoon art classes when she saw Dennis make the turn, almost a fishtailing one, into the driveway. Two steps at a time, he arrived on the porch in distracted fury, gave Jenny a grunting kiss on her cheek as he drew her toward him. Then he released her and headed into the house toward his upstairs office.

As soon as he arrived upstairs, he turned and descended rapidly to the porch.

Jenny tensed.

What Sarah asked after overhearing Jenny and Spuhn talking on the phone at the school the day before came to mind: "Why is Uncle Dennis like so uptight?"

Cicadas, the August complement to spring's mayflies, were sending an anxious wave of sound from the lawn, the shrubs and the woods. The afternoon was hot with clouds building in the west, the air heavy with anticipation of the thunderstorms arriving in the early evening.

"Benson is screwing us," Spuhn said. The statement was eruption, not communication. Spuhn's look was drawn. His green eyes were narrow and hard. He glanced at Jenny, then at the reach of the lawn, then back to Jenny, to the wooden floor of the porch.

"How?"

"Tonti should be right in that halftime program. All fat and sassy, he should be there. Hands down. The athletic director knows that, the trustees Diebold talks to, they know that."

Jenny knew that.

Tonti was that close to being done with the handwalk, that close to completing 313 miles on his hands, three years of labor at it. Putting him at midfield would give the university the benefit of all the handwalk's publicity, everything.

Jenny waited, ready to wrap into Dennis, ready to push his gloom away from him. The cicadas thrummed in the humid air. The August sun burned down. Sarah could manage the class until Jenny arrived at the school.

Benson, Benson, Benson. Even while running for the legislative seat made vacant by the stroke that had forced Democrat Joe Wahlig's retirement, Benson had the meanness and the time for thwarting Dennis Spuhn. Her husband's look indicated that, so far, Benson's major backer, Vic Krol, was prevailing. The Burger King franchise owner and former Iowa football star who had long filled the same funding role for Benson's employer, Congressman Pat "Patriot" Sawyer, would crowd out Spoon and Ronnie Tonti.

"The college says good idea, no room this time, maybe something at one of the basketball games. Diebold found out the Congressman's been sticking his nose in."

With Benson freely using the Congressman's influence, Spuhn had found his hopes for a place in the program blocked.

So far, Benson had found the right barrier. Vic Krol had laid down years of financial contributions to his alma mater.

So far, not forever. Solving the issue would come. First, Spuhn would withdraw, would give in to study of possibilities, connections, and levers. So far was not the last word when Dennis Spuhn wanted something a certain way. Jenny knew.

"Something will happen," Jenny said, speaking what she knew, advancing into Spuhn for a kiss before she picked up her art supplies and moved to the car.

Dennis now had the distracted air of the bridge player calculating the cards he could see and those he could ferret into view.

"There's chicken in the fridge," Jenny said.

"Okay."

"Go inside. It's too hot out here. And you should run after the rain stops, not now."

Jenny had forgotten the speech Dennis was giving that night at a program of the Quad Cities Boy Scout Leadership.

"Tank is one of the people Iowa invited. He'll be there."

Dennis was not expecting an answer, had only spoken the regret that Tank's selection for halftime or Tank's exclusion meant nothing for Spoon and Tonti. Anna was no longer alive. This season, Anna would not hear the cicadas or see the men and the trucks and the combines come into the fields for the harvest before the cold set in the ground. She would not be a means of Tank interfering, in case Tank's interference could sway any of the university officials.

Not sure what action to take but decided on action, Spuhn began organizing the forces he knew. Instructing his secretary Elaine in the recordings, he dictated letters and a company memo while standing in his upstairs office, while looking down at the spread of the *Morning Democrat*, the issue showing Benson flanked by two clean-cut, take-home-to-meet-Momma campaign staff as the candidate responded to the excited reach of some senior women at the Presbyterian Senior Home.

The first dictation would go to all restaurant managers but would apply narrowly to the single Scott County, legislative district 43 restaurant, the original Spoon where Brady Street met the interstate. "Spoon will not allow the use of its premises for campaigning by any candidate for political office. This includes appearances with or without staff for shaking hands with diners who are there to enjoy a meal. This includes the taking of campaign photographs. This includes passing out literature. Spoon is a restaurant, a place for enjoying good food. It is not a political meeting hall.

"Of course, Spoon is hospitable to every candidate who is ready to conduct himself as a regular patron. Expect the candidate to pay his bill."

Spuhn would repeat the instruction in a phone call to the Brady Street manager and during regular visits to the restaurants.

Most would know what Spuhn meant: the devil could sit, have his coffee replenished, and hold forth forever. Candidate Greg Benson couldn't come inside.

"Elaine," Spuhn said into the dictaphone, "get Jerry or one of the other people to pull a list of our Iowa students, A-sap, the ones now, the ones from the past two years. Oh, do we know what their majors are? Anyone on a team? Find out. I'd like that, too."

Two hours later, deciding not to wait until his secretary listened to the dictated tape, Spuhn called her and gave her the instruction.

"Elaine," he added, "make out a $500 personal check to the Marty Wahlig campaign. He's running for his dad's seat."

Then he changed into a clean outfit of chinos and button-down blue shirt, brown Gucci loafers with no socks, combed his hair, and left for the Boy Scouts events. Elaine had seen to stocking of the Corvette with coupons for the boys and their leaders.

The speech was a "you can do it" one Spuhn modified with references to merit badges and

Eagle Scout achievements. To Spoon, he applied a statistic he had read in a *Restaurant Management* article about the industry: nearly 40 percent of the kids, girls and boys, Spoon hired were former Scouts, some Explorers.

"So if you need someone to tie a good knot for you, come see us," he said. For added effect, he paused and swept the pleased boys and the scout leaders with a broad, handsome smile.

Spuhn promised that, when Ron Tonti was done with his handwalk across the whole state, he would come back to visit with everyone at the Spoon restaurant in Davenport. A rowdy trio, maybe eighth graders near the front, cheered.

At the end, the Scoutmaster and a serious, slender First Class Scout named Darryl presented Spuhn with a neckerchief slide carved into the familiar Spoon logo. Half a dozen members of Darryl's troop went efficiently into the audience of boys gathered in the school gymnasium and distributed the coupons Spuhn had brought.

Before Spuhn left, a photographer from the *Morning Democrat* composed a shot of Spuhn and Darryl joined in a Boy Scout handshake as the Scoutmaster looked on and Spuhn displayed the slide in his free hand.

So much for "be prepared," Spuhn thought to himself as he left the building without an umbrella or raincoat. The rain had arrived in a cold torrent that soaked him on the way to his car.

After the day's heat, the rain felt good. Briefly, Spuhn's mood was elevated from the rain's cool and the way the the speech had concluded with happy Scouts surging toward the boys handing out Spoon coupons.

The stop he made at the Brady Street restaurant restored the gloom.

The rain had lightened to a steady fall that would end in a short time. The clouds above were moving. Already the sky to the west showed end-of-day white at the horizon.

Spuhn saw the parking lot satisfactorily full but not completely full. Inside, he found customers delaying as they waited for the rain to stop. When they saw Spuhn enter, a couple of waitresses, high school students, busied themselves with menu stacking and placement of condiment and ketchup containers. The heightened activity spread to the rest from the evening manager, an ambitious 20 year old working on an associates degree at Scott County Community College. With her own example and with looks, Therese stirred activity aimed at fewer customers than Spuhn wished to see.

The manager knew Benson from the television news, and, Spuhn was sure, would bar Benson from any campaigning on the restaurant property.

Two of her personnel were Iowa students, she knew. They worked on weekends. A girl named Linda could be a student. Therese would see her the next day.

After dropping the dictation tape on Elaine's desk in Spoon's 3rd Street office, Spuhn drove home with the car's tires sounding on wet, shiny roads bordered occasionally by pools of runoff. The clouds had passed to the east, only threads of the clouds left for hiding, then revealing the rising moon.

Sarah was home, the black VW given her by her father parked in front, and radio station KQUD sounding through the closed door of her bedroom.

"Don't come in," she said when Spuhn knocked.

"Jenny at the school?"

"Yeah. She's into a painting thing."

Spuhn went to his office where he began working through news and industry magazines, some newspapers that gave him fodder for plans. Even as he tore pages for filing in folders he kept for subjects ranging from new businesses to government policies and locales, he remained intent on the true worry, his investors' and his board's growing unease with the slackened pace of the restaurants' same-store sales.

"We're up from last year," Spuhn argued, each time hearing that the pace lagged the new chains Woofer and Burger Palace as well as Burger King and McDonald's.

Spoon was expanding. Gross revenues were up.

But same-store sales were not rising as before.

And how could the pace increase enough to offset the board members' gloom about personal holdings in steel, in autos, in telecommunications, banking, in whatever else was being affected by the 1971 economy of almost six percent inflation? Certainly, the board knew what Spuhn knew, that the restaurants were just as susceptible as everyone else to employees' pressure for salary increases that outstripped productivity, were not immune from the widespread pessimism that was suddenly giving pause to consumer spending all over the country.

"This is why you diversify," Bob said, speaking of Spuhn and Jenny's personal investments in Spoon, in SI Data and the other data companies as well as interests in Klein Construction and some Klein developments, in investment funds of Madison Alberts and of Bob's own bank. Spuhn shared Randy Isaac's enthusiasm for IBM.

"Do you want me to find a buyer?"

"Hell, no, I don't want you to find a buyer. That's the last thing I want." Spuhn answered with a force that kept Bob Adamski from voicing the idea again, not if he wanted to keep wearing tailored shirts bought with fees from Dennis Spuhn.

The investment banker masked what he was thinking, the recognition of an entrepreneur beginning to believe his own bullshit.

"Certainly," Jenny's brother said.

What Spuhn wanted was a menu concoction from Jesus Hernandez's work, something of narcotic influence on the tastes of everyone in Iowa or passing through Iowa. Short of that, he wanted Ronnie Tonti hands down on the midfield of an Iowa football stadium filled with cheering throngs of hungry patrons. All the better if Tonti's handwalking trampled the presence of Vic Krol. And hoorah again if everything rubbed Greg Benson's face in the dirt.

Spuhn wouldn't have changed his schedule, anyway, but was glad of Jenny's absorption in her own work. She had accepted a Philadelphia collector's commission for two new pieces in her Compare and Contrast series and was also enthused about an entirely new work. As for Sarah, who knew what was going on with the reserved, womanly girl who was so popular with the young students of the art school and so mysterious in her other solitary interests? Curious, Jenny had taken to looking at the odometer of the Volkswagen. The miles didn't concern Spuhn the way they bothered Jenny; he remembered nights of circling the one-ways in Davenport, Rock Island and Moline with Clayton, Szabo and Yoder.

Before Jenny and Sarah rose, Spuhn was arrived already in Iowa City, where he spent time at SI Data with Randy Isaccs before going to the Iowa City restaurant in late morning.

Elaine's gathering of staff connections with the university had already produced a result.

"Does this help?" Donna Shaw, a timid, efficient assistant to the manager, asked. "A man who comes here sometimes with his family is the director of the marching band. My boyfriend knows him."

Spuhn didn't have to answer. The transformation Donna Shaw saw indicated that her name and her round, freckled face would be one remembered by the company CEO.

Of course! Hoorah! The band would be on the field no matter who was in the Athletic Department's lineup.

With Donna in shy awe beside him in the Corvette, Spuhn drove to meet the young woman's boyfriend and then went with the music student to call on the band director.

Spuhn's own celebrity helped.

Professor Adolpho Luis Capriles, a tall, gracious man whose Venezuelan parents had brought him and his two sisters to live in Miami during the 1950s, recognized and liked Cuban elements in the menu of Spoon. Spuhn himself Professor Capriles recognized from television and from articles. Professor Capriles' oldest son, Fernando, was determined to master handwalking.

"He is close. He will get it before too long."

Spuhn postponed his departure for Grinnell and Des Moines restaurant visits in order to meet Professor Capriles in between the last class of the day and the practice he and an assistant would conduct with the members of the marching band.

The band leader knew how to raise money and knew how to interpret the interests of someone who approached him.

A contribution to the scholarship fund? Spuhn was ready.

Funds for the purchase of forty-eight uniforms the following spring? Spuhn was ready.

Spoon advertising in the year 1971-72 programs of the music department? Spuhn would authorize the spending as soon as the University presented the proposal.

The rest, the part that interested Spuhn, was equally simple. Familiar with the Spoon restaurants and sharing his family's enthusiasm for the imminent completion of Ronnie Tonti's handwalk across the state, Professor Capriles was a showman who could envision the attention the marching band would receive when Ronnie Tonti, on his hands, led the musicians onto the Iowa field at halftime.

No, the drum major could not be followed by someone carrying a flag with the Spoon logo.

"I compliment you for trying, Dennis," said the amused Professor Capriles.

Before leaving for Grinnell, Spuhn returned to the Iowa City restaurant in search of Donna Shaw.

She beamed as Spuhn rushed and gave her a hug that ignored mustard and some meat drippings collected on the cuff of her Spoon uniform.

"Outstanding can-do attitude, everyone," Spuhn said to the surrounding staff members. "Hoorah!"

Few understood what made the CEO so animated and joyous but Spuhn's happiness was infectious. Handsome, slender, green-eyed and youthful, he had a look that made everyone sure of a right course, a success from the evening's proud conduct of Spoon's Iowa City restaurant.

Jubilant, jubilant, jubilant, Spuhn pulled onto westbound I-80 under a sky showing striations of orange, pink and purple at the western horizon.

Ronnie Tonti at the head of the marching band, at the initiation of the halftime program – under the nose of Greg Benson.

From Grinnell and then from Des Moines, Spuhn arranged the completion of the Spoon agreement with Professor Capriles and the Music Department of the University of Iowa.

"I'll be home Friday," Spuhn said when he called Jenny at her art school.

"Not Thursday?" she asked.

"No, had to stick around in Iowa City, get that done."

Jenny thought but didn't ask: "Don't you have anyone else? Why is it always Dennis Spuhn?"

"Jenny, we are going to kick ass and take names at the Iowa game."

Jenny already knew from his tone something wonderful had happened.

"Everything okay?"

"Yes, fine."

"Jenny, Diebold's calling. I have to go."

Then the connection ended. In the quiet of the art school, with the big riverside windows reflecting her, the canvas and the rest of the room, Jenny resumed her work, a representation of the broad, flooded Iowa River nearing absorption of a fragile spit holding one small tree.

Whooeee, the air in Louisiana August made a person sink down on whatever was near and just go still as a gator till rain or till the last little bit of sweat finished sticking any clothes to his back along with little insects, pollen, and tree fluff. Iowa was the same.

If Melinda Beasley came from LSU, the heat Tonti felt on his bare back would make the woman wonder if she had come north at all. Tonti added years to her, grew her from the college girl with dark bangs and white shorts into a woman with the same silky hair, big, dark eyes and tan legs.

Most likely, Dottie was on the lookout for any more letters from Louisiana. Tonti knew Dottie didn't need letters, only needed to look past his little laugh and see the picture pressing large from his brain: a dark-haired, pretty woman running toward the sensations of the river, of studies, of Ronnie Tonti.

The two college students moving beside him, the Tonti tenders, spoke about returning to Iowa City, the beginning of the new school year.

Together and separate, Tonti with his head down, the boy and the girl distant from Tonti in their own conversation, they kept to the schedule of westward movement.

Ronnie Tonti felt the sun as he moved on his hands toward Omaha in about forty days and toward Oakland in the meantime. According to the Tonti tenders, the little place was not much more than 30 miles from the end of the walk.

Sweat dripped from Tonti, dripped along his forearms onto the back of his hands, onto the packed ground of the shoulder of Route 6.

"Almost 300 miles," the small, freckled psychology student named Judy said to Tonti when they stopped at a picnic bench set in the shade of some oaks.

"You're almost done."

Yes, almost done. Then, Ed Sullivan? Johnny Carson? The Tonti tenders, all college wise, seemed sure. Get across Iowa on his hands and Ronnie Tonti would be so famous he'd have things coming to him from all directions.

Two more days this week, both of them going to be hot, dry, perfect for what Dennis Spuhn and everyone wanted.

Two more days, he would go back to Davenport, to Dottie, and, when Dottie went to her shift, to the girl with the need.

Darlin', lookie here, lookie here. For you, chère, Ronnie Tonti has him a eight inch dick and a pile-driving ass.

Omaha then. Maybe go look for Melinda Beasley, see what she's turned into back in Louisiana.

CHAPTER 33

If I die in a combat zone
Box me up and ship me home.
Pin my medals on my chest,
Tell my girl I did my best.

Until everything went topsy turvy, Dennis Spuhn's ebullient spirit, his child-waiting-for-Christmas impatience for the front and center, straight across midfield appearance of Ronnie Tonti, set high the mood of the household. Jenny took pleasure in it, without thinking about the cause. There was no need to consider such a thing: Spuhn was the barometer, always the barometer. When Spuhn was anxious, she and many others were on tiptoes. On days the world was Spuhn's oyster, pearls abounded for everyone in his reach. The influence of his boyish smile, the look of his green eyes, the bounce in his whole lean form were hard to avoid.

These September days were an extreme. The air cooled and dried, a stimulant for Spuhn and for Jenny when they expended their energy on runs along farmlands where, behind fences sheltering Queen Anne's Lace and sumac, high corn was drying into gold and heavy cattle were noses deep in abundant grass. In the woods, maples began to redden. At night, the cicadas sounded. The crepitation revealed a world surrounding Spoon, Jenny and detached, adolescent Sarah with energy, hope and, no doubt about it, looming joy.

Cardplayer that he was, Spuhn saw nothing but strength in his hand each time he reviewed it. Thousands would view the appearance of the handwalker who had been made the symbol of the restaurant chain that soon would extend from the Mississippi River to the Missouri River. Thousands would watch. Among the thousands would be the thwarted, outmaneuvered, diminished Greg Benson.

For spite, Greg Benson could read the cost-was-no-object double truck, full bleed in the gutter color ad Spuhn had approved for the center pages of the football program.

Because he had time and because the approaching event filled his thoughts, Spuhn tweaked plans. The band leader, Professor Capriles, accommodated Spuhn with tickets for four seats several rows above field level, behind the Iowa bench where Ron Tonti would conclude his handwalk. There would be t-shirts with the Spoon logo for fraternity brothers paid to raise a Spoon banner. Above the field, a plane would circle with a Spoon streamer.

Jenny's skepticism did not discourage Spuhn from hoping that Tank Vetrov would wear one of the t-shirts, too, when he lined up with the other champion athletes Iowa would celebrate that day - and maybe right next to Vic Krol, owner of the Burger King franchises.

For Sarah, the mood, good or bad, was of no apparent consequence. Now enrolled at St. Sebastian's, she left for school in her Volkswagen when she had to, returned home when she wanted, answered questions with her eyes glowering and her posture in stiff rebuff. The other students were okay, unbelievably straight, she said. She had a test, wanted to study for it. In her room with the door shut, she played Bob Dylan, Cat Stevens, Cream, Rolling Stones, other LPs at a volume that spread the music along the hallway toward other bedrooms and Spuhn's office.

Spuhn's good humor could withstand the irritant.

"Jenny, don't worry," Spuhn said. "She's new. School's only, what, less than ten days so far?"

Told of Sarah by his sister, mother of one of Sarah's art students, a St. Sebastian junior named Mike Weber called one night. What Jenny overheard of the call revealed a boy as shy as Sarah was withdrawn. More pause than conversation, the call ended with Sarah saying she had to do something.

"Was that the Weber from near Ridge Park? The one whose father manages the Sears?" Jenny asked.

"I don't know. Maybe," Sarah said. "We didn't talk about that."

"That's a nice family."

Sarah nodded and went back upstairs.

The girl was similarly withdrawn and cold when three other St. Sebastian students were "in the neighborhood" and dropped by one Thursday evening. Jenny opened the door on a gangly senior who did most of the talking. The other two classmates chimed in with excessive laughs when they weren't flipping their hair back from their foreheads. When they waited for Sarah to come down stairs, one of the boys made numbers of imaginary jump shots. Then, from the rear of the house, Jenny heard only the three boys.

"Not everyone jumps into things right away," Spuhn said.

"You do," Jenny said.

"Well, not everyone does," he answered. He was pleased, Jenny could see.

He also was absorbed in harvesting of all the good flowing from the approaching Iowa event. The halftime appearance would come nearly at the completion of the handwalk across the whole state. The Mayor's office in Omaha was helping line up officials for a welcome on the first of October, a date that gave Spoon some scheduling leeway in case of stormy weather. Spuhn was already preparing his board for a new capital raise, one tied to the initiation of new Spoons stretching across Nebraska.

Because of all the attention he needed to give Spoon, SI Data and his other businesses before October, Spuhn postponed a trip with Randy Isaacs to New York, where George Forrest and his partners were eager to launch a new fund for investment in several data enterprises they thought could be rolled into SI. The fund would sustain the organic expansion of SI as well as growth of SI through acquisition.

On the Monday before the September 25th halftime ceremony, Spuhn left in the slight pre-dawn chill of a rich fall day for a string of appointments that ordinarily would keep him away for an entire week. This time, he planned to get to Omaha and back, with stops in Iowa City and most of the restaurants, before Thursday night. Ronnie Tonti, safely close enough to Omaha to spit across the river by then, would spend the rest of the week and much of the next on promotional appointments in eastern Iowa. On Friday, the sunny, broad-shouldered performer would go to Iowa City with Spuhn for a TV news appearance and a *Daily Iowan* interview that would appear in the game day paper. The same night, Spuhn and Jenny would meet Tank Vetrov, driven to Iowa City by his principal and patron Tom Daniels for the Saturday appearance.

Exuberant each time, Spuhn called Jenny between appointments several times each day.

When the phone rang Thursday morning at the art school while Jenny was preparing for the day's sessions, she expected the call could be from Spuhn.

Instead, the call came from St. Sebastian, an office staff member alerting a parent or guardian about the absence of a student.

Jenny called the house twice without reaching Sarah, who must have overslept.

After waiting five minutes and making another unsuccessful attempt, Jenny decided to drive home, wake Sarah, scold her, and return to the school for the day's work.

The sight of Sarah's VW parked in front of the house confirmed the suspicion; Sarah, left alone, had turned Thursday into a Saturday, had failed to answer her alarm. Maybe she hadn't set one at all.Before entering the house, Jenny paused to notice a small deposit of red, some yellow, maple leaves blown onto the porch. Inside, she called upstairs for Sarah, and returned to the porch with a broom.

When she came back into the house and called upstairs again, the suspicious force of the bedroom door being flung open and the sound of Sarah's feet along the hallway to the bathroom brought Jenny to hasten up the stairs.

There was Ronnie Tonti coming naked out of the bedroom, then retreating into it as he shouted for Sarah and, Jenny thought, leaned against the closed door while he shouted and worked to dress himself.

Jenny moved past the bedroom and into the bathroom where Sarah, naked and shaking, was shrinking against the side of the bathtub. Jenny closed the door and locked it.

"I want to be dead, I want to be dead, I want to be dead," Sarah repeated, the moan changing to command to shaking whisper as she worked at her eyes with her long fingers.

Then Tonti was in the hallway, right at the door.

"Sarah," he shouted."Go away," Jenny called back. "You have to leave."

"Mrs. Jenny, you don't know what's happenin' here," Tonti said. His voice had the freckled, grinning innocence he usually affected.

"I sure do know what's going on," Jenny said. "You have to leave. Go. I'm calling the police."

"Just let me be dead," Sarah said between sobs.

Tonti began to bang on the door, so powerfully that it shook.

Jenny looked around the bathroom. Later, she would be glad that Spuhn allowed no corners cut in the house, had wanted solid oaken doors and trim everywhere, no hollow core material that would make the home less than equal to the baronial places crowning the Bettendorf river bluff.

Tonti threw himself at the door, so hard that the door shook in the frame. Then he took to kicking it as he demanded, "Sarah, open up, chère, open up."

"I want to be dead, I want to be dead" mixed with the noise of Tonti's kicking and his cries for Sarah to open.

Jenny pushed herself against the inside of the door.

Tonti's kicks began to open a split in a low panel.

Jenny looked around the bathroom for a plunger, a club she could use. Violently, she pulled at one of the towel racks, a thing of heavy, twisted brass affixed to plaster with screws. The plaster cracked. The screws gave way.

Sarah sobbed.

Tonti kicked at the opening he was making in the panel.

Jenny raised the brass club as Tonti began reaching up through the broken panel for the lock of the door.

Jenny brought the bar down on Tonti's hand, then brought it down again, brought it down again with an effect that made Tonti's shouting turn to screaming as his fingers turned limp and his blood began to stream.

"Go away. I'm calling the police," Jenny said.

She held the bar ready while, sounding little gasps of pain, Tonti withdrew his arm from the door.

"You're twice her age. She's a girl," Jenny screamed.

Sarah shivered with her legs drawn up and her face against her knees.

"She's old enough to bleed, she's old enough to butcher," Tonti said, rousing from his sad, pained breathing for the spiteful answer.

"You'll go to jail the rest of your life," Jenny said.

"Hell I will," Tonti answered. "Sarah, where the keys to the car?"

He had no answer from her.

"You two darlin's rest up. I'm gettin' a axe, some ol' sledge thing, from the garage."

Jenny heard him push his weight against the wall of the hallway and shove himself to standing. He had a heavy step along the hallway.

The yard outside, the whole property was too large for a call to any neighbor from the bathroom window. Jenny made calming noises to Sarah and caressed her shoulders for a moment as she brought the girl to stand. Jenny pulled a large towel from the bathtub rack and drew it around the girl.

Then Jenny waited, long enough for Tonti to arrive in the garage.

No sound came through the door.

Jenny kept the club in her grip, snatched the door open, and pulled Sarah by the hand. As quickly as Jenny could, she led Sarah to the head of the stairs.

They had just begun moving down the stairs, toward the front door and Jenny's car, when Tonti came out from hiding below them. He lunged and, midway up the stairs, grabbed Jenny by the hair, flung her so that her head struck the wall before she pitched forward down the stairs. Before Jenny could rise, Tonti had his weight on her back. In slitted, red-eyed rage, he drove his left fist down so that her face flattened against the floor. He repeated the strike. In his anger, he ignored the way the movement sent arcs of pain along the wrist and hand of his right arm.

"Stay there, you little bitch."

Jenny was conscious but unable to rise as Tonti led Sarah, whimpering, upstairs for the Volkswagen keys.

Then Jenny slipped into black until the opening of the front door roused her and she saw Sarah entering.

"Sarah, are you all right?" Jenny asked.

"Leave me alone."

Jenny sat up, a movement that made her head whirl. The sun had begun an afternoon slant that spread in golden, dust-flecked rays across the empty living and dining rooms. In the living room, a mantel clock ticked.

"Where is Tonti?"

"I hate you. I hate you, all of you."

Jenny used the bannister of the stairs and pulled herself up.

"I want to die."

"Where is Tonti now?"

"He's at his girlfriend's. Why do you need to know?"

Jenny didn't reply. She touched the side of her face. The expanse of the swelling went from her temple to her jawline.

"Sarah, stay here," Jenny said.

Sarah was already on the stairs. "Why? I want to go to my room."

"You need to stay here."

"I hate you. I want to die."

"Well, I don't want you to die. I want. . . everything to be all right."

Sarah plopped onto the second step, rested against the wall with her face turned down and her breath coming in sobs. She didn't resist as Jenny came to sit beside her and cradle her.

"I want to die." Sarah had trouble catching her breath.

"No."

"Yes. I want to die."

"No, we'll solve this."

Jenny wanted to call the police but she didn't want to leave Sarah, who could race upstairs, lock the bathroom, and begin ingesting whatever she could find in a medicine cabinet. Or Sarah could flee to the kitchen for slitting of her wrists.

The clock ticked off another 15 minutes, another half hour, as Jenny felt her own dizziness and stroked Sarah's arm.

The rays were approaching evening slant when Spuhn drove up, raced in his normal hurry into the house and froze at the sight of Jenny and Sarah. Sarah began to have trouble breathing as her sobbing grew loud.

"What happened to your face? Did you fall?"

Sarah stiffened.

"It's Ronnie Tonti," Jenny said. In a flat tone, she told what had happened.

Spuhn didn't come to her, just stood with his thoughts playing out in the set of his jaw, the stretch of his arms outward and up, the rub of his fingers through his hair, and through his hair again. Hands on his hips, he bent forward and then stood up, as if preparing for a race, as if filling his lungs for a start.

"Damn it, damn it, damn it. Where is he?"

"I don't know." Jenny began to stand. "I have to call the police. They need to arrest him."

"No."

"Yes. Sarah is underage."

"No."

"You didn't hear what he said. You didn't see how he looked."

"Don't tell anyone."

"Don't tell anyone?"

The space at the bottom of the stairway had become shadowed. Moving suddenly and decisively past them up the stairs, Spuhn said, "Don't call anyone, Jenny. I'm calling Diebold."

"Sarah has to go to the hospital, Dennis. Dennis, Sarah has to go to the hospital."

Spuhn didn't listen, didn't answer.

Sarah gave no resistance as Jenny led her upstairs for the packing of a small overnight bag and then drove her to the emergency room of Mercy Hospital. Jenny spent the next two hours deflecting inquiries as she arranged Sarah's admittance to the psychiatric wing.

"Let me call my brother first," Jenny said. "He and my sister-in-law don't know.'

"What about you?" The emergency physician asked, tilting Jenny's head back. "Did someone do this to you?" Beside the tall, crewcut man, a quiet resident stared at the side of Jenny's face as the doctor ran his fingers along the red puff of her wound.

"I bumped into something. I was in a hurry and fell on the stairs."

"Nothing's broken far as I can tell. You're getting a black eye."

The tall physician let the resident disinfect the area. The swelling had half-closed Jenny's right eye.

Once Sarah was sedated and under the watch of the psychiatric staff, Jenny went to the hospital lobby for a pay phone call to Spuhn.

"I have to find Tonti," he said. His tone was determined, cold.

"Won't the police find him?"

"The police don't know. Jenny, don't call the police. The Iowa game is Saturday."

Jenny pushed at the fold of the phone booth door so her conversation would not sound into the adjacent booth, where a woman with a high voice seemed to be talking with her sister about an aunt's admission.

"Dennis, did Diebold say not to call?"

Spuhn ignored that. "What did you do to his hand? Did you break anything when you hit him?"

"I hope I broke it in a million pieces."

"I have to go find him."

Jenny began to cry, her own sobbing a mirror of Sarah's that afternoon. Before she settled herself, she became aware that Spuhn had hung up.

Jenny was in a nightgown and holding ice wrapped in a thin towel against her face when Spuhn arrived home. He was alive with rage and agitation and cascading thoughts when he boomed into the bedroom, looked at Jenny in bed, and began.

"His hand is all messed up. His fingers are twice the size. You did a number on him."

Jenny stiffened and waited.

"It hurts him to even move his arm."

"My brother is flying here tomorrow morning."

Spuhn fussed with things on the top of his dresser - some coins, a fountain pen, several business cards - and didn't look at Jenny. The brightness of the overhead light made black mirrors of the room's windows. In the stillness, as Jenny felt the throbbing along the side of her face, as she carefully set her body so she wouldn't rest directly on the ache all along her right side, Spuhn ran fingers through his hair and stared at nothing in the corner of the ceiling.

"You think Tank will heal him? Tank can heal him, can't he?"

The question Spuhn put was also an answer. With excitement, he turned to the bed, leaned forward so his hands rested on it and depressed the side of the mattress. Jenny saw his face light with the rapture of someone struck, someone going to a meeting with Jesus.

Spuhn needed no word from her. The true believer delight in his face showed the bringing of Ronnie Tonti to Jenny's brother-in-law would restore Ronnie Tonti's fingers, his hand, his whole arm.

Jenny heard him, loud on the phone with Ronnie Tonti, as she fell miserably asleep with the overhead light shining down on the bed.

CHAPTER 34

Motivated!
Dedicated!
Alll rrright!

Even Dennis Spuhn, an uncaring churchgoer, would have recognized the contrast with the Centurion so frequently celebrated in sermons and in some St. Sebastian religion classes. That Roman official sent intermediaries to save Jesus Christ the trouble of traveling across Capernaum for the healing of a dying servant. A word would do. The man, despite his high station, was not worthy that the son of Almighty God would enter the house.

Not so Dennis Spuhn.

In between phone calls and the completion of appointments with the Iowa City television station and student newspaper, he went about the correction of the injury Jenny had inflicted. As a backup to what Nikolay Vetrov would do, Spuhn set Elaine to the finding of a hypnotist, an effort that came to naught when Elaine spoke with the most promising on a short list. The first two either insisted on a harmony of biorythmic cycles or required a two-session minimum. The last one would not return from a Los Angeles convention before the following Wednesday.

With a pale Ronnie Tonti protecting his right arm from the jarring of the Corvette on the graveled drive of the Blossom Motel where Tank Vetrov and Tom Daniels were sharing a room, Spuhn braked at the "Office" sign and found out from the polite woman inside that the two men were in a room midway along the low, yellow brick building. In another moment, Spuhn had Tonti at the door with him.

More placid than Spuhn remembered seeing him, Tank Vetrov answered the knock and stepped out into the cool evening with his visitors. Through the open door, Spuhn caught sight of some papers and an open bible on one of the beds.

Barely able to wait, Spuhn had to endure Tank's unhurried pace. A car passed one way, the two-lane county road returned to shadows, and then another car passed in the opposite direction under a sky with a pale, fattening moon coming into view.

Was this how Tank wrestled, how he toyed with another man before moving on him? Grateful for the way Tank was studying Tonti, Spuhn kept quiet.

Tank had been expecting them, had remained at the motel while Tom Daniels had dinner with Iowa City friends.

Now, with Spuhn and Tonti before him in the partly shadowed area beneath the motel's irregular overhang, Tank had the attentive look of a confessor, one who had acceded to Tom Daniels' insistence on a groomed appearance appropriate for an Iowa celebrity representing Harlan. Tank's face had only heavy evening growth flecked with some gray and his hair had been cut so that he had a clean line around his ears, barely enough length on top of his head for a part. Along with the small smile Tank showed the visitors, he gave them the gray-eyed fixity his wrestling opponents once knew.

Tank's steadiness heartened Spuhn, who had masked his distraction during the Iowa City sessions with the television and

Daily Iowan reporters. Pushing himself, he had made himself more charming and zestful than he felt, more the easy-going, charismatic young success than he was as he guided the interviews.

Ronnie Tonti, too, with his playfulness affected by the tenderness of his right hand and wrist, still had enough life for satisfaction of the willing young journalists, all of them long familiar with the Spoon restaurants and their celebrated, handsome founder.

Disposed to accept every lead from Dennis Spuhn, the young interviewers took for fact Spuhn's description of the soft charcoal gloves Tonti wore: in readying for the next day's halftime event, the broad-shouldered man with the Louisiana accent was preparing his hands with lotion that, each weekend, healed the little cuts suffered during the previous days of the week. Instead of shaking hands, Tonti answered introductions with a left-handed wave.

Left to his own inclinations, freed of the schedule with the Iowa City news groups, Spuhn would have driven Tonti for an interception of Tank and the Harlan school principal in Des Moines, in Newton, anywhere along the route toward Iowa City. No sending of an intermediary for Spuhn; he was right beside the injured handwalker, and would remain beside him until Tonti was cured by Tank or by the power of Spuhn's own spirit.

With his own will, he pressed to infuse Tonti with a maxim from *Think and Grow Rich*: "The starting point of all achievement is desire."

"Did you see the Iowa paper?" Spuhn asked Tank. "There is a page with your picture and everyone else, all you sports stars from the teams."

Tank closed the door of the motel room and moved along the front of the motel with Spuhn and Tonti following, all the way to a rusty barbed wire fence dividing the rectangular property of the motel from the surrounding cornfield. Two great, dry-leafed oaks inside the fence line provided a bower Tank's bearing made into a spiritual space.

"Tank, we're ready when you are," Spuhn said, no longer able to maintain patience. The ceremony, the manifestation of healing was all Spuhn wanted for the malleable Tonti. Every chance during the day, Spuhn had talked in sure terms about the healing Tank Vetrov would accomplish. Whether Tank could cure Tonti or not, Spuhn would make sure Tonti believed himself cured, at least long enough to get across the field among some strong Tonti Tenders ready to help keep the handwalker upright.

Spuhn didn't care what whooping dance, what incantation, what powders went into a firepit, as long as the powerful, intense former wrestler did something suggestive of curing Tonti's hurts. In military training, Spuhn had seen boots with contorted faces ignoring blisters across the whole ball of each foot, gasping from backaches that nearly brought tears with each movement. He himself had achieved his best time in a marathon run when he willed himself to ignore whatever a misstep in a shallow depression at mile six had done to his knee.

Tank's calm face did not reveal to Spuhn whether the man had the power of healing this evening.

The air was still. Stars were appearing in a clean sky.

After a long Siberian Stare, Tank closed his downcast eyes and crossed his arms on his chest. Spuhn and Tonti kept their eyes open as they mimicked the big man's meditation in the quiet beneath the trees.

"Dennis, Ronnie,' Tank said, "I am thankful to Jesus Christ, my lord and savior, for this gathering in his name."

"Amen," Tonti said, his old worship habits sparking to Tank's call and response.

"The Lord Jesus is good to us. . . '

"He is," Tonti said.

"... He is forgiving to us. A sparrow does not fall without Jesus Christ protecting that bird.""No."

"We are loved the way that bird is loved."

"Yes."

"Before we ask it, God knows what we need."

"Amen," Spuhn said, glad of what he saw in a sidelong glance at Tonti's believing face.

Tank tipped his head back and raised his eyes.

"Lord, this man is in pain."

"Yes," Tonti said.

"Lord, you know the pain we have in our hearts.""Yes."

"Lord, this man needs you tonight."

"Yes."

"Jesus, tonight this man is full of hurt in his heart. He is full of hurt in his limb."

Tank looked down long enough to find Tonti's right hand and to extend it tenderly skyward.

Spuhn saw Tonti wince, perhaps from apprehension and not from the feel of Tank's grip.

For a moment, his eyes closed and his lips moving slightly in private conversation, Tank moved his own hands along the length of Tonti's outstretched arm, slowly back and forth three times as he pushed his strong fingers along the curve of Tonti's wounded hand. He prayed out loud while maintaining the rigid press of his own grip on Tonti's wrist.

"Let this limb be strong, Jesus. Let it be strong to grip your grace. Let it be strong to grip the pathway of your salvation. Amen."

"Amen."

Spuhn looked and saw hope in Tonti's appearance.

The ruddy spirit and country smile came back on Ronnie Tonti's young face. He tested his arm with a looping movement and then the removal of the glove for a look at swollen fingers he was able to bend into a shallow curl. Tonti's smile was wide when he looked and met Spuhn's relieved look.

Hoorah! ""Whatever the mind can conceive and believe, the mind can achieve" with Positive Mental Attitude, Napoleon Hill had written in Spuhn's often-studied *Think and Grow Rich*. Frisky and giddy, Tonti seemed positive enough to overshadow a W. Clement Stone, positive enough to make the ebullient millionaire insurance executive seem in comparison like a first grader forgetting lines in front of a Parents Night audience. Hoorah!

Tonti tipped forward and pressed gingerly on the ground. Immediately returning to upright, he shook his arm and tenderly worked the knuckles and the wrist of his injured hand with the other.

"Far out, Tank. You did it. Far out," Spuhn cried.

In comparison to Spuhn's exhilaration, W. Clement Stone was shrunken and closed up like a box turtle.

Common sense, and awe, kept Tonti from saying then what he said to an exultant Spuhn on the way into Iowa City. "Whoooeeee, Jim, I wonder could he tighten up a couple nice pussies." What he didn't tell Spuhn was the image that had returned to his thoughts with the feeling in his arm: somehow, Melinda Beasly, woman now, seeking him for her Tonti study, would be at the end of the bridge when he arrived on his hands in Omaha. If he could cross Iowa on his hands, the chère could get to Omaha from Peoria.

Spuhn had the radio playing loud and was paying no attention to Tonti, was only visualizing the next day and trying to stay awake. Spuhn had slept little the previous night and then had been at battle alert all day.

In his room at the same Holiday Inn where Tonti was doubling up with a straight and narrow Tonti tender working his way through the university as a tennis team member, Spuhn made his first call to Jenny that day.

The call awakened her.

"Where are you?" she asked. Her voice was drowsy.

"Iowa City. Jenny, you should come. Tank fixed Tonti's hand."

Everything that came through the phone was a wish to go back to sleep.

"No. I'm going to the school. I'm not coming tomorrow."

"You should."

Jenny answered what Spuhn had not asked. "Bob came. He's going to take Sarah back to Connecticut. She has to stay at the hospital for a thirty day observation."

"Tell Bob to call me."

"He's at his hotel. Dennis, I'm going back to sleep."

If Jenny had turned to the game the following afternoon instead of immersing herself in the working of the swollen river on the canvas at the art school, she would have heard what eastern Iowa knew from a look out the window:

"A perfect day for football."

"Just glorious. And the Hawkeyes and the Nittany Lions of Penn State are ready for this one," the Hawkeye football commentators said to each other as they looked out at a sunny, sixty degree Iowa day and an Iowa Stadium with more than 40,000 fans settling into seats.

No fan, no player was as ready that day as Dennis Spuhn, who had been at work in his room before sunup with calls that reached the Iowa City manager as she finished a shower, again as she unfolded a fresh Spoon uniform, two more times before she left her apartment. Randy Isaacs, about to leave the lab and go home for a morning's sleep, had a typically exact report of a promising new agreement with a home appliance chain in Ohio and Pennsylvania. Isaacs, who had no undergrad loyalty to University teams and prized the quiet of the campus while games were played, declined Spuhn's offer of the ticket Jenny would not use. Spuhn would sit with his Spoon board member Howard Rowland, a Drake graduate who had invested in SI Data, and the civil engineer's petite, cheerful wife, an Iowa graduate who would be wearing the school's black and yellow.

Jack Diebold had left his hotel room already for a day of business socializing that included entertainment of two other couples with the lawyer and his wife midway up the Iowa stands at the 50.

After completing an hour of calls, Spuhn occupied himself with a run along the west bank of the Iowa River, then back along the east bank, through the University campus, where visitors were beginning to walk among students headed for Saturday morning labs or courses, and where busy fraternity and sorority houses were resuming festivities begun the night before. The brassy sound of a band rehearsing rang through the sunny, leafy morning.

The Iowa manager would see that someone went to the television station for a copy of the video once it aired as part of the pre-game coverage.

The football program sales department had supplied Spuhn with a copy of the game program carrying the two-page advertising spread.

Before showering, Spuhn read the *Daily Iowan* article a second time. The page three placement disappointed him but, in other respects, the young interviewer, Paula Krawiec, had followed Spuhn's didactic conversation lead. The comfortable friendliness of Ronnie Tonti came through the text and through the pair of photos accompanying the article; fortunately, neither photo showed clearly the gloves Tonti wore for the meeting. The errors in the story were in Spoon's favor: the Omaha restaurant was not open but would open soon enough, once George Forrest found the new investors and raised the capital. Spoon was not the largest restaurant chain in Iowa; it was the largest Iowa chain founded since 1960.

Paula Krawiec had also interviewed three of the former athletes who would be celebrated that day. Among them was Vic Krol. Spuhn was sorry to see the interview but glad that it included no photo except the one among the other past stars; the article paid more heed to the man's Iowa sports accomplishments than his business ones.

As Spuhn polished and buffed the light brown Gucci loafers he would wear without socks, Spuhn saw on television repeated weather reports promising perfect football temperature, repeated interviews with Iowa's young quarterback and a coach who spoke confidently and respectfully of the visiting team, a national news report of Philippine President Ferdinand Marcos' meeting with Secretary of State William P. Rogers, and then local Iowa news.

In Scott County, where he was campaigning for election to the state legislature, a camera-aware, muscular Greg Benson, American flag in his lapel, was declaiming to an American Legion audience about his rival's support for legislation favoring a large developer's design for housing that would be small and shabby. The plan would create an instant slum out of character with Davenport and Bettendorf standards. Benson had the shoulder roll of a fattened Angus and, in recent news articles, credentials that included sparking the St. Sebastian wrestling team in the 1964 season. Spuhn knew before Benson squared his beefy shoulders and spoke the name: Klein Construction.

What he glimpsed in a pan of the audience changed Spuhn's mind about checking with Jim Clayton, in case the former St. Sebastian classmate was in Iowa City: Spuhn wouldn't offer Jenny's game ticket to the lawyer. The extra ticket would be used by one of

Howard Rowland's business partners, an engineer who had graduated from Iowa in 1959.

Fully suited and wingtipped, sideburns only long enough to brush the boundary of corporate taste, Clayton let the camera catch him leaning forward and paying sycophantic attention to the oration of his Cutler & Mattingly client.

Ronnie Tonti was damp from showering and wound in a bath towel when the serious young tennis player answered the knock. Seeing Spuhn, Tonti turned from the television, grinned and raised his hand in the air.

"Well, don't you look all bright-eyed and bushy-tailed," Spuhn said.

"We just got up, Dennis ," said the student assigned to watch Tonti.

"You feelin' up to this today, Ronnie?" Spuhn asked.

"Mr. Dennis, like a tick on a fat dog this mawnin'". Tonti stretched both arms upward. The thumbnail of his right hand was dark and several fingers were swollen.

"Let's hope so."

Spuhn was at the hotel lobby, ready in a new, pale yellow Izod shirt with a Spoon logo three times the size of the brand's alligator, dark green slacks and a folded Armani sport coat 15 minutes before Tonti appeared. Like the tall Tonti tenders beside him, Tonti wore fresh, long-sleeved Spoon garb that would stand out as he led the Iowa band onto the field at halftime. The tennis player had wound Tonti's right wrist and fingers in flesh-colored gauze.

The group of them entered the white Chevrolet station wagon and went with the teen-aged Spoon worker who had been sent for them. In another 15 minutes, nearly an hour before kickoff, they were at Iowa Stadium. There, Spuhn went for a pay phone while the Tonti Tenders followed a band department staff member into the stadium area where they would watch the game and wait for the halftime appearance.

Just as the stadium crowd sat down again at the end of the Star-Spangled Banner and an official was beginning the coin flip, two naked men and a woman avoided a surprised referee and several security staff as they raced across the field, toward the Iowa student section. A number of Iowa and

Penn players hooted as they did nothing to help the pursuing security detail. Once across the field, the naked trio were swept up over the low rail, wrapped in blankets, and hidden among the Iowa students in the area below and to the left of Spuhn.

The Rowlands wanted the streakers to be arrested, the men drafted into the Army.

Spuhn's anxiety, as well as his impatience with looping, no-destination small talk made him an impolite host for Howard Rowland, his excited wife and his business partner. Marylyn Rowland answered the Hawkeye cheerleaders with a gusto that would have her hoarse before the game's end. She buried her face against her husband and hugged his arm each time a pass went skittering or a run came up short. During advertising timeouts, she quickly examined her makeup and the neatness of her compact, freshly streaked hairstyle before taking up with the Iowa couple on her right.

"We can win this," she said.

Spuhn's own prayer was similar, a determined, internal statement that Tonti, strong and hands down, would move across the field as steadily as a combine along a row of ready corn.

Halftime came.

The president of the Hawkeyes Alumni Association, a Toastmasters veteran with a bulk that amplified his baritone, introduced each former team star as the twelve men and three women spread in a line along the midfield stripe. Nikolay Vetrov raised his head as his description - Big Ten champion, undefeated at weight - echoed in the Stadium. The introductions continued. Tank composed himself with his hands clasped and his broad shoulders squared, his stare aimed at the ground; Spuhn could tell Tank was praying.

At the end, as the celebration concluded with the stadium ringing loud with applause and the line moving toward the sideline, Tank suddenly swerved and took the microphone from the surprised master of ceremonies.

"Iowa brothers and sisters," Tank called in full pulpit intensity. "Forgive me, the sinner who was proud, who thought victory was in sin, who thought happiness was in power. The psalm says,

"The lord heard my cry.
He drew me out of the pit of destruction,
out of the mud of the swamp;
he set my feet upon a crag;
he made firm my steps."

Program officials, careful of Tank's size, strength and determination, were reaching for retrieval of the microphone before Tank was halfway through the prayer. After one unplugged the mic and Tank's voice no longer rolled about the stadium, Spuhn only saw Tank pulling from the touch of an official.

With the mic useless, Tank lowered his head, extended his arms, and made a slow revolution that sent his plea to all in the stadium. Then, he knelt until two consoling state troopers prevailed on him to stand and move to the sidelines with them.

The crowd, through loyalty or excitement or through delight that the second half would begin soon, sent up cheers.

Along the sideline, the Iowa band massed, and then began to sound, a sign for a new roar from those in the stadium.

At the head, just before the drum major in a tall white hat banded with shining yellow, Ronnie Tonti, encircled by three tall, alert Tonti Tenders, rolled theatrically onto his hands, wobbled uncertainly for a moment, and laboriously, successfully navigated the crossing of nearly the full span of Iowa Stadium's 50 yardline. As Tonti came near, Spuhn saw him raised, supported by two tall Tenders.

On their way home, the game fans produced a tsunami of a statewide spike in Spoon sales.

CHAPTER 35

Hey, hey, sweet thing
How do you do?
Do you remember me
The way I remember you?

While the school was empty except for herself, Jenny paused several times for sight of the sunrise breaking red, then yellow over the flow of the Mississippi River below. At the Illinois side, two heavy barge strings appeared and passed with the help of the current.

They went by without being watched. Jenny let herself cry in the emptiness of the art school.

Shortly after calling her assistant and making arrangements for suspension of some classes, transfer of others to the affable, empty-nester landscape painter, Jenny completed the storing of some supplies and work, including two of her own. When the other teacher stopped at the school for class records and supplies, Jenny avoided "What happened to you?" by hiding and pretending to be busy in her own studio.

At ten, Jenny went to meet her brother at Bob's hotel.

The tired, somber expression on her brother's face as they drove to Mercy Hospital gave him a disheveled look, despite the cut of his sportcoat and a light blue Izod shirt that was seeing its first use. He answered with a small shrug and went back to watching the river through the slats of the bridge.

"What do they say about your eye?" he asked.

"You should have seen it Thursday." The swelling along Jenny's cheek and jaw had diminished enough that she was able to see again through her right eye. The wound was healing in hues of black, purple and yellow.

Conversation for her was an effort, as it was for Bob.

At the hospital, they returned to silence as they waited for admission to the wing where Sarah was being observed.

When the nurse came, Jenny meant to sit and wait but Bob told Jenny to come with him.

Of the three, Sarah was the settled one who could give comfort to her father as he stood by the bed and took in the sight of her.

"A bummer, huh?" she said, with a smile that applied the description to everything: the gown that covered her chest and arms, the plastic band she wore on her wrist, the hospital smell of medication and protocol.

Then the girl's resolve broke and she began to cry.

Bob, helpless and clumsy, rubbed Sarah's shoulder and surrendered his own expression to anguish while a nurse with a soft voice took Sarah's pulse and then gave her a pill.

Sarah, already sleepy, fluttered into slumber.

Bob reconfirmed his intention to stay at the hospital, to talk with Sarah's doctor, to be with her. For the sake of retrieving his bag, he accompanied Jenny to her car.

"I'll catch up to you," he said. "Thanks for picking me up."

They had talked enough about Ronnie Tonti the day before. The man was on their minds but not in their conversation, not while Bob was busy with Sarah's care and Jenny was weary, empty of everything but hurt.

In the quiet of the art school, she returned to making the last strokes on the canvas, the image of the swollen, relentless river, the Iowa, near to absorbing the point where a small tree, now a willow, was rooted. No longer the river as it once moved through the campus, the river in Jenny's painting was green, its breadth increasing as it took the soft banks along its relentless flow. The willow clung to land that would tear.

When Jenny finished, she stared long at the work.

Then she left a note with the address of the New York gallery where her other work was accumulating.

At about the same time Ronnie Tonti was tipping forward at midfield, Jenny made a phone call, her voice as flat as her eyes were dry. The call made, she cradled the phone and moved through the rest of the afternoon at a determined pace, as if beginning the kick of a race.

Spuhn came home in the dusk still showing pale pink and orange in the west. The cicadas were thrumming on trees with leaves hanging in still air headed down to 50 degrees.

The front door was open.

When he entered, Spuhn found a small suitcase, Jenny's blue Samsonite, just inside.

The set of Jenny's face made him quiet as she came down the stairs with a tan car coat over one arm. A sleeveless white silk blouse fit to the shape of her form. Spuhn recognized Jenny's dark green skirt as a modest, business-suited one she chose for travel. She had made up her face and had put on nylons.

Instead of exulting about the afternoon, Spuhn asked "Where are you going?"

"Marjorie's coming."

"Where are you going?" The CEO was coming out in him, the irritation of needing to ask the same question more than once.

'Marjorie's for awhile, then New York."

"You didn't answer the phone." He had called the studio and their home four times during the afternoon.

Jenny put on the car coat and buttoned it.

"How long you goin' be gone?"

Jenny's throat was dry. She answered with a little escape of air from her nostrils, a look into a corner. She finished buttoning the coat.

Spuhn looked at her face, the bones delicate, her dark eyebrows a contrast to the gold of her hair, gathered now in a pony tail that spread on her left shoulder. The cream and powder along her jaw, up to her right eye, were a failed mask for the long, pulpy injury from Tonti's blows.

"I'll meet Marjorie at the end of the drive."

Spuhn stepped out of her way, allowed her to move with her luggage in one hand, down the stairs and then the driveway.

He watched her progress on legs that proved the existence of God.

Before Marjorie came in a blue Pinto that had wheel wells and rear quarter panels caked gray from driving on country roads, Spuhn broke off staring down the darkening yard, went upstairs and made phone calls.

Tom Figel

Thomas Russell Figel, born in Chicago in 1946, is the firstborn of Don and Marge Figels' eleven children. After three years in seminaries of The Maryknoll Fathers, he graduated from Assumption High School, Davenport, Iowa and then from the University of Notre Dame, where his fortunate life came to include Nancy Carlin, who would join him as parent of four. A US Army draftee coaxed into becoming a paratrooper, he completed stateside service in Massachusetts. During a public relations career begun in Florida and concluded in Chicago, he used the GI Bill for an MBA from Northwestern University's Kellogg School. With Nancy, he moved from Chicago to Long Beach, CA during 2021. A favorite activity is to fill a minivan with grandchildren and head to the East Coast or Canada for parasitic stays with friends. He regrets the end of a time when young people could hitchhike. He is glad he caught the Sixties. During the mid-70s, he co-founded The Palm Beach County Algonquins.

Tom Figel is at work on a new novel.

Cover design by Creative Works

Florida native Robert W. Jahn founded Creative Works in 1970. The design firm now located in Daytona Beach, FL found immediate success in the U.S. and abroad. In recent years, Bob has organized Creative Works as a studio. The personal structure and the focus on a limited number of consultancies each year permit Bob, the Creator, to immerse himself deeply in the opportunities and needs of client enterprises. The studio's engagements range from community planning and architectural and interior design to the finish of medical and electronic products. The designer is a co-founder of The Palm Beach County Algonquins and a past member of the organization's Supreme Tribunal. See www.creativeworksusa.net.

Photographic Art of Mel Theobald

Chicago painter and photographic artist Mel Theobald, contributer of photographs appearing in *Hands Down*, is a native of central Illinois' Bloomington. His work is held in public and private collections around the world, including Russia, where his assistance to artists needing materials and tools before the fall of the Soviet Union has led to multiple visits and mutual admiration. His book *Inside the Enigma* documents his experience curating art exhibitions for the Russian Ministry of Culture (www.inside-theenigma.com). Mel's creative work underwent a metamorphosis from painting in 2001 when he began using technology to produce large scale digital photographs. See www.theobaldart.com.

CPSIA information can be obtained
at www.ICGtesting.com
Printed in the USA
LVHW080151090822
725499LV00015B/805